A GIFT OF LOVE

Jude Deveraux
Judith McNaught

A GIFT OF LOVE

Kimberly Cates
Andrea Kane
Judith O'Brien

POCKET BOOKS

New York   London   Toronto   Sydney   Tokyo   Singapore

POCKET BOOKS, a division of Simon & Schuster Inc.
1230 Avenue of the Americas, New York, NY 10020

ISBN: 0-671-53662-1

First Pocket Books hardcover printing November 1995

10 9 8 7 6 5 4 3 2 1

Contents

Judith McNaught

Double Exposure

One

OBLIVIOUS TO THE SPECTACULAR VIEW BEYOND THE GLASS
wall of the Houston high-rise that housed the offices of *Foster's
Beautiful Living* magazine, Diana Foster paced in front of her
desk with a telephone cradled between her shoulder and ear.

"Still no answer at the house?" asked Kristin Nordstrom, a
production assistant at the magazine.

Diana shook her head and hung the phone up, already
reaching into the credenza behind her desk for her handbag.
"Everyone is probably out in the garden, reinventing mulch or
something," she joked. "Did you ever notice," she continued
with a rueful smile as she shrugged into a lime green linen jacket
trimmed in white, "that when you have really exciting news, the
people you want to share it with are never where you can reach
them?"

"Well, how about if you tell me the news in the meantime,"
Kristin suggested teasingly.

Diana paused in the act of smoothing wrinkles from her
white skirt and flashed the other woman a smile, but she had to
look up to do it. At thirty-two, Kristin was two years older than
Diana and a full six feet tall, with the fair skin and blue eyes of
her Nordic ancestors. She was also conscientious, energetic, and
detail-oriented, three traits that made her an ideal member of
the production department.

"Okay, you've got it. I've just decided to shoot some of the photos for the 'Perfect Weddings' issue on location in Newport, Rhode Island. The opportunity dropped into my lap this morning, and it's going to put us under tremendous deadline pressure, but it's too good to pass up. In fact, if you're available I'd like to send you to Newport a week before the wedding to help our crew. Mike MacNeil and Corey will arrive a few days later. You can work with them while they shoot the actual photos. They're going to need an extra pair of hands, and it will give you an opportunity to find out what it's like to work on location, under pressure, in difficult conditions. How does that strike you?"

"Like a bolt of lightning," she said, her face illuminated by a broad smile. "I've always wanted to go on location with Corey's crew. Newport should provide a gorgeous setting for the layout," she said as Diana started for the door. "Diana, before you go, I want to thank you for everything you've done. You're a joy to work with—"

Diana waved off her gratitude with a smile. "Just keep trying to find Corey. Oh, and keep calling the house. If anyone answers, tell them to stay put until I get there. Tell them I have great news, but I want Corey there to hear it."

"I will. And when you see Corey, please tell her I'm excited about the chance to work with her." She paused, a funny, uncertain smile on her face. "Diana, does Corey realize how much she looks like Meg Ryan?"

"Take my advice and don't mention it to her," Diana warned with a laugh. "She gets accosted all the time by strangers who refuse to believe her when she tells them she *isn't* Meg Ryan, and some of them become downright unpleasant because they think she's trying to trick them."

The telephone rang, interrupting them, and Kristin reached

across the desk to answer it. "It's Corey," she said, holding the receiver toward Diana. "She's on the car phone."

"Thank heaven!" Diana said as she hurried forward and took the phone. "Corey, I've been trying to reach you all morning. Where have you been?"

Corey registered the excitement in her sister's voice, but at the moment her attention was concentrated on the driver of an orange pickup truck who was determined to merge into a space on the expressway that was already occupied by Corey's car. "I was at the printer's all morning," she said, deciding it was wiser to change lanes and let him win the bluff than to have an orange "pin stripe" embossed on the door of her burgundy car. "I wasn't happy with some of the shots I got for the barbecue layout for the next issue, and I brought him some different ones."

"Don't worry about that issue, it'll be fine. I have something more important to tell you—it's great news. Can you meet me at the house in twenty minutes? I'd like to tell everyone at once."

"Did I just hear you say *not* to worry about an issue?" Corey teased, amused and surprised by this unusual attitude of optimism from her eternally cautious sister. Glancing in the rearview mirror, she changed lanes so that she could take the exit for River Oaks, rather than continuing to the office as she'd originally intended. "I'm heading for the house, but I insist on some sort of hint now."

"Okay, here goes: What would you say if I told you an unbelievable opportunity for the 'Perfect Weddings' issue just fell into my lap! The mother of the bride, who is clearly anxious to further bolster her social status, wants us to feature her daughter's wedding in *Beautiful Living*. If we are willing to do that, she is willing to guarantee us that it will be done in authentic 'Foster Style,' under our supervision, *and* she is willing to pay whatever that costs, as well as all travel expenses for our staff."

For months, Corey and Diana had been discussing possible locations and themes for the "ideal" wedding they wanted to stage and feature in that issue, but so far they'd discarded all of them either because Diana thought they were too expensive or because Corey thought they were artistically unacceptable. Diana bore the full burden for all Foster Enterprises' financial matters, but the responsibility for the beautiful photographic layouts that appeared in Foster's publications was Corey's. "It sounds good from a budget standpoint, but what about the location? What sort of setting would we have?"

"Brace yourself," Diana said.

In the car, Corey smiled with helpless anticipation. "I'm braced. Tell me."

"The wedding is to take place on the lawn of the bride's uncle's home . . . a lovely little forty-five room 'cottage,' built in 1895, complete with frescoed ceilings, fabulous plasterwork . . . and undoubtedly hundreds of other little architectural goodies you could include in our next coffee-table book—you know," she said, "those big, fancy, beautiful books that you turn out in your spare time?"

"Don't keep me in suspense." Corey laughed, her enthusiasm soaring. "Where's the house?"

"Are you ready for this?"

"I think so."

"Newport, Rhode Island."

"Oh, my God, how perfect!" Corey breathed, her photographer's mind already envisioning scenic shots with fabulous yachts floating on sparkling blue water in the background.

"The bride's mother sent me pictures of her brother's house and grounds and then called me this morning after the package arrived. Based on something she let slip, I got the funny feeling he may be paying for the entire wedding. Oh, I forgot, she promised to provide us with six local people who'll work under our supervision. That should enable us to put some special touches in a few of the main rooms, so you'll have even more to photograph. All materials and freelance labor are at their expense, of course, and our people will have private rooms at the house. The hotels are already booked for the season, and you'll all need to work late anyway, so that's a practical solution. Also, they have servants and they'll have houseguests, so staying there to make certain no one tampers with our handiwork becomes a necessity."

"No problem, for an opportunity like this, I would work and sleep in Bluebeard's house."

Diana's voice lost a little of its happy confidence. "Yes, but can you do that in Spencer Addison's house?"

Corey's reply was instinctive and instantaneous. "I'd prefer Bluebeard."

"I know."

"Let's find another wedding to feature."

"Let's talk about it when you get home."

Two

BY THE TIME COREY TURNED OFF INWOOD DRIVE AND ONTO the long, treelined driveway that led to the house, she already knew she was going to go to Newport. Diana undoubtedly knew it too. Whatever either of them needed to do for the good of the other, or the good of the family, or the good of Foster Enterprises, they would do. Somehow, that had always been understood between them.

Corey's mother and grandmother would also have to go to Newport, because they were the creators of what was now popularly called the "Foster Style." It was a concept that Corey and Diana had managed to showcase and market on a national scale, via the magazine and a variety of books, but it was still a joint family venture. Her mother and grandmother would undoubtedly regard the chance to see Spencer again as a delightful side benefit rather than a repugnant drawback, but then he hadn't hurt them the way he'd hurt Corey.

Diana's car was already parked in front of the house, a sprawling Georgian-style mansion that served as the family's home as well as a sort of "testing ground" for many of the menus and home improvement projects that appeared regularly in *Foster's Beautiful Living*.

Corey turned off the ignition and looked up at the house that she and Diana had helped to protect and preserve. So many momentous events in her life were linked to this place, she thought as she leaned her head against the headrest, deliberately postponing going inside, where she would have to listen to a discussion of the Newport wedding. She had been thirteen and standing in the foyer when she had met Diana for the first time, and she'd met Spencer Addison a year later on the back lawn, when she attended her first grown-up party.

And here, in this house, she had learned to love and respect Robert Foster, a broad-shouldered giant of a man with a gentle heart and brilliant mind who later adopted her. He had met Corey's mother in Long Valley, when he bought the manufacturing company where she worked as a secretary, and the rest had seemed like a fairy tale. Entranced by Mary Britton's lovely face and warm smile, the Houston millionaire had taken her to dinner his first night in town and decided that same evening that Mary was the woman for him.

The following night, he appeared at Corey's grandparents'

house, where she and her mother lived, and began a whirlwind courtship that included the entire close-knit little family. Like a benevolent wizard, he materialized each evening with an armload of flowers and little gifts for everyone, and he stayed until the early hours of the morning, talking to the entire family until they went to bed and then sitting out on the swing in the backyard with his arm around Mary's shoulders.

Within two weeks, he'd befriended Corey, soothed all of her grandparents' possible objections to the marriage, and overridden Mary's own marital misgivings, then he whisked his new bride and her daughter from their little frame house on the outskirts of Long Valley into his private plane. A few hours later, he laughingly carried first Mary and then Corey over the threshold of his Houston home, and they had lived there ever since.

Diana had been vacationing in Europe with some school friends and their parents when the wedding took place, and Corey had dreaded meeting her new sister when she finally came home at the end of the summer. Diana was a year older, and supposed to be very smart. Corey was morbidly certain that besides all that Diana would be beautiful and sophisticated and the world's biggest snob.

On the day Diana returned from Europe, Corey hid on the balcony eavesdropping while her stepfather greeted his daughter in the living room and informed her that while Diana had been "lazin' around in Europe all summer," he had gotten her a new mother *and* a new sister.

He introduced Diana to Corey's mother, but Corey couldn't quite hear what they said to each other because their voices were too soft. At least Diana hadn't had a temper tantrum, as Corey had feared, and Corey tried to take some solace in that when her stepfather brought Diana into the foyer and called Corey to come downstairs.

Her knees knocking together, Corey had thrust out her chin and affected an "I don't care what you think of me" attitude as she walked stiffly down the staircase.

At first glance, Diana Foster was the personification of Corey's worst fears: Not only was she pretty and petite, with green eyes and shiny brown hair that tumbled in mahogany waves halfway down her back, she was also wearing an outfit that looked like it came right out of a teen magazine—a very short tan skirt with cream-colored tights and a plaid vest in shades of tan and blue, topped off by a tan blazer with an emblem on the pocket. She had breasts, too, Corey noticed glumly.

In comparison, Corey, who was two inches taller and wearing jeans, felt like a washed-out, overgrown lump of ugly clay with her ordinary blue eyes and streaky blond hair pulled up in a ponytail. In honor of the occasion, Corey was wearing her favorite sweatshirt—the one with a running quarter horse emblazoned in white across her flat chest. She tried to take some comfort from that as Diana stared at Corey in silence and Corey stared right back.

"Say something, girls!" Robert Foster commanded in his cheerful but authoritative voice. "You're sisters, now!"

"Hi," Diana mumbled.

"Hi," Corey replied.

Diana seemed to be staring directly at Corey's sweatshirt, and Corey's chin lifted defensively. Her grandmother in Long Valley had lovingly painted the horse on that sweatshirt, and if Diana Foster said one nasty word about it, Corey was fully prepared to shove her right off her dainty feet.

Finally, Diana broke the uneasy silence. "Do you—do you like horses?"

Wary, Corey shrugged and then nodded.

"After dinner, we could go over to Barb Hayward's house.

The Haywards have a great stable with racehorses. Barb's brother, Doug, has a polo pony, too."

"I've only ridden a few horses and they've been pretty gentle. I'm not good enough for racehorses."

"I'd rather pet them than ride them anytime. I got thrown last spring," Diana admitted, putting a hesitant foot on the first step and starting up toward her bedroom.

"You have to get right back on if you get thrown," Corey sagely advised, feeling remarkably buoyed by Diana's easy admission of her own shortcomings. She'd always wanted a sister, and maybe—just maybe—this dainty, beautiful brunette girl would do after all. Diana didn't *seem* like a snob.

They walked upstairs together and hesitated in the hallway in front of their separate doorways. From the living room below, they heard their parents merry laughter and the sound was so youthful and carefree that both girls smiled at each other as if they'd caught their grown-up parents acting like children. Feeling that she owed Diana some sort of comment or explanation, Corey said with frank honesty, "Your dad is real nice. My dad ran out on us when I was still a baby. They got divorced."

"My mom died when I was five." Diana tipped her head to the side, listening to the happy voices coming from the living room, "Your mom makes my dad laugh. She seems nice."

"She is."

"Is she strict?"

"Sometimes. A little bit. But then she feels guilty and she'll bake up a batch of brownies or a fresh strawberry pie for me—I mean us—before I—I mean we—go to bed."

"Wow, brownies," Diana muttered. "And fresh strawberry pie."

"My mom believes in everything being fresh whenever possible, and my grandma's the same way. No canned stuff. No boxed stuff. No frozen stuff."

"Wow," Diana muttered again. With a shudder she confided, "Conchita—our cook—puts jalapeño peppers in everything."

Corey giggled. "I know, but my mom's already kind of taken over the kitchen."

Suddenly she felt as if she—and her mother—had something nice to offer to Diana and her father, after all. "Now that my mom's your mom, too, you won't have to eat any more of Conchita's jalapeños." Teasingly she added, "Just think, no more chocolate cake with jalapeño frosting!"

Diana fell into the game at once. "No more jalapeño waffles with jalapeño syrup!"

They broke off, giggling, then their eyes met and they stopped, each feeling awkward and desperate, as if their future might somehow teeter on saying just the right thing during these first minutes together. Corey gathered the courage to speak first. "Your dad gave me a great camera for my birthday. I'll show you how it works and you can use it whenever you want."

"I guess he's 'our dad' from now on."

It was an offer to share him, and Corey bit down on her lip to keep it from trembling with emotion. "I—I always wanted a sister."

"Me, too."

"I like your outfit. It's neat."

Diana shrugged, her gaze on the flashy horse that seemed to be racing across Corey's shirt. "I like your sweatshirt!"

"You do? Really?"

"Really," she said with an emphatic nod.

"I'll call Grandma and tell her you like it. She'll make one just like it for you, only in your favorite color. Her name is Rose Britton, but she'll want you to call her Grandma, like I do."

A glow appeared in Diana's eyes. "Grandma? You come with a grandma, too?"

"Yep. Grandma's a terrific gardener, besides being an artist.

And Grandpa loves to garden, too, but he grows vegetables instead of flowers. And he can build anything! He can put a deck on your house, or build you a playhouse, or design neat things for the kitchen, just like that." Corey tried to snap her fingers for emphasis, but she was still a little nervous and failed. "He'll build you anything you'd like. All you have to do is ask him."

"You mean I'm going to have a grandpa, too?"

Corey nodded, then she watched in delight as Diana lifted her gaze to the ceiling and happily proclaimed, "A sister, and a mom, and a grandma, and a grandpa! This could be *very* cool!"

It only got better.

As Corey had predicted, her grandparents fell in love with Diana on her first visit, and both girls began spending so much time in Long Valley with Rose and Henry Britton that their father irritably announced he was feeling left out. The following spring, when Mary gently mentioned that she wished her parents lived closer, Robert happily solved everyone's problems by instructing an architect to draw up plans to renovate and enlarge the estate's guest cottage, then he stood back in considerable awe as Henry insisted on doing most of the carpentry. After that, it was only a small concession to add a greenhouse for Rose and a huge vegetable garden for Henry.

Robert's magnanimous gesture was repaid a hundredfold with savory meals of fresh fruits and vegetables grown on his own land and artfully presented amid centerpieces of flowers or whimsical baskets, or in "canoes" made from hollowed-out loaves of French bread. Even the location of meals changed according to the whim and mood of what Robert routinely referred to as "his ladies."

Sometimes they ate in the vast kitchen with its brick walls and copper pots hanging from an arched wall above the row of ovens and gas burners; sometimes they ate in the garden on place mats made from green and white striped cloth to match the umbrella above the table; sometimes they dined beside the pool on the low recliner chairs that Corey's grandfather had fashioned and built from strips of wood; sometimes they ate on a blanket on the lawn, but with crystal goblets and fine china for what Mary called "a special touch."

This flair for dining and entertaining earned Mary a great deal of praise a year after her wedding, when she gave her first big party as Robert Foster's wife. At the outset, she was alarmed and intimidated at the thought of entertaining Robert's friends, people who she feared would think they were her social superiors and who she was certain would look upon her as an interloper, but Corey and Diana weren't worried at all. They knew whatever she did, she did with love and with flair. Robert Foster felt the same way. Wrapping his arm around her shoulders, he said, "You'll dazzle 'em, darlin'—You just be your sweet self, and do things your own special way."

After a week of consultations with the entire family, Mary finally decided to have a Hawaiian luau at poolside beneath the palms on the lawn. And as Robert had cheerfully predicted, the guests were indeed dazzled—not only by the sumptuous food, gorgeously decorated tables, and authentic music, but by the hostess herself. On the arm of her husband, Mary moved among her guests, her slim figure wrapped in a lovely sarong, her free arm draped from wrist to elbow with spectacular leis made of homegrown orchids from their own greenhouse, and as she encountered each female guest, she presented her with a lei that matched the lady's apparel.

When several men complimented her on the amazingly tasty food and then expressed amused shock at the discovery that Robert Foster had plowed up part of his lawn for a vegetable garden, Mary signaled her father, who proudly offered tours of the garden by moonlight. As Henry Britton showed the tuxedo-clad gentlemen along the neat rows of organically grown vegetables, his enthusiasm was so contagious that before the night was over, several of the men had announced their desire to have vegetable gardens of their own.

When the ladies asked for the name of her caterer, Mary stunned them by naming her own family. Marge Crumbaker, the society gossip columnist for the *Houston Post* who was covering the party, also asked her what caterer as well as what florist she had used, and Mary grew tense, knowing she might seem like a fool, but she admitted the truth: despite the popular notion that all domestic duties were sheer drudgery, and that any intelligent woman would want to find other, more appropriate uses for her time, Mary loved to cook, garden, and sew. She was in the midst of confessing that she also enjoyed canning fruits and vegetables when she noticed an elderly, white-haired woman who was sitting slightly off to one side, rubbing her arms as if she were chilled. "Excuse me," Mary explained with an apologetic smile, "but I think Mrs. Bradley is cold, and I need to find her a wrap."

She sent Corey and Diana into the house to find a shawl, and when they returned, they found Mary talking to their grandmother about the interview with Marge Crumbaker. "I just know I made us all sound like *The Beverly Hillbillies!*" she confided miserably. "I don't even want to know what she says about us in that column." She took the shawl from the girls and asked her mother to bring it to Mrs. Bradley, then she melted into the crowd to look after her guests.

Corey and Diana were stricken at the possibility of being held up to public ridicule. "Do you think she'll make fun of us?" Diana asked.

With a reassuring smile, Rose put her arms around their

15

shoulders. "Not a chance," she whispered encouragingly, then she headed off to give Mrs. Bradley the shawl, hoping she was right.

Mrs. Bradley was glad for the lacy, handmade shawl. "I used to love to crochet," she said, holding it up to admire, her long, aristocratic fingers gnarled with arthritis. "Now I can't hold a hook in my hands, not even those big ones they sell in the stores."

"You need a hook with a large handle that's specially made to fit your hand," Rose said. She looked about for Henry, saw him standing nearby, talking to a middle-aged man about growing edible flowers, and signaled him to come over. When Henry heard the problem, he nodded at once. "What you need, ma'am, is a hook with a big, fat, wooden handle that's shaped to the grip of your hand, with small indentations low on the handle, so it won't slip out of your fingers."

"I don't think they make any like that," Mrs. Bradley said, looking hopeful and despondent at the same time.

"No, but I can make you one. You come by the day after tomorrow and plan to stay for a couple of hours so I can fit it to your grip." He touched her twisted fingers and added sympathetically, "Arthritis is a curse, but there's ways to work around it. Got a touch of it, myself."

As he walked away, Mrs. Bradley watched him as if he were some sort of mythical knight in shining armor. Slowly she transferred her gaze to Rose and politely excused her to return to the other guests. "My grandson, Spencer, is attending another party nearby. I asked him to come for me at eleven o'clock, to take me home. You needn't stay here on my account."

Rose passed a sweeping glance over the banquet tables and, satisfied that she wasn't needed elsewhere, she sat down beside Mrs. Bradley. "I'd rather talk with you. You'll need to use thick yarn with Henry's hook. I intended to teach Diana how to crochet and I showed her a picture of a place mat, hoping to spark her interest. She turned up her nose at the notion of crocheting rectangles. She suggested we make them in the shape of apples, lemons, strawberries, and things like that. She drew up some sketches. They were simple and bold. You'd enjoy making them."

"Diana?" Mrs. Bradley interrupted doubtfully. "You don't mean little Diana Foster?"

Grandma nodded proudly. "I do, indeed. That girl has an artistic streak a mile wide—they both do. She paints and does charcoal sketches that are excellent. And Corey's fascinated with photography, and quite good at it. Robert bought her developing equipment for her fourteenth birthday."

Mrs. Bradley leaned forward and followed Rose's gaze, smiling a little when she spotted the girls. "I don't envy your life when the boys discover those two," she chuckled.

Unaware that they were being scrutinized and discussed, Diana and Corey observed the festivities from the sidelines near the dessert tables. It was not the sort of gathering to which teenagers were invited, and so they were pretty much on their own. At their father's request, Corey had been acting as "roving photographer," moving from group to group, trying to capture the mood of the party and the faces of the guests without being too obvious or in the way.

"Are you ready to go inside?" Diana asked. "We could watch a movie."

Corey nodded. "As soon as I use up the rest of this roll of film." She looked about for a face she hadn't photographed yet, realized she hadn't taken many pictures of her own family, and scanned the crowd to see where they were.

"There's Grandma, over there," she said, starting forward. "Let's get a pict—" She stopped short, and her breath seemed to catch in her throat as a tall young man in a white dinner jacket suddenly strolled out of the crowd. "Oh, *wow!*" Corey breathed, unknowingly clutching Diana's wrist in a vice and stopping her short. "*Oh, wow . . .*" she whispered. "Who is that? He's over there, being introduced to Grandma," she clarified.

Diana followed the direction of her stare. "That's Spencer Addison. He's Mrs. Bradley's grandson, and when he isn't away at SMU, he lives with her. He always has." Racking her brain for any other tidbits of information she'd heard over the years, she added, "He has a mother somewhere and a half-sister who's a lot older, but he doesn't have much to do with them . . . Wait! I remember why he lives with his grandmother. His mother kept changing husbands, and so Mrs. Bradley decided Spencer should live with her a long time ago. He's nineteen or twenty, I don't know which."

Corey had never had a crush on a boy in her life, and until that moment she'd harbored considerable derision for all the girls she'd known who had. Boys were just boys and no big deal. Until that moment.

Choking back a surprised giggle at Corey's mesmerized expression, Diana said, "Do you want to meet him?"

"I'd rather marry him."

"First you have to meet him," Diana said with typical practicality and attention to protocol. "Then you can propose. Come on, before he leaves—"

In her haste, she grabbed Corey's hand, but Corey yanked it back in panic. "I can't, not now! I mean, I don't want to just barge up to him and shake his hand. I can't. He'll think I'm a jerk. He'll think I'm a kid."

"In the dark, you can pass for sixteen."

"Are you sure?" Corey asked, ready to rely completely on Diana's judgment. Although there was only a year's difference in their ages, to Corey, Diana was the epitome of youthful sophistication—poised, reserved, and outwardly confident. Earlier, Corey had felt she herself looked especially nice that night in her "nautical" outfit of wide-legged, navy blue pants and a short navy jacket trimmed in gold braid at the wrists with gold anchors appliquéd at the shoulders and gold stars on the lapels. Diana had helped her choose the clothes, then she'd styled Corey's heavy blond hair into a fashionable knot atop her head, which they'd both agreed gave Corey a more mature look. Now Corey waited in an agony of uncertainty while Diana gave her a close once-over.

"Yes. I'm sure."

"What if he thinks I'm a troll?"

"He won't think that."

"I won't know what to say to him!" Diana started forward, but Corey pulled her back again. "What'll I say? What'll I do?"

"I have an idea. No, bring the camera with you," Diana said when Corey started to put the camera down on a vacant lawn chair. "Don't worry."

Corey wasn't worried, she was petrified, but in the space of a moment, fate had thrust her out of childhood and onto a new path, and she was too brave and too excited to try to retreat to the safety of the old path.

"Hi, Spencer," Diana said when they reached their destination.

"Diana?" he said in the flattering tone of one who can scarcely believe his eyes. "You're all grown up."

"Oh, I hope not," she joked with a regal ease that Corey mentally vowed to copy. "I wanted to end up taller than this by the time I grew up!" Turning to Corey, she said, "This is my sister, Caroline."

The moment Corey yearned for and simultaneously dreaded had arrived. Grateful to Diana for using her real name, which

19

sounded older and more sophisticated, Corey forced her gaze up the front of his white pleated shirt, past his tanned jaw, until it finally collided with his amber eyes, and she felt a jolt that made her knees knock.

He held out his hand, and as if from far away, she heard his deep voice—a velvet voice, intimate and caressing as he repeated her name. "Caroline," he said.

"Yes," she breathed, gazing into his eyes and putting her trembling hand in his. His palm was warm and broad, and his fingers closed around hers. Her fingers tightened involuntarily on his, inadvertently preventing him from breaking the handclasp.

Beside her, Diana was rushing to her rescue, trying to distract Mrs. Bradley and their grandmother from Corey's enraptured pose. "Corey still has some film in her camera, Mrs. Bradley. We thought you might like to have a picture taken of you and Spencer, together."

"What a lovely idea!" Mrs. Bradley said, leaning around Diana and breaking the spell by addressing Corey directly. "Your grandmother tells me you're quite the young photographer!"

Corey looked over her shoulder at Mrs. Bradley and nodded, still gripping Spencer Addison's hand.

"How would you like Spencer and his grandmother to pose, Corey?" Diana hinted.

"Oh, pose. Yes." Corey loosened her grasp on his hand and slowly pulled her gaze from his. In a sudden flurry of motion, she stepped back and raised her camera, looked through the viewfinder, and aimed the camera straight at Spencer, nearly blinding him with the unexpected glare of her flash. He laughed, and she shot another picture.

"That was a little too quick," Corey said in breathless apology, hastily focusing again. This time he looked straight at her and smiled—a lazy grin that swept across his tanned features and touched his tawny eyes. Corey's heart did a somersault that she feared made her camera hand shake as she took that picture and the next one. Thrilled with the opportunity to have lots of pictures of him to look at in the morning, she forgot all about poor Mrs. Bradley and took two more shots of him in rapid succession.

"And now," Diana said, sounding as if she was about to choke on something, "how about a few shots of *Mrs. Bradley* with Spencer. If the pictures turn out," she added in a deeply meaningful voice aimed directly at Corey, "we could bring them over to *their house* in a couple days."

The realization that she'd completely forgotten about taking Mrs. Bradley's picture made Corey flush to the roots of her hair, and she immediately vowed to produce a photograph of the two of them that would do credit to a professional portrait photographer. With that goal in mind, the technicalities of photography temporarily replaced her preoccupation with her handsome subject. "The torchlight makes it tricky," she said. With the camera to her eye, she addressed Spencer. "If you could move over behind your grandmother's chair . . . Yes, just like that. Now, Mrs. Bradley, look at me . . . and you, too . . . Spencer . . ."

Saying his beautiful name sent shivers down her spine, and she paused to swallow. "Yes, that's good." Corey took the shot, but when the pair started to part, she wasn't at all satisfied with the stiffness of the pose she'd arranged. "Let's take just one more," she pleaded. She waited while Spencer stepped back into the frame. "This time, put your hand on your grandmother's left shoulder."

"Aye-aye, Admiral," he said, teasing her about her jaunty naval outfit, but following her order.

Corey held on to her composure at the endearing little joke, but she tucked his words away in her heart, to be savored later. "Mrs. Bradley, I'd like you to look at me. That's good," she said, scrutinizing the light playing on Spencer's features and its effect on the ultimate outcome. She liked the way his large hand looked as it rested almost protectively on his grandmother's shoulder. "Now, before I take the picture, I'd like you each to take a second and think of a *really* special time that you spent together, just the two of you when Spencer was a little boy. A trip to the zoo, maybe . . . or the day he got his first bicycle . . . or an ice cream cone he dropped and still wanted to eat . . ."

Through the viewfinder, she saw a fond grin drift over Spencer's face, and he glanced down at his grandmother's white head. At the same moment Mrs. Bradley's face softened with a smile of remembrance that made her eyes twinkle, and she looked up at him, spontaneously lifting her right hand and laying it over his. Corey snapped the shot and another immediately after, her heart pounding with delight at the unexpectedly intimate moment she was almost sure she'd captured on film.

She let the camera slide down and smiled at both of them, her eyes shining with hope. "I'll have these developed at a camera shop. I don't want to try to do it myself, they're too important."

"Thank you very much, Corey," Mrs. Bradley said with gruff pleasure, but her eyes were still shining with whatever memory Corey had evoked.

"I'd like a picture taken with you, too, Spence, and then we have to go or we'll be late!" a plaintive female voice said, and for the very first time, Corey realized that there was a girl with Spencer. A beautiful girl, with a small waist and big breasts and long, slender legs. Corey's heart sank, but she obediently stepped back to take the picture, then she waited until the flickering torchlight threw a shadow over her rival's face.

* * *

The following week, Corey's pictures were ready to be picked up and Marge Crumbaker's column appeared in the *Post*. The entire family gathered around the dining room table and held their breaths while Robert opened it to the society section. An entire page was covered with pictures of the guests and decorations, the food and flowers, and even the greenhouse and garden.

But it was Marge Crumbaker's column that made the family beam as Robert Foster proudly read her words aloud:

" 'As she presided over this lovely party and looked after her guests, Mrs. Robert Foster III (the former Mary Britton of Long Valley) displayed a graciousness, a hospitality, and an attention to her guests that will surely make her one of Houston's leading hostesses. Also present at the festivities were Mrs. Foster's parents, Mr. and Mrs. Henry Britton, who were kind enough to escort many fascinated guests and would-be gardeners and handymen (if we only had the time!) through the new garden, greenhouse, and workshop that Bob Foster has erected on the grounds of his River Oaks mansion. . . .' "

Three

THE PARTY HAD BEEN A GREAT SUCCESS AND SO WERE THE pictures Corey took of Spencer Addison and his grandmother. Corey was so excited that she ordered two enlargements of the best picture—one for Mrs. Bradley and one for herself.

The day they arrived, she placed her framed copy on her nightstand, then she stretched out on the bed on her back to make certain she could see his picture with her head on the pillow. Lifting her head, she peered at Diana, who was sitting at her feet. "Isn't he gorgeous?" she sighed. "He's Matt Dillon and Richard Gere rolled into one—only better looking. He's Tom Cruise and that guy Harrison whatshisname—"

"Ford," Diana provided with typical attention to details.

"Ford," Corey agreed, picking up the picture and holding it above her face. "I'm going to marry him someday. I just *know* I am."

Although Diana was a little older, and definitely wiser and more practical, she wasn't immune to Corey's contagious enthusiasm or the energy with which Corey always tackled life's obstacles. "In that case," Diana said, getting up and reaching for Corey's phone, "we'd better make sure your future husband is home before we take the other copy over to Mrs. Bradley. We can walk over there, it's only two miles."

Mrs. Bradley didn't merely like the photograph, she loved it. "What a talent you have!" she exclaimed, her arthritic hand trembling a little as she touched Spencer's face in the picture. "I shall place this on my dresser. No," she said, getting up, "I shall place it here in the living room where everyone can see it. Spencer," she called out as he bounded down the staircase, heading for the front door. In answer to her summons, he strolled into the living room, wearing tennis whites and carrying a tennis racket—looking to Corey even more gorgeous than he had in a tuxedo.

Oblivious to Corey's hectic color, Mrs. Bradley gestured toward the girls. "You know Diana, and I'm sure you remember Corey from the party Saturday night?"

If he had said no, Corey would have died of humiliation and disappointment right there—expired on Mrs. Bradley's Persian carpet and had to be carried out and buried.

Instead, he looked at Corey with a smile and then nodded. "Hi, ladies," he said, making Corey feel at least twenty.

"The girls have just brought me a very special gift." She

handed him the picture in its frame. "Remember when Corey asked us to think of a special moment while she took the picture?—look how it turned out!"

He took the picture, and to Corey's almost painful joy she saw his expression go from polite interest to one of surprised pleasure. "It's a wonderful picture, Corey," he said, turning the full force of his deep voice and magnetic gaze on her. "You're very talented." He returned the photograph to his grandmother, bent down, and brushed a quick kiss on her brow. "I have a tennis date at the club in thirty minutes," he told her. To the girls, he said, "Can I give you a ride home? It's on my way."

Riding beside Spencer Addison in his blue sports car with the convertible top down soared straight to the top of Corey's "Major Events of a Lifetime" list, and during the next several years, she managed to create a great many more events of a similar nature. In fact, she developed a positive genius for inventing reasons to visit his grandmother, whenever Spencer was home from college for an occasional weekend. His grandmother inadvertently collaborated in Corey's grand design by sending Spencer over to the Fosters' to deliver things she'd baked or to pick up some recipes or patterns she wanted to try with Grandpa's specially made crochet hook.

As the weeks passed, Corey used her interest in photography as an additional excuse to see Spencer and capture more treasured shots of him. Under the ploy of wanting to perfect her ability with "action photography," she went to Spencer's polo matches, his tennis matches, and anywhere else she could possibly go where he was likely to be. As her collection of his pictures grew, she started a special scrapbook and kept it under her bed, and when that was filled, she started another, and then another. Her favorite shots of him, however, were always displayed around her bedroom, where she could see them.

When her grandmother asked why most of the pictures in her

room were of Spencer Addison, Corey dissembled with a long, involved, and mostly trumped-up explanation about Spencer's unique photogenic qualities and how concentrating on a single "subject" in a variety of settings helped her to gauge her improvement as a photographer. For good measure, she threw in a lot of jargon about stop-action photography and the effect of aperture settings and shutter speeds on the final result. Her grandmother walked out of Corey's bedroom looking a little dazed and thoroughly confused, and did not broach the subject again.

The rest of the family undoubtedly suspected Corey's true feelings, but they were all kind enough not to tease her about them. The object of her unflagging devotion seemed perfectly at ease around her, as if he had no idea that she lived for his visits, and he visited often, although mostly on errands for his grandmother. The reasons he came to the house didn't matter to Corey; what mattered was that he was rarely in a hurry to *leave.*

If she had advance notice of his arrival, she spent hours in her room frantically restyling her hair, changing her clothes, and trying to decide on a good topic for conversation when she had a chance to talk to him. But regardless of how she looked, or what topics she chose, Spencer unfailingly treated her with a gentle courtesy that evolved into a kind of brotherly affection by the time she was fifteen. He took to calling her "Duchess" and teasing her about being beautiful. He admired her latest photos and joked with her and talked to her about college. Sometimes he even stayed for dinner.

Corey's mother said she thought he came over to the house and stayed for a while because he'd never had a real family, and so he enjoyed being with theirs. Corey's father thought Spencer enjoyed talking with him about the oil business. Corey's grandfather was equally certain that it was his garden and greenhouse that interested Spencer. Corey's grandmother was adamantly of the opinion that he knew the value of healthy cooking and eating, which was her forte.

Corey clung to the hope that he enjoyed seeing and talking to *her,* and Diana was young enough and loyal enough to completely agree with Corey.

Four

SOMEHOW, COREY MANAGED TO MAINTAIN THE FACADE OF wanting only a platonic friendship with him until she was sixteen. Until then she'd kept a tight rein on herself, partly because she was terrified of overwhelming him with her ardor and losing him completely, and partly because she hadn't found a risk-free opportunity to show him that she was old enough and more than ready for a romantic relationship with him.

Fate handed her that opportunity the week before Christmas. Spence had come over to the house to deliver an armload of Christmas gifts from his grandmother to each of the Fosters, but for Corey there was a special gift from him to her. He stayed for dinner and then for two games of chess with her grandfather. Corey waited until afterward, when the family had gone upstairs, then she insisted he wait while she opened his gift to her. Her hands shook uncontrollably as she spread the tissue in the big box aside and lifted out a large beautifully bound book of photographs by five of the world's leading photographers. "It's beautiful, Spence!" she breathed, "Thank you so much! I'll treasure it always."

She knew he was on his way to a Christmas party being given by some friends of his, but as she ushered him across the foyer in her new high heels, long plaid skirt, white silk blouse, and wine-colored velvet blazer, she had never felt more confident and mature. Because she'd known he was coming that night, she'd put her hair up into a chignon, with tendrils at her ears, because the style made her look older, and because Diana and she agreed it made her blue eyes look bigger.

"Merry Christmas, Corey," he said in the foyer as he turned to leave. Corey acted on sheer impulse because if she'd thought about it, she'd never have had the nerve. The house was decorated for the Christmas season in pine boughs and holly—and hanging from the crystal chandelier above the foyer was a giant bunch of mistletoe tied with red and gold ribbon. "Spence," she burst out, "don't you know it's bad luck not to honor the Christmas traditions of your friends when you're in their home?"

He turned, his hand already on the front door handle. "It is?"

Corey nodded slowly, her fingers clasped behind her back in a pose of nervous expectation.

"What tradition am I violating?"

In answer, she tipped her head back and looked meaningfully at the mistletoe overhead. "That one," she said, struggling to keep her voice steady. He looked up at the mistletoe, then down at her, and his expression was so dubious and hesitant that Corey abruptly lost much of her nerve.

"Of course," she fabricated hastily, "the tradition doesn't require you to kiss me. You can kiss anyone who lives in the house." Trying to turn it into a joke, she continued. "You can kiss a maid. Or Conchita. Or our cat. My dog . . ."

He laughed then and took his hand off the doorknob, but instead of leaning forward and kissing her cheek, which was about all she'd let herself hope he'd do, he hesitated, looking at her. "Are you sure you're old enough for me to do this?"

Corey got lost in those tawny eyes, mesmerized by something

she saw flickering in their depths. *Yes,* she told him silently, beckoning him to kiss her. *I know I'm old enough. I've been waiting forever.* She knew the answers were in her eyes, and she knew he saw them, and so she smiled a little, and with her hands still clasped behind her back, Corey softly and deliberately said, "No." It was an instinctive piece of highly effective flirtation, and just as instinctively he recognized it . . . and succumbed.

With a husky, startled laugh, he took her chin between his thumb and forefinger, tipped her head back, and brushed his lips slowly back and forth across hers . . . just once. It took only a moment for the kiss, but it was another, longer, moment before he took his hand from her chin and an even longer one before Corey opened her eyes. "Merry Christmas, Duchess," he said softly.

Corey felt the blast of icy air as he opened the door. When it closed behind him, she reached out automatically and switched off the foyer lights; then she stood there in the dark, reeling from the tenderness she'd heard in his voice after the kiss. For two years, she had fantasized about Spencer Addison, but not even in her fantasies had she ever imagined that his voice could be as stirring and as tender as a kiss.

Five

THE ONLY BLIGHT ON HER HAPPINESS WAS THAT SPENCER HAD said he planned to stay at college over spring break, studying for final exams, and that he didn't intend to be back in Houston until after he graduated in June.

Corey, who hadn't had much interest in dating, decided to use the months between January and June to broaden her knowledge of the workings of the male mind by going out regularly with a variety of boys. Spence was almost six years older than she, and a hundred times more worldly, and she was beginning to worry that her lack of dating experience would eventually embarrass him or somehow stop him from getting any more deeply involved with her.

She was popular at school and there were a gratifying number of boys who were eager to take her out, but it was Doug Hayward who quickly became her favorite and most constant escort, as well as her confidant.

Doug was a senior at her high school, the captain of the debate team, and the quarterback of their football team, but his greatest attraction from Corey's standpoint was that he, too, was hopelessly in love with someone else who lived far away. As a result, she could talk to him about Spence and get some male insight from an older boy who, like Spence, was smart and athletic and who also regarded her more as a sister than a real girlfriend.

It was Doug who tutored her on what "older men" liked in their girlfriends and who helped her come up with ideas to capture Spencer's attention and then his heart. Some of Doug's ideas were useful, some impractical, and some downright hilarious.

In May, just after Corey's seventeenth birthday, they had a long discussion about kissing techniques—a subject in which Corey felt woefully inexperienced—but when Doug earnestly attempted to demonstrate some of the techniques they'd discussed, they ended up convulsed with laughter. When he told her to slide her hand around his nape, Corey made a comic, threatening face and slid her hand around his throat instead. When he attempted to lightly kiss her ear, she got the giggles and laughed so hard she bumped his nose.

They were still laughing as he walked her to her front door that night. "Do me a favor," Doug joked, "if you ever tell Addison what we did tonight, don't mention my name. I don't want my right arm broken by some jealous running back before I ever get to play college football."

They'd already discussed the possibility of making Spence jealous as a way of forcing him to notice Corey, but the methods Doug came up with had seemed trite and transparent to Corey, and the outcome far too uncertain. "I can't see Spence getting jealous over anything connected with me," she said with a sigh, "let alone having him get physical about it."

"Don't bet *my* life on it. There's nothing like knowing your girl has been kissing someone else to make a sensible guy lose his mind. Believe me," he added as he left, "I know from experience."

Corey watched him walk down the sidewalk to his car in the driveway, her imagination running away with itself as his words revolved in her mind and an idea took shape.

She was still standing on the porch long after his taillights disappeared. By the time she finally went inside, she'd made a decision and was working out the fine details of the plan.

As soon as Spence came home in June, she had Diana suggest to their mother that Spence be invited to the house for dinner later in the week. Mrs. Foster readily complied. "Spence seemed delighted," she announced to the family when she hung up the phone in the kitchen.

"That young man appreciates the benefits of healthy home cooking," Rose said.

"He likes those father-son chats he and I have about business and making money," Mr. Foster asserted. "I've missed them, too."

"I'd better finish that project in the workshop," Henry mused aloud. "Spencer has an eye for fine woodwork. He should have gotten his degree in architecture instead of finance. He's fascinated with anything that has to do with building things."

Corey and Diana looked at each other with a conspiratorial smile. They didn't care why Spence came, so long as he came and stayed after dinner so that Corey could get him outside and execute her plan. Diana's contribution was to get everyone else to go to the movies once they'd had dinner and a little time to visit with him. Diana had chosen a movie that Corey had already seen so that no one would think it odd when Corey decided to stay home.

By the time Spence finally rang the doorbell, Corey was a mass of quivering nerves, but she managed to look serenely composed as she smiled into his eyes and gave him a quick, welcoming hug. She sat across from him at dinner, surreptitiously studying the changes that a half year had made in his beloved face, while he talked about attending graduate school in the fall. His tawny hair seemed a little darker to Corey, and the masculine planes of his face harder, but that lazy, heartstopping smile of his hadn't changed a bit. Every time he grinned at some quip of hers, Corey's heart melted, but when she smiled back at him, her expression was teasing, not worshipful. By her own count, she'd been out on forty-six dates with boys since he left her in the foyer at Christmas, and although the majority of them had been with Doug, her sixmonth crash course on dating, flirtation, and men in general had served her very well.

She was counting heavily on it as Diana herded the entire family into the car and Spence picked up his sport jacket, obviously intending to leave also. "Could you stay for a little while longer?" Corey asked, giving him what she hoped was a vaguely troubled look. "I—I need some advice."

He nodded, his forehead furrowing with concern. "What sort of advice, Duchess?"

"I don't want to talk about it here. Let's go outside. It's a beautiful evening, and I won't have to worry about our housekeeper overhearing us."

He walked beside her, his sport jacket slung over his shoulder and hooked on his thumb, and Corey wished she could feel one tenth as relaxed as he looked. The night was balmy, devoid for once of the awful humidity that made Houston summers into a steam bath. "Where do you want to sit?" he asked as she walked by two umbrellaed tables and headed toward the swimming pool further back on the lawn.

"Over here." Corey gestured to a lounge chair next to the swimming pool, waited until he sat down on it, then she boldly sat down beside him. Tipping her head back, she gazed up through a canopy of blooming crape myrtles to the stars twinkling in the moonless sky while she fought desperately to recover her fleeing courage. She made herself think only of his Christmas kiss and of the tenderness in his eyes and voice afterward. He had felt something special for her that night. She was still positive he had. Now she needed to make him remember it and feel it again. Somehow.

"Corey, what did you bring me out here to ask me?"

"It's a little difficult to explain," she said with a nervous laugh that caught in her throat. "I can't ask my mother because she'll get all upset," she added, deliberately eliminating what she knew would be his only escape routes from the discussion. "And I don't want to talk about it with Diana. She's all excited about starting college in the fall."

She stole a glance at him and saw him watching her with narrowed eyes. Drawing a fortifying breath, she plunged in. "Spence, do you remember when you kissed me at Christmas?"

His answer seemed a long time in coming. "Yes."

"At the time, you may have known I didn't have much experience . . . Did you know—notice—that?" The last question hadn't been in her rehearsed speech, and so she waited, wanting him to deny that he'd noticed. "Yes," he said flatly.

Irrationally, Corey was crushed. "Well, I've gotten a lot more experience since then! A *whole lot* more!" she informed him haughtily.

"Congratulations," he said shortly. "Now get to the point."

His tone was so sharp and impatient that Corey's head snapped around. Not once in all the times that she'd been with him had he *ever* spoken to her like that. "Never mind," she said, nervously rubbing her palms on her knees. "I'll find someone else to ask," she added, abruptly abandoning the whole scheme and starting to stand.

"Corey," he snapped, "are you pregnant?"

Corey gave a shriek of horrified laughter and dropped back to her seat, gaping at him. "From *kissing?*" she laughed, rolling her eyes. "What did you do, skip health and hygiene class in the sixth grade?"

For the second time in moments, she saw Spencer Addison exhibit another unprecedented emotion—chagrin. "I guess you aren't pregnant," he said wryly, shooting her a rueful smile.

Utterly delighted to have him off balance for a change, Corey continued to tease him, trying without success to control her wobbly grin. "Don't football players take biology at SMU? Listen, if *that's* why you have to go to graduate school, save the tuition and talk to Teddy Morris in Long Valley, Texas. His dad's a doctor, and when Teddy was only eight years old, he told us everything there is to know on the playground by the swings." Spencer's shoulders were shaking with laughter as Corey finished. "Of course, he used a pair of turtles for teaching tools. They *may* have mated by now."

With traces of a grin still tugging at the corners of his mouth, he shifted position so that his shoulders were against the raised back of the chaise lounge and his left leg was bent at the knee, resting beside Corey's hip. His right leg, which had been injured twice in games last year, was stretched out beside the chair, his heel resting on the flagstones. "Okay," he said mildly, folding his arms over his chest and lifting his brows, "let's hear it."

"Is your right knee bothering you?"

"Your *problem* is bothering me."

"You don't know what it is yet."

"*That's* the part that's bothering me."

The banter was so endearingly familiar, and he looked so relaxed and powerful—as if he could carry the entire world's problems on his wide shoulders—that Corey had a crazy impulse to simply curl up beside him and forget kissing. On the other hand, if she executed her plan successfully, she might end up stretched out beside him *and* being kissed. An infinitely preferable alternative, she decided as she paused for a quick mental check of her appearance to make certain she looked as desirable as possible. Something slinky and low-cut would have been preferable to the white shorts and sleeveless knit top she was wearing, but at least they showed off her tan well.

"Corey," he said in a no-nonsense tone, "the problem?"

Corey drew a long, fortifying breath. "It's about kissing . . ." she began haltingly.

"I already got that part. What do you want to know?"

"How can you tell when it's time to stop?"

"'How can you—?'" he repeated in disbelief; then he recovered and said flatly and piously, "When you're enjoying it too much, it's time to stop."

"Is that when *you* stop?" Corey countered.

He had the decency to look ashamed of his answer; then he looked annoyed. "This discussion is not about me."

"Okay," Corey said agreeably, rather enjoying his discomfi-ture, "then it's about someone else. Let's call him . . . Doug Johnson!"

"Let's drop the pretense," Spence said a little testily. "The fact is that you're seeing someone named Johnson and he's pushing for more than you want to give. If you want advice, I'll give it to you: Tell him to pound sand!"

Since she hadn't been certain what tactics Spence would use to evade her trap, Corey was ready with several variations of the same scheme, all of which were designed to maneuver him back onto the path. She tried out the first variation. "That won't help. I'm seeing lots of *different* people, actually, but things seem to go too fast after the kissing gets started."

"What are you asking me?" he said warily.

"I'd like to know how to tell when things are getting out of hand, and I'd like some specific guidelines."

"Well, you aren't going to get them from me."

"Fine," Corey said, defeated, but bluffing to save her pride. "But if I end up in a home for unwed mothers because you wouldn't tell me what I needed to know, then it's going to be as much your fault as mine!"

She made a move to stand, but he caught her wrist and jerked her back down onto the seat. "Oh, no you don't! You aren't going to end this discussion with a remark like that."

A moment ago, Corey thought she was defeated, but now she realized that victory was actually in her grasp. He was flounder-ing. Uncertain. Retreating from his original position. Corey prepared to advance, but *very* cautiously.

"What—exactly—do you need to know?" he asked, looking sublimely uncomfortable.

"I'd like you to tell me how to know when a kiss is going to get out of hand. There has to be some sort of clue."

Defeated by his own uncertainty, Spence leaned his head

back and closed his eyes. "There are several clues," he muttered, "and I think you already know damned well what they are."

Corey widened her eyes and innocently said, "If I knew what they are, why would I be asking you about them?"

"Corey, it is impossible for me to sit here and give you a play-by-play description of the stages of a kiss."

Corey opened the trapdoor and got ready to shove him in. "Could you demonstrate?"

"Absolutely not! But I can give you a good piece of advice: You're dating the wrong bunch of people if they're all pushing you for more than you want to give."

"Oh, I guess I didn't make myself clear. What I'm trying to say is that I think *I* might be the one who is giving the guys the wrong idea." Mentally, she stood beside the open door and made a sweeping gesture to him. "I think the problem may be how *I* kiss *them*."

Spence walked straight into her trap. "How the hell do you kiss?" he demanded, then he looked furious at his blunder. "Never mind," he said, leaning forward suddenly.

Corey put her hands on his shoulders and gently forced him back. "Now, don't get hysterical," she said in a soothing voice. "Just relax."

Beneath her palms his shoulders were still tensed, as if he wanted to bolt, and she had a fleeting image of him on the football field, only tonight he'd caught a pass he hadn't expected and didn't want, and now he couldn't find anyone else to hand it off to.

The thought made her smile into his narrowed eyes; it made her feel as if she, not he, were calling the plays for a change. It gave her confidence. It made her absurdly happy. "Spence," she said. "Just run the ball down the field. It's very simple. Honest."

Her ability to find humor in his predicament only made him

more irritable. "I cannot believe you seriously want me to do this!"

From beneath her lashes, Corey gave him a look of limpid appeal. "Who else can I possibly ask? I suppose I could ask Doug to show me what I do that—"

"Let's get on with it," he interrupted shortly.

His knee was still beside her hip, preventing her from moving closer to him. "Could you move your knee?"

Wordlessly, he shifted his left leg out of the way without altering the position of his upper body. Corey scooted closer, turning so that she could look at him.

"Now what?" he demanded, his arms crossed obstinately over his chest.

Corey had a rehearsed answer in mind for exactly this moment. "Now you pretend you're Doug—and I'll be me."

"I don't want to be Johnson," he said, sounding bitter about everything.

"Be anyone you like, but be a good sport, okay?"

"Fine," he clipped. "Now I'm being a good sport."

Corey waited for him to move, to reach for her, to do *something.* "You can start whenever you're ready," she said when he didn't budge.

He looked resentful. "Why do *I* have to start?"

Corey looked at his balky expression and felt an almost uncontrollable impulse to burst out laughing. She had started out tonight hoping to fulfill the most cherished dream of her lifetime—to be kissed by him—*really* kissed—by him. As badly as she'd wanted that, the prospect of it had made her feel nervous and inadequate. Now it was a foregone conclusion that she was going to be kissed, but it was Spencer who was uneasy and off balance, and it was she who was amused and very relaxed. "You have to start," she informed him, "because that's the way things . . . start." When he still didn't seem able to move, she peered at him with sham concern. "Do you *know* how to start?"

"I think so," he drawled.

"Because if you aren't certain, I can give you a hint. Most guys—"

Corey broke off as the absurdity of her suggestion registered on him, banishing his annoyance over his assigned task and making his eyes gleam with amusement.

"Most guys do what?" he asked with a grin as he reached out and moved her closer to his chest. "Is this how Johnson starts?" He bent his head and Corey braced herself for some sort of wild kiss that would make her faint. What she got was a swift clumsy kiss that was slightly off center and made her shake her head in the negative.

"No?" he joked. He pulled her forward into a bear hug and nipped her ear. "How was that?"

He was being playful, Corey realized, and she suddenly feared that this sort of kissing was all there was going to be. She resolved not to let all her carefully made plans lead only to this, but she couldn't help laughing as he quickened his demonstration of how he pictured poor imaginary Doug Johnson treating her. "I'll bet this technique is a real favorite of his," he said, starting to kiss her and deliberately bumping her nose instead. "Did I miss?" He switched to the other side and bumped her nose again. "Did I miss again?"

Laughing, Corey leaned her forehead against the solid wall of his chest and nodded.

He caught her chin, turned her face aside, and rubbed his nose against the side of her neck like a playful puppy. "Let me know when I'm driving you out of your mind with passion," he invited, and Corey laughed harder. "Am I great?" he asked, nuzzling the other side of her neck. "Or am I great?"

Her eyes swimming with mirth, Corey raised her gaze to his and nodded vigorously. "You're completely great—" she said, "but you just aren't—Doug."

He grinned back at her, sharing the joke, and in that prolonged moment of silent companionship, with his hands linked loosely behind her back and his eyes smiling into hers, Corey felt utterly content. Alive. At peace. So did he—she knew it with every beat of her heart. She knew it as surely as she knew he was about to kiss her again and that the joking was over.

His gaze holding hers, he tipped her chin up and slowly lowered his head. "It's time," he said softly, as his mouth descended, "for a more scientific approach to the problem."

At the first touch of his lips on hers, Corey's entire body stiffened with the shock of the contact. He obviously noticed her reaction, because he took his mouth away and touched it to her cheek, kissing her there as he continued in a throaty murmur, "In order for us to obtain reliable data . . ." His mouth slid slowly to her jaw. ". . . both parties have to . . ." His lips traced a warm path to her ear. ". . . collaborate in the . . ." He lifted his mouth slightly, his hand curving around her nape, tilting her face into better position. ". . . experiment."

His mouth captured hers in a slow, insistent kiss that steadily increased in pressure, forcing Corey's lips to part beneath his and setting off tremors of passion inside her that began to collide and combine with stunning force. With an inner moan of pleasure and need, Corey slid her hands up his chest and gave herself over to the kiss, letting him part her lips, yielding to the probing of his tongue, then welcoming it with mindless desperation.

His fingers shoved into the hair at her nape, loosening the pins that held her hair, and suddenly the mass of golden strands were pouring over them like a veil, and everything was out of control. She was kissing him back, falling forward into his arms while his tongue plunged into her mouth, breathlessly insistent, stroking and caressing.

His hands slid over her breasts, cupping them possessively, and Corey crushed her mouth to his, her nails digging into his arms, her body pressing intimately against his surging erection while his arm clamped around her hips, pressing her tighter to him, holding her as he rolled her onto her side.

Years of love and longing more than compensated for lack of experience, and Corey returned each endless, scorching kiss, her hands sliding over the bunched muscles of his back and shoulders, her parted lips surrendering to and then boldly conquering the man whose long fingers were caressing her breasts, tormenting her, tantalizing her with the same promise of pleasure her mouth was giving him. Time ceased to exist for her, obliterated by the turbulence of raging desire and a sensual mouth that was hungrily devouring hers with increasing urgency . . . and a knee that was nudging her legs apart while his hands . . . stopped.

He tore his mouth from hers and lifted off her so abruptly that Corey felt completely disoriented, and when she saw the awful expression on his face, she was afraid to breathe.

His brows were drawn together into a dark frown of utter disbelief as he stared down at their bodies, then he seemed to notice that his hand was still on her breast and he jerked it away, glaring at his own palm as if it had somehow offended him. His accusing gaze snapped from his hand to her face, and his expression slowly transformed from angry to utterly thunderstruck.

Understanding dawned, and Corey expelled her breath on a rush of joyous relief. He had lost control and he didn't like it. He hadn't imagined she would ever be able to do that to him, but she had done it. *She* had done that to him. Filled with pride

41

and satisfaction and a world of love, Corey smiled slumberously at him, her hand still resting on his chest. "How'd I do?"

"That depends on what you were *trying* to do," he said curtly.

She leaned up on her elbow, so happy that she had been able to make him want her that nothing he could have said would have spoiled her joy. "Now that you've had a demonstration," she teased, "would you care to tell me at what point things got out of hand?

"No," he said, and sat up.

Corey sat up beside him, thoroughly enjoying the situation, her smile disarmingly innocent. "But you were supposed to notice and tell me if things got out of hand because of something *I* did. Do you need another demonstration?"

"No more demonstrations." He stood as he said it. "Your father would get out his shotgun if he knew what happened out here tonight, and he'd be justified."

"Nothing happened."

"If this is your idea of 'nothing,' then that's why the boys in your life are trying to take things too far."

She walked beside him trying to look deeply concerned when she felt like laughing with delight. "Would you say, then, that things went too far between us?"

"They didn't go too far. They *could* have gone too far."

Six

HE LEFT, AND COREY DIDN'T SEE HIM AGAIN UNTIL THE following Thanksgiving. When he finally came over to the house, Corey had the feeling that she couldn't have gotten him off to a solitary spot if her life depended upon it, and she told herself that if the kiss hadn't affected him, he wouldn't be so wary.

Diana was inclined to agree, and Corey again enlisted her aid in helping to accomplish her dream, a dream she'd cherished for years. She wanted it to come true so fiercely, so completely, that she couldn't believe fate would ever prevent it. In order to accomplish her goal, she was careful toward the end of Spence's visit to seem a little distracted and just a touch sad. Once she'd made certain he couldn't help but notice, Corey left him alone in the living room with Diana, then she hid around the corner to see how things went. "Poor Corey," Diana said—as they'd rehearsed.

"What's wrong?" Spence asked quickly, and Diana's heart soared at how concerned he sounded.

"She's been looking forward to the Christmas dance at school all semester. She's on the decorations committee and everything. She's had the dress she's going to wear for months."

"What's the problem?"

"The problem is that Doug Johnson was going to take her— he's on Baylor's football team—but he phoned this morning to tell her that his family has decided to go to Bermuda for Christmas, and they won't even consider letting him stay behind. I feel terrible for Corey."

"She's better off not going out with jocks, anyway. You know what they're like and what they think they're entitled to from any girl they honor with a few hours of their time."

"You were a jock," Diana said with a laugh.

"And that's how I know what I know."

"The point is, she's not going to be able to go. The dance is a big thing, especially for graduating seniors."

"Why doesn't she ask someone else to take her?" he suggested, sounding puzzled that Diana was bringing the problem to him.

"Corey has lots of friends, but they already have their own dates."

To Corey it seemed like hours before he said, "Are you suggesting I take her?"

"That's entirely up to you." Diana got up then and headed out of the room, and as she passed Corey in the dining room, they exchanged a silent "high five." Corey was halfway into the living room before she remembered to wipe the grin off her face and replace it with a more woebegone expression, but Spencer didn't notice; he was putting on his jacket to leave.

"My mother is coming home for Christmas," he said.

"That will be nice."

"I'm looking forward to seeing her," he admitted, looking a little embarrassed by his sentimentality. "The point is," he continued abruptly, "I haven't seen her in three years. Diana explained that you don't have a date for the Christmas dance. I'll be in Houston, so if you don't mind having an old man take you to your dance, and you can't find anyone else, then I will."

Corey felt faint with joy and relief, but she was wise enough to refrain from a display of too much exultation and risk suffocating him. "It's very nice of you to offer."

"I'm on my way back to Dallas. You can tell me when I come home Christmas week if you want me to take you."

"Oh, I do," Corey said quickly. "I can tell you right now. The dance is the twenty-first. Could you pick me up at seven?"

"Sure. No problem. And if you get a better offer, just let me know." He turned on the front step as he zipped up his jacket, and Corey said in a daring, grown-up way, "You're a complete sweetheart, Spence."

In answer, he chucked her under the chin as if she were a six-year-old and left.

Seven

ON DECEMBER 21 AT SEVEN, WHEN COREY CAME DOWNSTAIRS in her gown of royal blue silk and matching blue high heels, she didn't look or feel like a child. She was a woman, her eyes shining with love and anticipation; she was Cinderella on the way to her ball, watching for her Prince Charming at the living room window.

Prince Charming was late.

When he hadn't arrived by seven forty-five, Corey called his house. She knew his grandmother wasn't planning to return from Scottsdale until the next day and that she'd given the servants some time off before Christmas, so when no one answered the phone at the Bradleys', Corey was certain it was because Spence was on his way.

When he still wasn't there at eight fifteen, her father gently suggested that he go over to the house and see what was keeping Spence or if something was wrong over there. In an agony of suspense and foreboding, Corey waited for her father to return, certain that only death or injury would keep Spence from honoring his commitment.

Twenty minutes later, Mr. Foster came back. Corey took one look at his angry eyes and hesitant expression, and she knew the news was bad. It was worse than bad; it was devastating: Her father had spoken with the family chauffeur, who lived in an apartment above the garage, and the chauffeur had told him that Spencer had decided not to come home for the holidays, after all. According to the chauffeur, Spencer's mother, who'd been expected for Christmas, had decided to go to Paris instead, and as a result, Spencer's grandmother had decided to extend her stay in Scottsdale until the New Year.

Corey listened to that shattering recitation in anguished disbelief, fighting back tears. Unable to bear either sympathy or righteous indignation from her family, she went upstairs to her room and took off the beautiful gown she'd chosen with such care to dazzle and impress him. For the next week, she jumped every time the phone rang, convinced he would call to explain and apologize.

On New Year's Day, when he had not done either one, Corey calmly removed the blue gown from her closet and carefully packed it in a box, then she removed every single picture of him from all the walls, mirrors, and bulletin boards in her room.

Afterward, she went downstairs and asked her family never to mention to Spencer that she had waited for him or had been disappointed in any way that he failed to show up. Still furious at the hurt Corey had suffered, Mr. Foster argued vehemently that Spencer was getting off much too lightly and deserved to be horsewhipped, at least verbally if not physically! Corey calmly replied that she didn't want to give Spencer the satisfaction of knowing she'd waited and watched and worried. "Let him think I went to the dance with someone else," she said firmly.

When Mr. Foster still argued that, as Corey's father, he was entitled to the satisfaction of "having a few words with that young man," Corey's mother had put her hand on his arm and said, "Corey's pride is more important, and that's what she's saving with her plan."

Diana, who was as angry with Spencer as her father was, nevertheless sided with Corey. "I'd love to give him a good swift kick, too, Daddy, but Corey's right. We shouldn't say anything to make him think he was ever that important to her."

The next day, Corey donated the beautiful blue gown to a charity resale shop.

She burned the unmounted photographs.

The photo albums she'd kept under her bed were too big and too handsome to burn, so she packed them into a large box along with the framed photographs she'd taken of him. She lugged them up to the attic, intending the remove the pictures some day and use the albums and frames for photographs of more worthy subjects than Spencer Addison.

When she went to bed that night, Corey did not cry, nor did she let herself ever again fantasize about Spencer Addison. She had packed away more than his pictures that day; she had put away the last traces of adolescence with all its lovely, impossible dreams.

After that, fate presented her with only two opportunities to see Spencer, had she wanted an excuse to talk to him—his grandmother's funeral that spring and his wedding to a New York debutante that summer. Corey attended the funeral with her family, but when they went to talk to Spencer, she deliberately let herself be obscured by the crowd of mourners. With her gaze on the flower-strewn coffin, Corey paid her last respects to the elderly woman in silence, with a prayer, while tears of sorrow slid unnoticed down her cheeks. And then she left.

She did not attend Spencer's wedding with her family either, even though it took place in Houston, where the bride's maternal grandparents lived, nor did she attend the reception. She spent his wedding night doing exactly what she knew he would be doing that night: she went to bed with Doug Hayward.

Unfortunately the young man to whom she had chosen to surrender her virginity was a much better friend and confidant than he was a lover, and she ended up weeping her heart out in his awkward embrace.

In time, she forgot about Spencer entirely. There were other, better, things to concentrate on, to anticipate and celebrate.

For one thing, the Foster family was becoming quite famous. The family's joint interest in gardening, cooking, and handiwork that had seemed like a lark to many had become something of a trend, popularized by Marge Crumbaker, who continued to give it glowing mentions in her column.

During Corey's freshman year at college, an editor at *Better Homes and Gardens* saw one of the columns, and after coming out to the house and attending a Fourth of July party, the editor decided to do a huge feature on what she dubbed "Entertaining—Foster Style."

When the magazine came out, there were pictures featuring tables set with Grandma's hand-painted china and handmade place mats, with beautiful flower arrangements that Corey's mother created from flowers taken from their own garden and their little greenhouse. Also included were pictures of some of the family's favorite meals, beautifully photographed and described in detail, with recipes and directions for growing the fresh herbs, fruits, and vegetables that were used for the family meals. But the most memorable part of the article came at the end, where Corey's mother had tried to describe her feelings about what she and her family did and why they did it: "I think the real pleasure of having a party, or preparing a meal, or planning a garden, or creating a furnished room, comes from doing it with people you love. That way there's satisfaction in the effort, no matter how that effort turns out."

The magazine dubbed that last sentence, "The Foster Ideal," and the phrase stuck. After that, other magazines contacted the Fosters asking for articles and pictures, for which they were willing to pay. Corey's mother and grandparents were only able to produce the raw material, so Diana wrote the articles and Corey took the photographs.

In the beginning, it had all been a family hobby.

Robert Foster died of a stroke five months after the stock market made its downward plunge in 1987. When his attorney and accountant gave the family the details of his dire financial situation, they understood why he'd been so tense and preoccupied during the last year, and why he had wanted to shield them. After that the family hobby became a business that enabled them to survive. Marge Crumbaker's columns had already made Mary Foster into a celebrity hostess, but in the aftermath of Robert's death, that no longer had any meaning to anyone, particularly his grieving family.

In the end, it was Elyse Lanier, the wife of one of Houston's leading entrepreneurs, who hit upon a way to help them stay afloat. A few weeks after Robert's death, she phoned Mary and gently asked her if she'd be willing to accept the responsibility for the food and decorations for the Orchid Ball. When Mary said yes, Elyse used her considerable influence to make the rest of the ball's committee agree.

It was the first time in the ball's history that one person had ever been entrusted with so much. On Elyse's part, it had been an act of friendship and support, one that Mary never forgot. Several years later, when Elyse's husband was elected Houston's mayor, Mary finally found a way to express her gratitude. She did it in the form of a large picnic basket, the size of a compact car, which bore a huge red, white, and blue ribbon when it was delivered to the Laniers.

In it were hand-painted dishes, wineglasses, coffee cups, candlesticks, napkin rings, and salt and pepper shakers, along with handmade napkins and place mats. It was a full picnic service for twenty-four people. Each piece was lovingly crafted. Each item bore the Laniers' monogram in red, white, and blue.

Despite the Fosters' instant renown as Houston society's "caterers of choice" after the Orchid Ball, there would never have been enough money to maintain their house or their living style from catering alone, and the hard work quickly began taking a heavy toll on Corey's mother and grandparents.

In the end, it was Diana who decided the family should be capitalizing on the fame they'd acquired in various home and entertainment magazines, rather than trying to run a catering business for which they were actually ill-equiped. She was the daughter of an entrepreneur, and although Robert Foster had suffered the fate of many other wealthy Texans in the seventies and eighties, Diana had clearly inherited his proclivity for business.

She drew up a business plan, packed up the magazine articles and recipes that had been published over the years, and put together a large collection of Corey's photographs taken of family projects.

"If we're going to do this," she announced to Corey as she left to see a banker friend of her father's, "we have to do it big and with plenty of financial backing. Otherwise we'll fail, not from lack of ability, but from lack of funds to keep us going for the first two years."

Somehow, she got the funds they needed.

The first issue of *Foster's Beautiful Living* magazine came out the following year, and although there were some difficult, and even terrifying, setbacks along the way, the magazine caught on with the public. Foster Enterprises began putting out recipe books and then coffee-table books, where Corey's photography won acclaim and generated even more income for the family.

All of that had led up to Newport, Corey thought wryly. After more than a decade of years and dozens of cameras, she had come full circle: she was about to take a camera with her and go see Spencer Addison again . . .

Corey pulled out of her reverie, glanced at her watch, and hastily opened the car door. As she walked up the front steps of the house, she suddenly realized that the prospect of seeing Spencer again no longer upset her. For more than a half hour, she'd been sitting in the car, dredging up old and awful memories that she'd buried in the attic with all his pictures and photo albums. Now that she'd taken out the memories and examined them as an adult, they no longer hurt.

She had been a dreamy adolescent with an enduring crush on "an older man." He had been the unwilling, and in the end, unkind, recipient of her adoration. It was as simple as that.

She was no longer an adolescent, she was nearly twenty-nine, with a large group of friends, a long list of accomplishments behind her, and an exciting life ahead of her.

He was . . . a stranger. A stranger whose marriage had ended five years after it began and who had stayed on the East Coast, where he'd developed some sort of pleasant relationship with his only remaining relatives—his half-sister and his niece, who was about to be married.

Now that she'd thought the whole thing through, she could hardly believe she'd reacted so badly to the thought of seeing him. The prospect of photographing that wedding and featuring it in *Beautiful Living* was challenging and exciting to her professionally and she *was* a professional. In fact, her feelings for him were so totally impersonal, and her infatuation with him so silly in retrospect, that she decided she really ought to ship the box in the attic to Newport, along with the other supplies that would be sent ahead. She had no use for those photographs, but they were a chronicle of his youth, and he might like to have them.

Her family was seated at the kitchen table with lists spread everywhere. "Hi, guys," Corey said with a grin as she slid into a chair. "Who's going to Newport with me?"

Her answer was relieved smiles from her mother, her grandmother, her grandfather, and Diana.

"Everyone is going but me," Henry Britton said, glancing at the walker he used now to get around. "You girls always get to have all the fun!"

Eight

COREY'S PLANE WAS TWO HOURS LATE, AND IT WAS NEARLY SIX o'clock by the time the taxi turned down a quiet street lined with palatial homes built at the turn of the century when the Vanderbilts and Goulds spent summers in Newport. Spence's house was at the end of the road, and one of the most imposing of them all.

Shaped like a wide U that faced the street, it was a three-story masterpiece of architecture and craftsmanship with soaring white columns that marched across the front and joined both wings. No matter how Corey felt about Spencer Addison, she adored his house on sight. A high wrought-iron fence surrounded the lush lawns, and the driveway was secured by a pair of ornate gates that swung open electronically after the cab driver gave her name on the intercom.

A butler answered the front door, and she followed him across an octagonal foyer that was easily sixty feet across with pale green marble pillars supporting a gallery above. It was a rotunda meant to welcome bejeweled women in fabulous ball gowns and furs, Corey thought wryly, not modern businesswomen in dark suits and definitely not a female photographer in a turquoise silk shirt and white gabardine pants with a matching jacket over her arm. If jewels were the ticket of admission, she'd never have gotten in the front door of this place, not even with the wide gold bracelet at her wrist or the turquoise and gold earrings at her ears. These were authentic pieces and very fine, but this place called out for emeralds and rubies. "Could you tell me where I'll find the group from *Beautiful Living* magazine?" she asked the butler as they approached the main staircase.

"I believe they are out on the back lawn, Miss Foster. If you wish, I can show you to them now and have your suitcases taken upstairs to your room." Corey was more anxious to see how things were progressing outside than she was to unpack, so she accepted the butler's offer and followed in his wake.

In contrast to the foyer, which had been quiet and serene, nearly all the other rooms she passed were hotbeds of activity, with furniture being rearranged and wedding decorations being put up.

Her mother's handiwork was clearly evident in the dining room, where a forty-foot table had been set with exquisite china and crystal on handmade lace cloths, but the unmistakable "Foster Signature" would be the individual centerpieces that would be placed on the table the morning of the wedding for each pair of diners. All of the centerpieces would contain the same kinds of flowers, but each arrangement would be unique, and all of them were meant to be taken home by the ladies whose places at the table they had adorned during dinner, a token—Mrs. Foster said in her monthly column in *Beautiful Living* magazine—of the hostess's affection for her guests.

The author of that column was standing on the back lawn, oblivious to the glorious expanse of blue water or the pink and gold sunset taking place on the horizon as she directed four of the six freelance helpers that Spencer's sister had provided. Corey's grandmother was standing beside her, irritably shooing away her two assistants with the obvious intention of rearranging the wires that were being wound in and around the framework of the flowered arches the bride would walk under on her wedding day.

Corey came up behind them and gave them both a hug. "How's it going?"

"About like you'd expect," Corey's mother said, kissing her cheek.

"Chaos!" Her grandmother said flatly. Age had not made many changes in her except that she had acquired a disconcerting bluntness that her doctor said was common to many of the elderly. If something was true, she came right out and said it, though never with any malice. "Angela—the bride's mother— is interfering with everything and getting underfoot."

"How's the bride holding up?" Corey asked, avoiding asking about Spencer.

"Oh, she's a sweet enough girl," Gram said. "Pretty, too. Her name is Joy. She's dumber than a box of rocks," she added as she walked off to correct one of her helpers.

Stifling a nervous laugh, Corey glanced over her shoulder, then exchanged knowing glances with her mother, who said a little worriedly, "I know how important it is to use real events like this for our magazine layouts, but they're very wearing on Gram these days. She doesn't like working under any sort of deadline pressure anymore."

"I know," Corey said, "but she always insists she wants to be part of it." She looked around at the bustle and activity taking place on the grounds, at the newly erected gazebo being covered in climbing roses, at the banquet tables beneath the big white tent near the water, and she smiled at the transformation taking place. "It's going to be splendid."

"Tell that to the bride's mother before she drives us all crazy. Poor Spence. If he doesn't strangle Angela before this is over, it will be a miracle. When she isn't worrying, she's complaining, and she's nipping at his heels like a hyperactive terrier all the time. She's the one who wanted Joy's wedding to take place

54

here, and she's the one who wanted *us* here, and it's Spence who's paying the bill. Diana was right about that. Spence never complains and Angela never stops."

"I wonder why he's paying for the wedding when Angela's husband is supposedly a German aristocrat with relatives all over the social register."

Mrs. Foster paused to pick up a long strip of crepe paper skittering across the grass near her foot. "According to what Joy told me—and the child is quite a chatterbox—Mr. Reichardt has noble ancestors but little money to go with it. At least not the sort of money Spence has, and when you think about it, Angela and Joy are really his only family. I mean, his father remarried when Spence was still a baby and never wanted anything to do with him, and when his mother was alive, she was too busy enjoying herself to ever bother with him. To be fair to Mr. Reichardt, Joy isn't his daughter. Joy's father was Angela's second husband. Or was it her third? Anyway, according to Joy, Spence is paying the bill because his sister thinks it's important that Joy be married in a style that befits the step-daughter of a fancy German aristocrat."

Corey chuckled at the problems of the rich and multimarried. "What's the groom like?"

"Richard? I don't know really. I haven't seen him, and Joy doesn't talk about him. She spends most of her time with the caterer's son, whose name is Will. I gather they've known each other for several years, and they seem to enjoy each other's company. By the way, have you seen Spence yet?"

Corey shook her head as she reached up to shove her hair off her forehead. "I'm sure we'll bump into each other sooner or later."

Mrs. Foster nodded toward three people walking their way. "Here come Mr. and Mrs. Reichardt with Joy. Dinner is in two hours, and I suggest you say hello to them and then excuse yourself to go unpack. The next two hours will be the last peace and quiet you get until you leave this madhouse in three days."

"Sounds like a good idea. I have some phone calls to make before dinner, anyway."

"By the way," she added, "Gram and I eat in the little room by the kitchen, not in the dining room with the family."

Corey heard that with a sharp twist of annoyance. "Are you telling me that Spencer is treating us like servants?"

"No, no, no," Mrs. Foster said with a laugh. "We prefer to eat in the kitchen. Believe me, it's much more pleasant than listening to Mr. and Mrs. Reichardt and the two other couples who are friends of theirs and staying here for the wedding. Joy usually eats in the kitchen with us. She likes it better there, too."

Mrs. Foster had likened Angela to a terrier, but Corey thought it a false analogy after meeting the trio. With close-cropped, white-blond hair and brown eyes, Angela was as exotically elegant—and as nervous—as a Russian wolfhound. Her husband, Peter, was a Doberman pinscher—sleek, aristocratically aloof, and temperamental. Joy was . . . Joy was a cute cocker spaniel, with wavy, light brown hair, and soft, inquisitive brown eyes. As soon as the introductions were over, the wolfhound and the Doberman ganged up on Corey's poor mother and dragged her off to show her something they didn't like about the way the living room was being decorated, leaving Corey alone with Joy.

"I'll show you up to your room," the eighteen-year-old volunteered as Corey started toward the house.

"If you have something else to do, I can ask the butler where it is."

"Oh, I don't mind," Joy said, coming to heel on Corey's left and trotting off beside her toward the house. "I've been looking forward to meeting you. You have such a nice family."

"Thank you," Corey answered, a little startled by what she instantly sensed was a very genuine girl who was far more interested in getting to know Corey than she was in talking about herself or her wedding.

A flagstone terrace with French doors wrapped around the back and right side of the house, which both had spectacular water views. Corey started across the terrace toward the doors at the back, but Joy turned right. "Come this way, it's quicker," she told Corey. "We'll cut through Uncle Spence's study and avoid—"

Corey stopped short, intending to insist on *not* using that entrance, but she was too late. Spencer Addison was walking across the terrace, heading toward the steps that led down to the side lawn, and even if she hadn't seen his face, Corey would have recognized that long, brisk stride.

He saw her and stopped abruptly, a welcoming grin sweeping over his tanned face as he shoved his hands into his pockets and waited for her and Joy to reach him. Once that special smile of his had made her heart thunder, but now she felt only a swift, sharp jolt of recognition. At thirty-four, wearing casual gray pants and a white shirt with the sleeves rolled back on his forearms, he *still* managed to look every bit as handsome and sexy as he had when he was twenty-three years old.

He turned up the heat of his smile as she came close, and when he spoke, his baritone voice was richer, more intimate than she remembered. "Hello, Corey," he said as he slid his hands out of his pockets and made a move to hug her.

Corey responded with a smile that was appropriate for greeting a casual acquaintance whom one hasn't seen for many years—a friendly, serene smile, but not too personal. "Hello,

Spence," she replied and deliberately held out only one hand so that he had to settle for a handshake. No hug.

He understood it and he settled for it, but his handclasp lasted longer than was necessary, and so she ended it.

"I see you've already met Joy," he said, shifting the conversation to include his niece. To her he added a mild reproof, "I thought you were going to tell me when Corey arrived."

"I just arrived a few minutes ago," Corey said. Once, the thought that he wanted to see her or was eager to see her, as his words implied, would have sent her spirits soaring. Now, she was older and wiser and doing a rather excellent job, she thought, of handling this first meeting and remembering that Spencer was and had always been all charm and sex appeal and no substance. She glanced at her watch and then apologetically at him. "If you'll excuse me, I have some phone calls to make before dinner." On the off chance that Spencer intended to volunteer, she directed her request specifically to Joy, "Would you mind showing me where my room is now?"

"Oh, sure," Joy said happily, falling into step beside her. "I know exactly where it is."

With a polite nod in Spence's direction, Corey left him standing on the terrace. He turned and watched her walk away; she knew he did because she could see his reflection in the glass panes of his study doors, but the knowledge scarcely affected her. She was completely in control and proud of it. She couldn't deny the jolt of nerves she'd felt at the first sight of him, or the increase in her pulse rate when he smiled into her eyes and took her hand in his, but she attributed all that to a natural phenomenon, a sort of irritating but understandable response to an old, forgotten stimulus. Long ago, he had affected her that way, and even though her emotions were no longer engaged, her body was reacting like one of Pavlov's dogs to the sound of a bell.

Joy led her through the foyer and up a sweeping staircase with beautiful wrought-iron scrollwork. The staircase ended in a wide gallery that wrapped around the foyer on three sides. Long hallways branched off the gallery at regular intervals, and Joy headed down the first of them, then continued walking until they came to a pair of double doors at the end. As she reached for the brass door handles, she confided with a smile, "My mother and stepfather wanted their friends to have this, but Uncle Spence said it was 'reserved' for you." She threw open the doors with a flourish and stepped aside to give Corey her first, unobstructed view, then she looked expectantly at her, waiting for reaction.

Corey was speechless.

"It's called the Duchess Suite," Joy provided helpfully.

In dumbstruck silence, Corey walked slowly into a vast room that looked as if it belonged in Nicholas and Alexandra's summer palace. The suite was decorated entirely in pale blue and gold. Above the bed an ornately carved golden crown secured panels of ice blue silk that draped the bed at its corners, ending in graceful swirls on the pale blue carpet. The thick, tufted coverlet was of blue satin and so was the headboard with its arched gilt frame.

"It's called that because the original owner of the house had a daughter who became the duchess of Claymore when she married. This was the room she used whenever she came home from England, and it was called the Duchess Suite from then on."

Corey found it hard to concentrate on Joy's narrative as she looked around. The draperies at the windows were of blue silk with elaborate swags fringed in gold, and in the corner was a French secretary with carved panels on the doors and a dainty chair pulled up in front of it that was also upholstered in blue.

"When my uncle bought the house a few years ago, he had

the entire place renovated and all the furniture in all the guest rooms restored, so that they all look pretty much the way they did a hundred years ago, when the house was built."

Corey pulled out of her daze, and turned to Joy. "It's— breathtaking. I've only seen rooms like this in pictures of European palaces."

Joy nodded, and added with a grin, "Uncle Spence said he used to call you Duchess when you were my age. I guess that's why he wanted you to have this suite."

That announcement had a definite softening effect on Corey's attitude toward Spence. He'd been inexcusably thoughtless of her feelings as a young man, but he'd evidently mellowed a little with age. It hit her then that she was giving him far too much credit for what was a very small gesture that hadn't inconvenienced him in the slightest.

"Dinner's at eight o'clock. I'll see you then," Joy added as she left.

Nine

FROWNING WITH INDECISION, COREY HESITATED IN FRONT OF the mirror in her room and studied her appearance. The black jersey jumpsuit she'd decided to wear had narrow black shoulder straps attached to the bodice with a pair of golden loops, a scooped neckline, and a low back. It clung to her figure like a soft glove, ending in a gentle flair at her ankles, but she wasn't certain if it was too dressy for dining next to the kitchen, or perhaps too casual for this house. It would definitely make a good impression on Spence though . . . *Spence!*

Angry at herself for even considering his reaction, she stepped into a pair of flat-heeled sandals, clipped on a pair of gold disks at her ears, and snapped the wide gold cuff she'd worn earlier onto her wrist. She took a step toward the door, then a step back toward the mirror to check her face and hair. She was wearing her hair down tonight, loose around her shoulders; she no longer had to worry that Spencer Addison might think she was too young for him. She needed a little more lipstick, she decided, and quickly applied some. She glanced at her watch and could not believe how late it was. It was fifteen minutes after eight. She had just taken exactly twice as long to get ready as she had the night of the last Orchid Ball in Houston. Thoroughly disgusted, she turned her back on the mirror and marched to the door.

The little room by the kitchen was not the dark cubbyhole Corey had imagined, but rather a cozy alcove behind the kitchen that had a large, semicircular booth in it surrounded by tall windows that looked out on the darkened lawn. Corey heard her mother's voice as she rounded the corner, and she was already smiling at the sound when she walked into the room.

And saw Spence.

He was sitting at one end of the booth, his left arm stretched casually across the top of it, grinning down at Corey's mother, who was seated on his immediate left. Corey's grandmother was next to Corey's mother, facing the kitchen doorway, and Joy was seated next to her. The table had been set for five people. Four of them were already there. He was staying to eat with them.

Corey's smile froze, her step faltered, but she recovered just as her grandmother saw her and announced her arrival to the gathering. "Here's Corey, now. You're late, dear. My, you look nice tonight! Is that a new outfit?"

Corey felt like sinking through the floor. The implication was that she'd dressed especially for the occasion, which of course she had, and she was horribly certain that Spencer had noticed.

Spencer Addison had definitely noticed how she looked.

At the moment, what he noticed most was that her entire body had stiffened when she saw him sitting at the table. She hadn't expected him to be there, Spence realized. And she didn't want him there. The realization baffled and hurt him.

He watched her moving toward the booth with that same easy grace she'd had as a teenager, and he smiled at her. In return, she smiled *through* him, and he had a sudden insane impulse to get up out of the booth, block her path, and say, *Dammit, Corey, look at me!* He still could hardly believe that this cool, composed young woman who seemed to scarcely remember him was the same Corey Foster he'd known.

One thing hadn't changed about her, Spence noted—she still lit up a room when she walked into it. Within moments after she slid in across from him and started talking with the others, the entire atmosphere at the table seemed to brighten. At least that much about tonight was the same as it had been so long ago. Except, in those days, Corey had been glad to see him.

An image of those days danced in his mind . . . recollections of an adorable kid with a camera around her neck who popped up at his tennis matches. *"I got a great shot of your first serve, Spence."* It had been a lousy serve, and he'd said as much. *"I know,"* she'd agreed with that infectious smile of hers, *"but my shot of it was just great."*

He remembered the times when he'd gone over to the house unexpectedly. She had been so glad to see him then, her smile dawning like sunshine. *"Hi, Spence! I didn't know you were coming over."*

And then, one day, when she was about fifteen, he looked

around and saw her walking toward him across the back lawn, her honey-colored hair blowing around her shoulders, sun-streaked and glinting in the sun, her eyes the bright clear blue of a summer sky. A golden girl—all sparkle and zest, long legs and laughing face. She had been his golden girl from that day on—changeable, constant, glowing.

Even now, he could see her standing beneath the mistletoe, her hands clasped behind her back. She was sixteen and looking very grown up.

"Don't you know it's bad luck not to honor the Christmas traditions of your friends in their homes . . ."

He had hesitated. *"Are you certain you're old enough for this?"*

Of course, he'd known she had a fierce crush on him, and he'd known the time would come when she would grow up, grow out of it, and grow away from him. It was natural, inevitable that boys her own age would replace him in her heart. It was right that should happen.

He'd expected it, and even so, it had bothered him a little when it happened. More than a little. He hadn't even seen the change coming until the night she asked him to be a kissing partner in an experiment. God, he had felt like such a pervert for what he'd done to her that night, and even worse for what he had wanted to do to her—to a *seventeen-year-old* girl!

His golden girl.

He'd forgotten about her Christmas dance, and that was all it took to sever whatever feeble feelings she had left for him. She went with someone else, a last-minute substitute, which was what he had been. According to his grandmother, she went with someone closer to her own age "and a far more suitable companion for an innocent girl" than Spence was. Corey was so involved with her own life by then that she hadn't even bothered to say anything to him at his grandmother's funeral a few months later. Diana had excused her by saying Corey had an afternoon date. She hadn't bothered to attend his wedding either, even though she could have brought her date . . .

The conversation swirled around him at the table as one course followed another, and he participated now and then, but with only half his attention. He preferred to watch Corey when she wasn't looking at him, and since she never glanced in his direction for more than a moment, he had plenty of opportunity. He was genuinely surprised when dessert was served; he'd eaten without tasting his food, and he certainly didn't want any dessert.

What he did want he could not have: just this one night, just for this one meal, he had wanted it to be the way it had been the last time he had had dinner with her family. That was the night Diana had asked him to volunteer to take Corey to her school dance. She had a new man in her life by then—Doug somebody—and several others, as well.

Spence had already been relegated to least-important man in her life, but at least she'd still been able to spare a smile for him. The fact that she now found him completely dispensable in his own damned house at his own damned table was worse than annoying; it was terribly disappointing. And he knew exactly why it was. He'd been looking forward more than he wanted to admit to seeing her again, to having her happy family around him again. When he'd seen her coming across the back lawn earlier today, with her sun-streaked hair blowing in the breeze, he'd thought . . . He'd thought a lot of stupid, impossible things.

"Uncle Spence?" Joy's puzzled voice cut through his thoughts, and Spence looked at her. "Is something wrong with your glass?"

"My what?"

"Your water glass. You've been staring at it and turning it around in your hand."

Spence straightened in his seat and prepared to pay attention to the present and forget the past. "I'm sorry. My mind was on something else. What have you all been talking about?"

"The wedding mostly, but we're all bored with that subject. Anyway, everything's all taken care of."

Corey sensed instinctively that Spence was about to join in the conversation, and since she was more comfortable not having to talk to him, she tried to keep everyone focused on Joy. "We're not bored with the wedding at all," Corey said quickly. "And even though you think everything is taken care of, there are always last-minute details that people forget. Sometimes they're really important."

"Like what?" Joy asked.

Corey thought madly for something to discuss that hadn't already been covered. "Well, *um* . . . did you remember to apply for a marriage license?"

"No, but the judge is going to bring it with him."

"I don't think you can do that," Corey said, wondering if Angela, in her preoccupation with making the wedding into a social extravaganza, had failed to handle the more mundane, less showy details. "I've been a bridesmaid in several weddings, and you always have to apply for a license in advance, then there's a waiting period of a few days, oh—and blood tests."

Joy shivered at the mention of blood. "I get faint at the sight of needles, so I don't have to have one. The judge who's performing the wedding is a friend of Uncle Spence's, and he has the right to decide. He said I didn't need one."

"Yes, but what about the license and the waiting period?"

Spence spoke for the first time in fifteen minutes, and even though Corey was braced for the sound of his deep voice, it still did funny things to her heart. Nostalgia, she was learning, was not a feeble force. "It's all taken care of," he said. "There's no waiting period in Rhode Island."

"I see," Corey said, looking away from him the instant he finished speaking. Rather than try to think of another topic, she did what the others were doing and began to eat her dessert. Unfortunately, Joy wasn't interested in her own slice of cheesecake; she was interested in Corey and Spence. "It's funny," she said, looking from Spence to Corey and back to Spence, "but I thought you two used to be good friends."

Spence was so annoyed with Corey for treating him like an insignificant nonentity that he abruptly decided to make his presence, and his feelings, known. "So did I," he said curtly. He had slammed the conversational ball directly into Corey's court, and with amused satisfaction, he noticed that the "gallery" of three all turned to her to see how she was going to return it.

Corey lifted her head and met his challenging look. Mentally she reached across the table and flipped his plate into his lap, but all she did was smile and shrug. "We were."

"But you don't seem to have anything to say to each other," Joy said, looking baffled and a little disappointed. The gallery looked to the right at Spence, then to their left, at Corey, but Corey had cleverly eaten a bite of cheesecake, effectively forcing Spence to deal with that issue. "It was a long time ago," he said flatly.

"Yes, but Uncle Spence, only *two days ago* you were upset because Corey delayed her flight for a day. I started thinking maybe there'd been a—like, relationship—between you two when you were younger."

Now, when he didn't want Corey's attention, he got it. In fact, he got everybody's attention. Corey lifted her brows and gave him a serenely amused look that managed to convey that he deserved whatever embarrassment he suffered in a conversational confrontation that he had provoked. The other three spectators waited expectantly. "I was not upset because she delayed her flight," Spence said. "I was upset because I thought she had canceled her trip." They continued to look at him until he was prodded into a half lie. "Corey is an excellent photographer, and she was part of the 'deal' your mother made with the magazine to cover your wedding. It was a legal, binding contract. Naturally, I expected Corey to honor her commitments."

Corey's mouth dropped open at that enormous piece of hypocrisy, and her mother, who sensed Corey's impulse to throw her cheesecake into Spence's face, rushed to the rescue. "Corey always honors her commitments," she told Joy with gentle firmness. "She has very *strong* feelings about that."

"Actually," Corey added, heading off what she felt certain would be another probing question from Joy, "Spence was a friend of the whole family's, not of mine in particular."

Corey was pleased with that explanation, and Joy looked satisfied, but unfortunately Corey's grandmother was neither. "I don't think that's entirely true, Corey."

"Yes, Gram," Corey said in a warning voice, "it is."

"Well, maybe it is, dear, but you were the only one in the house who wallpapered your bedroom with his pictures."

Corey wanted to kill her, but at the moment all she could do was argue on a technicality. "I did not *wallpaper* my room with his pictures."

"That room was a shrine to Spencer," the elderly lady argued. "If you'd lit candles in there, people would have prayed. Goodness, you even had photograph albums filled with his pictures under your bed."

"Then what happened?" Joy asked.

"*Nothing* happened," Corey said, aiming a quelling look at her grandmother.

"You mean, one day you just—just stopped caring about Uncle Spence and took down his pictures? Just like that?"

Corey gave her a bright smile and nodded. "Just like that."

"I didn't know it could happen that way," Joy said somberly. "A person can just stop caring—for no reason?" For the first time since her questions had begun, Corey had the feeling that Joy wasn't merely curious, she was troubled.

Corey's grandmother obviously noticed the same thing and attributed Joy's anxiety to bridal nerves. Patting Joy's clenched hand, she offered reassurance: "Corey had a very good reason, dear. One you will never have, I'm sure."

"She did?"

"Yes. Spence broke her heart."

Mentally, Corey threw up her hands and yielded to the inevitable. Short of gagging her grandmother with a napkin and dragging her out of the booth by her ankles, Corey knew there was nothing to stop what was to come. Torn between misery and mirth, she waited for her dignity to be sacrificed on the altar of truth, for the sake of a nervous bride-to-be. Since she couldn't prevent it, and since she knew Spence was also going to suffer some unpleasant moments, she leaned back, folded her arms, and decided to enjoy his discomfort. He looked completely flabbergasted, Corey noted with some amusement, his coffee cup arrested halfway to his mouth.

"I did what?" he said irately, and actually looked to Corey as if he expected *her* to come to his rescue by denying it. In answer she lifted her brows and gave him an unsympathetic shrug.

"You broke her heart," Corey's grandmother asserted.

"And just exactly how did I do that?" he demanded.

She gave him a deeply censorious look for failing to own up

to his wrongdoing and retaliated by addressing her answer to his niece, instead. "When Corey was a senior in high school, your uncle asked to take her to the Christmas formal. I've never seen Corey so excited. She and Diana—Corey's sister—shopped for weeks for just the right gown to dazzle him, and they finally found it. When the big day arrived, Corey spent most of it in her room primping. Then, just before Spence was due to arrive, she came downstairs. My, how she sparkled in that gown! She looked so beautiful and grown-up that her grandpa and I had tears in our eyes. We took pictures of course, but we saved some film so Corey would have pictures of Spence with her."

She paused for a sip of water, letting the suspense build, and Corey had the fleeting thought that her grandmother had a previously undiscovered flair for high drama. Poor Joy was on the edge of her seat, frowning at her uncle for whatever he'd done to spoil such a night. Spence was frowning at Corey's grandmother, and Corey's mother was frowning at her plate. Corey was beginning to enjoy herself.

"Then what happened?" Joy implored.

Corey's grandmother carefully put her glass where it had been, then she lifted her sorrowful gaze to Joy. "Your uncle stood her up."

Joy turned a look of such disbelief, such accusation on Spence that Corey almost pitied him. "Uncle Spence," she breathed, "you *didn't!*"

"He did," Corey's grandmother averred flatly. Spence opened his mouth to explain, but she wasn't through with him. "It broke my heart the way Corey kept watching for him at the window. She could not believe he wasn't coming."

"And so you missed the formal?" Joy asked Corey, displaying the sort of appalled sympathy that only females are capable of feeling for each under those particular circumstances.

"No, she did not," Spence said.

69

"Oh, yes she did."

"I think you're mistaken about that and some other things," Spence said, his jaw tight with annoyance at being made to look like an even bigger villain than he'd actually been. "I did stand Corey up that night," he said, addressing his defense mostly to his wide-eyed niece. "I forgot I was supposed to take Corey to the dance, and I went to Aspen for the holidays instead of going home to Houston. It's obvious now that I shouldn't have let my grandmother handle my apology, but she was very upset and very insistent. I'm guilty of those two things, but the rest of the story you just heard"—he hesitated, searching for a respectful way to say Corey's grandmother was completely wrong—"isn't the way I remember it. Corey already had a date for the dance, and she already had her gown, but her date had to cancel at the last minute. The other boys she knew who would have taken her already had dates of their own, so Diana suggested I offer to take Corey, which I did. I was not a volunteer, I was a recruit, and the only reason Corey wanted to go with me was there wasn't anyone else available—except for her very last choice, which was whoever she called in as a last-minute substitute for me. I," he finished bluntly, "was her next-to-last choice."

Having had his say, he gave Corey's grandmother a conciliatory smile and said, "My memory isn't the greatest either, but I have a very clear recollection of all that because I felt very badly when I realized I'd forgotten about the dance. I was very relieved when I was told that Corey went with someone else."

"You would have had a clearer recollection," Gram informed him smugly, "if you had been there, as I was, when she went upstairs in that beautiful blue gown—the gown she bought had to be royal blue because that was your favorite color—and took it off. I don't know what gave you the idea you weren't her first choice, but I do know that if you had heard her crying

70

herself to sleep, as I did that night, you would never forget the sound of it either. She was beyond heartbroken. It was pitiful!"

Although some of what he'd heard didn't make sense, as Spence stared at the elderly woman, he knew instinctively she was telling the truth. His niece knew it, too. Filled with shame, he looked at their accusing faces while his mind tormented him with images of his golden girl coming down the stairs in her royal blue gown and waiting for him at the windows. He thought of Corey crying herself to sleep in a bedroom filled with his pictures, and he felt physically ill. He didn't know why she'd invented a story about needing a substitute date for the dance, but when he looked at Mrs. Foster, who was avoiding his gaze, one thing was obvious: everybody had known how Corey felt about him back then, but him.

He looked at Corey, but she had leaned her elbows on the table and covered her face with her hands, and he couldn't see her face. His jaw tight with self-disgust, he glared at his water glass, thinking of the barb he'd thrown earlier about honoring commitments. No wonder she couldn't stand the sight of him!

Across the table, Corey looked between her fingers at the stricken expression on Spence's face and then the satisfied smile on her grandmother's, and the whole scenario was so beyond her worst imaginings that she had an uncontrollable impulse to . . . giggle.

"Corey," Spence said, lifting his eyes to her covered face, prepared to take whatever verbal flogging she wanted to give him. "I didn't know. I didn't realize—" he began awkwardly, and to his horror, her shoulders started to shake. She was crying!

"Corey, please don't—!" he said desperately, afraid to reach for her and make things worse.

Her shoulders shook harder.

"I'm sorry," he said in an aching voice. "I don't know what else to say—"

Her hands fell away, and Spence stared in disbelief at a pair of laughing blue eyes that were regarding him with amused sympathy, not animosity. "If I were you," she advised in a laughter-choked voice, "I'd leave it right there and say good night. If Gram isn't convinced you feel guilty enough, this could actually get worse." Her transformation from cool stranger to his enchanting ally was so sudden, so undeserved, and so poignantly familiar that Spence felt a surge of pure tenderness pour through him.

He slid out of the booth, gave Corey's grandmother a wink, and held his hand out to Corey. "In that case, I'd rather do my groveling outside, and deprive her of the opportunity to witness it."

"I really ought to let you do it," Corey said with that infectious smile he'd always loved, "but you're already too late. I'd already forgiven and forgotten the whole thing. In fact, I shipped those old photograph albums here with some of my equipment and supplies. I intended to give them to you. So, as you can see, there's no need to go outside *or* grovel."

Spence put his hand firmly beneath her elbow. "I insist," he said with quiet implacability.

Joy slid out of the booth behind Corey. "I guess I'd better spend some time with Mom and Peter and their guests."

Mrs. Foster waited until the three were well out of earshot. "Mother," she said with a sigh, "I cannot believe you did that."

"I only said what was true, dear."

"Sometimes the truth hurts people."

"Truth is truth," the elderly lady said smugly as she eased her way out of the booth. "And the truth is that Spencer deserved a thrashing for what he did that night, and Corey deserved an apology. I accomplished both tonight, and they're both better off for it."

"If you're hoping that they'll fall in love now that you've cleared the way, you're very wrong. Corey is the living example of 'once burned, twice shy.' You've said that a hundred times about her."

"Well, that's the truth, too."

"Do you think," Mrs. Foster said, her mind shifting away from Corey and Spence and back to the basic problem, "you could just *think* about the truth, and not say it quite so often?"

"I don't think so."

Mrs. Foster stepped aside so that her mother could precede her down the hall. "Why not?"

"I'm seventy-one years old. I don't think I should waste any more of my time on words that don't mean anything. Besides, at my age, I'm allowed to be eccentric."

Ten

LAUGHTER AND RAISED VOICES ECHOED FROM THE DINING room, where Angela's dinner party was in full swing, but outside the night was soft and hushed as they strolled across the side lawn toward the water. Corey was amazed at how utterly relaxed and at peace she felt, walking at Spence's side. She could not remember ever being near him when she'd felt anything but an excited, nerve-racking tension, and she vastly preferred this new feeling.

She no longer had anything to hide or regret—her grandmother's dissertation at dinner had exposed her girlhood infatuation, laid it bare for all to see, and in the process she'd revealed it to Corey for exactly what it was—a very sweet, adolescent infatuation with an unknowing victim, not the painfully embarrassing, neurotic obsession with a selfish monster she'd feared it was. Spence's tanned face had actually paled while he listened to her grandmother's eloquent description of what Corey had "suffered" at his hands.

Before she had left for Newport, Corey had forced herself to view the whole awful debacle with philosophical indifference, but she was still hurt by it. Tonight, she had ended up laughing at herself in her grandmother's dramatic tale, and then laughing at the "villain" and trying to rescue him from any more guilt than he was already being made to feel. Confession, she decided, was definitely good for the soul, even if that confession was forced out of you by your grandmother. She had finally put an end to any and all attachment she ever had to Spence; all that was left was nostalgia, and her freedom gave her a sensation of sublime serenity.

He stopped beneath a big tree near the water's edge, and Corey leaned her shoulders against it, looking out at the crescent of twinkling lights from houses in the distance, waiting for him to say whatever he'd brought her out here to say. When he didn't seem to know how to begin, she found his uncharacteristic uncertainty a little touching and extremely amusing.

Spence gazed at her pretty profile, trying to gauge her mood. "What are you thinking about?" he asked finally.

"I'm thinking that I've never known you to be at a loss for words before."

"I don't quite know where to begin."

She crossed her arms over her chest, lifted her brows, and tipped her head toward the water in a silent, joking suggestion. "Want some help?"

"I don't think so," he said warily. She laughed, and the sound

74

of it made him laugh, and suddenly everything was the way it had always been with them, only better, richer for him because he was beginning to understand its value. He was shamefully pleased that she'd had his pictures all over her room and belatedly delighted that she'd evidently wanted him to take her to her Christmas dance from the very beginning.

Rather than start with the dance, he started with the pictures. "Did you really have my pictures all over your room?" he teased, gentling his tone so she wouldn't think he was gloating.

"Everywhere," she admitted, smiling at the memory; then she looked up at him and said, "You surely had to have known I had a terrible crush on you when I was tagging after you taking pictures of you."

"I did. Only I thought it ended when you were seventeen."

"Really? Why?"

"Why?" he uttered, a little dumbfounded that she didn't know. "I suppose I regarded it as a clue when you asked me to help you practice kissing techniques so that you could use them on some guy named . . ." He searched his memory for a name. "Doug!"

Corey nodded. "Doug Johnson."

"Right. Johnson. In fact, Diana told me Johnson had planned to take you to the Christmas dance and then had to cancel at the last minute, which was why I volunteered. I naturally assumed you had a crush on him after that, not me. How could I have possibly thought you cared about me after all that?" He waited for her to see the logic in his thinking, and when she only regarded him in amused silence, he said, "Well?"

"There was no Doug Johnson."

"What do you mean 'there was no Doug Johnson'?"

"I wanted you to kiss me, so I invented Doug Johnson and used him as an excuse. I wanted you to take me to the

Christmas formal, so I used Doug's name again. The only reason I dated boys was so that I'd know how to act on a date with *you,* when you asked me." She gave him a sideways smile, and Spence had an insane impulse to lean down and kiss it off her lips—an impulse that approached a compulsion when she shook her head at the memory of her infatuation and added softly, "It was you. It was always you. From the night I met you at the luau until a week after the dance, when you didn't call to apologize or explain, it was only you."

"Corey, there was another reason I forgot about the dance and went to Aspen. I'd expected my mother to come to Houston for Christmas, and I was looking forward to it more than I let anyone know. I'd been making excuses for her absence and lack of interest my whole life, and although it sounds absurd now, I actually thought that if she got to know me as an adult, then maybe we could have some sort of relationship. When she phoned at the last minute to say she'd decided to go to Paris instead, I ran out of excuses for her. I got drunk with some friends, none of whom had 'normal families,' and we all decided to go to Aspen, where one of them had a house, and forget Christmas."

"I understand," Corey said. "You'd told me you were looking forward to her visit, but I'd already guessed she was more important to you than you wanted anyone to know. You were a hobby of mine, remember. There wasn't much about you I didn't know or try to find out."

Flattered and touched, Spence braced his palm high on the tree trunk, longing to lean down and kiss her, but there was one more thing he needed to say. "I should have called you to explain, or at least apologize, but I let my grandmother convince me that I'd already done enough damage and that I should stay completely out of your life. She told me that you went to the dance with someone else—which she believed—

and that I was not a fit companion for an innocent young girl—which she also believed. I already felt like a complete pervert for what I did to you that night by the pool, so her tirade hit me in a very vulnerable place."

Corey saw his gaze drop to her lips and a little of her newfound serenity deserted her even before he said in a husky voice, "Now that we've finished the explanations, there's only one thing left to do."

"What's that?" Corey asked warily.

"We have to kiss and make up. It's traditional."

Corey pressed further back against the tree trunk. "Why don't we just shake hands, instead."

He smiled solemnly and shook his head. "Don't you know it's bad luck not to honor the traditions of your host?"

The forgotten sweetness of the memory was nothing compared to what she felt as he laid his palm against her cheek and whispered, "A golden girl told me that one Christmas, a long time ago." He bent his head and brushed a kiss slowly over her lips, and Corey managed to savor the moment without participating, but Spence wasn't finished. "If you don't kiss me back," he coaxed, sliding his mouth over her cheek, "the tradition isn't fulfilled. And that means *very* bad luck." His tongue lazily traced the curve of her ear, sending shivers down her spine to her toes, and Corey smiled helplessly, tipping her head back a little as he traced a warm path down her neck. "*Extremely* bad luck," he warned, retracing his path, and then the teasing was over. He cradled her face in his palms, his thumbs slowly caressing her cheeks, and Corey was mesmerized by the intensity in his eyes. "Have you any idea," he said gruffly, "how much I hated Doug Johnson after that night?"

Corey tried to smile and felt the sudden, inexplicable sting of tears instead.

"Have you any idea," he whispered as his mouth descended

purposefully toward hers, "how long I've wanted to do this . . ."

Corey felt her defenses crumbling and tried to forestall him with humor. "I'm not completely sure I'm old enough."

A sensual smile curved his lips, and she watched them form a single word: "Tough," he said, and curved her into his arms, capturing her lips in a kiss that was as rough and tender as his answer had been.

Corey told herself there was no danger in a kiss, no defeat in cooperating just a little, as she slid her hands up his hard chest and yielded to the coaxing insistence of his tongue. She was wrong. The instant she did, his arms tightened and his mouth opened over hers in a fierce, demanding kiss that assaulted her newfound serenity and made her clutch his broad shoulders for balance in a world that was beginning to spin. His tongue drove into her mouth, and with a silent cry of despair, Corey wrapped her arms around his neck and kissed him back.

She leaned into him and forced him to gentle the kiss by softly stroking his tongue with hers and felt the gasp of his breath as he drew her tighter to him, his arm angling over her hips to hold her pressed to his rigid thighs. She kissed him slowly, sliding her fingers over his jaw and around his nape, and he let her set the pace, his hand drifting in a slow caress over her spine and bottom, his mouth moving endlessly on hers, following her lead. And just when Corey was beginning to feel in complete control, he took it away. His fingers shoved into the hair at her nape, and he ground his lips into hers, pressing her back against the tree with his body, freeing his hands to rush over her breasts, then slowly covering and caressing them until Corey thought she would die of the sweet torment and the longing for more.

Time ceased to exist, measured only in a series of endless,

shattering kisses and arousing caresses that began slowly and built toward a crescendo; then they pulled apart. So they could begin all over again.

Corey heard herself moan when he tore his mouth from hers for the very last time. He buried his face in her neck, then he drew a long, labored breath and tightened his arms around her, holding her face against his heart.

She stayed there, her eyes closed tightly against the moment when her mind would take over and rage against the stupidity, the insanity of what she'd just done to herself, but it was already too late. Reality was setting in. She was clearly mentally ill! She had some sort of sick obsession with Spencer Addison. She had tossed away her adolescence on him, and now, all he had to do was say something sweet—and she fell into his arms like a lovesick idiot. She had never in her life felt as she had tonight except once . . . long ago on a summer night by the swimming pool. A tear dropped from her eye and raced down her cheek. She did not mean anything to him, and she never had . . .

"Corey," he said in a roughened voice as he touched his lips to her hair. "Would you care to explain to me why I seem to lose my mind the moment I touch you?"

Her heart did a somersault, her mind went into silent shock. For the second time tonight, she had an absurd impulse to laugh and cry at the same time. "We are both clearly insane," she said, but overall, she felt much better than she had the moment before. She moved away from him, and he put his arm around her shoulders, walking with her back to the house.

Lost in her own thoughts, Corey scarcely noticed that he was walking her to her room until they'd turned down the hall and she saw the double doors of the Duchess Suite in front of her. She turned in front of them and looked up at him. This last half hour was the closest thing to a date they'd ever had, and she had an irreverent impulse to smile at him and say, "Thank you for a lovely evening." Instead she said, "Since we've already kissed good night, I guess there's nothing else to do or say."

He grinned at her and braced his hand against the doorframe, relaxed and confident. A little too confident, she thought. "We could always do it again," he suggested.

"I don't think that would be a good idea," she lied.

"In that case, you could invite me in for a nightcap."

"I think that's an even worse idea," she primly informed him.

"Liar," he said with a grin, then he bent and gave her a hard swift kiss and opened the door. Corey walked serenely into her room, closed the door, and collapsed against it, dazed by the last half hour she'd spent in his arms. Her gaze landed on the clock on the little secretary. It was almost midnight. They'd been outside for well over an hour.

Eleven

STANDING ON THE BACK LAWN, COREY WATCHED MIKE MacNeil and Kristin Nordstrom setting up some of the camera equipment for exterior shots of the work underway, but there was little the pair could do until tomorrow, when the flowers were in place on the bridal arches and the banquet tables beneath the white tent were decked out in "Foster Style." At the moment, there was a small army of gardeners, carpenters, and florists bumping into the caterers, who were scheduled to serve a rehearsal dinner on the terrace tonight after the rehearsal itself was over.

To Corey's trained eye, everything looked as if it was going very well. She saw Joy talking earnestly to one of the caterer's staff, and whatever she was saying to the young man made him smile at her and the rest of his companions guffaw. The caterers were a family operation, Corey knew, and besides being very good, they obviously enjoyed working together. She saw Corey and waved, and Corey waved back, then she headed over to Mike and Kristin, who'd arrived that morning in a van. "How's it going, Mike?"

"Everything's under control. No problems." He was five feet four inches tall, fifty pounds overweight, and he looked as if he were about to collapse on top of the heavy trunk he was dragging across the grass. Corey knew better than to offer to help. "How do you like your new location assistant?"

He looked over his shoulder at Kristin, who was effortlessly carrying an identical trunk. "Couldn't you have found someone a little taller and a little more robust?" he asked wryly.

Since Corey had more than enough work to occupy her, she watched for a few minutes and then headed back to the house.

Back to Spence.

She'd fallen asleep with her arms around her pillow, thinking of him, and today, she could think of little else. He wasn't helping, either. This morning, he'd strolled into the little breakfast room where they'd dined last night, and in full view of Corey's mother and grandmother and his astonished niece, he'd rumpled Corey's hair and pressed a kiss on her cheek.

At noon, she saw him coming down a crowded hallway near his study with a sheaf of papers in his hand that he appeared to be engrossed in reading. Without looking up, he nodded to a houseguest and moved around three servants. As he passed Corey, seemingly without seeing her, he made a sharp turn and walked straight into her, backing her through an open doorway and straight into a closet, closing its door behind them. While she was still sputtering, he dropped the papers, pulled her into his arms, and kissed her senseless. "I've missed you," he said just before he let her go. "And don't make plans for dinner. We're dining alone tonight on your balcony. My balcony overlooks the back lawn, which means we'd have as much privacy as we have in the halls."

Corey knew she should object, but she didn't want to. She was leaving on Sunday, which gave her only tonight and tomorrow night to see him. "Only if you promise to behave," she said instead.

"Oh, I will—" he agreed solemnly, then he pulled her back into his arms and kissed her until she was clinging to him, "—just like this." He let her go with a familiar smack on her rump. "Now get out of here before I decide to keep you here and we end up suffocating. There's no air in this damned closet."

The entire time they'd kissed there'd been a parade of footsteps down the hall and Corey shook her head. "No, you go first and make certain the coast is clear."

"Corey," he said, "I can't leave this closet right now. I'm in no state to greet houseguests, believe me."

Embarrassed and pleased, she put her ear to the door, then stealthily reached for the handle when the coast seemed clear. "I ought to lock you in here," she tossed over her shoulder.

"Try it and I'll pound on the door and tell everyone you've stolen the silver."

Corey was smiling at that memory when she saw Joy walking slowly and dejectedly toward a stand of trees on the perimeter of the lawn. She looked so miserable that Corey hesitated and then went after her. "Joy—is something wrong?" she said, coming up behind her.

"I'd rather not talk about it," she said, hastily brushing her fingertips over her cheeks before she turned and gave Corey a watery smile.

"If you don't want to tell me why you're crying, then will you talk to your mother or someone else? You shouldn't be upset like this on the day before your wedding. Richard will be here tonight. He won't want to see you unhappy."

"Richard's very sensible, and he'll say I'm being foolish. So will everyone." She shrugged and started slowly to the house. "Let's talk about something else. Tell me more about you and Uncle Spence." She hesitated, and then said in a voice tinged with desperation, "Do you think you really loved him when you were my age?"

If the question had been asked in idle curiosity, Corey would have sidestepped it, but she had the feeling that Joy was turning to her for help and that anything other than the truth might somehow do a great disservice to her. "I want to answer you honestly, but it's hard for me to look back at my feelings for him without also realizing how hopeless and one-sided they were, and then to discredit them because of it."

"Would you have eloped with him?"

The question was so unexpected that Corey laughed and nodded. "Only if he'd asked me."

"What if he hadn't been from a wealthy family?"

"I only wanted him, nothing else would have mattered."

"So you did love him?"

"I—" Corey hesitated, looking back. "I believed in him. I admired and respected him. And I did it for all the *right* reasons, even then. I didn't care that he was a football hero at college, or what kind of car he had. I wanted to make him happy, and he always seemed to enjoy being with me, so I truly believed I could." With a rueful smile, she admitted, "I used to lie in bed at night, imagining that I was going to have his baby, and that he was asleep beside me with his arms around me, and that he was happy about the baby. It was one of my favorite fantasies, out of about ten thousand fantasies. If all those things add up to love, then yes, I did love him. And I'll tell you a secret," Corey finished wryly, "I have never felt that way about anyone else since."

"Is that why you've never gotten married?"

"In a way, it is. On the one hand, I don't want to risk feeling that way about anyone again—I was completely obsessed. On the other hand, I'd never settle for anything less if I were to marry someone." They'd arrived at the house, and to Corey's surprise, Joy gave her a hug. "Thank you," she said fiercely.

Corey watched her walk back across the lawn toward the caterers, then she started slowly toward the dining room, where she was planning to spend the rest of the afternoon taking photographs, but she felt uneasy. She decided to talk to Spence about Joy. Something was wrong.

Twelve

TRYING NOT TO MAKE A SOUND, COREY REPOSITIONED AN antique candelabra on the dining room table. From the head of the table, out of range of the shot she was setting up, Spence said, "Don't worry about making noise. Do what you need to do."

He had brought his paperwork there so they could be together while she worked. Corey was afraid to admit to herself how much she loved his company and how wonderful it felt to have him pursuing her after all these years. "I don't want to distract you."

A lazy, intimate smile swept across his handsome face. "In that case, you'll have to pack up and leave Newport."

Corey knew exactly what he meant, but the sweetness of flirting with him, and even getting the upper hand, was too tempting to pass up. "Be patient. We'll be out of here Sunday morning, and you'll have this ramshackle old house all to yourself again."

"That isn't what I meant, and you know it," he said calmly, refusing to participate in her game.

That surprised her. Sometimes, she was positive they were indulging in a long-overdue flirtation, but just when she'd adjusted to that and tried to play by the rules, he ended the game and turned serious on her.

"Can you stay a few days longer?"

Corey hesitated, struggling to resist the temptation. "No, I can't. I have assignments already booked for the next six months."

She waited, half in hope, half in fear, that he'd urge her to stay longer and she would agree. He didn't. Evidently he wasn't *that* serious. Refusing to acknowledge that it hurt her, Corey turned her attention to safer matters and glanced at the papers spread out in front of him. "What are you working on?"

"I'm considering the pros and cons of a business deal; weighing all the alternatives, balancing the element of risk with the possibilities of gain; going over the research. The usual process of decision making."

"It isn't usual for me," Corey admitted, crouching down and eyeing the effect of the flower arrangement with the candles and heirloom china. "If I went through all of that, I'd never be able to make any decision at all." Satisfied, she walked over to the tripod and took the picture, then she adjusted for a slightly different angle that would catch the rays of the sun dancing off the crystal and snapped off two more shots.

Spence watched her, admiring her deft skill for a moment, then turning his attention to her other more alluring attributes. He studied the curve of her cheek, the generous softness of her mouth, and watched the sunlight dancing on her hair. She'd pulled the wavy mass up into a ponytail with tendrils at her ears, and it made her look about eighteen years old again. She was wearing white shorts and a T-shirt, and he indulged himself with a leisurely visual caress of her long slim legs and her full breasts while he imagined how she was going to feel in his arms in bed tonight.

She could set him on fire with a kiss, and tonight he intended to fan that fire and let it blaze out of control until it consumed them both. And then he was going to build it up again. He was going to make love to her until she pleaded with him to stop, and then he was going to make her plead for him to start again.

They were meant for each other; he knew that now just as surely as he knew Corey didn't want to trust him with her heart again. He could persuade her to give him her body tonight, but he needed time to persuade her to give him her heart, and she was trying not to give him that time. He already knew how amazingly steadfast she was once she made up her mind; she had been steadfast in her devotion to him years ago, and now she was just as dedicated to keeping her emotional distance from him. For the first time in his adult life, Spence felt powerless and fearful, because short of tying Corey up, he couldn't think of a way to make her give him the time to prove himself.

"Stop staring at me," she said with a smothered laugh, without glancing in his direction.

"How do you know I am?"

"I can feel your eyes on me."

He heard the tiny tremble in her voice, and he smiled, then he returned to the discussion they'd been having about decision making. "What method do you prefer for making your decisions?"

Corey looked over her shoulder. "Seriously?"

"I'm very serious," he said, his voice deep with meaning.

Corey ignored that. "For the most part, I act on instinct and impulse. I seem to know in here"—she touched her heart—"what decisions are best. I've learned that from experience."

"That's a risky way to handle important things."

"That's the only way I can handle them at all. The truth is, if I spend too much time weighing alternatives, balancing the risk against the gain, I become paralyzed with uncertainty, and I end up making no decision at all. My judgment is best when I rely on impulse and instinct."

"That's probably a part of your artistic nature."

Corey smiled. "Maybe, but it's just as likely that it's genetic. My mother is the same way. If you give either of us too much time to think, or offer us too many possibilities, we don't act at all. She told me once that if my stepfather hadn't rushed her into marriage before she could sort out all the drawbacks from the benefits, if she hadn't been forced to act on instinct instead of logic, that she wouldn't have married him at all."

Mentally, Spence filed that revealing information about Corey away for future use.

"Is that why you've never married—too many possibilities for failure and too much time to think about all of them?"

"Could be," Corey evaded, and quickly turned the discussion back to him. "What happened to your marriage?"

"Nothing happened to it," he said dryly, then he realized that he wanted her to understand. "Sheila's parents had died the year before my grandmother died, and neither of us had anyone else. When we realized we had only that in common and very little else, we decided to get a divorce while we were still able to be civil to each other."

Corey opened her camera case and carefully slid the camera

into its compartment, then she turned around and leaned against the dining room table, her forehead furrowed into a frown. "Spence . . . speaking of marriage, I wanted to talk to you about Joy. I don't know that she's certain she's doing the right thing. Does she have anyone she confides in? I mean, where are her friends, her bridesmaids, her *fiancé?*"

She half expected him to wave the matter off; instead he leaned his head back and ran his hand around behind his neck as if the subject somehow made his muscles tense. "Her mother has picked her friends, her bridesmaids, *and* her fiancé," he said bitterly. "Joy isn't stupid, she's simply never been allowed to think for herself. Angela has made every decision for her and then inflicted them on her."

"What's her fiancé like?"

"In my opinion, he's a twenty-five-year-old egomaniac who is marrying Joy because she's pliable and will reinforce his own inflated opinion of himself. I also think he likes having a connection through marriage to German nobility. On the other hand, the last time I saw the two of them together, Joy seemed to like him very much."

"Will you talk to her?" Corey asked as she turned back and finished packing up her equipment.

"Yes," he said, his voice so near that his breath stirred the hair on her nape, then his lips grazed her skin and Corey felt an alarming jolt from even that simple contact. "Will you mind having a late dinner? Although I don't give a damn about any of these people, I do have a duty as host to fulfill at the rehearsal dinner."

He'd asked her to join him downstairs during the rehearsal festivities, but she'd declined. Corey knew it was insanity to have dinner with him in her room, but she told herself she'd keep things under control, and that they weren't even eating on the bed, they were eating on the *balcony*—"A late dinner is fine. It will give me a chance to take a nap."

"That's a *very* good idea," he said, and with such emphasis that Corey turned around and tried to see his face. He looked completely innocent.

Thirteen

ALTHOUGH COREY'S BALCONY FACED THE SIDE LAWN, ANOTHER set of her windows offered a perfect view of the party taking place on the terrace below and an ideal chance to observe Spence without fear of having him know it. It occurred to her that she'd been with him for only two days and she was right back where she'd begun—watching for a glimpse of him. Sighing, she leaned her shoulder against the window frame, but she continued to watch.

He was a man of great contrasts, she thought tenderly—a tall, powerfully built man who exuded a tough, hard-bitten strength that was at complete variance to the sensuality of his mouth and the glamour of his sudden smile. He looked as if he could still carry a football and plow his way through a defensive line, and yet he exuded the relaxed elegance of a man who was born to preside over a mansion like this one.

Tonight, he was playing his role of host with ease, appearing to listen intently to what a group of men were telling him, but Corey saw him look at his watch for the third time in ten minutes. He'd had dinner sent up five minutes ago, and the table on the balcony was already set with china and silver and covered platters. She glanced at the clock and watched the minute hand make its last small lurch. It was ten o'clock. She looked out the window and smothered a laugh as Spence abruptly put his drink down, nodded briefly to the men who were talking to him, and left them there, his long, swift strides taking him straight toward the doors that led into the house. He'd fulfilled his social obligations; now he was in a hurry.

Because he wanted to have dinner with her.

And after dinner, he intended to have Corey for dessert.

Wryly, Corey glanced at the table on the balcony, where a hurricane lamp was already casting its mellow glow. It was a perfect seduction scene—a private balcony, candlelight, champagne chilling in a bucket, music in the distance, and a very large, luxurious bed with satin sheets within immediate reach. She was immensely flattered by his attention to detail, but she was not going to let him make love to her. If she did, the desolation she would feel when he kissed her good-bye and sent her on her way would make the episode eleven years ago pale in comparison.

Corey was very clear on all that. What she was not clear about was why he suddenly seemed to find her so irresistible. Last night, as she had lain awake, trying to find a reason for his display of passion, she'd decided it was a case of guilt over the picture her grandmother had painted for him of Corey waiting at the window for him to take her to the dance.

That theory was invalidated by the way he'd behaved today—he was in serious amorous pursuit, and he was using an entire arsenal of sensual weapons on her, from his voice to his hands. He'd even asked her to extend her trip, though he'd backed off without pressing her. It didn't make sense. Outside, on the lawn, there were stunning women who put Corey completely in the shade, and she'd watched several of them trying to flirt with him. Spence was gorgeous, sexy, and rich. He had an unlimited supply of women who were just like him from

90

which to choose. *That* was the real reason he'd never been interested in Corey, not even when she was almost eighteen and the age difference between them wouldn't have mattered so much.

Now he was suddenly pursuing her with single-minded determination, and she knew there had to be an explanation. It was possible he simply enjoyed the novelty of trying to seduce a childhood friend. She shoved that thought aside; it was completely unjust. Spence wasn't cynical or jaded; she wouldn't be so helplessly in love with him now if he was.

Corey moved away from the window so that he wouldn't see her there and guess she'd been watching him on the terrace.

When there was no answer to his knock, Spence tried the knob and let himself in. He was halfway across the suite when he saw Corey outside on the balcony, standing at the balustrade in a long, bright green silk shift that covered her from her neck to her ankles with the exception of a slash at the neck. She was waiting for him, he thought with an inner grin. After all these years, his golden girl was waiting for him again. Fate had given him a second chance he didn't deserve, and he intended to seize it any way he could.

Dinner with Corey was one of the most enjoyable meals he'd had in years. She regaled him with funny stories about events in his life that he'd almost forgotten. Afterward, they sipped brandy and Corey got out one of the photo albums she'd brought to give him. The light from the hurricane lamp wasn't very good, but Corey argued that bad lighting was a help, not hindrance, for viewing her earliest photographic attempts. Spence let her have her way because the champagne and brandy were having a mellowing effect on her, and he wanted her to be relaxed tonight.

With his elbow on the table and his chin on his fist, he divided his attention between her animated face and the pictures she was showing him. "Why did you keep that shot?" he asked, pointing to a picture of a girl in riding breeches who was sprawled on the ground in a sitting position, her hair half-covering her face.

Corey gave him a winsome smile, but he had the feeling she was a little embarrassed. "Actually, that was one of my favorites for a while. I gather you don't recognize her?"

"Not with her hair in her face."

"That happens to be Lisa Murphy. You took her out during your junior year of college when you were home during the summer."

Understanding dawned and Spence swallowed a laugh. "I take it you didn't like her very much?"

"Not after she took me aside and told me I was a pest and that I should stay away from you. We were all at a charity horse show that day. Actually, I didn't even know you were going to be there."

The last page contained one of the snapshots of Spence with his grandmother that Corey had taken at the luau. They looked at it in silence for a moment. "She was very special," Corey said softly, touching her fingertip to the elderly lady's cheek.

"So were you," he said quietly, as he closed the album. "Even then."

Corey knew instinctively that the part of the evening she longed for and dreaded was about to begin. She took the coward's way and tried to forestall the inevitable with humor and a change of location. "I'm sure you didn't think I was 'special' when I was hanging out of trees taking pictures of you," she joked, walking over to the balustrade.

He walked up behind her and put his hands on her shoulders. "I always thought you were special, Corey." When she didn't reply, he said, "Would you be surprised if I told you I have a picture of you?"

"Was it one of the ones I used to stick in your wallet when you weren't looking?"

An instant ago he was about to kiss her, and he ended up burying his laughing face in her hair instead. "Did you really do that?"

"No, but I considered it."

"The picture I have of you is from the front of *Beautiful Living*."

"I hope you found enough room for it somewhere," she joked. "It's only an inch tall."

He brushed his lips over her temple, his voice a tender murmur. "I want a larger photograph that shows the way you glow in the moonlight when you're in my arms."

Corey tried not to let what he was saying or doing affect her, but warmth was already spreading through her entire body, and when he slid his arm around her waist and drew her against his full length, she felt an ache of longing begin to build. "I'm insane about you," he whispered.

"Spence," she pleaded softly, "don't do this to me." But it was too late, he was already turning her in his arms, and when his mouth opened over hers, insistent and hungry, Corey gave herself up to the torrid kiss, surrendered to the turbulence that followed in the wake of male hands that caressed her breasts and slid down her spine, forcing her into vibrant contact with his arousal. When he finally lifted his mouth from hers, Corey felt seared by the kiss and branded with his body.

"Stay for a few days," he whispered, rubbing his jaw against her hair.

A few days . . . She deserved a few sweet days to remember and cherish. And then regret. "I—I have to work for a living—a schedule—"

He shoved his hands through the sides of her hair and turned her face up to his. "Put me on your schedule. I have work for you."

She thought he was joking about it being work, and she leaned her forehead against his chest. She was going to stay with him. God help her, she was going to do it. "What you're suggesting is not work," she said, her voice trembling with fear and love.

Spence sensed that she was wavering, and he pressed the advantage he'd gained before she could change her mind. "I'm serious," he said, using the only method he'd been able to think of all day that might make her agree to stay. "I've been putting together notes for a book on this house and several others built at the same time. I need photographs to accompany the text, and you could—"

She shoved him away so abruptly that he almost lost his balance. "So that's what this whole seduction routine has been about!" She wrapped her arms around her middle and backed away, her voice shaking with tears and fury. "You wanted something!" He reached for her, but she jerked free and backed away. "Get out of here."

"Listen to me!" Spence caught her just inside the open doors. "I love you!"

"If you want me to take pictures of this place, then call the William Morris Agency in New York and talk to my agent, but first you'd better send him a blank check!"

"Corey, shut up and listen to me. I invented all that about the book. I'm in love with you."

"You lying, conniving—Get out of here!"

She was trying so damned hard not to cry, and he knew she'd hate him more if she broke down in front of him. He dropped his arms to his sides, but he wasn't giving up. "We'll talk about this in the morning."

By the time Spence reached his own room, the enormity of his mistake had hit him. No matter what he tried to tell her in the morning, she wasn't going to believe him. After this, there was no way he could prove to her that he had no ulterior motives and that all he wanted was her.

Furious with his blunder, he yanked off his jacket and unbuttoned his shirt while he let himself consider the one ugly possibility that had been there all along: Corey wasn't in love with him. He knew damned well she felt *something* for him; it ignited the moment he touched her, but he could be mistaking that "something" for love. He was on his way to the liquor cabinet when he passed his bed and saw the note propped on his pillows.

It was a hastily written letter from Joy, telling him that she was eloping with Will Marcillo, the caterer's son, and asking Spence to tell her mother in the morning. The rest of the letter was a desperate effort on his niece's part to make Spence understand why a conversation she'd had with Corey earlier that day had convinced her she had to marry the man she loved. According to Joy's disjointed explanation, Corey had admitted to her that she had never loved anyone but Spence and she wanted to have his babies, but she was afraid to risk her feelings again. That, according to Joy, was exactly how she herself had felt about Will, only Joy was no longer afraid to take the risk.

Spence read the letter again, then he put it down on a table and stared at his bed, his mind whirling with Joy's revelations, fitting them together with the things he'd discovered about Corey and then coming to a full stop at the impossible predicament he'd put himself in tonight by lying to her about his motives for wanting her to stay.

According to Joy's note, Corey loved him. She wanted to have his babies. She was afraid to take a risk.

According to Corey, she either acted on impulse and instinct, or else she lost her courage and didn't act at all.

Spence had inadvertently fixed it so that nothing he *said* would make Corey believe he wanted only her. Tomorrow a wedding was scheduled to take place, but there was no bride and no groom. He couldn't say anything to make her believe him, but there was a possibility he might still be able to *do* something. He hesitated for a moment, and then he made his decision and picked up the telephone.

Judge Lattimore had just gotten home from the rehearsal dinner. He was very surprised to hear from Spence. He was more surprised when he understood why.

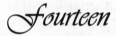

Fourteen

COREY WAS ALREADY SETTING UP EQUIPMENT FOR THE WEDding shots on the lawn at seven o'clock in the morning when she was handed a note from Spence telling her to come to his study immediately. Convinced he had some new form of lie to tell her, she circumvented him by taking Mike and Kristin with her.

Anger made her steps long and fast as she walked across the lawn. She still could hardly believe he'd done what he had, merely to get free professional photographs for his damned book. On the other hand, Corey's freelance fees were very high, and she'd lived among the wealthy long enough to know how incredibly cheap some of them were when it came to spending money on anything other than themselves. Cheap was bad enough, but deceitful and manipulative were unforgivable, and to use her as he had—to touch her and kiss her—and then to tell her he *loved* her. That was obscene.

As soon as she stepped into his study, Corey realized she needn't have worried that he had any sort of cozy tryst in mind. Angela was seated in a chair wearing a dressing robe and clutching a handkerchief; her husband was standing rigidly beside her chair in his robe, looking poised to attack. Spence looked immune to whatever drama had taken place in there. With his hip perched on the edge of his desk and his weight braced on the opposite foot, he was looking out the window, idly turning a paperweight on his desk.

He looked up at Corey as she walked in with her assistants, but instead of the animosity or the cajolery she expected to see, he looked perfectly composed, as if last night hadn't happened. He nodded toward the chairs at his desk in an invitation for Corey, Mike, and Kristin to have a seat. Unable to bear the suspense, Corey looked from him to Angela. "What's wrong?"

"She's gone, that's what's wrong!" Angela cried. "That nitwit has eloped with that—that busboy! I shouldn't have named her Joy, I should have called her Disaster!"

Corey sank down into the chair, her shock giving way to happiness for Joy and then to the awful realization that Joy's last-minute elopement was a calamity for Corey and the magazine. It was too late to substitute another wedding for the next issue, much too late. They were already at deadline now.

"I notified the groom's family an hour ago," Spence told her. "They'll speak to as many of their guests as they can reach. Those guests who can't be reached will be met here by one of their relatives, who will explain the situation."

"This is a nightmare!" Angela gritted.

"It's also created an enormous problem for Corey's magazine. They've invested a great deal of time and money in all this." He paused to let that sink in before he continued. "I've had longer than anyone else to consider alternatives, and I think

I've come up with a plausible solution. I suggest we let Corey go ahead and photograph the wedding."

"There isn't going to *be* a wedding!" Angela burst out bitterly.

"What I'm suggesting is that Corey be allowed to photograph everything—"

"Except the bride and groom who *won't be here!*" Angela exploded.

"Corey can use stand-ins," Spencer explained.

Corey understood exactly what he was suggesting, and she rushed in to help him explain, her mind already racing ahead to the angles she'd use to get appealing photographs without revealing the faces of the bride and groom. "Mrs. Reichardt, we can take long shots of another couple dressed as a bride and groom. What I need is a crowd in the background . . . It doesn't have to be a large one, but—"

"Absolutely not!" said his sister.

"I won't have it!" Mr. Reichardt stormed.

Spence's voice had a razor edge to it that Corey had never heard before. "*You* haven't paid for it, I have." He shifted his attention back to his sister and continued, "Angela, I understand how you feel, but we have a moral and ethical obligation to do what we can to make certain Corey's magazine doesn't suffer because of Joy's . . . impulsiveness."

Corey listened to him in stunned silence, trying to understand how his mind worked. Last night, she'd decided that he was so cheap that he'd been romancing her in the hope of getting free photography for his book. This morning, he was lecturing about ethics and morality and passing up an opportunity to cancel everything associated with the wedding, forfeit what deposits he had to forfeit, and still save himself a small fortune.

"But what will we tell *our* guests?" Angela demanded. "Some of the guests are friends of yours, too, don't forget that."

"We will tell them we're delighted with the bride's decision, and sorry that she can't be here . . . but that we'd like them all to celebrate at the reception as if the newlyweds were present." Finished, he looked to Corey for approval, and she gave it to him in the form of a relieved smile, but in fairness to Angela she added, "It is very unusual."

"So are many of the wedding guests," Spence said dryly. "They'll probably enjoy the novelty of a reception for a canceled wedding. That's something they won't have already done. A new experience, you might say, for a bunch of jaded cynics."

Angela looked ready to hit him. She surged to her feet and stormed out of the room with Reichardt at her side.

Spence waited until they were gone, then he said briskly, "Okay, let's handle the details. We need a bride and a groom and a judge."

Corey knew he was waiting for her to speak, but as she looked at the forceful, dynamic man who was willing to help shoulder her burdens, her heart was reclassifying him from enemy, to ally and friend, and there was nothing she could do to stop it. He saw the change reflected in her eyes and his tone softened to a caress. "I'll find a stand-in for the judge."

"In that case, all we need are stand-ins for the bride and groom." Corey looked at Kristin and Mike. "How about you two?"

"Get serious," Mike said. "I'm fifty pounds overweight and Kristin is six inches taller than me. The caption beneath our picture would have to read 'Pillsbury Doughboy Weds the Green Giant.'"

"Stop thinking about food," Kristin chided, "and start thinking of solutions."

Silence ensued for a long moment before Spence finally said

in a tone of exasperated amusement, "What am I, chopped liver?"

Corey shook her head. "I can't use you for the groom."

A look of surprised hurt flashed across his eyes. "As I recall you used to find me rather photogenic. Now that I'm older, are you afraid I'll break your lens?"

"You'd be more likely to melt it," she said wryly, imagining his tall, muscular physique in a raven black tuxedo with a snowy shirt contrasting against his tanned skin.

"Then what's the problem?"

"You'll be busy with the guests, making explanations and trying to keep them smiling." She paused to make her point. "Spence, it's imperative that I have lots of happy faces in these shots. Their success depends much more on the mood of the crowd than on my technique."

"I can accomplish that and still be the 'groom.' I'll tell the staff to open up all six of the bars on the lawn and keep passing drinks until the last guest leaves or we run out of liquor. If necessary, we'll have taxis lined up in front in case they're needed."

"In that case," Corey said with a relieved sigh, "the job is yours. Kristin, you get to be the bride. Spence is several inches taller than you."

Spence opened his mouth to object, but Kristin beat him to it. "I'd have to lose twenty pounds to get into Joy's wedding gown, and it would still only hit me at the knees."

"Corey, there's only one solution and it's obvious," Spence said flatly. "You'll have to be the bride."

"I can't be the bride; I'm the photographer, remember? We'll have to ask someone else."

"Even I cannot trample on good taste to the extent of asking a wedding guest to put on Joy's gown and play bride for us. You have several tripods here. You can set up the shot, rush into the picture, and have Mike or Kristin press the button. That's all there is to it."

Corey bit her lip, considering his suggestion. She didn't need more than a couple shots of the bride and groom—one in the garden beneath the gazebo, the other somewhere at the reception off to the side, so using tripods wasn't a problem. "Okay."

"Would anyone like a glass of champagne?" Spence offered, looking completely satisfied with the situation. "It's customary to toast Corey and me."

"Don't make jokes like that," Corey warned, and the tension in her voice surprised everyone, including her.

"Bridal nerves," Spence surmised, and Mike guffawed.

They got up to leave, but Spence laid a detaining hand on Corey's arm. "I want to ask you for a favor," he said when the others were gone. "I understand how you felt last night, but for the rest of the day, I'd like you to pretend it never happened."

When Corey eyed him in dubious silence, he grinned and said, "No favor, no wedding. I'll cancel it and the deal's off."

He was completely unpredictable, inscrutable, and utterly irresistible with that teasing glint in his eyes. "You are completely unscrupulous," she informed him, but without any force.

"Lady, I am the best friend you've ever had," he countered, and when she gaped at the arrogance of that claim, he explained, "I have, in my possession, Joy's elopement letter. In it, she says very clearly that it was her conversation with *you* yesterday that convinced her she'd regret it for the rest of her life if she didn't marry the man she loved. Contrary to what my sister thinks, you brought all this on yourself. Now, do I get my favor or do I cancel the wedding?"

"You win," Corey agreed, laughing. She wasn't certain whether she was relieved or disappointed that he didn't want to talk about last night.

"No dark thoughts about me for the rest of the day— agreed?" When she nodded, Spence said, "Good. Now, is there anything else I can do to make things easier for you before the wedding?"

Corey shook her head. "You've already accomplished a great deal. I'm very grateful," she said earnestly. "And very impressed," she reluctantly admitted, tossing him a grin over her shoulder as she left.

Spence studied the easy grace of her movements while he considered her last remark. If Corey was "very impressed" by what she knew he'd accomplished, she'd be dazzled by the rest of it. Upstairs, Joy's wedding gown was already being altered to the size of one of Corey's dresses. In Houston, Spence's attorney was drawing up a letter notifying the tenants in his grandmother's house that their lease was being terminated, and preparing a large check from Spence to compensate them. In Newport, Judge Lawrence Lattimore was on the phone with a sleepy clerk from City Hall who was being talked into issuing a marriage license on a Saturday.

All things considered, Spence decided, it had not been a bad morning's work.

Even so, he had the disquieting feeling that he was forgetting something important—something other than informing Corey that she was about to become a bride. He hoped to God that she'd been sincere about her love of spontaneity and acting on instinct; he hoped she'd been sincere when she told Joy she'd always loved him and wanted to have his babies.

That last part didn't bother him as much as the first. Corey loved him, he knew she did, but he wasn't thrilled about the sort of wedding she was about to have.

Of course, based on their early history, she was bound to feel an enormous amount of satisfaction at having forced him to go to such bizarre lengths in order to get her to the altar.

He smiled to himself, imagining the tales she would tell their children about this day, but his smile faded as he walked out of his study and stood on the terrace, watching the sailboats gliding across the water. If he was mistaken, she was going to be furious, and if he wasn't mistaken, then he shouldn't be feeling quite this uneasy. On the other hand, he could merely be suffering from an ordinary case of wedding nerves.

Spence turned his back on the view and walked over to his desk to make some more phone calls. At the very worst, Corey could get an annulment and no one would ever need to know they'd been married.

Fifteen

STANDING NEAR A ROSE-COVERED GAZEBO WHERE HE WAS about to be married by a thoroughly inebriated judge to a totally unsuspecting photographer, Spence chatted amiably with two women who didn't know they were about to become his in-laws.

Corey had wanted happy faces for her pictures, and he'd provided two hundred of them for her, with the aid of an amazing quantity of French champagne, a fortune in Russian caviar, and a brief, amusing speech he'd given that had gained their full cooperation. In fact, all the guests seemed to be having a thoroughly enjoyable time.

The bridegroom certainly was.

Lifting his champagne glass to his mouth, Spence watched his bride-to-be study the angle of the sun as she readied the last of the tripods for the shots of the actual wedding. The long train of her ten-thousand-dollar wedding gown had gotten in her way, so she'd tied it up into a makeshift bustle, and her long lace veil was currently slung over her shoulders like a crumpled stole. He decided she was the most exquisite creature alive. Utterly fetching. Completely unself-conscious. And she was about to become his. He watched her hurrying toward him, her eyes glowing with pleasure at the shot she'd lined up. "I think we're all set," she told him.

"It's a good thing," Spence chuckled. "Lattimore is roasting alive in that gazebo in those robes you've made him wear for the last hour, and he's been quenching a very big thirst."

Corey's grandmother summed it up differently as she reached up to rearrange Corey's veil. "That judge is drunk!" she declared.

"It's okay, Gram," Corey said, twisting around to watch her mother unwind her train and stretch it out carefully behind her. "He isn't really a judge. Spencer says he's a plumber."

"He's a lush, that's what he is."

"How's my hair?" Corey asked when they were finished.

Spence particularly loved her hair today, even though it wasn't loose around her shoulders the way he wanted to see it tonight, in bed. They'd pinned it up into curls at the crown to keep it from looking untidy in the pictures. "It looks fine," Mrs. Foster declared, reaching up to straighten the headpiece.

Spence offered Corey his arm and grinned. He was so damned happy, he couldn't stop smiling. "Ready?" he asked.

"Wait," Corey said as she straightened his black tie. Spence envisioned a lifetime of Corey straightening his ties.

Corey felt a sharp ache in her chest as she looked up at the elegant man in a tailor-made tuxedo who was smiling down at her with all the tenderness of a real bridegroom. She'd dreamed this dream a thousand times in years gone by, and now it was only make-believe. To her horror, she felt the sting of tears and hid them quickly behind an overbright smile.

"Will I do?" Spence asked, his deep voice strangely husky.

Corey nodded, swallowed, and smiled gaily. "We look like Ken and Barbie. Let's go."

Before they could take the first step onto the white carpet that stretched between the rows of chairs and into the gazebo, someone in the front row turned around and good-naturedly called, "Hey, Spence, can we get this thing going? It's hot as hell out here."

It hit Spence at that moment what he'd forgotten. He looked around for something to use and saw a piece of gold wired ribbon lying in the grass.

"Ready?" Lattimore said, running his finger around the collar of his robe.

"Ready," Spence said.

"Okay if we make it sh . . . short?"

"That's fine," Corey said, but she was leaning back, trying to see where Kristin was with the spare camera they'd decided to use for extra shots.

"Miss . . . uh . . . Foster?"

"Yes?"

"It's cushtomary to look at the groom."

"Oh, sorry," Corey said. He'd been very nice and very cooperative, and if he wanted to play his part to the fullest, she didn't mind in the least.

"Place your hand in Spence's hand." On the right, Corey saw Kristin move into position and lift her camera.

"Do you, Spencer Addison, take Cor . . . er . . . Caroline Foster to be your lawfully wedded wife so long as you both shall live?" the judge said so quickly the words ran together.

Spence smiled into her eyes. "I do."

Corey's smile wavered.

"Do you, Caroline Foster, take Spencer Addison to be your

lawfully wedded wife . . . husband . . . so long as you both shall live?"

Alarm bells began ringing in Corey's brain, but they sprang from a source she couldn't understand.

"For God's sake, Corey," Spence teased gently, "don't jilt me at the altar."

"It would serve you right," she said on a breathless laugh, trying to concentrate on the whereabouts of Mike.

"Come on. Say yes."

She didn't want to. It seemed wrong to perpetrate this sham. "This isn't a movie, these are still shots," she said.

Spence reached out and took her chin between his thumb and forefinger, tipping her face up to his. "Say yes."

"Why?"

"Say yes."

He bent his head and as his lips moved closer to hers, she could almost hear Kristin rushing forward for this unexpected shot.

"You can't kiss her until she says yes," Lattimore warned in a slur.

"Say yes, Corey," Spence whispered, his mouth so close to hers that his breath touched her face. "So the nice judge will let me kiss you."

Corey felt a helpless giggle well up inside her at his cajolery and his insistence on being kissed. "Yes," she whispered, laughing, "but it better be a very good k—"

His mouth swooped down, smothering her voice, and his arms closed around her with stunning force, gathering her to him, stifling her laughter while the judge happily proclaimed, "I now pronounce you man and wife, give her the ring." The crowd erupted into laughing applause.

Caught completely off guard by the deep, demanding kiss,

Corey clutched his shoulders for balance as her senses reeled; then she flattened her hands, forcing him away. "Stop," she whispered, tearing her mouth from his. "That's enough. Really."

He let her go, but he laced his fingers tightly through hers and kept them there while something round and scratchy slid against her knuckle.

"I need to change out of this gown," Corey said as soon as they stepped out of the gazebo.

"Before you go—we have to—" the judge began, but Spence intervened. "You can congratulate me in a few minutes, Larry," he said smoothly. "I'll meet you in the library, where it's quiet, as soon as I take Corey upstairs. There's a cab out front to take you home after we talk."

In the space of time it took to leave the gazebo and start down the hall to her suite, Corey's emotions had plummeted from an enthusiastic high over the outstanding photographs she was certain they'd gotten to an inexplicable depression, which she tried to rationalize as a normal letdown after a day of extraordinary tension and hard work. She knew Spence wasn't to blame. He'd played his role as surrogate bridegroom with a combination of unshakable calm and boyish enthusiasm that had been utterly charming.

She was still trying to sort out her tangled emotions when he opened the door to her suite and stepped aside, but when she started to walk past him, he stopped her. "What's wrong, beautiful?"

"Oh, please," she said on a choking laugh, "don't say anything sweet, or I'll burst into tears."

"You were a gorgeous bride."

"I'm warning you," she said chokily.

He drew her into his arms, cupping the back of her head and

pressing her face to his heart in a gesture that was so tender and so unexpected that it moved her another step closer to tears. "It was such an awful farce," she whispered.

"Most weddings are an awful farce," he said in quiet amusement. "It's what comes afterward that matters."

"I suppose so," she said absently.

"Think about the weddings you've seen," he continued, ignoring the startled looks of several wedding guests who saw them through the open door as the guests walked down the hall. "Half the time the groom is hungover or the bridge has morning sickness. It's pitiful," he teased.

Her shoulders shook with a teary laugh, and Spence smiled because the sound of her laughter had always delighted him, and making her laugh had always made him feel as if he were better, stronger, nicer than he really was. "All things considered, this is about as close to a perfect wedding as you could hope for."

"Not to me it isn't. I want a Christmas wedding."

"Is that the only thing you dislike about this wedding—the season of the year, I mean? If there's anything I can do to make you happier about all this, tell me and I'll do it."

You could love me, Corey thought before she could stop herself, then she pushed the thought aside. "There is absolutely nothing more you can do beyond what you've done. I'm being ridiculous and overemotional. Weddings do that to me," she lied with a smile as she stepped back.

He accepted that. "I'll deal with Lattimore, and then I want to change clothes. In the meantime, I'll have some champage sent up here, and then I'll come up and share it with you, how does that sound?"

"Fine," she said.

Sixteen

A SHOWER HAD PARTIALLY REVIVED COREY'S SPIRITS, AND SHE surveyed the selection of clothes hanging in her closet, wondering what the appropriate attire was for a stand-in bride who was about to have champagne with a surrogate groom after their pretend wedding. "This will work," she said with relief as reached for the billowy cream silk pants and long tunic she'd brought along because they were flexible enough to wear to almost any social event in a Newport mansion.

She was standing in front of the bathroom mirror, brushing her hair, when she heard Spence knock on the door and then let himself in. "I'll be right there," she called, pausing long enough to put on pearl earrings. She straightened and stepped back from the mirror. She looked much happier and more contented than she felt, she decided with relief. Because what she felt was . . . haunted. She had worn a bridal gown and veil and stood beside Spence in a rose-covered gazebo while he held her hand in his, smiling tenderly into her eyes. He had even slipped a ring on her finger afterward. . . . The memories of their "wedding" seemed to be permanently imprinted on her mind. No, she told herself, not permanently, only temporarily. Memories would soon give way to the reality. The wedding had been a hoax, the "ring" a piece of gold ribbon with a wire in it. The reality made her ache.

Spence had taken off his tuxedo jacket, loosened his tie, and opened the top buttons of his formal shirt. He looked every bit as sexy and elegant that way as he had during the wedding; he did not, however, look nearly as relaxed. His jaw was rigid, and his movements were abrupt as he ignored the champagne chilling in a gold bucket and jerked the stopper out of one of the liquor decanters on the cabinet. He poured some into a crystal tumbler and lifted the glass to his mouth. "What are you doing?" Corey asked, watching him take two deep swallows of straight bourbon.

He lowered the glass and looked at her over his shoulder. "I'm having a very stiff drink. And now I'll fix one for you."

"No thanks," Corey said with a shudder. "I'd rather have the champagne."

"Take my advice," he said almost bitterly, "have a regular drink."

"Why?"

"Because you're going to need it." He fixed her a drink that at least had ice cubes and some club soda to dilute it and handed it to her. Corey sipped it, waiting for him to explain, but instead of talking, he stared at the glass in his hand.

"Spence, whatever is wrong, it can't be worse than you're making it seem to me right now."

"I hope you still feel that way in a few minutes," he said grimly.

"What *is* it?" Corey said desperately. "Is someone ill?"

"No." He put down his drink, then he walked over to the fireplace and braced his hands on the mantel, staring into the empty grate. It was a pose of such abject defeat that Corey felt a fierce surge of protective tenderness. She walked up behind him and laid her hand on his broad shoulder. It was the first time since coming to Newport that she had voluntarily touched him except when he was kissing her, and she felt his muscles tense beneath her hand. "Please don't make me wonder like this, you're scaring me!"

"An hour ago, my idiotic niece called to tell me she was now married to her beloved restauranteur."

"So far, that sounds good."

"That was the only good part of the phone call."

Visions of car crashes and ambulances flashed through Corey's mind. "What was the bad part, Spence?"

He hesitated, then he turned and looked directly at her. "The bad part is that, during our conversation, we also discussed the elopement letter she left for me last night. It appears that in her haste to explain how you'd influenced her decision to elope, Joy was a little remiss about the verbs she used. Specifically, she failed to clearly differentiate between past and present tense."

"What do you mean she explained *how* I influenced her?" Corey asked warily.

"Read the letter," he said, taking two folded pieces of paper out of his pants pocket and handing Corey the one on top.

Corey saw at a glance what he was talking about.

Corey told me she loved you and wanted to have your baby, she said you're the only man she's ever felt that way about, and that's why she's never married anyone else. Uncle Spence, I love Will. I want to have his babies someday. That's why I can't marry anyone else. . . .

Despite the mortification she felt, Corey managed to affect a calm, dismissive smile as she handed the letter back to him. "In the first place, I was describing how I felt about you when I was a teenager, not an adult. Secondly, the conclusion she drew about why I haven't married was hers, not mine."

"As you can see, that's not quite the way it read."

"Is—is that all that's bothering you?" Corey said, relieved that he wasn't going to challenge her explanation.

Instead of answering, he shoved his hands into his pockets and studied her in impassive silence for so long that Corey took a nervous sip of her drink. "What's bothering me," he said bluntly, "is that I don't know how you feel about me now."

111

Since she didn't have the slightest idea how he felt about her and he wasn't volunteering any information about it, Corey didn't think he had any right to ask the question or expect an answer. "I think you're one of the handsomest men I've ever married!" she joked.

He was not amused. "This is no time to be evasive, believe me."

"What do you mean?"

"I mean that I know damned well you feel something for me now, even if it's just common garden-variety lust."

She gaped at him. "Does your ego need a boost?"

"Answer the question," he ordered.

Struggling desperately to put a light tone on the matter and end it, she said, "Let me put it this way: If we ever do an article on 'Great Kissing,' you'll be featured in the Top Ten, and I'll give you my vote. Well?" she teased. "What do you think?"

"I think you'd be accused of bias for voting for your own husband."

"Don't call yourself my husband," Corey said. "It isn't funny."

"It isn't a joke."

"That's what I just said," Corey pointed out impatiently.

"We're married, Corey."

"Don't be ridiculous."

"It may sound ridiculous, but it is also true."

Corey searched his impassive features, shaking her head in denial of what she saw in his eyes. "The wedding ceremony was a sham. The judge was a plumber."

"No, his father and his uncle are plumbers. He's a judge."

"I don't believe you."

Instead of replying, he handed the second folded piece of paper to her.

Corey opened it and stared. It was a copy of a marriage

license with Corey's name on it and Spence's name on it. It was dated that day and signed by Judge Lawrence E. Lattimore.

"We're married, Corey."

Her hand closed into an involuntary fist, crumpling the paper; her chest constricted into a knot of confused anguish. "Were you playing some sort of sick joke on me?" she whispered. "Why would you want to humiliate this way?"

"Try to understand. I told you what Joy said, and I thought this was what you wanted—"

"You arrogant bastard!" she whispered brokenly. "Are you trying to tell me that you actually married me out of pity and guilt, and you thought I'd *like* it? Am I so pathetic to you that you thought I'd be happy to settle for getting married at someone else's wedding, in someone else's gown, with a piece of wire ribbon for a wedding ring?"

Spence saw the tears in her eyes, and he caught her by the shoulders. "Listen to me! Corey, I married you because I love you."

"You love me," she scoffed, her shoulders shaking with laughter, her face wet with tears. "You love me. . . ."

"Yes, dammit, I do."

She laughed harder and the tears came faster. "You don't even know what love is," she sobbed. "You 'loved me' so much that you didn't even bother to propose. You didn't see anything wrong with turning my wedding into one great big joke."

From her perspective it was all true, Spence knew that, and the knowedge was as painful to him as the tears racing down her pale cheeks and the anguish in her eyes. "I understand how you feel about me right now."

"Oh, no you don't!" She twisted out of his grasp and angrily brushed tears off her pale cheeks. "But I'll try to make it clear once and for all: I don't want you! I didn't want you before, I don't want you now, and I will never want you!" Her palm crashed against his cheek with enough force to snap his head sideways. "Is *that* clear enough for you?" Whirling on her heel, Corey started for the closet where her suitcases were. "I'm not spending the night in the same house with you! When I get to Houston, I'm going to start annulment proceedings, and if you dare try to oppose me, I'll have you and that drunken judge arrested in less time than it took you to arrange this marriage! Is *that* clear?"

"I have no intention of opposing an annulment," he said in a glacial voice. "In fact," he added as he tossed something onto the bed and walked to the door, "I suggest you use that to cover the cost of your attorney." The door slammed shut behind him.

Corey collapsed against the wall and buried her face in her hands, her body shaking with silent sobs.

At last, a numbness finally swept over her, and she shoved away from the wall and went over to the telephone. She asked the servant who answered to locate her mother and grandmother and tell them to come up to her room immediately, then she instructed him to find Mike MacNeil and have him call her.

When Mike called, Corey told him something had come up, and she had to fly home tonight. The phone rang as soon as she hung it up. "Miss Foster," the butler coolly informed her, "Mr. Addison's car is on its way to the front and will be waiting for you there as soon as you are ready to leave."

Despite the fact that she was desperate to get out of that house, Corey was irrationally infuriated at being summarily ejected from the premises that way. She finished packing in record time and closed her suitcases. As she put the last one on the floor, she remembered the object her "husband" had tossed onto the bed. Expecting to see a money clip with bills in it, she glanced toward the head of the bed, where she thought it had landed.

Lying atop a pile of ice blue satin pillows, glittering in the pale light from the setting sun, was a spectacular diamond ring that looked as if it should have belonged to a duchess.

Her mother and grandmother knocked on her door, and Corey called to them to come in while she picked up her purse and reached for her suitcases. Mrs. Foster took one look at Corey's pale face, saw the suitcases, and came to a full stop. "Dear God, what's wrong?"

Corey told them in a few brief sentences and nodded toward the ring on the bed as she left. "Please see that he gets that back. Then tell him if he ever comes near me again, I'll swear out a warrant!"

After Corey left, Mrs. Foster looked at her mother in stunned silence, then she finally said, "What a stupid thing for Spence to have done!"

"He deserves to be horsewhipped," Gram decreed without animosity.

"Corey will never forgive him for this. Never. And Spence is impossibly proud. He won't ask her again," said Mrs. Foster with a sigh.

Her mother walked over to the bed and picked up the ring, turning it in her fingers with a smile. "Spence will have to send a bodyguard with Corey when she wears this."

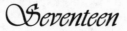

Seventeen

"WHAT DO YOU MEAN HE WON'T SIGN THE RELEASES SO THAT we can use the pictures we took in Newport?" Corey exploded.

"I didn't say he had flatly refused to sign them," Diana said carefully. In the week since Corey had been back from New-

115

port, she'd thrown herself into a dozen projects to keep from thinking about either her marriage or the annulment proceedings she'd started, and she looked exhausted. "He said he would sign them, but only if you brought them to him personally tomorrow tonight."

"I am not going back to Newport," she warned.

"You won't have to. Spence will be in Houston taking care of some business."

"I don't want to see him in Houston or anywhere else."

"I think he knows that," Diana said wryly. "You not only started annulment proceedings, you asked for a legal injunction to prevent him from coming near you."

"What do you think he'd do if we put the magazine out without the releases?"

"He said to tell you that if we do, his attorneys will dine on our corporate carcass."

"I hate that man," she said wearily.

Diana wisely refrained from arguing that point and stuck to the matter at hand. "There's a relatively painless way around this. He said he's staying at the River Oaks house, so tomorrow night—"

Furious at the control he was exerting over the magazine and over her, Corey said, "Tomorrow night is the Orchid Ball. He'll have to sign the releases during the day, instead."

"I explained to Spence we're one of the sponsors and have to be there. Spence said he would expect you at the house before the ball, at seven o'clock."

"I am not going there alone."

"Okay," Diana said, sounding as relieved as she felt. "Mother and I will wait in the car for you while you're with Spence, then we'll leave from there."

Eighteen

COREY HADN'T BEEN BACK TO SPENCE'S HOUSE SINCE HIS grandmother lived there, and it seemed strange to be returning after so many years.

She knew he'd leased the house to tenants who'd kept most of the servants on, and the place was as beautifully maintained as it had always been. Since Spence was staying there now, Corey assumed either he had decided to sell it and it was vacant, or else the people who'd lived there for years had moved out.

All the carriage lights were lit on the front porch, just as they'd always been whenever guests were expected, but tonight, a strange colorful glow was visible through the closed draperies in what Corey knew was the living room.

"I won't be long," Corey told Diana and her mother as she got out of the car and walked up the front steps.

Clutching the release form in her hand, she rang the bell, her heart drumming harder as footsteps sounded in the foyer, and harder still when the door swung open and Mrs. Bradley's former housekeeper said with a warm smile, "Good evening, Miss Foster. Mr. Addison is waiting for you in the living room."

Corey nodded, then she walked through the dimly lit foyer. Bracing herself for the impact of seeing Spence for the first time since that hideous scene in Newport, Corey rounded the corner and walked into the living room.

Then she braced herself again, trying to assimilate what she was seeing.

Spence was near the middle of the candlelit room, leaning casually against the grand piano with his arms crossed over his chest.

He was wearing a tuxedo.

The room was decked out for Christmas.

"Merry Christmas, Corey," he said quietly.

Corey's disoriented gaze drifted over the thick garlands draping the mantel, to the beribboned mistletoe on the chandelier overhead, to the huge Christmas tree in the corner with its red ornaments and twinkling lights, then it came to a stop at a small mountain of presents beneath the tree. All of them were wrapped in gold foil, and all of them had huge white tags on them.

And all the tags said "Corey."

"I cheated you out of a Christmas dance and a Christmas wedding," he said solemnly. "I'd like to give them to you anyway. I still can, if you'll let me."

Spence had envisioned a dozen possible reactions from her, from laughter to fury, but he had never considered the possibility that Corey would turn her back on him and bend her head and start to cry. When she did, his heart sank with defeat. He reached for her and dropped his hands, and then he heard her choking whisper: "All I've ever wanted was you." Relief made him rough as he spun her around and yanked her into his arms, wrapping them tightly around her.

His wife laid her hand against his jaw and tenderly spread her fingers over his cheek. "All I've ever wanted was you."

In the car outside, Mrs. Foster looked at the embracing couple silhouetted against the draperies. Her son-in-law was kissing her daughter as if he never intended to stop or let her go. "I don't think there's any need for us to wait," she told Diana with a happy sigh. "Corey won't be going anywhere tonight."

"Yes she will," Diana said with absolute certainty as she put her car into gear. "Spence cheated her out of one Christmas dance, and he intends to make up for it tonight."

"You don't mean he intends to take her to the ball," Mrs. Foster said worriedly. "The tickets have been sold out for months."

"Spence managed to reserve somehow, and we're sitting together at it." With a fond smile, she added, "We shouldn't have any trouble finding the table. It has an unusual centerpiece. Instead of white orchids, it has a big red sleigh filled with holly."

Epilogue

WRAPPED IN A RED VELVET ROBE, COREY STOOD AT THE windows of the chalet, looking out across the snowy, moon-swept hills of Vermont, where they had decided to spend their first real Christmas. Her husband insisted this was also their second honeymoon—the one they would have had if Corey had gotten her Christmas wedding—and he was playing the role of ardent bridegroom with passion and élan.

She turned and walked over to the bed where Spence was asleep, then she leaned down and pressed a kiss to his forehead. It was almost dawn, and he'd made love to her until they were both exhausted, but it was Christmas morning, and she was absurdly anxious to see him open his presents. He gave her presents all the time, and she'd shopped for months for just the right gifts for him.

A smile touched his lips. "Why are you awake?" he asked without opening his eyes.

"It's Christmas morning. I want to give you a present. Do you mind?"

"Not at all," he said with a husky laugh and pulled her down on top of him.

"This is not your present," she informed him, propping her

elbows on his chest as he opened her robe. "You've already had this one."

"I like having *two* of the same presents," he persisted, tracing his finger down the valley between her breasts.

"Two Christmases and two honeymoons, all in one year," she answered on a breathless laugh as his mouth traced a seductive path where his hand had been. "Are we always going to do everything in twos?"

The answer to that question appeared nine months later in the birth announcement section of *People* magazine:

It's a "double exposure" for Spencer Addison and his wife, photographer Corey Foster—identical twins named Molly and Mary, born September 25th.

JUDITH McNAUGHT soared to stardom with her stunning bestseller *Whitney, My Love.* Since then, she has gone on to win the hearts of millions of readers around the world with such breathtaking novels as *Once and Always* and the *New York Times* bestsellers *Something Wonderful, A Kingdom of Dreams, Almost Heaven, Paradise, Perfect,* and *Until You.* Judith McNaught lives in Houston, Texas, where she is currently working on her next novel, *Remember When,* coming soon from Pocket Books.

Jude Deveraux

Just Curious

One

"I DON'T BELIEVE IN MIRACLES," KAREN SAID, LOOKING AT HER sister-in-law with her lips pressed tightly together. Sunlight shone on Karen's shiny-clean face, making her look like the "before" photo of a model without makeup. But lack of makeup only revealed perfect skin, high cheekbones, and eyes like dark emeralds.

"I never said a word about miracles," Ann replied, her voice showing her exasperation. She was as dark as Karen was fair, half a foot shorter, and voluptuous. "All I said was that you should go to the Christmas dance at the club. What's so miraculous about that?"

"You said that I might meet someone wonderful and get married again," Karen answered, refusing to remember the car wreck that had taken her beloved husband from her.

"Okay, so shoot me, I apologize." Squinting her eyes at her once-beautiful sister-in-law, Ann found it difficult to believe that she used to be eaten up with jealousy over Karen's looks. Now Karen's hair hung lank and lifeless about her shoulders, with split ends up to her ears. She hadn't a trace of makeup on and with her pale coloring, Karen looked like a teenager without it. Instead of the elegant clothes she used to wear, she now had on an old sweat suit that Ann knew had belonged to Karen's deceased husband, Ray.

"You used to be the most gorgeous girl at the country club," Ann said wistfully. "I remember seeing you and Ray dance at Christmas. Remember that red dress you had, slit so high your tonsils were visible? But how you and Ray looked when you danced together was worth it! Those legs of yours had every man in the room drooling. Every man in Denver was drooling! Except my Charlie, of course, *he* never looked."

Over her teacup, Karen gave a faint smile. "Key words in that are 'girl' and 'Ray.' Neither of which I am or have any longer."

"Give me a break!" Ann wailed. "You sound as though you're ninety-two years old and should be choosing your coffin. You turned thirty, that's all. I hit thirty-five this year and age hasn't stopped me." At that Ann got up, her hand at her back, and waddled over to the sink to get another cup of herbal tea. She was so hugely pregnant she could hardly reach the kettle.

"Point made," Karen said. "But no matter how young or old I am, that doesn't bring Ray back." When she said the name, there was reverence in her voice, as though she were speaking the name of a deity.

Ann gave a great sigh, for they'd had this conversation many times. "Ray was my brother and I loved him very much, but, Karen, Ray is dead. And he's been dead for two years. It's time you started living again."

"You don't understand about Ray and me. We were . . ."

Ann's face was full of sympathy, and reaching across the table, she clasped Karen's wrist and squeezed. "I know he was everything to you, but you have a lot to offer some man. A man who is alive."

"No!" Karen said sharply. "No man on earth could fill Ray's shoes, and I'd never allow anyone to try." Abruptly, she got up from the table and walked to the window. "No one understands. Ray and I were more than just married, we were partners. We were equals; we shared everything. Ray asked my opinion about everything, from the business to the color of his socks. He made me feel useful. Can you understand that? Every man I've met before or since Ray seems to want a woman to sit still and look pretty. The minute you start telling him your opinions, he asks the waiter to give him the check."

There was nothing that Ann could say to contradict Karen, for Ann had seen firsthand what a good marriage they'd had. But now Ann was sick with seeing her beloved sister-in-law hide herself away from the world, so she wasn't about to tell Karen that she'd never find anyone who was half the man Ray was.

"All right," Ann said, "I'll stop. If you are bound and determined to commit suttee for Ray, so be it." Hesitantly, she gave her sister-in-law's back a hard look. "Tell me about that job of yours." Her tone of voice told what she thought of Karen's job.

Turning away from the window, Karen laughed. "Ann, no one could ever doubt your opinions on anything. First you don't like that I love my husband and second you don't approve of my job."

"So sue me. I think you're worth more than eternal widow-hood and death-by-typing."

Karen could never bear her sister-in-law any animosity because Ann truly did think Karen was the best there was, and it had nothing to do with their being related by marriage. "My job is fine," she said, sitting back down at the table. "Everyone is well and everything is going fine."

"That boring, huh?"

Karen laughed. "Not horribly boring, just a little bit boring."

"So why don't you quit?" Before Karen could answer, Ann held up her hand. "I apologize. It's none of my business if you, with all your brains, want to bury yourself in some typing pool." Ann's eyes lit up. "So anyway, tell me about your divine, gorgeous boss. How is that beautiful man?"

Karen smiled—and ignored the reference to her boss. "The other women in the pool gave me a birthday party last week." At that she lifted her eyebrows in challenge, for Ann was always saying snide things about the six women Karen worked with.

"Oh? And what did they give you? A hand-crocheted shawl, or maybe a rocking chair and a couple of cats?"

"Support hose," she said, then laughed. "No, no, I'm kidding. Just the usual things. Actually, they chipped in together and got me a very nice gift."

"And what was that?"

Karen took a drink of her tea. "Aneyeglassesholder."

"A what?"

Karen's eyes twinkled. "A holder for my eyeglasses. You know, one of those string things that goes around your neck. It's a very nice one, eighteen-karat gold. With little, ah, cats on the clasp."

Ann didn't smile. "Karen, you have to get out of there. The combined age of those women must be three hundred years. And didn't they notice that you don't wear glasses?"

"Three hundred and seventy-seven." When Ann looked at her in question, Karen said, "Their ages total three hundred and seventy-seven years. I added it up one day. And they said they knew I didn't wear glasses, but that as a woman who had just turned thirty I would soon need to."

"For an ancient like you, support hose are just around the corner."

"Actually, Miss Johnson gave me a pair last Christmas. She's seventy-one and swears by them."

At that Ann did laugh. "Oh, Karen, this is serious. You have to get out of there."

"*Mmmmm*," Karen said, looking down at her cup. "My job has its uses."

"What are you up to?" Ann snapped.

Karen gave her sister-in-law a look of innocence. "I have no idea what you mean."

For a moment Ann leaned back against the bench and studied her sister-in-law. "At last I am beginning to understand. You are much too clever to throw away everything. So help me, Karen Lawrence, if you don't tell me everything and tell me *now*, I'll think of some dreadful way to punish you. Like maybe not allowing you to see my baby until she's three years old."

When Karen's face turned white, Ann knew she had her. "Tell!"

"It's a nice job and the people I work with are—"

Suddenly, Ann's face lit up. "Don't you play the martyr to *me*. I've known you since you were eight years old, remember? You take extra work from those old biddies so you'll know everything that's going on. I'll bet you know more about what's going on in that company than Taggert does." Ann smiled at her own cleverness. "And you let your looks go so you don't intimidate anyone. If that dragon Miss Gresham saw you as you looked a couple of years ago, she'd find some reason to fire you."

Karen's blush was enough to tell her that she was right.

"Pardon my stupidity," Ann said, "but why don't you get a job that pays a little more than being a secretary?"

"I tried!" Karen said vehemently. "I applied at dozens of companies, but they wouldn't consider me because I don't have a university degree. Eight years of managing a hardware store means nothing to a personnel director."

"You only quadrupled that store's profits."

"Whatever. That doesn't matter. Only that piece of paper saying I sat through years of boring classes means anything."

"So why don't you go back to school and get that piece of paper?"

"I *am* going to school!" Karen took a drink of her tea to calm herself.

"Look, Ann, I know you mean well, but I know what I'm doing. I know I'll never find another man like Ray who I can work *with,* so maybe I can learn enough to open a shop of my own. I have the money from the sale of Ray's half of the hardware store, and I'm managing to save most of what I earn from this job. Meanwhile, I am learning everything about running a company the size of Taggert's."

Karen smiled. "I'm not really an idiot about my little old ladies. They think they use me to do their work, but truthfully, I'm very selective about what I agree to do. Everything in that office, from every department, goes across my desk. And since I always make myself available for all weekends and holidays, I always see what's most urgent."

"And what do you plan to do with all this knowledge?"

"Open a business somewhere. Retail. It's what I know, although without Ray there to do the selling, I don't know how I'll cope."

"You should get married again!" Ann said forcefully.

"But I don't *want* to get married!" Karen nearly shouted. "I'm just going to get pregnant!" After she'd said it, Karen looked at her friend in horror. "Please forget that I said that," she whispered. "Look, I better go. I have things—"

"Move from that seat and you're dead," Ann said levelly.

With a great sigh, Karen collapsed back against the upholstered banquette in Ann's sunny kitchen. "Don't do this to me. Please, Ann."

"Do what?" she asked innocently.

"Pry and snoop and generally interfere in something that is none of your business."

"I can't imagine what you could be referring to. I've never done anything like that in my life. Now tell me everything."

Karen tried to change the subject. "Another gorgeous woman came out of Taggert's office in tears last week," she said, referring to her boss, a man who seemed to drive Ann mad with desire. But Karen was sure that was because she didn't know him.

"What do you mean, you're 'going' to get pregnant?" Ann persisted.

"An hour after she left, a jeweler showed up at Taggert's office with a briefcase and two armed guards. We all figure he was buying her off. Drying her tears with emeralds, so to speak."

"Have you done anything yet about getting pregnant?"

"And on Friday we heard that Taggert was engaged—again. But not to the woman who'd left his office. This time he's engaged to a redhead." She leaned across the table to Ann. "And Saturday I typed the prenuptial agreement."

That got Ann's attention. "What was in it?"

Karen leaned back again, her face showing her distaste. "He's a bastard, Ann. He really is. I know he's very good looking and he's rich beyond imagining, but as a human, he's not worth much. I know these . . . these social belles of his are probably just after his money—they certainly couldn't like *him*—but they are human beings and, as such, they are worthy of kindness."

"Will you get off your pulpit and tell me what the prenupt said?"

"The woman, his bride, had to agree to give up all rights to anything that was purchased with his money during the marriage. As far as I could tell, she wasn't allowed to own anything. In the event of a divorce, even the clothing he bought her would remain with him."

"Really? And what was he planning to do with women's clothing?" Ann wiggled her eyebrows.

"Nothing interesting, I'm sure. He'd just find another gorgeous gold digger who fit them. Or maybe he'd sell them so he could buy a case of engagement rings, since he gives them out so often."

"What is it you dislike about the man so much?" Ann asked. "He gave you a job, didn't he?"

"Oh, yes, he has an office full of women. I swear he instructs personnel to hire them by the length of their legs. He surrounds himself with beautiful women executives."

"So what's your complaint?"

"He never allows them to *do* anything!" Karen said with passion. "Taggert makes every decision himself. As far as I know he doesn't even ask his team of beauties what they think should be done, much less allow them to actually do it." She gripped her cup handle until it nearly snapped. "McAllister Taggert could live on a desert island all by himself. He needs no other person in life."

"He seems to need women," Ann said softly. She'd met Karen's boss twice and she'd been thoroughly charmed by him.

"He's the proverbial American playboy," Karen said. "The longer the legs, and the longer the hair, the more he likes them. Beautiful and dumb, that's what he likes." She smiled maliciously. "However, so far none of them have been stupid enough to marry him when they discover that all they get out of the marriage is *him*."

"Well . . ." Ann said, seeing the anger in Karen's face, "maybe we should change the subject. How are you planning to get a baby if you run from every man who looks at you? I mean, the way you dress now is calculated to keep men at a distance, isn't it?"

"My! but that was good tea," Karen said. "You are certainly a good cook, Ann, and I've enjoyed our visit immensely, but I need to go now." With that she rose and headed for the kitchen door.

"Ow!" Ann yelled. "I'm going into labor! Help me."

The blood seemed to drain from Karen's face as she ran to her friend. "Lean back, rest. I'll call the hospital."

But as Karen reached the phone, Ann said in a normal voice, "I think it's passed, but you better stay here until Charlie gets home. Just in case. You know."

After a moment of looking at Ann with anger, Karen admitted defeat and sat back down. "All right, what is it you want to know?"

"I don't know why, but I seem to be very interested in babies lately. Must be something I ate. But anyway, when you mentioned babies, it made me want to hear all of it."

"There is *nothing* to tell. Really nothing. I just . . ."

"Just what?" Ann urged.

"I just regret that Ray and I never had children. We both thought we had all the time in the world."

Ann didn't say anything, just gave Karen time to sort out her thoughts and talk. "Recently, I went to a fertility clinic and had a complete examination. I seem to be perfectly healthy."

When Karen said no more, Ann said softly, "So you've been to a clinic and now what?"

"I am to choose a donor from a catalog," Karen said simply.

Ann's sense of the absurd got the better of her. "Ah, then you get the turkey baster out and—"

Karen didn't laugh as her eyes flashed angrily. "You can afford to be smug since you have a loving husband who can do the job, but what am I supposed to do? Put an ad in the paper for a donor? 'One lonely widow wants child but no husband. Apply box three-five-six.'"

"If you got out more and met some men you might—" Ann

stopped because she could see that Karen was getting angry. "I know, why don't you ask that gorgeous boss of yours to do the job? He beats a turkey baster any day."

For a moment Karen tried to stay annoyed but Ann's persistence thawed her. "Mr. Taggert, rather than a raise," Karen mimicked, "would you mind very much giving me a bit of semen? I brought a jar, and, no, I don't mind waiting."

Ann laughed, for this was the old Karen, the one she'd rarely seen in the last two years.

Karen continued to smile. "According to my charts, I'm at peak fertility on Christmas Day, so maybe I'll just wait up for Santa Claus."

"Beats milk and cookies," Ann said. "But won't you feel bad for all the children he neglects because he spent the whole night at *your* house?"

Ann laughed so hard at her own joke that she let out a scream.

"It wasn't *that* funny," Karen said. "Maybe Santa's helpers could—Ann? Are you all right?"

"Call Charlie," she whispered, clutching her big stomach; then as another contraction hit her, she said, "The hell with Charlie, call the hospital and tell them to rush a delivery of morphine. This *hurts!*"

Shaking, Karen went to the phone and called.

"Idiot!" Karen said, looking at herself in the mirror and seeing the tears seeping out of the corner of her eyes. Tearing off a paper towel from the dispenser on the restroom wall, she dabbed at the tears, then saw that her eyes were red. Which of course made sense since she'd now been crying for most of twenty-four hours.

"Everyone cries at the birth of a baby," she muttered to no one. "People cry at all truly happy occasions, such as weddings and engagement announcements and at the birth of every baby."

Pausing in her wiping, she looked in the mirror and knew that she was lying to herself. Last night she'd held Ann's new daughter in her arms and she'd wanted that child so much that she'd nearly walked out the door with her. Frowning, Ann had taken her baby from her sister-in-law. "You can't have mine," she said. "Get your own."

To cover her embarrassment, Karen had tried to make jokes about her feelings, but they had fallen flat, and in the end, she'd left Ann's hospital room feeling the worst she had since Ray's death.

So now Karen was at the office and she was nearly overpowered with a sense of longing for a home and family. Making another attempt to mop up her face, she heard voices at the door, and without thinking, she scurried into an open stall and locked the door behind her. She did *not* want anyone to see her. Today was the office Christmas party and everyone was in high good spirits. Between the promise of limitless free food and drink this afternoon and a generous bonus received from Montgomery-Taggert Enterprises this morning, the whole office was a cauldron of merriment.

If Karen hadn't already been in a bad mood, she would have been when she realized that one of the two women who entered was Loretta Simons, a woman who considered herself the resident authority on McAllister J. Taggert. Karen knew she was trapped inside the stall, for if she tried to leave the restroom, Loretta would catch her and badger her into hearing more about the wonders of the saintly M.J. Taggert.

"Have you seen him yet?" Loretta gushed in a way that some people reserved for the Sistine Chapel. "He's the most beautiful creature on earth, tall, handsome, kind, understanding."

"But what about that woman this morning?" the second

woman asked. If she hadn't heard all about Taggert, then she had to be the new executive assistant, and Loretta was breaking her in. "She didn't seem to think he was so wonderful."

At that, Karen, hidden in her stall, smiled. Her sentiments exactly.

"But you, my dear, have no idea what that darling man has been through," Loretta said as though talking about a war veteran.

Standing against the wall, Karen put her head back and wanted to cry out in frustration. Did Loretta never talk about anything but the Great Jilt? the Great Tragedy of McAllister Taggert? Wasn't there anything else in her life?

"Three years ago Mr. Taggert was madly, insanely in love with a young woman named Elaine Wentlow." Loretta said the name as though it were something vile and disgusting. "More than anything in life he wanted to marry her and raise a family. He wanted his own home, his own place of security. He wanted—"

Karen rolled her eyes, for Loretta was adding more to the tale each time she told it: fewer facts, more melodrama. Now Loretta was on to the magnificence of the wedding that Taggert had alone planned and paid for. According to Loretta, his fiancée had spent all her time having her nails done.

"And she left him?" the new assistant asked, her voice properly awed.

"She left that dear man standing at the front of the church before seven hundred guests who had flown in from all over the world."

"How awful," the assistant said. "He must have been humiliated. What was her reason? And if she did have a good reason, couldn't she have done it in a more caring manner?"

Karen tightened her jaw. It was her belief that Taggert waited until the night before or the day of the wedding to present his bride with one of his loathsome prenuptial agreements, letting her know just what he thought of her. Of course Karen could never say that, as she was not supposed to be typing Taggert's private work. That was the job of his personal secretary. But beautiful Miss Gresham was much too important to actually feed data into a computer terminal, so she gave the work to the person who had been with the company the longest: Miss Johnson. But then Miss Johnson was past seventy and too rickety to do a lot of typing. Knowing she'd lose her job if she admitted this, and since she had a rather startling number of cats to feed, Miss Johnson secretly gave all of Taggert's private work to Karen.

"So that's why all the women since then have left him?" the assistant asked. "I mean, there was that woman this morning."

Karen didn't have to hear Loretta's recapping of the events of this morning, as it was all the office staff could talk of. What with the Christmas party and the bonus, yet another of Taggert's women dumping him was almost more excitement than they could bear. Karen was genuinely concerned for Miss Johnson's heart.

This morning, minutes after the bonuses had been handed out, a tall, gorgeous redhead had stormed into the offices with a ring box in her trembling hand. The outside receptionist hadn't needed to ask who she was or what her errand was, for angry women with ring boxes in their hands were a common sight in the offices of M.J. Taggert. One by one, all doors had been opened to her, until she was inside the inner sanctum: Taggert's office.

Fifteen minutes later, the redhead had emerged, crying, ring box gone, but clutching a jeweler's box that was about the right size to hold a bracelet.

"How could they do this to him?" the women in the office had whispered, all their anger descending onto the head of the woman. "He's such a lovely man, so kind, so considerate," they said.

"His only problem is that he falls in love with the wrong women. If he could just find a *good* woman, she'd love him forever" was the conclusion that was always drawn. "He just needs a woman who understands what pain he has been through."

After this pronouncement, every woman in the office under fifty-five would head for the restroom, where she'd spend her lunch hour trying to make herself as alluring as possible.

Except Karen. Karen would remain at her desk, forcing herself to keep her opinions to herself.

Now Loretta gave a sigh that made the stall door rattle against its lock. Since Loretta had told every female in the office all about the divine Mr. Taggert, she wasn't worried about anyone overhearing.

"So now he's free again," Loretta said, her voice heavy with the sadness—and hope—at such a state. "He's still looking for his true love, and someday some very lucky woman is going to become Mrs. McAllister Taggert."

At that the assistant murmured in agreement. "The way that woman treated him was tragic. Even if she hated him, she should have thought of the wedding guests."

At those words, Karen could have groaned, for she knew that Loretta had recruited yet another soldier for her little army that constantly played worship-the-boss.

"What are you doing?" Karen heard Loretta ask.

"Filling in the correct name," the assistant answered.

A moment later, Loretta gave a sigh that had to have come straight from her heart. "Oh, yes, I like that. Yes, I like that very much. Now we must go. We wouldn't want to miss even a second of the Christmas party." She paused, then said suggestively, "There's no telling what can happen under the mistletoe."

Karen waited for a minute after the women were gone, then, allowing her pent-up breath to escape, she left the stall. Looking in the mirror, she saw that the time she'd spent hiding had allowed her eyes to clear. After washing her hands, she went to the towel holder and there she saw what the women had just been talking about. Long ago some woman (probably Loretta) had stolen a photograph of Taggert and hung it on the wall of the women's restroom. Then she'd glued a nameplate (also probably stolen) under it. But now, on the wall above the plate was written "Miserably Jilted" before the *M.J. Taggert.*

Looking at it for a moment, Karen shook her head in disgust, then with a smirk, she withdrew a permanent black marker from her handbag, crossed out the handwritten words, and replaced them with, "Magnificently Jettisoned."

For the first time that day, she smiled, then she left the restroom feeling much better. So much better, in fact, that she allowed herself to be pulled into the elevator by fellow employees to go upstairs to the huge Taggert Christmas party.

One whole floor of the building owned by the Taggerts had been set aside for conferences and meetings. Instead of being divided into offices of more or less equal space, the floor had been arranged as though it were a sumptuously, if rather oddly, decorated house. There was a room with tatami mats, shoji screens, and jade objects that was used for Japanese clients. Colefax and Fowler had made an English room that looked like something from Chatsworth. For clients with a scholarly bent there was a library with several thousand books in handsome pecan-wood cases. There was a kitchen for the resident chef and a kitchen for clients who liked to rustle up their own grub. A Santa Fe room dripped beaded moccasins and leather shirts with horsehair tassels.

And there was a big, empty room that could be filled with whatever was needed for the moment, such as an enormous Christmas tree bearing what looked to be half a ton of white and silver ornaments. All the employees looked forward to seeing that tree, each year "done" by some up-and-coming young designer, each year different, each year perfect. This tree would be a source of discussion for weeks to come.

Personally, Karen liked the tree in the day-care center better. It was never more than four feet tall so the children could reach most of it, and it was covered with things the children of the employees had made, such as paper chains and popcorn strings.

Now, making her way toward the day-care center, she was stopped by three men from accounting who'd obviously had too much to drink and were wearing silly paper hats. For a moment they tried to get Karen to go with them, but when they realized who she was, they backed off. Long ago she'd taught the men of the office that she was off limits, whether it was during regular work hours or in a more informal situation like this one.

"Sorry," they murmured and moved past her.

The day-care center was overflowing with children, for the families of the Taggerts who owned the building were there.

"If you say nothing else about the Taggerts, they are fertile," Miss Johnson had once said, making everyone except Karen laugh.

And they were a nice group, Karen admitted to herself. Just because she didn't like McAllister was no reason to dislike the entire family. They were always polite to everyone, but they kept to themselves; but then with a family the size of theirs, they probably didn't have time for outsiders. Now, looking into the chaos of the children's playroom, Karen seemed to see doubles of everyone, for twins ran in the Taggert family to an extraordinary degree. There were adult twins and toddler twins and babies that looked so much alike they could have been clones.

And no one, including Karen, could tell them apart. Mac had twin brothers who had offices in the same building, and whenever either of them arrived, the question "Which are you?" was always asked.

Someone shoved a drink into Karen's hand saying, "Loosen up, baby," but she didn't so much as take a sip. What with spending most of the night in the hospital to be near Ann, she'd not eaten since yesterday evening and she knew that whatever she drank would go straight to her head.

As she stood in the corridor looking in at the playroom, it seemed to her that she'd never seen so many children in her life: nursing babies, crawling, taking first steps, two with books in their hands, one eating a crayon, an adorable little girl with pigtails down her back, two beautiful identical twin boys playing with identical fire trucks.

"Karen, you are a masochist," she whispered to herself, then turned on her heel and walked briskly down the corridor to the elevator. The lift going down was empty, and once she was inside, loneliness swept over her. She had been planning to spend Christmas with Ann and Charlie, but now that they had the new baby, they wouldn't want to be bothered with a former sister-in-law.

Stopping in the office she shared with the other secretaries, Karen started to gather her things so she could go home, but on second thought she decided to finish two letters and get them out. There was nothing urgent, but why wait?

Two hours later Karen had finished all that she'd left on her desk and all that three of the other secretaries had left on their desks.

Stretching, gathering up the personal letters she'd typed for Taggert, one about some land he was buying in Tokyo and the other a letter to his cousin, she walked down the corridor to Taggert's private suite. Knocking first as she always did, then realizing that she was alone on the floor, she opened the door. It was odd to see this inner sanctum without the formidable Miss Gresham in it. Like a lion guarding a temple, the woman hovered over Taggert possessively, never allowing anyone who didn't have necessary business to see him.

So now Karen couldn't help herself as she walked softly about the room, which she'd been told had been decorated to Miss Gresham's exquisite taste. The room was all white and silver, just like the tree—and just as cold, Karen thought.

Carefully, she put the letters on Miss Gresham's desk and started to leave, then, on second thought, she looked toward the double doors that led into *his* office. As far as she knew none of the women in the secretarial pool had seen inside that office, and Karen, as much as anyone else, was very curious to see inside those doors.

Karen well knew that the security guard would be by soon, but she'd just heard him walking in the hall, keys jangling, and if she was caught, she could tell him that she had been told to put the papers in Taggert's office.

Silently, as though she were a thief, she opened the door to the office and looked inside. "Hello? Anyone here?" Of course, she knew that she'd probably drop dead of a heart attack if anyone answered, but still she was cautious.

While looking around, she put the letters on his desk. She had to admit that he had the ability to hire a good decorator;

certainly no mere businessman could have chosen the furnishings of his office, because there wasn't one piece of black leather or chrome in sight. Instead, the office looked as though it had been taken intact from a French chateau, complete with carved paneling, worn flagstones on the floor, and a big fireplace dominating one wall. The tapestry-upholstered furniture looked well worn and fabulously comfortable.

Against a wall was a bookshelf filled with books, one shelf covered with framed photographs, and Karen was drawn to them. Inspecting them, she figured that it would take a calculator to add up all the children in the photos. At the end was a silver-framed photo of a young man holding up a string of fish. He was obviously a Taggert, but not one Karen had seen before. Curious, she picked up the picture and looked at the man.

"Seen all you want?" came a rich baritone that made Karen jump so high she dropped the photo onto the flagstones—where the glass promptly shattered.

"I . . . I'm sorry," she stuttered. "I didn't know anyone was here." Bending to pick up the picture, she looked up into the dark eyes of McAllister Taggert as all six feet of him loomed over her. "I will pay for the damage," she said nervously, trying to gather the pieces of broken glass.

He didn't say a word, just glared down at her, frowning.

With as much in her hand as she could pick up, she stood and started to hand the pieces to him, but when he didn't take them, she set them down on the end of the shelf. "I don't think the photo is damaged," she said. "I, uh, is that one of your brothers? I don't believe I've seen him before."

At that Taggert's eyes widened and Karen was quite suddenly afraid of him. They were alone on the floor and all she really knew about him personally was that a lot of women had refused to marry him. Was it because of his loathsome prenuptial agreements or was it because of something else? His violent temper maybe?

"I must go," she whispered, then turned on her heel and ran from his office.

Karen didn't stop running until she'd reached the elevator and punched the down button. Right now all she wanted on earth was to go home to familiar surroundings and try her best to get over her embarrassment. Caught like a teenage girl snooping in her boss's office! How could she have been so stupid?

When the elevator door opened, it was packed with merrymakers going up to the party three floors above, and even though Karen protested loudly that she wanted to go down, they pulled her in with them and took her back to the party.

The first thing she saw was a waiter with a tray of glasses full of champagne, and Karen downed two of them immediately. Feeling much better, she was able to calm her frazzled nerves. So she was caught snooping in the boss's office. So what? Worse things have happened to a person. By her third glass of wine, she'd managed to convince herself that nothing at all had happened.

Standing before her now was a woman with her arms full of a hefty little boy and juggling an enormous diaper bag while she frantically tried to open a stroller.

"Could I help?" Karen asked.

"Oh, would you please?" the woman answered, stepping back from the stroller as she obviously thought Karen meant to help her with that.

But instead, Karen took the child out of her arms and for a moment clasped him tightly to her.

"He doesn't usually like strangers, but he likes you." The

woman smiled. "You wouldn't mind watching him for a few moments, would you? I'd love to get something to eat."

Holding the boy close to her, while he snuggled his sweet-smelling head into her shoulder, Karen whispered, "I'll keep him forever."

At that a look of fright crossed the woman's face. Snatching her child away from Karen, she hurried down the hall.

Moments ago Karen had thought she'd never before been so embarrassed, but this was worse than being caught snooping. "What is *wrong* with you?" she hissed to herself, then strode toward the elevators. She would go home now and never leave her house again in her life.

As soon as she got into the elevator, she realized that she'd left her handbag and coat in her office on the ninth floor. If it weren't zero degrees outside and her car keys weren't in her purse, she'd have left things where they were, but she had to return. Leaning her head back against the wall, she knew she'd had too much wine, but she also knew without a doubt that after Christmas she'd no longer have a job. As soon as Taggert told his formidable secretary that he'd caught an unknown woman—for Karen was sure the great and very busy McAllister Taggert had never so much as looked at someone as lowly as her—in his office, Karen would be dismissed.

On the wall of the elevator was a bronze plaque that listed all the Taggerts in the building, and toward the bottom it looked as though Loretta's new recruit had been busy again, for a piece of paper had been glued over McAllister Taggert's name that read, "Marvelous Jaguar." Smiling, Karen took a pen out of her pocket and changed it to, "Macho Jackass."

When the elevator stopped, she didn't know whether it was the wine or her defiance, but she felt better. However, she did not want another encounter with Taggert. While holding the door open, she carefully looked up and down both corridors to see if anyone was about. Clear. Tiptoeing, she went down the carpeted hall to the secretaries' office and, as silently as possible, removed her coat from the back of the chair and her purse from the drawer. As she was on her way out, she stopped by Miss Johnson's desk to get notes from her drawer. This way she'd have work to fill her time over Christmas.

"Snooping again?"

Karen paused with her hand on the drawer handle; she didn't have to look up to know who it was. McAllister J. Taggert. Had she not had so much to drink, she would have politely excused herself, but since she was sure she was going to be fired anyway, what did it matter? "Sorry about your office. I was sure you'd be out proposing marriage to someone."

With all the haughtiness she could muster, she tried to march past him.

"You don't like me much, do you?"

Turning, she looked him in the eyes, those dark, heavily fringed eyes that made all the women in the office melt with desire. But they didn't do much for Karen since she kept seeing the tears of the women who'd been jilted by him. "I've typed your last three prenuptial agreements. I know the truth about what you're like."

He looked confused. "But I thought Miss Gresham—"

"And risk breaking those nails on a keyboard? Not likely." With that, Karen swept past him on her way to the elevator.

But Taggert caught her arm.

For a moment fear ran through her. What did she really know about this man? And they were alone on this floor. If she screamed, no one would hear her.

At her look, his face stiffened and he released her arm. "Mrs. Lawrence, I can assure you that I have no intention of harming you in any way."

146

"How do you know my name?"

Smiling, he looked at her. "While you were gone, I made a few calls about you."

"You were spying on me?" she asked, aghast.

"Just curious. As you were about my office."

Karen took another step toward the elevator, but again he caught her arm.

"Wait, Mrs. Lawrence, I want to offer you a job over Christmas."

Karen punched the elevator button with a vengeance while he stood too close, looking down at her. "And what would that job be? Marriage to you?"

"In a manner of speaking, yes," he answered as he looked from her eyes to her toes and back up again.

Karen hit the elevator button so hard it was a wonder the button didn't go through the wall.

"Mrs. Lawrence, I am not making a pass at you. I am offering you a job. A legitimate job for which you will be paid, and paid well."

Karen kept hitting the button and looking up at the floors shown over both doors. Both elevators were stuck on the floor where the party was.

"In the calls I made I discovered that you've worked the last two Christmases when no one else would. I also found out that you are the Ice Maiden of the office. You once stapled a man's tie to your desk when he was leaning over you asking for a date."

Karen turned red, but she didn't look at him.

"Mrs. Lawrence," he said stiffly, as though what he said were very difficult for him. "Whatever may be your opinion of me, you could not have heard that I've ever made an improper advance toward a woman who works for me. My offer is for a job, an unusual job, but nothing else. I apologize for whatever

I've done to give you the impression that I was offering more." With that he turned and walked away.

As Karen watched, one elevator went straight from the twelfth floor down to the first, skipping her on nine. Reluctantly, she turned to look at his retreating back. Suddenly, the image of her empty house appeared before her eyes, the tiny tree with not much under it. Whatever she thought of how he treated women in his personal life, Taggert was always respectful to his employees. And no matter how hard a woman worked to compromise him, he didn't fall for it. Two years ago when a secretary said he'd made a pass at her, everyone laughed at her so hard, she found another job three weeks later.

Taking a deep breath, Karen followed him. "All right," she said when she was just behind him, "I'll listen."

Ten minutes later she was ensconced in Taggert's beautiful office; a fire burned in the fireplace, making a delightful rosy glow on the table that was loaded with delicious food and what seemed to be a limitless supply of cold champagne. At first Karen had thought of resisting such temptation, but then she thought of telling Ann that she'd eaten lobster and champagne with the boss and she began to nibble.

While Karen ate and drank, Taggert started to talk. "I guess you've heard by now about Lisa."

"The redhead?"

"*Mmmm,* yes, the redhead." He refilled her glass. "On the twenty-fourth of December, two days from now, Lisa and I were to be in the wedding of a good friend of mine who lives in Virginia. It's to be a huge wedding, with over six hundred guests flying in from all over the world."

For a moment he just looked at her, saying nothing. "And?" she asked after a while. "What do you need me for? To type your friend's prenupt?"

McAllister spread a cracker with pâté de foie gras and held it out to her. "I no longer have a fiancée."

Karen took a drink of the wine, then reached for the cracker. "Excuse my ignorance, but I don't see what that has to do with me."

"You will fit the dress."

Maybe it was because her mind was a bit fuzzy with drink, but it took her a moment to comprehend, and when she did, she laughed. "You want me to pose as your fiancée and be a bridesmaid of some woman I've never met? And who has never met me?"

"Exactly."

"How many bottles of this have *you* drunk?"

McAllister smiled. "I'm not drunk and I'm absolutely serious. Want to hear more?"

Part of Karen's brain said that she should go home, get away from this crazy man, but what was waiting for her at home? She didn't even have a cat that needed her. "I'm listening."

"I don't know if you've heard, but three years ago I was . . ." He hesitated and she saw his eyelashes flutter quite attractively. "Three years ago I was left at the altar of my own wedding by the woman I planned to spend the rest of my life with."

Karen drained her glass. "Did she find out that you were refusing to say the lines 'with thee my worldly goods I share'?"

For a moment McAllister sat there and stared, then he smiled in a way that could only be called dazzling. And Karen had to blink; he really was gorgeous, with his dark hair and eyes and a hint of a dimple in one cheek. No wonder so many women fell for him. "I think, Mrs. Lawrence, that you and I are going to get along fine."

That brought Karen up short. She was going to have to establish boundaries *now*. "No, I don't think we will, since I do not believe your tragic little-boy-lost story. I have no idea what really happened at your wedding or all those other times women refused to marry you, but I can assure you I am not one of these lovesick secretaries who think you were 'Miserably Jilted.' I think you were—" She halted before she said too much.

Enlightenment lit his face. "You think I was 'Magnificently Jettisoned.' Or do you think I am a 'Macho Jackass'? Well, well, so now at last I know who the office wordsmith is."

Karen couldn't speak because she was too embarrassed—and *how* had he found this out so quickly?

For a moment longer he looked at her in speculation, then his face changed from feel-sorry-for-me to that of one friend talking to another. "What happened back then is between Elaine and me and will remain between us, but the truth is, the groom is her relative and she is going to be at the wedding. If I show up alone, with yet another fiancée having left me, it will be, to put it kindly, embarrassing. And then there is the matter of the wedding. If there are seven male attendants and only six female, women get a bit out-of-sorts about things like that."

"So hire someone from an escort service. Hire an actress."

"I thought of that, but who knows what you get? She could audition Lady Macbeth at the reception. Or she could turn out to know half the men there in a way that could be awkward."

"Surely, Mr. Taggert, you must have a little black book full of names of women who would love to go anywhere with you and do anything."

"That's just the problem. They are all women who . . . well, they like me and after this . . . Well . . ."

"I see. How do you get rid of them? You could always ask them to marry you. That seems to cure every woman of you forever."

150

"See? You're perfect for this. All anyone has to do is see the way you look at me and they'll know we're about to separate. Next week when I announce our split, no one will be surprised."

"What's in it for me?"

"I'll pay you whatever you like."

"One of the engagement rings you give out by the gross?" She knew she was being rude, but the champagne was giving her courage and with every discourteous thing she said to him, his eyes twinkled more.

"Ouch! Is that what people say about me?"

"Don't try your sad-little-boy act on me. I typed those prenuptial agreements, remember? I know what you are *really* like."

"And that is?"

"Incapable of trust, maybe incapable of love. You like the idea of marriage, but actually sharing yourself, and above all sharing your money, with another human, terrifies you. In fact, as far as I can tell, you don't share anything with anyone."

For a moment, he gaped at her, then he smiled. "You certainly have me in a nutshell, but coldhearted as I am, it still embarrassed me that Elaine left me so publicly. That wedding cost me thirty-two thousand dollars, none of which was refundable, and I had to send the gifts back."

Refusing to give in to his play for sympathy, she repeated, "What's in it for me? And I don't want money. I have money of my own."

"Yes. Fifty-two thousand and thirty-eight cents, to be exact."

Karen nearly choked on her champagne. "How—?"

"My family owns the bank in this building. I took a guess that it might be the bank you use, so I tapped into the files after you left my office."

"*More* spying!"

"More curiosity. I was checking to see who you were. I am offering you legitimate employment, and since this is a very personal job, I wanted to know more about you. Besides, I like to know more about a woman than just the package." Taking a sip from his champagne glass, he looked at her the way a dark, romantic hero looks at a helpless damsel.

But Karen wasn't affected. She'd had other men look at her like that, and she'd had one man look at her in love. The difference between the two was everything. "I can see why women say yes to you," she said coolly, lifting her glass to him.

At her detachment, he gave a genuine smile. "All right, I can see that you're not impressed by me, so, now shall we talk business, Mrs. Lawrence? I want to hire you as my escort for three days. Since I am at your mercy, you can name your price."

Karen drained her glass. What was this, her sixth? Whatever the number, all she could feel was courage running through her veins. "If I were to do this, I wouldn't want money."

"Ah, I see. What do you want then? A promotion? To be made head secretary? Maybe you'd like a vice presidency?"

"And sit in a windowed office doing nothing all day? No, thank you."

McAllister blinked at her words, then waited for her to say more. When she was silent, he said, "You want stock in the company? No?" When she still said nothing, he leaned back in his chair and looked at her in speculation. "You want something money can't buy, don't you?"

"Yes," she said softly.

He looked at her for a long moment. "Am I to figure out what money can't buy? Happiness?"

Karen shook her head.

"Love? Surely you don't want love from someone like me?" His face showed his bafflement. "I'm afraid you have me stumped."

"A baby."

At that McAllister spilled champagne down the front of his shirt. As he mopped himself up, he looked at her with eyes full of interest. "Oh, Mrs. Lawrence, I like this much better than parting with my money." As he reached for her hand, she grabbed a sharp little fish knife.

"Don't touch me."

Leaning back, McAllister refilled both their glasses. "Would you be so kind as to inform me how I'm to give you a baby without touching you?"

"In a jar."

"Ah, I see, you want a test-tube baby." His voice lowered and his eyes grew sympathetic. "Are your eggs—?"

"My eggs are perfectly all right, thank you," she snapped. "I don't want to put my eggs in a jar, but I want you to put your . . . your . . . in a jar."

"Yes, now I understand." Looking at her, he sipped his drink. "What I don't understand is, why me? I mean, since you don't like me or exactly think I'm of good moral character, why would you want me to be the father of your child?"

"Two reasons. The alternative is going to a clinic, where I can choose a man off a computer data bank. Maybe he's healthy but what about his relatives? Whatever I may think of you, your family is very nice and, according to the local papers, has been nice for generations. And I know what you and your relatives look like."

"I'm not the only one who has been snooping. And the second reason?"

"If I have your child—in a manner of speaking—later you won't come to me asking me for money."

It was as though this statement were too outlandish for McAllister to comprehend, because for a moment he sat there blinking in consternation. Then he laughed, a deep rumbling sound that came from inside his chest. "Mrs. Lawrence, I do believe we are going to get along splendidly." He extended his right hand. "All right, we have a bargain."

For just a moment Karen allowed her hand to be enveloped in his large warm one, and she allowed her eyes to meet his and to see the way they crinkled into a smile.

Abruptly, she pulled away from his touch. "Where and when?" she asked.

"My car will pick you up at six A.M. tomorrow, and we'll leave on the first flight to New York."

"I thought your friend lived in Virginia," she said suspiciously.

"He does, but I thought we'd go to New York first and outfit you," he said bluntly, sounding as though she were a naked native he, the great white hunter, had found.

For a moment Karen hid her face behind the champagne glass so he wouldn't see her expression. "Ah, yes, I see. Based on what I've seen, you like your fiancées to be well coifed and well dressed."

"Doesn't every man?"

"Only men who can't see beneath the surface."

"Ouch!"

Karen blushed. "I apologize. If I am to pretend to be your fiancée, I will try to curb my tongue." She gave him a hard look. "I won't have to play the doting, adoring female, will I?"

"Since no other woman to whom I have been engaged has, I see no reason you should. Have some more champagne, Mrs. Lawrence."

"No, thank you," Karen said, standing, then working hard not to wobble on her feet. Champagne, firelight, and a dark-haired, hot-eyed man were not conducive to making a woman remember her vows of chastity. "I will see you at the airport

154

tomorrow, but, please, there'll be no need to stop in New York." When he started to say something, she smiled. "Trust me."

"All right," he said, raising his glass. "To tomorrow."

Karen left the room, gathered her things, and took the elevator downstairs. Since she didn't feel steady enough to drive, she had the security man call a cab to take her to a small shopping mall south of Denver.

"Bunny?" Karen asked tentatively as a woman locked the door of the beauty salon. Looking at Bunny's hair, Karen couldn't decide if it had been dyed apricot or peach. Whatever, it was an extraordinary shade.

"Yes?" the woman asked, turning, looking at Karen with no recognition in her eyes.

"You don't remember me?"

For a moment Bunny looked puzzled, then her fine pale skin crinkled in pleasure. "Karen? Could that be you under that . . . that . . . ?"

"Hair," Karen supplied.

"Maybe you call it hair but not from where I'm standing. And look at your face! Did you take vows? Is that why it's so shiny and clean?"

Karen laughed. One of her few luxuries while married to Ray had been having Bunny do her hair and give her advice on makeup and nails, and pretty much anything else in life. For all that Bunny was an excellent hairdresser, she was also like a therapist to her clients—and as discreet as though she'd taken an oath. A woman knew she could tell Bunny anything and it would go no further.

"Could you do my hair?" Karen asked shyly.

"Sure. Call in the morning and—"

"No, now. I have to leave on a plane early in the morning."

Bunny didn't put up with such nonsense. "I have a hungry husband waiting at home, and I've been on my feet for nine hours. You should have come earlier."

"Could I bribe you with a story? A very, very good story?"

Bunny looked skeptical. "How good a story?"

"You know my gorgeous boss? McAllister Taggert? I'm probably going to have his baby and he's never touched me—nor is he going to."

Bunny didn't miss a beat as she shoved the key back into the lock. "I predict that that hair of yours is going to take half the night."

"What about your husband?"

"Let him open his own cans."

Two

KAREN SETTLED BACK IN THE WIDE SEAT OF THE AIRPLANE, business class, and sipped her glass of orange juice. Beside her, McAllister Taggert already had his nose in the papers in his briefcase. Early this morning when she'd arrived at the airport, she was escorted to a lounge that she'd had no idea existed at the Denver airport.

Unobtrusively, she'd taken a chair across from him, and he hadn't bothered to greet her or even look at her. Ten minutes later, idly, he'd glanced up, lost in thought, then back down at his papers. Karen then had the great satisfaction of seeing him pause and look back at her—a long, slow look that went from her head to her toes then back up again.

"You *are* Karen Lawrence, aren't you?" he asked, making her smile, and making her sure that the three hours at Bunny's, with her head covered in foil, her face slathered in mud, then another three hours at home trying on everything in her closet, had been worth it.

He told her he had to work on the trip to Virginia, then looked back down at his papers, but several times he glanced at Karen. All in all, she found those looks quite gratifying.

Now, on the plane, she sat beside him, sipping orange juice and growing more bored by the minute. "Anything I can do to help?" she asked, nodding toward his papers.

He smiled at her in that way men do when they think a woman is pretty but had somehow managed to be born without a brain. "If I'd brought a computer, you could type for me, but actually, no, I have nothing for you to do. I just have some decisions to make."

Ah, yes, she thought, Men's Work. "Such as?" she urged.

A slight frown crossed his handsome brow. Obviously he liked his women to remain silent. "Just buying and selling," he answered quickly, in a tone that was meant to make her stop asking childish questions.

"And exactly what are you considering buying or selling this morning?"

The small frown changed to one that made his brows meet in the middle over the bridge of his nose. Love is such a funny thing, she thought. Had Ray looked at her like that, she would have backed off immediately, but this man did not frighten her a bit.

When he saw that she wasn't going to stop questioning him, he snapped, "I'm thinking of purchasing a small publishing company," then looked back at his papers.

"Ah," she said. "Coleman and Brown Press. Bad covers, mostly reprints. A few good books on regional history, but the covers were so bad no one bought the books."

McAllister looked at her as though she should mind her own business. "If I decide to buy it, I'll hire a new art director who can design good covers."

"Can't. The publisher is sleeping with her."

McAllister had just put his glass of orange juice to his lips and at Karen's words he nearly choked. "What?"

"I was curious, so when the publisher's secretary came to deliver the financial sheets to you I asked her to have lunch with me. She told me that the publisher—who is married and has three children—has been having a long-term affair with the art director. If he fires her, she'll blab to his wife—whose family owns the publishing house. It's a very sticky situation."

Mac blinked at her. "So what do you recommend?" he asked with great sarcasm.

"Buy the house and put some competent people in there, then consolidate several of the small history books into one fat one and sell it as a textbook on Colorado history to the schools. There's a great deal of money to be made in textbooks."

For a long moment Mac just looked at her. "And you found out all this because you were curious, right?"

Turning away, Karen looked out the window and knew she'd never missed Ray more than she did in that moment. Ray used to listen to her; he liked her ideas and her input. Unfortunately, she'd found that most men's minds were as closed as this man's.

It wasn't until the plane had taken off and they were cruising that he spoke to her again. "What other things have you looked into?" he asked softly. "Jet engines? Sewage plants? Road building equipment?"

She knew he was being ironic, but at the same time, she could hear that he actually wanted to know. "I'm only interested in the small things, especially the local Denver places."

"Such as?" he asked, one eyebrow raised.

"Lawson's Department Store," she answered quickly.

At that he smiled indulgently. "That place is an eyesore to downtown Denver. I already have an excellent offer from Glitter and Sass."

"Those stores that sell leather and chains?" she asked with a curled lip.

"More like leather and rhinestones." Leaning back in the seat, he looked at her in speculation. "And who would *you* sell it to?" When she didn't answer, he gave her a little smile. "Come on, don't chicken out on me now. If you're going to tell me how to run my business, don't stop after one suggestion."

"All right," she said defiantly. "I'd open a store that sells baby paraphernalia." At that she expected him to turn away in disgust, but he didn't. He just sat there, patiently waiting for her to continue.

She took a deep breath. "In England they have stores called Mothercare that sell everything for babies: maternity wear, strollers, nursery furniture, diapers, the works. In America you have to go to different stores for different items, and when you're eight-months pregnant and your feet are swollen and you have two other kids, it's not easy schlepping to five different stores trying to get what you need for the baby. I don't know from experience, but it seems that it would be a wonderful convenience to be able to buy everything from one store."

"And what would you call this store?" he asked quietly.

"Sanctuary?" she answered innocently, making him laugh.

McAllister took a piece of paper and a pen from his briefcase and handed it to her. "Here. Write down all you know or think about Coleman and Brown Press. All of it, gossip, everything. I want to know how I can make that place a going concern."

Karen used all her strength to keep from smiling, but it was no use. She had a feeling he'd never before asked a woman her opinion of what he should buy or sell. His branch of Montgomery-Taggert was very small, and he had a few women executives, but everyone knew that McAllister Taggert was a law unto himself. He infuriated people in his employ by his stubborn insistence on doing things his own way. It further infuriated them that he was pretty much always right.

But now he was asking *her* opinion! "Aye, aye, sir," Karen said mockingly as she started to write, but out of the corner of her eye, she could see just a bit of a smile playing about his lips.

If Karen thought she was going to get any warmth out of Taggert, the notion was short-lived, for what time during the flight he didn't have his nose buried in papers, he was on the telephone. He ate with one hand, papers in the other. When they landed at Dulles Airport, outside DC, he handed her three one-hundred-dollar bills, said, "Green hanging," then nodded toward the baggage carousel. Karen was tempted to give the porter one bill as a tip, but instead, she paid the five dollars out of her own pocket, then tried to find Taggert. He found her, rental car keys in his hand, and quickly, they went outside into the crisp, cold air to the car.

Once inside the warmth of the car, it felt almost intimate to be alone with him and she looked about for something to say. "If I'm to pretend to be your fiancée, shouldn't I know something about you?"

"What do you want to know?" he asked in a way that made Karen give him a look of disgust.

"Nothing really. I'm sure that knowing you are rich is enough for any woman."

Karen had expected the jab to make him laugh or respond sarcastically, but it didn't. Instead, he just looked straight ahead, his brow creased in concentration. For the rest of the drive,

Karen didn't bother to talk. She decided if anyone asked why she was planning to marry M.J. Taggert, she'd say, "Alimony."

He drove them through the highways of Virginia to Alexandria, then through wooded countryside, past beautiful houses until he reached a graveled road and made a sharp right. Minutes later a house came into view and it was the place where all little girls dreamed of spending Christmas: three stories, tall pillars in front, perfectly spaced windows. She half expected George and Martha Washington to greet them.

The front lawn and what she could see of the rolling gardens in the back were alive with people playing touch football, gathering armloads of wood, or just strolling. And there seemed to be children everywhere.

The moment the car was spotted, what seemed to be a herd of people descended on them, opening the door and pulling Karen out. They introduced themselves as Laura and Deborah and Larry and Dave and—

One very good looking man grabbed her and kissed her soundly on the mouth. "Oh!" was all Karen could say as she stared at him.

"I'm Steve," he offered in explanation. "The bridegroom? Didn't Mac tell you about me?"

Karen didn't think about what she was saying. "Taggert never speaks to me unless he wants something," she blurted, then stared wide-eyed. These people were his friends, what would they think of her!?

To Karen's consternation, they burst into laughter.

"Mac, at last you found a woman who knows the true you," Steve yelled across the roof of the car as he put one arm around Karen's shoulders, then a pretty woman put another arm around her, and they led her into the house, all of them laughing.

They led her past heavenly rooms with huge fireplaces that blazed cheerfully, then up a grand staircase, down two halls to a wide white door. Steve opened it. "He's all yours," he said, laughing, then pushed her inside and closed the door behind her.

Taggert was in the room, their suitcases were already placed on luggage racks, and there was only one bed. "There's been a mistake," Karen said.

Mac frowned down at the bed. "I've already tried to rectify this, but it's impossible. The house is full. Every bed, cot, and couch is already assigned. Look," he said, frowning, "if you're afraid I'm going to attack you in the night, I can see if a hotel room can be found for you."

There was something about his attitude that always seemed to rub her the wrong way. "At least with a full house if I scream, I'll be heard."

He gave her a little half-smile then started unbuttoning his shirt. "I need to take a shower. The wedding rehearsal is in an hour." He was looking at her as though he expected her to be a heroine from a Regency romance and flee the room in fear at the very thought of a man undressing. But she wasn't going to let him intimidate her. "Please don't steam up the mirror," she said, chin in the air, then turned away as though sharing a room with a strange man was of no consequence to her.

With a bit of a chuckle, he went into the bathroom, leaving the door ajar for the steam to escape.

When he was out of sight, Karen let her breath escape and her shoulders relax. The room was lovely, all green silk and Federal furniture, and as she heard the shower running, she happily unpacked suitcases. It wasn't until she was finished that she realized that, out of habit, she'd unpacked Taggert's case too. As she put his shoes in the closet next to hers, Karen almost burst into tears. It had been so long since a man's shoes had been next to her own.

When she turned, Taggert was standing there, his hair wet, his big body encased in a terry-cloth robe, and he was watching her.

"I, ah, I didn't mean to unpack your case, but, uh . . . Habit," she finally managed to say before escaping into the bathroom and firmly closing the door behind her.

She took as long as she dared in the bathroom and was very pleased to see that he was gone when she reentered the room. After dressing as quickly as she could, she left the bedroom and ran down the stairs to join the rest of the wedding party, who were piling into cars headed to the church for the rehearsal.

All the way to the church, her annoyance toward Taggert built. If she was supposed to be his fiancée, shouldn't he be showing her some consideration? Instead, he dropped her at the front door and expected her to find her own way among strangers. No wonder so many women refused to marry him, she thought. They were all obviously women of sense and intelligence.

At the church the rehearsal went off smoothly until at the end, when Taggert was to be the first to start down the aisle. He was to walk to the center, offer his arm to Karen, then walk with her out of the church. Maybe he hadn't heard what was said, but whatever his excuse, he walked to the center of the aisle, then started down alone, without Karen.

It was too much for her. "You know how Taggert is," she said, "he thinks he can partner himself."

Everyone in the church burst into laughter, and Taggert, turning, saw his mistake. With a great show of gallantry, he returned, bowed, and offered his arm to Karen.

"Getting me back for all those weekends of typing?" he said under his breath.

"Getting you back for all those women who were too timid to stand up to you," she said, smiling wickedly.

"I am not the monster you think I am."

"I shall ask Elaine's opinion on that. By the way, when is she coming?"

From the look on his face as they reached the back of the church, Karen regretted her remark.

"Christmas Day," he said softly, then turned away from her.

The rehearsal dinner was loud, with everyone talking at once about summers they had spent together and places they had visited. At first Karen looked at her food and listened but didn't participate in the conversation among these people who knew each other so well. Taggert sat on the other side of the big table, at the opposite end from her, and he, too, was quiet. Every once in a while, Karen glanced toward him and thought she saw him looking at her, but he turned away so quickly that she wasn't sure.

"Karen," one of the women said and the whole table quietened. "Where is your engagement ring?"

She didn't hesitate before she spoke. "Taggert had bought all the store had, so they're awaiting a new shipment of diamonds. He buys them by the dozen, you know."

The windows of the restaurant nearly exploded with the laughter of the diners, and even Mac laughed as Steve, next to him, slapped him on the back.

There were calls of, "I think you ought to keep this one, Mac," and, "It looks as though your taste in women is improving."

For the rest of the meal, Karen wasn't allowed to sit in silence. The two women across from her asked many questions about what she did and where she'd grown up and all the

normal questions that people ask. When she told them that
Mac was her boss, they were fascinated and wanted to know
what it was like working for him.

"Lonely," she answered. "He doesn't need any of us, except
to type a letter now and then."

Through all of this, Taggert ate his dinner without saying a
word, but Karen could feel his eyes on her and even when Steve
leaned forward to say something to him, Mac's eyes never left
Karen's face.

It wasn't until they were alone in "their" room that Karen
thought maybe she'd gone a little too far. "About tonight . . ."
she began as he walked past her out of the bathroom. "Maybe I
shouldn't have—"

"Going to chicken out on me now?" he asked, his face very
close to hers.

Inconsequentially, Karen thought, he has a beautiful mouth.
But she recovered herself and stood up straight. "No, of course
not."

"Good. Now, what did you do with my sweatpants?"

"Isn't it a little late for sports?" she said without thinking, not
that it was any of her business what he did when.

Mac gave her a one-sided smile. "Unless you want me
sleeping raw, they're the only alternative."

"Third drawer left," she said as she scurried into the bathroom. When she emerged, swathed in a puritanical white cotton
nightgown, he was already in bed, and there was a long, thick
bolster pillow down the center of the bed. Slipping into the
vacant side of the bed, she said, "Where did you get this?"

"Stole it."

"So I guess some poor unfortunate is sleeping on a couch
without a back cushion."

"Want me to take it back? You could sleep snuggled up with

me or, better yet, we could have a serious discussion about this jar that you want me to—"

"Good night," she said firmly, then turned on her side away from him, but she was smiling as she fell asleep.

Three

KAREN AWOKE TO THE SIGHT OF A GORGEOUS MAN WEARING only a thick white towel about his waist, standing before the bathroom mirror shaving. In those few minutes before she awoke fully and remembered where she was, she had a vision of him coming toward her, kissing her, then tossing the towel aside and climbing into bed with her. For just those few seconds she could remember clearly how it felt to have a man in her arms, the size of him, the warmth of his skin, the weight of him, the—

"Want to share that thought?" he asked, not turning his head but looking at her in the mirror.

Turning away so he couldn't see her red face, she rolled out of bed, grabbed her robe, and moved toward the closet, out of his line of vision.

"What do you have planned for today?" he asked, coming out of the bathroom, still wearing only that tiny towel and wiping excess lather from his face.

Karen flung open a closet door so she couldn't see him. Did he work out every day? He must to keep his body looking like that. And was that warm honey his natural skin color? "Shopping," she mumbled.

"Shopping?" he asked, moving around the door to the other side of her. "As in Christmas shopping?"

"I, ah," she said, studiously looking at the clothes hanging inside, yet seeing nothing. "Yes, Christmas shopping. And a wedding gift." She took a deep breath. She *had* to get hold of herself! Turning, she looked into his eyes—and not one inch lower. "Tomorrow is Christmas and if I'm to spend it with these people, I can't very well turn up empty-handed. Do you know a good shopping mall around here?"

"Tysons Corner," he said quickly. "One of the best in the country. And I need to buy gifts, too, so I'll go with you."

"No!" Karen blurted, then tried to recover herself. "I mean, I concentrate better when I'm by myself." Even as she said it, she knew it was a lie. Christmas shopping alone became a chore.

"And how will you know who to buy for? Even how many kids are here? I assume you want to buy for the kids."

"Write down all the names for me and I'll get everything." She did not want to spend the day with this man—and it was getting very difficult to keep her eyes off the muscles of his chest.

"I don't have a pencil," he said, smiling. "Everything is in my head."

Karen almost smiled back at him. "You can dictate them to me. Besides, wouldn't you rather stay here and play football with the other guys?"

"I am a fat, out-of-shape desk jockey and they'd cream me."

At that Karen did laugh, for there was no one who was less out of shape than he was.

Without waiting for her to say yes, he grabbed a terry-cloth robe from the closet, put it on, then kissed her cheek. "Pick me out some clothes, would you? I have to make some calls. I'll be back for you in thirty minutes."

Before Karen could protest, he was out of the room, the door closed behind him. Of course, she thought, feminists everywhere would shudder at the notion of her choosing the clothing of an autocratic, arrogant, presumptuous man like Mac Taggert. But by the time she'd completed this thought, she had draped a pair of dark wool trousers, an Italian shirt, and a heavenly English sweater across the bed. Shaking her head in disgust at herself, she went into the bathroom.

An hour later, after a quick breakfast, she and Mac were walking to the rental car, and on the lawn were the bridegroom and other men playing ball. Steve shouted to Mac, asking him to come play with them.

"She's forcing me to go shopping with her," he yelled back.

"Ha!" Karen called to them over the roof of the car. "Like I need a man to go shopping with me, right? Truth is, he's afraid to stay here because you might hurt him."

Ignoring the laughter of the men, Mac shouted, "What do you want us to get you for a wedding gift?"

"From you, Taggert?" Steve called. "A Lamborghini. But from her, I'll take anything she offers."

"I'll second that," one of the other men called, then they all laughed in a very complimentary way.

Feeling quite flattered, Karen smiled brilliantly at all the young men playing touch football and she smiled even more brightly when she saw that Mac was frowning. "What a very nice group of people," she said as she got into the car.

Mac, his body twisted as he looked out the back window while he drove the car out in reverse, maneuvering it around the many other vehicles in the drive, didn't answer her.

Maybe it was because of the men's flirting with her and Mac's resultant silence, but by the time they arrived at the beautiful Tysons Corner mall, Karen was in very good spirits.

"Where do we begin?" she asked as soon as they'd entered the center of the mall near Hecht's. Looking up at him, she saw that male shrug that meant that she was in charge. "Elephant time," she muttered.

"I beg your pardon," he said stiffly.

"It's what I used to say when I was with my husband and we

went shopping together. He'd refuse to participate in deciding what to buy anyone, but he'd carry anything I handed him. I called him my elephant."

For a moment Mac seemed to consider this, then he solemnly lifted his right arm, clenched his fist, and made his biceps bulge through his sweater. "I can carry anything you can pack onto me."

Karen laughed. "We shall see about that. By the way, if, as you said, 'we' are giving gifts, who's paying for these things?"

"Me?" he said with a mock sigh, as though he'd always paid for everything she'd ever bought.

"Perfect," she said over her shoulder as she took a right and headed for Nordstrom's. "Your money, my taste."

"Just give me a peanut now and then and I'll be fine," he said from behind her.

Three hours later, Karen was exhausted but exhilarated. She'd completely forgotten what it was like to shop with a man. He never wanted to take the time to consider which of any two purchases was better. "This one," he'd say, or, "What does it matter?" And when it came to gift suggestions, he could rarely think past the music store. Twice she had him sit on benches, surrounded by shopping bags, while she went into stores and purchased sets of soaps and lotions, and some fruit and cheese baskets. She almost couldn't get him out of the Rand McNally shop, where he purchased a huge 3-D puzzle of the Empire State Building. And they visited all nine toy stores and made purchases from each one, so many purchases in fact that Karen suspected that they'd bought more toys than there were children.

"Does lunch come with this trip?" he asked after they'd visited the very last toy store the mall had to offer.

"Are you *sure* you want to eat? I think there was a toy car still left in that last store. Maybe you should go back and get it."

"Food, woman!" he growled, leading the way to the Nordstrom's cafe, where they placed their orders, then took their drinks and found a seat where Mac could put all the bags, for he wouldn't allow Karen to carry anything.

"You're a good elephant," she said as soon as they were seated, smiling at him.

After they were situated, he looked at her. "What plans have you made for Lawson's Department Store?"

Karen was in too good a mood to lie. "You don't have to patronize me. And you don't have to listen to my childish ideas. For all that this has been great fun today, you and I both know that as soon as we get back to Denver, it will end. You're the boss and I'm just a typist."

"Just a typist, are you?" he said, one eyebrow raised as he reached down the neck of his sweater to his shirt pocket and pulled out several folded fax sheets. "You, your husband, and Stanley Thompson owned Thompson's Hardware Store for six years. You and your husband were everything to the store. Stanley Thompson was dead weight."

As Karen looked at him in astonishment, he continued.

"After you two were married, Ray worked two jobs, while you typed manuscripts at home. You two saved every penny you had and bought a half share in Thompson's Hardware and you turned the place around. Ray knew about machines; you knew everything else. You wrote ads that made people come to the store and you handled the money, telling Ray how much you could and could not afford. It was your idea to add the little garden center and bring in women customers, and that was the most profitable part of the store. After Ray died you found out that the only way Thompson had originally been willing to sell to him was on the condition that on Ray's death he could buy you out for fifty grand."

"It was fair at the time the deal was made," Karen said defensively, as though he were saying that Ray had made a bad contract.

"Yes, at the time of purchase, half a share was only worth thirty thousand, but by the time he'd died, you and Ray had built up the business so a half share was worth a great deal more than fifty grand."

"I could have stayed as a full partner," Karen said softly.

"If you shared Stanley Thompson's bed."

"You do snoop, don't you?"

"Just curious," he said, eyes twinkling at her as their food was set before her. After the waitress left, he said, "You want to tell me about your ideas for this store for mothers?"

"I haven't really thought about it, just some vague ideas," she said, playing with the straw in her glass of iced tea.

At that Mac gave a little snort of laughter and pushed a pen and a napkin toward her. "If you had unlimited money and owned Lawson's Department Store, what would you do with it?"

Karen hesitated but not for long. Truth was, she *had* thought about this for quite some time. "I'd put a children's play area in the center so mothers could watch their children at all times. If a mother is to be there a while, I'd tag the kids. You know, like clothing in department stores, so if the children wander outside the play area or someone tries to take them, bells go off as they exit the store."

Mac said nothing but his eyebrows were raised in question.

"They put tags on clothing so people can't steal them and children are a great deal more important than shirts, aren't they? And how can a woman try on clothes in comfort with a four-year-old screaming at her?"

After taking a bite of her food, she continued. "Surrounding

171

the play area I'd have different departments: maternity wear, furniture, layettes, books on the various aspects of raising children, all the visual things. And I'd have clerks who were extremely experienced. And fat."

Mac smiled patronizingly at that.

"No, really. My sister-in-law just had a baby, and she was constantly complaining about anorexic sales girls who looked at her with pity every time she asked if they had something in extra large. And I'd have trained bra fitters and I'd have free brochures of local organizations the women could contact if they needed help or information, such as La Leche League. And of course we'd have contact with a local obstetrician in case of mishaps in the store. And—"

She broke off as she glanced at his face. He was laughing at her!

"Haven't thought about it much, have you?"

She smiled. "Well, maybe just a bit."

"Where are your financials? And don't you dare tell me you haven't worked out to the penny how much opening a store like this would cost."

Karen took a few bites. "I have done a bit of number crunching."

"When we get back to Denver, you can put them on my desk and I'll—" He broke off because Karen had removed a computer disk from her handbag. Taking it, he looked down at it and frowned. "When were you going to present me with this?"

She knew what he meant. He thought *this* was the real reason she'd agreed to this weekend. She was just one of the hundreds of people who tried to see him about or mail him their schemes for getting rich. Karen snatched the disk out of his hands. "I was *never* planning to show it to you or anyone else," she said through her teeth. "Millions of people have dreams in their heads and that's just where they stay: in their heads."

Angrily, she grabbed her purse and coat from beside her. "Excuse me, but I think this has all been a mistake. I think I'd better leave now."

Mac caught her arm and pulled her back down into the booth. "I'm sorry. I apologize. Really, I do."

"Would you please release me?"

"No, because you'll run."

"Then I'll scream."

"No you won't. You allowed Stanley Thompson to rob you blind and you didn't scream then because you didn't want to make a scene for his family. You, Karen, are not the screaming type."

She looked at his big, tanned hand clasping her wrist. He was right, she was not a screamer—or much of a fighter. Maybe she needed Ray standing behind her telling her she could do anything before she believed in herself.

Mac's hand moved so his fingers were entwined with hers, and Karen made no attempt to pull away as he held her hand in his.

"Look, Karen, I know what you think of me, but it's not true. Have you ever told anyone else about your ideas for the baby store?"

"No," she said softly.

"But you must have been working on this idea since before Ray died. Did you tell him?"

"No." She and Ray'd had as much as they could handle with the hardware store. And she'd never wanted to give him the idea that she wanted something different—or even something more.

"Then I am honored by your confiding in me," Mac said, and when Karen gave him a look of suspicion, he said, "Really, I

173

am." Pausing a moment, he looked down at their two hands entwined. "All those prenuptial agreements were only to see if she *would* sign."

Karen looked at him in disbelief.

"Honest. If any of those women had signed, I'd have torn it up immediately. But all I ever heard was, 'Daddy doesn't think I should sign,' or, 'My lawyer advises me not to sign.' All I wanted was to be *sure* that the woman wanted me and not my family's wealth."

"Rather a hateful little trick, wasn't it?"

"Not as hateful as marrying me and four years later going through a divorce. And what if we had kids?"

In spite of herself, Karen felt herself curling her fingers around his. "And what about Elaine?"

"Elaine was different," he said softly, then pulled his hand from hers.

As Karen opened her mouth to ask another question, he said, "Ready?" and the way he said it was a command.

Minutes later they were again in the mainstream of the mall, Mac moving ahead, loaded down with shopping bags. Behind him, thoughtful, Karen followed—until she was pulled up short at the sight of a shop full of the most beautiful clothes for children she had ever seen. In the window was hanging a christening gown of fine cotton, hand-tucked, dripping soft cotton lace.

"Want to go in?" Mac said softly from over her head.

"No, of course not," Karen said sharply, turning away.

But Mac, already large, was made even larger by all the bags he was holding and he blocked her exit as he moved forward.

"Really, I don't want . . ." she began, but she stopped speaking as soon as she was inside the store. Never had she allowed herself to look at baby clothes as something for a child *she* might have. For others, yes, but never for herself.

As though in a trance, she went toward the pretty dresses hanging on racks at eye level.

Mac, who had been relieved of his bags by a kind saleswoman, came up behind her. "Not those. The first Taggert baby is always a boy."

"Nothing is ever 'always,'" Karen told him, taking down a white cotton dress hand-embroidered with pale pink and blue flowers.

"Here, this is much better," he said as he held up a red and blue striped shirt. "Good for playing football."

"I am *not* going to allow my son to play football," she told him, replacing the dress and looking at some white suits made for what could only be a little prince. "Football is much too dangerous."

"He's my son too and I say—"

It suddenly occurred to Karen what they were talking about, that they might have a baby together but it wouldn't be *theirs*. Not in any real sense. It wouldn't be . . . Before she could put together another thought, she ran from the store and was staring in the window of Brentano's when Mac found her.

"You mind if we sit awhile?" he asked, and all Karen could do was nod her head. Her embarrassment over what had happened in the baby store was still too fresh to allow her to speak.

She sat, he piled shopping bags around her, then he went to get the two of them ice cream cones, and for a while they sat in silence with their ice cream.

"Why didn't you and your husband have children?" he asked softly.

"We thought we had all the time in the world, so we put it off," she answered simply.

For a moment Mac was silent. "Did you love him very much?"

"Yes, very, very much."

"He was a very lucky man," Mac said and reached out to take her hand. "I envy him."

For a moment Karen looked into his eyes, and for the first time since Ray's death she saw another man. Not Ray superimposed over another man's features, but she saw Mac Taggert for himself. I could love again, she thought, and in that moment it was as though all the ice she had protectively put around her heart melted.

"Karen, I—" Mac began as he moved toward her as though he meant to kiss her right there in the midst of Tysons Corner mall.

"My goodness!" Karen said. "Just look at the time. I have an appointment at the hairdresser for the wedding tonight, and I'm barely going to make it. It's here in the mall but on the next level, so I'd better run."

"When did you make an appointment?" he asked, sounding for all the world like a husband who couldn't believe she'd done anything without his knowledge.

"In between toy stores." She stood. "I have to go," she said, then started walking. "I'll meet you back here in two hours," she called over her shoulder, then disappeared around the corner before he could say another word.

The truth was, she had half an hour before her appointment, but she wanted to get a Christmas gift for Mac. And she wanted to get away from him. She could not possibly fall in love with a man like Mac Taggert. "He's out of your league, Karen," she told herself. A man like him needed a woman whose father was the ambassador to some glamorous country, a woman who could identify one caviar from another, who could . . . could . . .

"Idiot!" she told herself. You are as bad as all the others, thinking you're in love with him. Or worse! Thinking he is in love with *you.*

By the time she met him two hours later, she had managed to calm herself and regain her equilibrium. She saw him sitting on the bench, looking very pleased with himself. "What have you done?" she asked suspiciously.

"Merely had everything wrapped and labeled, and now they are all in the car."

"I am impressed," she said, wide-eyed.

"Stop laughing at me and let's go," he said, taking her arm. "Is that shellac they used on your hair? Or did they give you a wig made out of wood?"

"It's lacquer and I think it looks great."

"*Hmmm,*" was all he'd say as they hurried to the car.

Back at the house, everything was chaos as people scurried to get ready for the wedding. It seemed that nearly everyone had lost a vital piece of clothing and now was frantically trying to find it. When Mac closed the door to "their" bedroom, it was like a haven of calm, and when Karen came out of the bathroom, the bed was covered with boxes and a couple of hanging bags full of clothes.

"It all came while you were in there," he said, and when Karen started to comment that she'd heard no one enter, Mac scurried into the bathroom.

One box contained silk underwear, all of it white: lacy bra, teddy, and white stockings that ended mid-thigh in lacy elastic. Never before had she heard of a wedding providing underwear along with the dress.

"You don't have time to examine everything," Mac said as he entered the room.

"But—"

"Get dressed!"

177

As she picked up the underwear, then the dress that must have been made of three hundred yards of chiffon, she looked at the narrow space in the bathroom and back at the voluminous skirt.

"I won't attack you if I see you in your underwear—but only if you make the same promise to me," Mac said, deadpan.

Karen started to protest but then smiled devilishly. "All right, you're on," she said as she took the white silk underwear and went into the bathroom. Moments later she emerged wearing makeup and her underwear and nothing else—and she knew that she looked great. She wasn't very large above the waist, but, as many people had told her, she had the legs of a showgirl.

"Do you know where—" Mac said as he turned toward her, then Karen had the great, oh, the enormous, satisfaction of seeing all the color drain from his face as he stared at her.

"Do I know where what is?" she asked innocently.

But Mac couldn't say a word as he stood there, his hands frozen, one held outstretched, the other trying to fasten the cuff link on his shirt.

"Could I help you with that?" she asked, striding toward him as he stared at her speechlessly. As sweetly as she could, she fastened first one then the other of his cuff links, then smiled up at him. "Anything else you need?"

When he didn't answer, she smiled again and started to walk away from him, knowing that the back view of her was as good as the front. Thank you, Nordic Track, she thought.

But she had no more time for thought because Mac grabbed her shoulder and pulled her into his arms, then brought his lips down on hers. How could she have forgotten? she wondered. She'd nearly forgotten the deliciousness of a kiss.

He kissed her long and thoroughly, and his big hands caressed her body, pulling her close to him.

Had it not been for the loud knock on the door and the call, "Ready to leave for the church?" Karen wasn't sure what would have happened. Even so, she had to push her way out of his arms, and it was with great reluctance that she did so. Her heart was pounding and her breath was fast.

"We must get dressed," she managed to say while he silently stared at her. With shaking hands, she picked up her dress and tried to get it on over her head without mussing her hair. She wasn't surprised when Mac helped her pull the dress down over her body, then zipped it up the back. And it seemed natural to help him into the coat of his tuxedo.

It wasn't until they started to leave the room that he spoke. "I almost forgot to give you your bridesmaid gift." Out of his pocket he pulled a two-strand pearl necklace and an earring with a long drop pearl.

"They're beautiful," Karen said. "The pearls almost look real."

"They do, don't they?" he said as he fished out the second earring, then he fastened the necklace on while she put on the earrings.

"Do I look okay?" she asked in earnest.

"No one will look at the bride."

It was a cliché, but the way he said it made her feel beautiful.

The wedding was enchanting. For all the chaos beforehand, everything went smoothly, and the reception was filled with laughter and champagne. Mac disappeared with a group of men he hadn't seen in years, and for a few moments Karen was alone at a table.

"Do you know how to dance?"

Karen looked up at Mac. "Wasn't that in your report about me? Or did your spies forget such unimportant things as dancing?"

With a laugh, he pulled her out of her chair and led her onto the dance floor. To say they danced splendidly together was an understatement.

Steve sailed by, his lovely bride, Catherine, in his arms, and told Mac he should keep "this one."

Mac smiled. "You know that no woman wants me for long."

After Steve had laughed and moved away, Karen frowned up at Mac. "Why don't you tell them the truth? Everyone blames you for all the breakups."

Mac pulled her closer into his arms. "Be careful, Mrs. Lawrence, it almost sounds as though you're beginning to like me."

"Ha! All I want from you is—"

"A child," he said softly. "You want to have my child."

"Only because you're—"

"What am I? Intelligent? A prince among men?"

"You're a reverse prince. When a woman kisses you, you turn into a frog."

"I didn't with the first kiss. Want to try again?"

For a minute he looked down at her and she thought he was going to kiss her again. But he didn't and she knew that her disappointment showed on her face.

Hours later she once again found herself alone in a room with Mac. When she returned from the bathroom wearing her chaste white nightgown, he was standing by the window, his back to her, looking out into the night.

"The bathroom is yours," she said.

"I'm going out," he said firmly.

To her horror, Karen said, "Why?" then put her hand to her mouth. What he did was none of her business. Stiffening her body, she forced a smile. "Of course." She gave a great yawn. "See you in the morning."

Mac grabbed her shoulders. "Karen, it's not what you think."

"I have no right to think anything at all. You're free to do what you like."

Quickly, he pulled her to him, and held her tightly. "If I stay in this room tonight, I'll make love to you. I know I will. I won't be able to stop myself." Without giving her a chance to reply, he left her alone in the room.

"Right," Karen said to the closed door. "And next week it would be business as usual, the little fling with your typist forgotten. Better not to do anything that could get you sued."

She went to bed and only went to sleep after she had vented her frustration on the thick pillow separating the two halves of the bed.

Hours later she was sleeping so soundly she didn't hear him return, slip into bed beside her or feel him press a soft kiss on her forehead before he himself tried to sleep.

Four

KAREN AWOKE CHRISTMAS MORNING TO SCREAMS. THINKING the house was on fire, she flung back the covers and started to leave the bed—but Mac's strong hand stopped her.

"Kids," he muttered, head buried in the pillow.

As the screaming increased, Karen pulled away from him, but his hand crept up her arm and pulled her down into the bed beside him. During the night the bolster pillow that separated them had slipped down (or been pushed) until it was nearer their knees.

Mac's hand crept upward into Karen's hair. He still had his face buried, still wasn't looking at her, but she could see his black glossy hair, could feel his warmth. The room was dim and the noise outside their room seemed very far away.

As he pulled her down to his level, as his face came next to hers and as his lips touched hers, he whispered, "Kids. Christmas. You know how they are."

"I was an only child. I had breakfast before opening my presents."

"*Mmmmm,*" was all he said as he kissed her, kissed her warmly, softly.

With the touch of his lips it was as though time fell away: to be in bed with a warm, sleepy man as he pulled her into his arms felt so very familiar. And so very right. It was easy to slide down so her body was stretched alongside his, to slip her arms about his neck and return his kiss with all the enthusiasm she felt.

Suddenly, the door flew open and in rushed two kids holding toys aloft, brandishing them over the heads of the couple in bed. Bewildered, Karen pulled her face away from Mac's and looked up at the toys the children were waving in the air. The girl had a Barbie doll in an outrageous dress with a handful of accessories worthy of any call girl, while the boy held a box full of trains.

In spite of this confusion, Mac was still kissing her neck while Karen was half on top of him and trying to look at the children's new toys.

Before she could make a suitable comment, because Mac was kissing her throat, a third child came tearing in through the open door with an airplane in his hand, whereupon he crashed into the other two children and sent them flying. Everything— dolls, trains, children—landed on Mac's head.

Instantly the little girl started screaming that her doll was hurt, while the two boys tumbled to the floor in a fistfight over who had pushed whom. Getting out of bed, Karen scrambled to find the missing pieces belonging to the toys, but it was several minutes before she could find everything and get the children settled.

"Wait," she said to Mac as she picked toys out of the covers, "there seems to be a red high heel in your ear."

"It's not the first time," he muttered, annoyed that the children had interrupted them.

Giving him a quelling look, Karen rounded up the children and pushed them out the door.

Once they were alone again, Mac put his hands behind his head and watched her move about the room as she gathered her clothes. "Our kids will have better manners."

Karen was looking for her belt. "I hope our kids are just as happy and excited as they are and that they—" With a red face, she broke off, glanced at him lying there, grinning at her, then she scurried into the bathroom to get dressed.

But Mac bounded out of the bed and caught her before she could close the door. "Come on, Only Child, you're going to miss all the fun."

"I can't go downstairs in my nightgown and robe!"

"Everyone else will be," he said, pulling her, grabbing a T-shirt as he passed a chair.

Mac was right. Downstairs under the Christmas tree was chaos, with an ocean of torn wrapping paper and children everywhere. Adults were sitting in the midst of everything, exchanging gifts and laughing—and ignoring the children as best they could.

"Ah, the lovebirds," someone called. "You'd better get over here and see what Santa brought you."

"By the looks of them, I think Santa's already delivered," someone else called, making Karen drop Mac's hand, which she had been holding rather tightly.

It didn't take her long before she plunged into the middle of the paper and the people, and sat on the carpet beside a red wagon with a ribbon tied about its handle. She was pleased that no one had yet opened the gifts she and Mac had purchased and she could have the pleasure of seeing their faces. However, she was surprised when people began heaping gifts into her lap. Each one had a tag telling who had given her the gift, but when she thanked them she saw a look of surprise on their faces, then they'd glance at Mac.

It didn't take her long to figure things out. He was sitting beside her, opening gifts, his face as innocent as a sleeping child's. "You were busy while I was at the hairdresser's, weren't you?" she asked softly, so just he heard. It was obvious that he had purchased all her gifts, had them wrapped, then labeled them as coming from his friends.

He didn't bother to deny it, but just smiled, his thick, black lashes half lowered. "Like your gifts?"

Her lap and some of the floor around her were covered with beautiful objects: a cashmere sweater, a music box, a pair of gold earrings, three pairs of slouchy socks, a silver picture frame.

"What did *I* give you?" Steve called. He and Catherine had postponed their honeymoon until the day after Christmas.

Karen laughed. "Let's see," she said, picking up tags. "I think you gave me the string bikini."

"The *what?*" Mac blurted then turned red when everyone burst out laughing. "Okay, okay," he said, smiling, but he put his arm possessively around Karen's shoulders.

A woman who was Steve's cousin looked at Karen thoughtfully. "You know, Karen, I have met all of Mac's fiancées, and I can tell him now that I've never liked any of them, but you, Karen, I like. You are the first one who has ever looked at Mac with love in her eyes."

"Actually, I forgot my contact lenses," Karen said, "and—" She was halted by boos that made her blush and look down at her lap. Mac's arm tightened about her shoulders.

"So when's the wedding?" someone asked.

Mac didn't hesitate. "As soon as I can persuade her. Look, she won't even wear my ring."

"Maybe it's worn out from being slipped on and off the fingers of so many other women," Steve called, and everyone laughed.

It was at that moment that Steve's mother, Rita, stepped in from the kitchen. "Stop it, all of you! You're embarrassing Karen. And I need help in the kitchen!"

To Karen's consternation, the room cleared instantly. Within thirty seconds, there wasn't a single male, young or old, in the huge room, only women, girls, and a mountain of gifts and torn paper. "Works every time," Steve's mom said with a grin. "Now, come on, ladies, let's go gossip."

Laughing, the women went upstairs to dress before settling into their various tasks. Alone in the bedroom she shared with Mac, Karen dumped her gifts onto the bed and looked at them. It hadn't taken much sleuthing to find out that everything she'd received as a gift since she'd arrived had been from Mac. She'd been curious to find out what the other women had received as bridesmaid's gifts and was told the gifts had been given out last week. Hadn't she received hers?

More questioning had revealed that pearl necklaces and earrings had *not* been the gifts given. "If you're referring to the pearls you had on last night," one of the women said, "and if they were a gift from Mac, then you can bet your bank account that they are real."

Karen blinked. "So I guess the bride didn't give out complete sets of white silk underwear."

She'd said it more to herself than to the other women around her, but they heard and set up a howl of laughter that made Karen blush.

So now, alone in their room, she looked at what he'd heaped on her and knew she'd trade everything for an extra hour with

Mac. Tomorrow they'd return to Denver and by the day after they'd be separated forever. Or at least as good as, she thought, remembering the office, with her desk about a million miles from his.

Turning, she noticed an envelope on the pillow, and when she moved the scarf she'd tossed onto the bed, she saw that it had "Merry Christmas, Karen" written on it.

Opening it, she saw that it was a short contract signed by Mac and witnessed by Steve. Quickly, she scanned it and saw that it gave her control of a business to be housed in Lawson's Department Store. Mac would put up the capital and she'd supply the expertise. She was to have complete control to run the business in whatever way she saw fit and she was to repay him at five percent interest starting two years after the store opened.

"It's too much," she said aloud. "I didn't want—"

She stopped when she saw that there was a letter with the contract.

My dearest Karen,

I know that your first instinct will be to throw this in my face, but I beg you to reconsider. I am a businessman and you have the knowledge and experience to run a business that I believe will show a profit. I am not giving you this contract because I think you are beautiful and funny and excellent company, and because I enjoy being with you. I did this because I was forced to—by my constantly pregnant sisters-in-law. I have been told that I may not return home if I sell leather instead of diapers in that old department store.

Please don't turn me down.

Your future partner,
McAllister J. Taggert

For a moment Karen's head reeled with the meaning of what he'd written. But it wasn't the business offer that made her dizzy, it was the "beautiful and funny and excellent company, and because I enjoy being with you" that was about to do her in.

"Stop it!" she commanded herself. "He's not for you. He has women by the truckload and . . . And . . ." She went into the bathroom, where she stared at herself in the mirror. "And, you, you complete and total idiot, are in love with him."

Turning away, she turned on the shower. "Business," she told herself. "Keep it to business and nothing else."

But it wasn't easy to do that. When she went downstairs, she was wearing jeans and a red cashmere sweater set that Mac had given her (under the label of "Rita," Steve's mother) and the pearls that she couldn't help touching often. She would, of course, have to return them to him. They were much too expensive a gift.

People were slowly beginning to move about, some trying to clear the living room, some going outside to play games with the men, and some, like Karen, going to the kitchen to help prepare the Christmas feast.

Somewhere during the last days she had heard it mentioned that Steve's mother was Mac's mother's best friend. Not that it was any of Karen's business, but didn't best friends tell each other everything? And hadn't about thirty-five people mentioned that Elaine was supposed to show up this afternoon?

Karen was curious to know if Rita knew anything about the truth behind the breakup of Elaine and Mac.

She spent hours in the kitchen, chopping and peeling, while hearing some outrageous stories about Steve's family and a few about Mac's. Outside the kitchen window she could see Mac, wearing tight cotton-knit pants and an armless sweatshirt, playing touch football. Several times, whenever he made a goal or lost a goal, he looked at her in the window and waved. Happily, Karen waved back. She hadn't had a family in so long, and never had she known all the noise and confusion of this one, with children running around the kitchen, people laughing and, in the living room, singing carols. It was all the noise that small families missed.

She nearly jumped when Rita spoke behind her. "You like all this, don't you? You're happy in the midst of wrapping paper and kids screaming and stuffing onions inside some poor murdered creature, aren't you?"

"Yes, very," Karen answered honestly.

"Mac is a very good man."

Karen didn't say anything. Maybe he was and maybe he wasn't. The only thing she knew for sure was that he wasn't hers. "Do you know the truth about Elaine?"

She and Rita were alone in the kitchen, as most of the work was done, and for a moment Rita looked at Karen as though considering whether or not to tell her. "I have been sworn to secrecy," Rita said, looking down at her knife.

Karen drew in her breath. A woman admitting that she knew a secret meant that half the battle was won. All Rita needed was a bit of urging. But Karen hesitated. Part of her wanted to know and part of her didn't want to hear. What had made the woman walk out of her wedding like that? What had Mac done to her? "I would truly like to know," she said with feeling.

Rita stared into Karen's eyes for a moment, then smiled and looked back down at her knife. "You really do love him, don't you?"

"Yes," was all Karen could say; she didn't dare allow herself to say another word.

"Elaine was madly in love with some poor artist who all of us could see was more interested in her trust fund than he was in her. But love is blind and Elaine fought for him with all she had. Her father sent the artist—not that he ever painted anything—a letter saying that if he married Elaine, her trust fund would be cut off. He enclosed a check for twenty thousand dollars that would only be honored if the man left Elaine. When Elaine got home that night, her artist was gone. She blamed her father for everything, and said that if he wanted her to marry a rich man then she would."

Pausing, Rita looked at Karen with her lips tight. "Elaine systematically went after Mac, the oldest of the Taggerts who wasn't yet married. She's beautiful, talented, and confident. Mac didn't have a chance. The night before the wedding her artist came back, and when Mac returned to their apartment, he found them in bed together."

Rita gave Karen time to assimilate this information before continuing. "Mac refused to marry her, but, being the gentleman he is, he allowed everyone to think that Elaine was the one who walked out on him. Since then he's been scared to death of marriage. He wants to get married, to have his own home, but I think he purposely chooses women who only want his money, then he tests them with some ridiculous prenuptial agreement and when they won't sign, it reinforces his belief that that's all women want from him. I'm glad to see that at last he's going to allow that wound to heal. I'm glad he's going to marry you, someone who actually loves him."

Karen didn't look up from the celery she was dicing for the salad.

"I'm telling you this because Mac has some sort of misguided sense of honor toward Elaine, so I didn't think he would ever tell you. And there're only two people outside of them who know the truth—his mother and I."

"But you told me this because I love him?"

"And because he loves you," Rita answered simply.

Karen smiled indulgently. "No he doesn't. We're not really engaged. He hired me to be his escort for the wedding and to—" She broke off because Rita was smiling at her in a *very* smug way.

"Karen, get real. Mac doesn't need to hire a woman for anything. He has women making fools of themselves wherever he goes. His mother is constantly complaining about the way the women who work for him make believe he comes with the job. She says he has two women executives so crazy about him they think that any work he gives them is proof of his love for them. His mother tells him to fire them, but Mac is so softhearted he won't. So he pays them outrageous salaries then does all the work himself."

"And the women complain to everyone because he doesn't share the load," Karen said softly.

"Probably. But Mac always takes the blame rather than allow a woman to look bad. His mother wanted to tell the world about Elaine, but Mac wouldn't allow it. Mac is from another era in time."

"Yes," Karen said in agreement. "I believe he is."

"Speak of the devil," Rita said, "a car just pulled up and it's Elaine. Karen! don't look like that. Go out there and—"

Karen was looking out the kitchen window. The arrival of Elaine had stopped the ball game because *all* the men had run toward the car to help the elegant, beautiful, exquisite Elaine out of the backseat of the long, black limo. And at the head of the crowd was McAllister Taggert.

"If you'll excuse me, I have to . . . to . . ." Karen could think of nothing she needed to do, so she turned and ran out of the kitchen, then ran up the stairs to her bedroom.

Five

THIRTY MINUTES LATER, KAREN FELT THAT SHE HAD LECTURED herself enough, and maybe she now had enough control to meet Elaine and not thrust a knife into her cold heart. Unfortunately, just outside the bedroom door, she found Elaine flanked by Steve and Mac.

Up close, Elaine was even more beautiful than she was from a distance. She was tall, blonde, cool-looking, and sophisticated enough to make Karen feel completely gauche. Elaine was exactly what Karen had envisioned as a woman Mac should marry. No doubt her father *was* the ambassador to some elegant foreign country, and no doubt she had a master's degree in something sophisticated and useless, like Chinese philosophy.

Just looking at Elaine made Karen feel as if she were wearing overalls and had straw sticking out of her hair. No wonder Mac had fallen head over heels in love with her, she thought.

Pausing at the head of the stairs, Elaine gave Mac a look that could warm a steel I-beam, while Mac just stared at her like a lost puppy, his heart in his eyes. He still loves her, Karen thought, and, against her best self-control, a flash of rage ran through her.

Steve paused only long enough to introduce Karen as Mac's fiancée, then he ran down the hall, football in hand, leaving the three of them alone.

"Still trying to get a woman to marry you, Mac?" Elaine asked softly, her eyes on Mac, as though Karen didn't exist.

"Still paying men to marry *you,* Elaine?" Karen shot back, then had the satisfaction of seeing Elaine's perfectly composed face crumble just before she turned and ran down the stairs. Obviously she'd thought her secret was safe forever and she could taunt Mac at will.

What Karen was not prepared for was Mac's reaction. His strong hand clamped around her upper arm and he half pulled her into their bedroom. When the door was shut, he faced her. "I didn't like that!" he said angrily, his face near hers. "What happened between Elaine and me is our business and no one else's, and I won't have you or anyone else sneering at her."

Karen straightened her body, ordering her muscles to remain rigid. If she hadn't, she would have collapsed on the bed in tears. What did it matter to her that McAllister Taggert was in love with a woman who had publicly made him a laughing-stock? "Certainly, Mr. Taggert," she said stiffly, then turned toward the door.

But Mac caught her, shoved her against the wall, and kissed her hungrily. For a moment Karen's pride made her fight him off, but it wasn't long before she was pulling him closer to her, her hands in his hair, her fingers gouging into his back.

"I hate you," she managed to say as he kissed her neck, his hands moving all over her body.

"Yes, I know. You hate me as much as I hate you."

Later, she didn't know how it happened, but one minute they were against the wall, fully clothed, and the next they were naked and writhing on the bed. Karen had been celibate for over two years and the only way she had remained that way was by repressing all sexual desire. The combination of her anger at Mac and now his soft caresses made her erupt into flames, all her desires exploding at once.

Mac was a worthy opponent and his passion matched hers as he entered her with force, then more gently as he put his mouth over Karen's to keep her from crying out.

It didn't take long, but in those few minutes, a lamp fell crashing to the floor, Karen fell off the bed, and Mac lifted her so her feet were on the floor, her back on the bed.

When Mac came inside her, Karen wrapped her legs about his waist and pulled his body down onto hers, holding him tightly. Her heart was pounding, her breath ragged.

It was several minutes before she could think again, and when she did, she was embarrassed and ashamed. What must he think of her? The poor, uneducated little secretary making a fool of herself over the boss?

"Please," she whispered. "Let me up."

Slowly, Mac raised his head and looked down at her, and when she turned her head away, he put his hand on her chin and made her meet his eyes. "What's this?" he asked teasingly. "My little lioness can't be shy, can she?"

Karen looked away from him. "I would like to get up."

But Mac didn't allow her to move away from him. Instead, he pulled her onto the bed, wrapped his big naked body about hers, drew the bedspread over them, then said, "Tell me what's wrong."

Karen was having trouble thinking, for somehow, this cozy cuddling, their bodies naked, was more intimate than what they had just done. "You—I—" she said, but no coherent words came out of her mouth.

"We made love," he said softly as he planted a kiss onto the top of her head. "It's something I've wanted to do for what seems like years."

"You never knew I existed until a few days ago."

"True, but I've made up in intensity for what I've lacked in time."

She tried to push away from him, but he held her tight.

"I'm not releasing you until you tell me what's wrong."

"What's *wrong?!*" she said with feeling, pushing away enough to look at him. "I am one of your secretaries, one step up from the custodian, and you're the boss and . . . and . . ."

"And what?"

"And you're in love with Elaine!" she spat at him. After all, how could she make more of a fool of herself than she already had?

To her great annoyance, Mac cuddled her closer and she could feel him chuckling against her.

"*Ow!* What was that for?" he asked when she pinched him.

This time she almost got away before he pulled her back. "I am *not* one of your bimbos. I am *not* after your money. In fact I want nothing whatever from you, not a business, not anything. Including ever seeing you—" She broke off as he kissed her. "Again," she whispered, finishing her sentence.

"Gladly," he said, pretending to misunderstand.

It was when his hand moved to her breast and Karen could feel herself wanting him again, and feel that he was again ready, that she pushed away from him. She didn't try to get off the bed, but she looked him in the eyes and said, "No."

"All right," he said, removing his hands from her body. "Tell me what's bothering you. Just don't leave. Please?"

Karen turned on her back, the spread covering her, none of her body touching his. "I didn't mean for this to happen. I just wanted—" At that she turned to look at him. By her calculations, she was at peak fertility today and after what they had just done, maybe she was pregnant.

As though reading her mind, he lifted her hand and kissed it, first the palm, then the back of her hand. When he started kissing her fingertips, she pulled away from him.

But Mac drew her back into his arms, holding her tightly. "I don't love Elaine."

"That's not what I saw, and you defended her!"

194

"Whatever bad I wish to befall Elaine, it isn't worse than what has happened to her. A man married her for her money. I know how that feels, so I have only pity for her. If it helps her to make snide remarks to me, let her. At least *I'm* not married to her." His voice lowered. "And she's not the mother of my children."

"Do you have many?" she asked as though making conversation. More than anything, she wanted to remain cool and detached. Wasn't it all right in this day and age to have affairs with men? She was positively primitive to believe that people who went to bed together should get married.

"Maybe we made my first one today," he said softly, then held her as she tried to get away from him.

"It is *not* a laughing matter. I wanted you to be a donor, not a . . . a . . ."

"Lover? Karen, please listen to me. Today wasn't a mistake. I've never before been to bed with a woman without using protection." He lifted her chin to look into her eyes. "I love you, Karen. If you'll have me, I'll try to make you a good husband."

"Me and all the rest of the free world," she said before she thought, then was horrified when she saw the hurt in his eyes. Instantly, he turned away and started to get out of bed.

"I'm sorry," she said, flinging herself onto his back as he sat on the edge of the bed. "Please, I didn't mean that. You don't have to marry me or even ask me to marry you. I know your streak of nobility, how you're a chivalrous knight and—"

Turning, he smiled to her. "Is that what you think of me? You think I ask every woman I go to bed with to marry me?"

Her face gave a positive answer to that.

Mac's face softened with his merriment. "Sweetheart," he said, smoothing a strand of hair behind her ears. "I don't know what's made you decide I'm a saint, but I'm not. Your first opinion of me was the most accurate any woman's ever had. You want to know the truth?"

Karen nodded, her eyes wide, then he pulled her into his arms and lay down beside her on the bed, her head on his shoulder.

"I was never in love with Elaine. Not really. I know that now, but it was flattering to have someone like her allow me to chase her."

"Didn't *she* chase *you?*" Karen said, then bit her tongue for giving away too much information.

Mac just smiled. "You have to remember that I've been around Elaine most of my life, and she was the one all of us boys went after. But she was unattainable. She was gorgeous, and by the time she was fourteen, she was built. We used to take bets on who could get Elaine to go out with him, but none of us ever succeeded. She studied for her final exams the night of our high school prom; she must have turned down every guy in the school."

"So you wanted what you couldn't have?" she said with sarcasm.

"Of course. Doesn't everyone?"

Karen was too interested in the story to think about philosophy. "But *you* got her."

"In a way. About four years ago she came to my office telling me she wanted me to help her with some investments and I—"

"Made a fool of yourself over her and asked her to marry you so you could show the other guys that *you* won."

"In a word, yes."

At that, Karen had to laugh. "So the artist saved you, didn't he?"

Mac hesitated before he answered. "Someday I want to know how you wheedled this information out of my mother. Or whomever she told who told *you.*"

"*Mmmm,*" was all Karen would answer. "So what about all the other women you asked to marry you?"

He paused, staring off into space. "You know, it was really quite odd, but every woman on earth seemed to think that after what happened with Elaine, I was dying to get married. Maybe they thought I wanted to show Elaine that I could get another woman if I wanted one."

"So they flung themselves on you," Karen said sarcastically. "You had nothing to do with all those engagement rings and prenuptial agreements."

He didn't laugh in return, but instead, turned so his face was above hers. "I'm serious. Two weeks ago I would have told you that I'd been in love with Elaine and maybe that I loved each of those beautiful girls I was engaged to. But now I know that I didn't love any of them, because when I'm with you, Karen, I don't have to be who I'm not. You're the first woman who has looked at me as just a man, not one of the rich Taggerts, not as a way to jump-start her own career. You saw *me* and nothing else."

He kissed her cheek. "I know it's sudden and I know you'll want to take time to think about this, and I'd love to court you, but I want to warn you what I'm after. I mean to marry you."

Karen's impulse was to throw her arms about his neck and say, "Yes, yes, yes," but instead she looked away for a moment, as though contemplating whether to marry him or not. When she looked back at him, her eyes were serious. "By courting do you mean candlelight dinners and roses?"

"How about trips to Paris, a cruise down the Nile, and skiing in the Rockies?"

"Perhaps," she said.

Pulling back, he looked at her speculatively. "How about I buy you two more buildings in cities of your choice for those baby stores of yours and set you up with a state-of-the-art accounting system?"

"Oh!" she said, startled. "With an instant inventory system?"

"Karen, honey, if you marry me, I'll give you the private code to my own accounting system and you can snoop to your heart's content."

"You do know how to court a girl, don't you?"

"*Mmmm,*" was all he said as he moved his leg on top of hers. "Did you know that twins run in my family?"

"I have seen a bit of evidence of that fact."

He was kissing her neck as his hand moved downward. "I don't know if you know this, but the way twins are made is to make love twice in the same day."

"Is that so? And here the medical people think it has to do with the way an egg divides."

"No. The more love, the more kids."

Turning her hips toward his, she put her arms about his neck. "Let's try for quintuplets."

"I *knew* there was a reason I loved you," he murmured before his mouth closed over hers.

Epilogue

"KAREN!" SAID A WOMAN BEHIND HER, MAKING KAREN TURN so quickly she dropped her packages. She was in a mall, people bustling about, and it took Karen a moment to recognize Rita, the woman she'd met on that remarkable weekend she'd spent with Mac.

To the consternation of both of them, Karen burst into tears.

With a motherly arm about the younger woman's shoulders, Rita led Karen to a tiled seat surrounding a quietly splashing fountain, then handed her a clean tissue and waited while Karen calmed herself.

"I am so sorry. I have no idea what is wrong with me. I seem to be bursting into tears constantly. I really am glad to see you. How is everyone? Steve?"

"Fine," Rita said, smiling. "Everyone is fine. So, when is your baby due?"

For several minutes Karen worked to control her tears. "Is it that obvious?"

"Only to another mother. Now, why don't you tell me what is bothering you. Something wrong between you and Mac? He *is* marrying you, isn't he?"

Karen blew her nose. "Yes, we're to be married in two months in a perfect little ceremony. You're on the guest list." She looked down at her sodden tissue. "Nothing is wrong. Nothing at all. It's just—"

"Come on, you can tell me."

"I'm not sure Mac wants to marry me," she burst out. "I tricked him. I . . . I seduced him. I wanted a baby so much, and he—" She broke off because Rita was laughing.

"I beg your pardon," Karen said stiffly, and started to get up. "I did not mean to amuse you with my problems."

Rita grabbed Karen's arm and pulled her to sit back down. "I'm sorry, I didn't mean to laugh; it's just that I've never seen a man pursue a woman as hard as Mac pursued you. Whatever could have made you think he doesn't want to marry you?"

"You really have no idea what you're talking about. If you knew the truth about what went on between us, you'd know that this will be more of a business arrangement than a real marriage. Everything was my idea and—"

"Karen, forgive me, but you're the one who doesn't know what you're talking about. Did you know that there were only to be six bridesmaids in the wedding? Mac called Steve in a panic, said he'd met the love of his life and he had to have an excuse to spend the weekend with her. The addition of another bridesmaid to the wedding was *his* idea. He paid triple price for a custom-made dress in your size, then paid for a tux for a friend of his so there'd be a seventh groomsman."

Karen stared at Rita. "Love of his life? But he told me just after he met me about his problem with finding someone to fit the dress."

"Steve and Catherine have plenty of friends, they didn't need one of Mac's girlfriends. Certainly not when his girlfriends changed as often as Mac's did."

Karen shook her head. "But I don't understand. I don't think he'd even seen me before the night of the Christmas party. What made him make up such a story? Why would he want to? I don't understand."

Rita smiled. "There's a saying in the Taggert family, 'Marry the one who can tell the twins apart.'"

Karen's face showed no understanding.

"In Mac's office, there is a photo of a man holding a string of fish, isn't there?"

Karen searched her memory, then remembered that night when she'd been snooping in Mac's office and picked up the photo from the shelf, then dropped it when Mac's voice startled her. "Yes, I remember the picture. It's one of his brothers, isn't it? I remember saying that I'd never seen the man before."

Rita smiled knowingly. "That was a photo of Mac's twin, a man who looks exactly like Mac."

"He doesn't look anything like him! Mac is *much* better looking than that man. He—" She stopped, then looked away from Rita's laughter, taking a moment to compose herself, then looked back. "He made up the whole bridesmaid story?" she asked softly.

"Completely. He offered to pay for the entire wedding if Steve would allow you to be in the ceremony. And he gave Steve free use of his precious speedboat for six months in return for putting both of you in the same bedroom. Those earrings Mac gave you came from the family vault, an heirloom, something given only to wives. Not girlfriends, wives. And I happen to know that twice that weekend he called home and told his family in detail about you, telling them how intelligent and beautiful you were and that he was doing everything he could to make you love him."

Rita gave Karen's hand a squeeze. "You must have noticed how tongue-tied Mac was around you. We were all laughing because he was so afraid of saying the wrong thing that often he wouldn't say anything. He told Steve that he kept pretending to ignore you because he'd been told by a man in the office that you ran from any man who showed the least interest in you."

"He told his sisters-in-law about the store I wanted to open," she said softly.

"Dear, if he wasn't with you, he was talking about you."

"But I thought he asked me to marry him because . . ." She broke off, looking into Rita's eyes. "Because I asked for something from him."

"I have never seen a man fall as hard in love with a woman at first sight as he fell for you. He said you picked up a photo in his office, he looked into your eyes, and he fell in love with you in that single moment."

"Why didn't he tell *me*?" Karen said.

"You mean Mac hasn't told you that he loves you?" Rita asked in horror.

"Yes, he has, many times, but I . . ." Karen stood. She wasn't going to say out loud that she hadn't believed him, that she couldn't believe that a man like McAllister Taggert could . . .

"I have to go," Karen said abruptly. "I have to—Oh, Rita, thank you," she said, then as Rita stood, she hugged her enthusiastically. "Thank you more than you could possibly know. You have made me the happiest woman on earth. I have to go and tell Mac that . . . that . . ."

Rita laughed. "Go! What are you waiting for? Go!"

But Karen was already gone.

JUDE DEVERAUX is the author of eighteen *New York Times* bestsellers. She began writing in 1976 and to date there are more than 30 million copies of her books in print. Her marvelous novels include *Sweetbriar, Twin of Ice, Twin of Fire,* and the magnificent James River trilogy: *Counterfeit Lady, Lost Lady,* and *River Lady.* In *The Velvet Promise, Highland Velvet, Velvet Song,* and *Velvet Angel,* Jude Deveraux created the unforgettable Montgomery family, who fought for love and honor from Scotland's fierce Highlands to the royal courts of medieval England. With *The Maiden, The Taming, The Conquest,* and the soon-to-be-published *The Heiress,* she returned to the medieval setting she immortalized so lovingly in the Velvet saga, while *The Duchess* features the Montgomerys in late nineteenth-century Scotland. In *Wishes, The Temptress, The Raider, The Princess, The Awakening, A Knight in Shining Armor, Mountain Laurel, Eternity, Sweet Liar* and *The Invitation,* she brought the proud Montgomery heritage to a new land, America. In *Remembrance,* she returned to the time-travel theme of her beloved *A Knight in Shining Armor.* All of these captivating Jude Deveraux romances are available from Pocket Books.

Kimberly Cates

Gabriel's Angel

To those who make the fires of Christmas remembrance burn brightest in my heart. Thank you for these precious memories of Christmas long ago:

My daughter, Kate, at three years old, crawling inside her giant Christmas stocking until nothing but her shiny patent leather shoes stuck out as she rummaged for treasures.

My husband, Dave, who tucked my engagement ring inside an antique pudding mold and promised me happily ever after on Christmas Eve.

My parents, Warren and Shirley Ostrom, who gave me a childhood full of such Christmas magic, it's impossible to choose only one memory. Thank you for Santa Claus visits, making pepparkauka, and even for making us eat lutevisk before we opened presents. (David and I laugh for hours now about our creative ways of feeding it to the dog.)

And to my brother, David, who spent an entire Christmas Eve doing battle with the gold and silver knights Mom and Dad let us open early. Waging war against you that day is one of my most beloved memories.

Remembrance, like candles, burns brightest at Christmas.
—Charles Dickens

Prologue

THE CHILD STOLE THROUGH THE LONDON STREETS LIKE A ragged ghost, a ravenous stomach and hungry amber eyes held together by a bundle of rags. Dark hollows dug into her wind-stung cheeks, and her legs were leaden from tramping through the snow. Her burning throat was raw from hurling Christmas carols out against the keening wind in an effort to tempt passersby to purchase the rolls of music clutched in her chilblained fingers.

There were too many left unsold, she thought, the knot of desperation twisting tighter beneath her ribs. But the weather this Christmas season had been too bitter for even the most kindhearted to pause and buy a ballad seller's wares.

She wanted nothing more than to curl up and sleep, to dream of a roaring fire and steaming meat pies and the mama she'd never known. But she didn't dare go home to the tiny room above the Red Dog Inn. Not yet. She could make excuses for the unsold bundle of ballads she still carried until her face was as blue as her half-frozen fingers, but it wouldn't matter if Da was drunk. Worse still, if Da was sober, he'd fall to his knees and beg her forgiveness, tears streaking his face.

I'm sorry, mo chroi, *but the pain . . . I cannot bear to live without my sweet Moira . . .*

Pain . . . from loss of the mother she didn't remember, from the hopelessness that cut its teeth on Thomas MacShane's dreams and roughened the voice once heralded as the sweetest tenor in all Ireland, turning it hoarse and uncertain.

He meant to do better by her, Alaina knew. But then the sadness would become too fierce again, and he would find the coins she'd hidden in their tiny room and embrace the only love left to him—a bottle of gin.

A brutal gust of wind twisted her ragged skirts, curling like icy tentacles about her bare legs. She gritted her teeth as the cold knifed into her very bones.

There was no use crying, she reasoned, charging into the snow-swept street. It wouldn't change anything. It never did. She'd trudge through the city selling ballads until one day she surrendered to one of the brothel rats that were already eyeing her with a feral gleam. She'd be just like the rest—all of the girls who had scrabbled out a living near Fleet Street—trading her body for a full belly or a pretty bit of ribbon.

"Look out, girl!" The cry made her jump out of the way just as two burly men in servants' livery nearly ran over her. She rounded on the men, ready to curse them, but she suddenly glimpsed what they were leading.

A pony, its coat as golden as a new-minted crown, its cream mane and tail impossibly long. A saddle trimmed in silver graced its back, a blue and gold caparison decking it like a knight's steed of old.

"'Twill make a wondrous gift for young Master Tristan." The taller man's voice drifted back as he eyed the pony. "I cannot wait to see his face when he sees what Father Christmas has brought him."

A gift? This pony was to belong to some boy? Alaina stared after them, envy warming the blood in her veins. She watched the pony with awe-filled eyes and knew she'd never seen anything so beautiful. She couldn't bear to see it disappear. Not yet. She scrambled after them through a maze of streets that led to grand town houses with windows glowing like jewels.

She stole after the pony through the gates of a huge brick town house, where the men tied the pony to a hitching post and disappeared inside. Ever so stealthily, she crept toward that gleaming, wondrous pony, stretching out one finger to touch it. It whickered, turning to nibble at the end of her shawl.

"You're so beautiful," she whispered, marveling at the creature's warmth as she slipped her half-frozen hand into the nook between the pony's mane and its silky neck.

She didn't hear the door to the town house open, or anything else, until one of the outraged servants bellowed. "You, there! What are you doing?"

She glanced up, but the man's cry was lost in a boy's shout of exultation.

Ebony hair gleaming, his cravat askew, a boy of about twelve pelted down the town house steps at breakneck speed to fling himself at the pony. Seeing Alaina, he came to a halt, looking into her face. Astonishment widened the most sparkling chocolate-hued eyes Alaina had ever seen.

"I said get away from here, you little beggar!" the servant bellowed in a voice she knew presaged a cuff on the shoulder.

The boy stepped between them. "Don't! She's not hurting anything." He smiled, and Alaina felt an odd fizzy sensation in her chest. "Hullo. I'm Tristan Ramsey. What's your name?"

It took Alaina a moment to realize he was speaking directly to her. Boys teased and tormented, shoved and slapped, their greatest delight was making smaller children miserable. They didn't smile so warmly, speak so kindly. She regarded Tristan Ramsey warily, half expecting him to pinch her.

"My name's Alaina," she volunteered at last.

He stroked the pony's soft nose with paint-smudged fingers, awe and delight shining in his face.

"Isn't this the most stupendous pony you've ever seen, Alaina?" Tristan asked. She nodded. "I'm going to call him Galahad. You know, like the knight in the legends of King Arthur."

She'd never heard that tale, but if this boy loved it, it must be wonderful. She wished she could curl up at his feet, listening as she sometimes did when her father told stories of enchanted swans and fairy kings from Ireland. Her longing must have shone in her face, for suddenly she was aware of the boy's gaze on her in solemn contemplation.

Her cheeks burned beneath the grit that smudged them. She tucked her feet deeper beneath the hem of her gown and tugged her shawl over a ragged hole where her knee showed through.

He looked away, as if he understood her discomfort, then he gave a magnificent shrug. "You know, since I've got Galahad, there's not a thing more I could wish for in the world. So I won't be needing this." He rummaged in his pocket, grasped her hand, and put something into it. The object was hard, round, and warm from his pocket. Alaina glanced down and almost dropped it.

"It's—it's a whole guinea!" she gasped, as stunned as if he'd just handed her angel's wings.

"My Christmas guinea. I want you to have it."

"I can't," Alaina choked out.

"I don't need money," he said grandly. "I'm going to be the greatest artist who ever lived. The minute I'm old enough, I'm going off to Rome to see what Michelangelo's done, and then I'm going to paint something even more stupendous."

Alaina's mouth rounded in awe at the confidence in his

210

words, a fiery determination that would have seemed odd on any other boy's face. Maybe that was why he didn't pinch her. He was saving up his pinches for this Mikey Angelo.

"You'd better take it," Tristan said, forcing her fingers to curl over the coin. "It's my Christmas wish that you do, and Christmas wishes are magic."

Alaina stared up at the boy, memorizing his face. A stubborn chin, a generous mouth that seemed made for laughter, eyes black and dancing with imps of mischief, yet shining with a kindness only too rare. In that moment, she would have merrily followed Tristan Ramsey and his pony anywhere.

"Magic," she breathed, gazing down at the slivers of gold guinea shimmering between her grubby fingers. Her heart felt too big for her chest. Her eyes burned with something shamefully like tears. She clutched the coin tight and ran toward the gate before Tristan could see her cry, but she didn't stumble out into the street.

She hid behind the gatepost until everyone had returned to the house, then she crept to one shining window and peered inside. She watched the family at their Christmas revelry until dawn came, oblivious to the biting cold, the keening wind, the dark night, forgetting that her father was waiting.

When the last wassail had been drunk, the last sweet plum popped into sugar-spangled mouths, and the last kiss had been stolen beneath the kissing bough, Alaina tore herself away from the Ramseys' window.

Guilt jabbed like a sharp stone beneath her rag-wrapped feet, blistering her with the knowledge that it was nearly dawn. Her Da would be worried. But even if she'd been missing for weeks on end, Da would forgive her the instant he saw that she'd earned a whole guinea.

He'd reach out his hand, his fingers shaking, and clutch the gold piece to his chest, praising the saints and his sweet Moira, promising Alaina a warm new shawl, coal for the fire, a feast fit for one of Ireland's ancient High Kings. And then the guinea would vanish: all those solemn promises as much fantasy as the tales he'd always spun for her—of how he'd stolen her shawl pin from a fairy king's cloak and how they'd have a lovely cottage one day, with fine fat geese in the yard and coverlets made of swansdown.

A sick churning gripped Alaina's stomach at the image of that shiny coin disappearing into Da's grimy pocket.

No. Tristan Ramsey's Christmas guinea was hers. She'd never spend the boy's gift, no matter how hungry and cold she got. She'd keep it forever to remind her of a boy named Tristan with a dazzling smile and laughing eyes and a pony named Galahad. She'd keep it to remind her of Christmas magic and wishes that would come true if she just believed strongly enough.

She swore to herself she would come to the window every Christmas to watch holly being festooned across the mantel and charades being played before the fire. And she would imagine what it would be like to see Tristan's dark eyes gazing down into her own as if all the wishes in the heavens had finally come true.

One

Sixteen years later . . .

NO ONE SHOULD BE ALONE AT CHRISTMAS, BUT ALAINA MacShane had never been anything else. She pressed her mittened hand against the frost-etched windowpane and groped for the courage to peer one last time through the glass. To finally say farewell to a dream that could not come true.

Tonight she would say good-bye to things she could never have, to holiday laughter and love-filled embraces welcoming her home, garlands of holly, Christmas puddings, kissing boughs.

And Tristan Ramsey.

Her fingers burned to bury themselves in midnight waves of hair she had never touched. Her mouth craved the honeyed power of lips she had never tasted. Her body trembled with a desperate need for the passion that burned, like black fire, in his eyes.

She had loved him forever, but it was time to face the truth. It was time to leave London forever. For no matter how many Christmases she stood waiting at the window, no holiday magic could pull her into the drawing room filled with Tristan's laughter. No star-kissed wish could transform her into a woman Tristan could take into his arms and welcome into a world of bright holly and tender caresses.

She had been confronted with that painful reality years before, when she'd been seventeen—watching as Tristan fell in love with his father's ward, a golden-curled beauty as fragile as a Christmas rose. He'd spent that Christmas bundling his dreams into a dozen trunks and setting out to build a future with his bride, a future Alaina could never share.

Heartbroken, she had stayed away from the window for seven Christmases after that, assuring herself that Tristan didn't need her, that she had no right to watch over him any longer. But no matter how far she ran, she could never escape the mystical link forged between them on that long-ago Christmas when he had pressed the Christmas guinea into her hand. She would carry it into a bleak eternity without him.

Fingers of wind tugged at her serviceable gray bonnet,

whipping auburn hair across eyes that blurred with tears. She dashed them away, wondering how it was possible to grieve so terribly at the loss of something you'd never had.

She sucked in a steadying breath and steeled herself to look in the window one last Christmas, knowing what she'd see: firelight flashing off of glorious satin gowns, starched cravats tied to perfection beneath hard masculine jaws, reckless games and spritely dancing, and the tempting green sphere of the kissing bough dangling from the ceiling, its ribbons and apples and candles all aglow.

But as she peered through the pane of glass that had separated her for so many years from the celebration beyond, she raised a stunned hand to lips that suddenly trembled. Not so much as a sprig of mistletoe adorned the room; the chamber was cloaked in funereal gloom.

Where was everyone? The mob of Tristan's laughing sisters, the portly papa and rosy-cheeked mother, who bustled so tenderly about her brood? Where was Tristan?

Was it possible that in the years she'd stayed away, they had left the lovely house for good? Loss ripped through her, as though her own family had vanished.

Then, suddenly, she saw him. Garbed in shirtsleeves, he sat in a leather chair, broad shoulders bent, elbows on his black-breeched knees. His dark hair had been tousled by restless fingers, the hard planes and angles of his face buried in one splayed hand.

"Tristan," she whispered aloud, but he couldn't hear her. He could never know that she was there. "Oh, God, Tristan, what is it? What's wrong?" she asked, as if the heavens themselves might answer.

At that instant, the chamber door opened and a boy of about seven entered. Tristan's son. The certainty wrung Alaina's heart. Garbed in a little nightshirt, he had his mother's golden curls.

Yet his face was a miniature of Tristan's own. Pale and sad, the child squared his narrow shoulders as if he were struggling valiantly to be brave.

The Tristan she had watched over for so long would have gathered his son in his arms, offered solace as he had to the beggar child so long ago. But this Tristan hesitated for a heartbeat, as if he wanted to touch the boy, then levered himself from the chair and walked away.

Alaina wanted to catch hold of him, to shake him, demand to know what had driven the light from his eyes, the tenderness from his heart. She wanted to understand. But that was as impossible as touching those firmly molded lips with her own.

She was shaken from her imaginings as the boy approached the window with dragging steps. Alaina drew back into the shadows, hiding as those chubby child-hands opened the casement and the little boy leaned out into the night.

Moonlight shimmered in eyes that seemed far too old for a child's face; snowflakes dusted a freckled nose and baby-pink lips clamped tight against sorrow. He peered up to the heavens as if there were answers written there that he alone could see.

"Mama?" he called in an uncertain treble voice. "It's me. Gabriel. Are you out there in the stars?"

Alaina bit down hard on her lip. How many times had she told her hurts and her sorrows and even her joys to the night sky, as if it were only a fragile veil obscuring her mother's face?

"Papa says that you're in heaven now," the boy said. "He says you listen to my prayers. But I don't believe him anymore. He always said Christmas wishes would come true, but I asked for you to get better last Christmas, and you left me when spring came anyway. You didn't come back no matter how hard I prayed. I don't care if we never have a Yule log or Christmas pudding or play Snap Dragon again. I don't even care if I don't get a pony like Papa did. Christmas is just for babies." A wistful sigh put the lie to those brash words. "I only wish that . . ." His chin trembled. Alaina could see how much effort it took for him to quell it. "No. It doesn't matter. I could wish and wish forever that Papa would laugh again, but it won't ever happen. There is no magic, Mama." His voice dropped low. "Maybe there aren't even any angels."

Tears wet Alaina's face as Tristan's child closed the window. Her heart ached with the memory of his small, sad face and Tristan's own, so drastically changed.

How much had he loved his wife? Alaina wondered, quiet anguish gripping her. Had Tristan loved his bride as deeply as her father had loved her mother—all but flinging himself in his wife's grave once she was gone? Only a man who loved with all his heart could be so altered by his wife's death.

She shivered at the hot imprint of jealousy in her soul—resentment toward the woman who had shared Tristan's life, his bed, given him a son. Irrational guilt weighed her down, as if the very fact that she'd stayed away for so long had let some sinister force slip through the window to harm the woman she had envied.

"Nine o'clock, an' all's well."

She heard the watchman calling out the hour and felt a swift jab of panic. She had to go. She'd finally saved enough to leave all this behind, to make a life for herself far away from the London slums, in a place where no one would know who she was or where she had come from. A hundred genteel doors closed in her face had left her no other choice.

There is no magic . . . Gabriel's voice echoed in her mind. *Christmas wishes don't come true . . .*

She swallowed hard, her fingers touching her own talisman tucked beneath the bodice of her gown—a coin suspended between her breasts by a ragged ribbon. The makeshift necklace had been a constant reminder of the healing warmth of the Christmas guinea from Tristan's pocket—a warmth that had threaded through her whole life, changed it forever, as if the coin truly were infused with some mystical power. For countless Christmases she had watched over Tristan, clutching tight to that magic.

Could she abandon him now? She had watched, helpless, as her father sank into an abyss of grief and bitterness. She couldn't forsake Tristan to Thomas MacShane's fate, leave him in bitter darkness, no matter what the cost to herself.

She turned her gaze to the sky, its horizon roiling with purple-black clouds, the wind gusting a bitter cold warning. She should hasten back to her room far across town before the storm struck, finish her preparations for leaving London.

But a force more powerful than logic drew her fingers to the reticule where she'd tucked the precious coins she had hoarded for so many years, "stitching her way to America" in Miss Crumb's Millinery.

The weight of the coins wasn't half so heavy as the weight of Tristan Ramsey's shattered dreams. Surely there was time for her to make a little bit of magic—for Tristan, and for the little boy who talked to angels.

The boy had cried himself to sleep again.

Tristan stood beside his son's bed, gazing down at that cherublike face, his heart raw with regret. Traces of salty tears still lingered on the boy's cheek, and one arm was curled about a rag-stuffed pony, his last Christmas gift from his mama.

Damnation, what a disaster this Christmas holiday had turned into. It had seemed simple enough at the outset—find the boy a temporary governess, then pack him onto a coach bound for Beth's house in Yorkshire. Gabriel could admire his newborn cousin and join in the family's revels, while Tristan—Tristan could remain behind, where his brooding wouldn't dampen the Christmas joy of those who loved him.

But he had failed as miserably in finding a governess as he had at everything else where his son was concerned. And Gabriel had resisted the notion of traveling to his aunt's with a determination that had been as odd as it was irritating.

Blast it, Tristan thought, he should have slung Gabriel into the coach kicking and screaming if necessary.

But his son would never have stooped to such a childish display. The boy had seemed old, deep down in his soul, from the time he'd taken his first toddling steps. His huge, dark eyes were so earnest, devoid of mischief and laughter, filled instead with determination. To do what? To be a little man? To take care of his mama while his father . . . Tristan's throat constricted.

No. There was no point raking it open again. He had done his best to remedy the situation once and for all. The decision he'd made was best for everyone. The sooner it was over the better. Tristan's jaw knotted. In two weeks his son would be gone.

He should leave the boy's room at once, get to the mounds of paperwork he'd brought from the office. Ramsey and Ramsey could always provide enough business to bury a dozen men. Yet tonight he couldn't seem to force himself away from where Gabriel lay sleeping. Some demonic part of Tristan wanted to make sure he would remember his child innocent in slumber, not realizing that this was the last Christmas Eve he would sleep in his own small bed.

Tristan stiffened, an odd, grating sound coming from the floor below making his muscles tense. What the devil could be making that racket? Burrows or Cook banking the fire? No. The old butler and his apple-cheeked wife had long since gone to their quarters, their rheumy old eyes as wistful for past Christmases as his son's bright ones.

A metallic ring echoed up the stairway, then was silenced, as if someone was trying to be stealthy, quiet.

He crossed soundlessly to Gabriel's open door and leaned out into the hallway. A muffled thud rasped at his ears—footsteps. He froze.

Housebreakers? He'd heard they loved nothing more than plying their trade at Christmas, when so many families were off visiting. If Tristan hadn't been in the house, they could have filled their bags with silver plate till they split and no one would have been the wiser. At night, Cook plugged up her ears with wool batting to muffle her husband's snoring, and old Burrows would have slept through the battle of Waterloo even if his mattress had been balanced atop one of Wellington's cannons.

Casting one more glance at his sleeping son, Tristan stole down the hall, pausing at his own bedchamber long enough to secure his pistol. He loaded it hastily, then made his way to the head of the stairs, his heart hammering, his jaw set, grim.

His roiling emotions shifted into feral protectiveness. At last there was an enemy he could fight, something besides the phantoms in his own embattled soul.

Nerves strung tight as wire, Tristan made his way down the staircase, the sounds growing louder, more distinct. The drawing room—that was where the noise was coming from. His jaw clenched grimly. What if there were more than one thief? What if they were armed? Would Burrows or Cook hear the scuffle? What would happen to Gabriel if . . . if what? If Tristan died?

His hand tightened around the pistol, the thought slashing, ruthless. His death would make little difference to his son's future. It had already been decided, the plan put into motion. Tristan approached the drawing room door—closed, no doubt, in an effort to muffle the sound of the brigands ransacking the room. His left hand reached for the door latch, a hundred grim scenarios playing in his mind. Then, ever so stealthily, he opened the door.

Two

IF A HORDE OF MURDERERS HAD TAKEN UP RESIDENCE IN THE room, they could have merrily cut Tristan to ribbons while he stood there, paralyzed with shock.

A precarious tower, constructed of a gaming table, Tristan's leather wing chair, two Chippendale side chairs, and a silk-embroidered footstool, teetered in the far corner of the room, atop which a fiery-haired woman in a dove-gray gown stood on tiptoe, like an angel on a church spire. A hammer was clamped between her knees. Three nails bristled from the crease of her lips as she hummed a muffled tune and wrestled to hang a monstrosity constructed of Christmas greenery, apples, bright ribbons, and candles from the nail in the ceiling.

A kissing bough? The realization crept through Tristan's befuddled brain.

"What the devil?" he roared, his finger tightening reflexively on the pistol's trigger. The weapon exploded. Plaster shattered. The woman screamed, wheeling around in white-faced shock. The hammer clattered to the ground. Nails rained down as the tower gave a horrendous shudder. Tristan glimpsed amber eyes widening in alarm as the chair four levels down skidded off the edge of the table. The woman grabbed for the rim of the kissing bough in a desperate effort to regain her balance, but her fingers tore free.

Instinctively Tristan flung the pistol aside and dove toward her, as if he could somehow keep her from falling. But the furniture clattered to the floor with a deafening racket, the woman crashing atop Tristan. He heard a hollow thud and a sharp cry of pain as the force of the woman's fall knocked them both to the floor.

He swore, grappling for her wrists, rolling her beneath him while she struggled like a wildcat. "Hold still! Damn you—" He snarled, forcing her into submission with the weight of his body. He gritted his teeth as the soft pillows of her breasts crushed beneath his chest, her skirts tangled about her thighs, and her legs were pinned beneath the weight of his own. She smelled of wintertime—snowflakes and ivy—her eyes snapping gold fire in a pale heart-shaped face haloed by wild waves of auburn hair.

"Who the devil are you?" Tristan grated, stunned at the fierce jolt of awareness that sizzled through every sinew of his body. "And what are you doing in my house?"

"My name is Alaina MacShane. I was h-hanging a kissing bough," the woman choked out. "Do you always shoot people for that offense?"

"Only when they break into my house to do so. Did someone send you here? Blast it, if one of my sisters took it into their heads to interfere—"

"No. I broke into your house of m-my own accord."

Tristan wondered if one of the chairs had crashed down on his head. "You broke into my house to decorate it for Christmas? What kind of lunatic are you?"

"One who will soon have a lump on her head big enough to match the dome on St. Paul's Cathedral." The woman gave a futile tug against his grasp. "I'm not a lunatic. I only wanted to . . . You have a child here. He deserves a little Christmas magic."

Blast it, was his family responsible for this? Tristan wondered.

They'd bludgeoned him with pleas about Christmas until his head ached. Hearing the same condemnation from a stranger made his features harden, a muscle in his jaw tic dangerously.

"Take this rubbish and get out of my house," he said, dragging her to her feet. "And tell whoever sent you that my son is my concern. Christmas can go to blazes for all I care! And you with it!"

"Papa?" The soft voice came from beyond the door.

"Gabriel, get back to your room this instant!" Tristan bellowed.

But it was too late. The child, a pale ghost in a white nightshirt, had stolen into the room, his beloved stuffed pony clutched beneath his arm. Gabriel's sleep-heavy eyes skated past the pieces of furniture strewn across the floor, past the two disheveled figures, then caught on the kissing bough still swinging wildly from the nail overhead.

"Oh, Papa!" Gabriel cried, rushing closer, breathless. The child's eyes rounded with wonder, then swept an awed path from the kissing bough to Alaina MacShane. Gabriel caught his breath, as if afraid he would shatter some enchantress's spell. "So . . . so beautiful!" Gabriel gaped at the woman as if she were spun of moonbeams. It irritated Tristan that he wasn't certain whether his son was rhapsodizing over the kissing bough or the woman standing beneath it.

Displays of delight were so rare in the solemn boy that it was like acid in the raw places in Tristan's soul. "I had nothing to do with this nonsense. This—this . . . thief is responsible for this disaster."

"I'm not a thief!" the woman protested.

"She's right, Papa! She couldn't be a thief," Gabriel piped up. "She didn't take anything. She brought things. Holly and ivy and Christmas candles."

Tristan ground his teeth so hard his jaw ached. "Gabriel, I'm not going to argue with you. Get upstairs. And *you*." He threw a glare back at the woman. "You take this rubbish and get out of here before I turn you over to the authorities."

The woman's chin jutted up at a stubborn angle. "Go ahead. It would be worth it just to hear you attempt to explain my crime to the constables."

"No!" Gabriel cried, and flung himself between them. The stuffed pony tumbled to the floor, the child twining his arms about the woman's skirts.

"Hush, *mo chroi*," the woman soothed. "It's all right."

"He wants to send you away!" Gabriel cried, casting a glare at Tristan. "I won't let you do it, Papa! She's mine! I wished her here!"

"Wished her here?" Tristan gaped, stunned at the passionate fury in the boy. His son, who had always treated Tristan with the stiff courtesy accorded a stranger, was clinging to Alaina as if she were the only safe haven left in his little world. It hurt Tristan far more than he would have believed possible.

"Gabriel, we cannot keep this woman here. God only knows where she came from!"

"God *does* know!" The child's face set in stubborn lines that mirrored Tristan's own. "She's an angel. *My* angel. I asked for help, and Mama sent her, just like I asked."

The fierce certainty in the boy's voice twisted in Tristan's gut like a knife.

"Gabriel, hush, now." The woman called his son by name, stroking his silky golden curls. How the devil had she known Gabriel's name? His own? Tristan fought off a ripple of unease. His sisters must have told her . . . or whoever else was behind this plot. The idea of spinning out private wounds before a stranger made him feel violated. And when Tristan got his hands on the person responsible . . .

"Gabriel, look at her!" Tristan dragged his fingers through his hair, struggling for patience. "This is no angel. If she had wings, don't you think she might have used them to fly instead of building towers and landing on top of me and bruising the devil out of both of us?"

"Mama said angels come in all different shapes and sorts. She said that you should always be good because you never know when one will plop right down in front of you."

The words lanced through Tristan's chest. Gabriel believed this fable with his whole heart—believed in angels and that his mother had answered his prayers. Was there any way to tell a grieving child that neither miracle was possible?

Tristan crossed to his son, then sank to one knee so that his eyes were level with the boy's.

"Gabriel, maybe your mama was right. But this woman isn't an angel. She doesn't belong here."

"You can't send her away!" Dark eyes blazed with their first bout of defiance. "I won't let you."

"Actually, Gabriel, I have a . . ." The woman paused, obviously groping for an explanation. ". . . a coach I need to catch."

Gabriel's brow crinkled. "A coach to go to heaven? I thought you just flew where you wanted to go." He turned to Tristan. "Please, Papa. I never asked for anything, ever. I didn't even care that you forgot Christmas . . . at least not so very much. But I want to keep her!"

"She's not a puppy, Gabriel!" Tristan snapped, battling against the conflicting emotions inside him. "You can't keep a woman."

"God sent her," the boy asserted stubbornly.

"God would have done better to send a governess."

"Maybe He *did!* She's my governess!" Gabriel brightened. "You were so angry when Miss Grimwiddle didn't come. Maybe God heard you shouting."

Tristan ground his teeth, grappling for patience.

"For God's sake—" he began, then stopped. "No, blast it, God has had more than enough to do with this disaster."

"Please, stop it. Both of you," Alaina pleaded. "I think it will be best if I just go on my way."

"No!" Gabriel clung even tighter to Alaina's skirts, tears welling in his eyes, a thin note of hysteria in his voice. "Papa, look at all the Christmas pretties. She put everything in exactly the right place. Just the way Grandmother used to. How could she do that if she wasn't an angel?"

"Don't be absurd." Tristan tried to dismiss the observation, yet as his gaze skimmed over the mantel festooned with holly, he was stunned to realize that the scarlet ribbons and gilded bits of fruit were all tucked in the exact places where his mother had put them every year.

A chill coursed beneath Tristan's skin. How the devil had a complete stranger known where to put things, down to the tiniest red bow? Surely someone from his infernal meddling family must be responsible for dropping this disaster of a woman in the middle of his drawing room. He couldn't even contemplate any other possibility.

He dragged his gaze back to the woman, who was gently but firmly disentangling herself from his son's clinging arms. It was all Tristan could do not to snatch Gabriel away, then fling Alaina MacShane out the door and nail it shut behind her.

He grabbed hold of Gabriel, tugging him away from the woman as she went to the door, her lovely face filled with dismay and pain as she gazed into the distraught features of the child.

She started to say something, then tugged open the door. A blast of snow swirled in on a bitter-cold wind, knocking her back a step. A wall of falling snow obscured everything an arm's length from the door, obliterating the stone wall, the iron gates, and the street beyond, until it seemed as if an evil spell had cast the house adrift in a sea of white.

A blizzard. Hell, yes, the way his luck had been holding lately there would have to be a goddamn blizzard! Why hadn't he noticed the wind beginning to howl?

Alaina caught her lip between her teeth, eyeing the blinding wall of white with barely concealed trepidation.

"Perhaps I'll have to take a sled to heaven, Gabriel," she said with a wan smile.

"No! You can't go out in the storm!" Gabriel wailed. "Papa, you can't let her go into the snow! She could get lost, Papa, or hurt! What if she fell down and nobody could find her until she was all frozen up?"

"Surely an angel's wings could manage navigating through a little snow, wouldn't you think, Miss MacShane?" Tristan's mouth twisted with grim amusement. "Or are they rather impractical after all? Made for gliding over silver clouds and through star fields. Not for everyday use?"

"I'm certain I can manage somehow."

If only she could, Tristan thought in disgust. But no. She'd probably build a tower out of coach seats and hitching posts and land smack outside Gabriel's window or be killed by some cutthroat when she tried to stick a sprig of holly in his buttonhole.

"No thank you," Tristan snapped, dragging her back into the room by an elbow and thumping the door shut against the storm. "I have enough on my conscience without adding a frozen angel to the list."

Gabriel gave a skip of delight, his bare feet leaving little prints in the layer of snow dusting the entryway. "You can come upstairs and tuck me into bed, Alaina," he said. "Did my mama tell you about how she did that, every night?"

As his son slipped one small hand trustingly into Alaina's

own, Tristan's fists knotted with anger and frustration. Damn the woman! He'd said she could spend the night, not drive him insane filling Gabriel's head with more nonsense.

But unless he was willing to forcibly pry Gabriel away from her, he had no choice but to allow her to ascend the stairs and plunge deeper into his home, and into the hidden pain that limned each silent corridor, every shadowy corner, where joy had once sparkled with abandon.

Tristan glared after her, hating her, yet unable to take his eyes from her lithe form as Gabriel led her up the stairs and back to the nursery where Tristan himself had dreamed as a child. Impossible dreams, caught ever so briefly by paint-smudged fingers before reality stole them away.

Tristan followed them to Gabriel's bedchamber. He leaned against the wall in the shadows, achingly aware of the woman, his dark eyes never leaving her and his son.

The nursery was always painfully tidy—the condition wrenching at Tristan's heart because no nurse or governess or upstairs maid had enforced this rigid code. Gabriel had done so himself, as if the child instinctively feared that the slightest mistake or mess or disturbance would have dire consequences. Consequences like being sent away.

Tristan's chest ached as Gabriel tunneled under his covers, his "angel" sitting down on the edge of his bed as if she had tucked him in a hundred times before and listened to him lisp his child prayers. As if she belonged there far more than the child's own father did.

Gabriel clung to her hand, fighting against sleep, and Tristan could almost taste his son's fear. "Promise you won't go away without saying good-bye . . . like . . . Mama did," the boy pleaded, gazing up into eyes as golden as heaven's gates. "I won't sleep unless you promise . . ."

A soft sound tore from the woman's throat, and she scooped

227

Gabriel into her arms, comforter and all, crooning some half-forgotten lullaby. But she didn't make promises she couldn't keep. The realization flayed Tristan's nerves, setting them even more on edge.

No matter how he tried to resist it, her voice entranced him as she sang the soft, lilting melody. Haunting, ethereal, it curled around the battered places in Tristan's soul like crystal-cold water after an eternity of thirst.

Every fiber of his being seemed to be captured by this woman who had come from nowhere. His gaze traced the fragile curves of her face—high cheekbones, thick lashes, a delicate, up-turned nose sprinkled with a dusting of freckles. She had that almost otherworldly beauty that could only be born of Irish mists and magic, that impossible coloring God's hand had stroked into rose blooms and sweet cream, polished amber and starless nights.

Tristan remembered in excruciating detail what her breasts had felt like, pressing sweetly against his chest, how that riot of auburn hair had smelled, like cinnamon and honey. How close her lips had been to his own when she'd lain beneath him on the drawing room floor, the soft curve of her mouth temptation incarnate.

Temptation? Or a wild enchantment that induced madness? For only a madman would be leaning against a wall, watching a stranger with his son, furious with the woman, wanting to hurl her out of his house, out of his life, while at the same time some demon buried deep within him, all but forgotten, yearned to draw Gabriel's angel into his arms. He wanted to hold her as a man holds a woman, wanted to taste her, to touch her, to draw her to his own bed, where she would soothe him in a way different from the way she'd soothed his son.

Tristan stifled a groan, furious at his own weakness. It was nothing but a stab of lust. God knew, there had been no one since Charlotte, and in the last years of their marriage, she and Tristan had found it as difficult to touch each other's bodies as it was to touch each other's hearts.

Relief surged through Tristan as he saw that Gabriel had finally surrendered to sleep. He crossed to his son's bed and with one strong hand encircled the woman's wrist. She looked up at him, her eyes wide and golden and agonizingly familiar, though he was certain he'd never seen her before.

Drawing her to her feet, he tugged her out of the nursery. In the corridor, Tristan turned her to face him, her back to the wall, her auburn hair forbidden fire against the cream-colored plasterwork. A need fiercer than any he'd ever known swept through him, a need to kiss her until her knees melted, his heart healed. The image jolted through him, apalling in its vividness. Sickened by himself, he released her, aware that if he scrubbed his hands until they bled, he'd never be free of the feel of Alaina MacShane, the soft warmth of her wrist pulsing beneath his palm, the bone-melting heat of the kiss they would never share.

"You owe me an explanation, angel," he grated, latching on to anger to suppress desire, confusion, longing. "What the devil is this all about?"

Three

"WHEN GABRIEL OPENED THE DRAWING ROOM WINDOW, I heard him wishing on the stars," Alaina said, her voice musical as meadow breezes. "He sounded so sad and so lonely."

Tristan flinched, but his eyes grew even harder. "My son is none of your concern."

"I'm afraid you're mistaken. You heard Gabriel. He . . . wished me here."

If she'd slapped him, she couldn't have fed his fury more. "Blast it, leave off this lunacy. You're no more an angel than you are the bloody queen! And wishes are nonsense. The boy knows that better than anyone. He spent last Christmas wishing for his mother to get well, and that was a waste of time. Three weeks later she was dead. Now, who the devil sent you here? Which of my meddling sisters—"

"Beth didn't send me, and Allison wouldn't dare—"

"They didn't send you, but you know their names?" Tristan's lip curled in a bitter sneer. "How much did they offer you to kick up this nonsense? I made it clear to them that Christmas was over for eternity as far as I'm concerned."

"I'm certain they wouldn't defy you. They adore you—"

"Damnation, you speak as if you're a family friend."

Color stung the woman's cheeks. "I'm not. I just . . . just wanted to take away the sadness in Gabriel's eyes. It's as simple as that."

"Simple? None of this is simple. You break into my house, dragging Christmas rubbish in your wake. You work my son into a frenzy, until he believes you're some sort of angel." He paced away from her, so he wouldn't be distracted by the spicy tang that clung to her hair.

"God knows, you'd think they'd dress you better if you came from heaven. Blast, that's right. Your clothes . . . What the devil would my sisters be doing associating with someone like you? I can't imagine you're one of their acquaintances. Even their servants wear better clothes."

The woman's chin bumped up a notch. "If I'd known breaking into someone's house was a formal occasion, I would have dressed in my Sunday best."

In a heartbeat his hands flashed out, encircling her arms, drawing her mere inches away from the hard plane of his body. Her face swam before him—all creamy curves and peach glow, her breath wisping warm against his lips, taunting him to taste her. "Don't toy with me, girl. You listen to my son's dreams, hang the kissing bough where it's dangled every Christmas since before I was born, and you know my sisters by name. Damn it, who are you?"

He could see the woman grope desperately for an answer. In the end, she clutched on to Gabriel's staunch belief. "If you don't believe in angels, what can I possibly tell you?"

Tristan shoved her away as if she'd burned him.

"All right," he snarled. "Keep your secrets. First thing in the morning, I want you out of this house. Before Gabriel wakes up."

"I understand."

"Do you? Do you understand half the damage you've done here tonight?"

"By trying to give a child a Christmas? If that's a crime, I'll gladly be condemned. There are countless people who would be thrilled if they had your blessings. A warm house, a loving family, years of Christmas memories. And a fine, healthy son who adores you. If I were you, I wouldn't waste time feeling sorry for myself!"

The words lashed Tristan's raw emotions. "Don't you *dare* criticize me over things you know nothing about. Apparently it was my son's wish that brought you here. You may sleep in the chamber across the hall. In the morning, I will see to it personally that you are delivered wherever the hell you are going. Is that understood?"

"Perfectly," she said, a soft mourning clinging to her lips. She looked at him as if he'd failed her somehow, as if she were grieving . . . because he was prepared to forfeit his son? He didn't even know the blasted woman!

"Good night, Miss MacShane," he snapped. "One final word:

Stay away from my son. I won't have you building up hopes that will only end in disillusionment. He's had enough pain to last him two lifetimes. I will be leaving for my place of business tomorrow at nine o'clock. On the way to the office I will deposit you in a coach that will take you wherever you are going."

"You can't mean that!"

"I may be a cad, madam, but I would hardly dump you in the streets."

"I don't care if you dump me into the Thames! You can't possibly mean that you intend to leave Gabriel alone tomorrow! It's Christmas Day!"

"I am familiar with the calendar, Miss MacShane. The date has no meaning for me—unless I care to remember it as the day the doctors told me my wife was going to die."

Alaina's lovely face went ashen, dismay flooding into rare amber eyes. She reached out, taking his large hand in her small, warm one. It seemed an eternity since anyone had touched him.

"I'm sorry, Tristan." She called him by name, that lilting Irish voice wrapping about the syllables with unbearable sweetness, as if she'd used it a thousand times. "But your wife is dead. Gabriel is alive. This is the child's first Christmas without his mother. You should make this holiday as bright as possible for him, so he won't spend the time remembering—"

"You think a kissing bough and some holly can make Gabriel forget the loss of his mother?" Tristan demanded, pulling away from her tender grasp.

"No. But I—"

"Miss MacShane, my son will remain in my household another two weeks only. If I chose to carpet this house in holly, it wouldn't change anything. His mother is dead. And he will be far better off settled elsewhere."

Dismay flooded her face. "Tristan, you're sending your own son away? You're his father!"

Guilt lanced deep. "I'm closing up the house and selling it. I'll take rooms above my office, and Gabriel will live with his aunt. It will be better not to foster any tender memories this Christmas that would make the parting more difficult."

She was gaping at him as if he'd plunged a knife in her breast. He could feel her bleeding for the child, her eyes huge and heavy with the sorrow Tristan had brought to her. Why the devil should a complete stranger be so devastated by his decision? Why did her reaction lance to the farthest reaches of Tristan's soul, making him feel barren and brutal and lost?

"I was wrong about you." Her voice cracked on a whisper. "You don't deserve a son like Gabriel."

Anguish coursed through Tristan, because he knew that she was right. He sucked in a burning breath, his gaze searing into hers.

"When you talk to God tonight, Miss MacShane, perhaps you can convince him to make other arrangements for the child." Tristan spun on his heel and stalked away to his cold, empty bed, a lifetime of regret, and to dreams he knew would be haunted by an auburn-haired angel.

Alaina stared after him, feeling battered, bewildered. What had happened to him in the years she'd been away? What horrible events had transformed the laughing, sensitive, kind Tristan she had known into this cold embittered man? A man who treated his son like a stranger—who would leave the child alone on Christmas, then cast him onto an aunt's doorstep because it was no longer convenient to keep him?

She shivered, as disillusioned as if she had scooped up a handful of jewels and discovered that they were bits of colored glass, cutting her, deep.

There isn't any magic . . . Gabriel's voice echoed in her mind.

When you talk to God . . . *make other arrangements* . . . Tristan's cold words hung like a challenge in the room. She might have been able to hate him, if she'd not seen his eyes—dark and wounded and hopeless.

Her chin jutted up in sudden defiance. Perhaps she would make other arrangements after all.

TRISTAN HAD AWAKENED ON MANY CHRISTMAS MORNINGS, yet never one so bleak as this. He stared at his reflection in the mirror, his hands fumbling over the knot of his cravat. Dark circles smudged the skin beneath his eyes; there was an unaccustomed pallor to his face. Lines of strain carved deep about his mouth. He looked as if he'd spent the night battling for his soul. In a way, he supposed he had—with a flame-haired angel who had drifted into his world with the subtle magic of a child's Christmas wish.

He had spent hours wrestling with the mad notion that the woman might be the answer to his problems—the temporary governess he needed so desperately—and then had raged at himself for even considering such insanity. The woman was a total stranger, quite possibly touched in the head. And Gabriel would have a difficult enough time adjusting to the changes about to take place in his life without Alaina MacShane whispering to him about star wishes and angels and Christmas magic.

She was nothing but trouble. Tristan was certain of it. Then why had he spent his own dreams reaching for her in the night—his hands closing on coverlets, his fevered mind conjuring images of petal-soft skin and fiery hair and golden eyes with all the joy and pain and compassion of the heavens above?

He'd spent his dreams trying to explain to her how he'd lost his soul somewhere on a journey he'd never intended to make. And he'd begged forgiveness of an angel he wanted to fall into his arms.

But she'd only said to him, in that sad, soft voice, what he already knew . . .

You don't deserve a son like Gabriel.

Tristan yanked at the knot of his cravat, the neckcloth impossibly mussed, the face above it set in the lines of the damned. She would be gone, soon. Out of his house. Out of his life. Like Gabriel.

He opened the door and stalked down to her chamber, intending to get the parting over with as hastily as possible—hopefully before Gabriel awakened, Gabriel with his unnatural attachment to the woman who had brought a wisp of Christmas into his life.

Yet, as he approached the doorway where he'd left Alaina MacShane the night before, he saw it stood wide open, sunshine streaming through it to pool in the corridor.

He hastened his step, glancing into the room. It was as if she had never existed. Nothing was out of place, the coverlets smooth. His heart gave an odd thud. She was gone.

He should be rejoicing. If he'd had any sense at all, he would have flung the woman out last night, before she could stir up trouble in the first place. What insanity had prompted him to allow a complete stranger to sleep under his roof anyway? It would serve him right if the woman had stolen every bit of silver in the place.

But there had been only one treasure Alaina MacShane had shown interest in, Tristan realized with a jolt. Gabriel, with his angel-gold curls and dark, solemn eyes. Gabriel, who had trusted her completely.

Tristan swore, alarm making his heart pound with dread. He raced to his son's room, his belly knotted, his fists clenched, his mind in fierce denial. The nursery was silent. The bed . . .

Tristan ran over to it, his gaze fixing on the smooth coverlets, the pillow still crushed into a soft hollow where Gabriel had dreamed. Yet most horrifying of all was the fact that the threadbare stuffed horse lay there, abandoned. Even if Gabriel had been swept up to heaven, he would have clutched that treasured toy.

What if the woman had stolen Gabriel away? Taken him? And the child had gone with her believing that she was an angel sent by his mother?

Perhaps you can convince God to make other arrangements . . . the bitter words of the night before echoed in his mind.

He wheeled, then raced through the corridor, bellowing his son's name, desperation squeezing his heart. Cook hobbled from the kitchen; Burrows hastened to Tristan as fast as his gouty leg could carry him.

"Master Tristan, what is it? What's wrong?" Burrows demanded.

"It's Gabriel. Have you seen Gabriel?"

Cook paled. "Why, no, sir. I thought he was still abed. Didn't wake him, poor lamb. No point, what with Christmas canceled."

"Sweet Jesus," Tristan gasped, more prayer than curse. "Search the house—every cranny. There was a woman here last night—She must've taken him."

"A woman, sir?" Burrows gaped at him as if he'd said a

mermaid had taken up residence in Cook's washtub. "But how . . . Who . . ."

"She broke into the house, and I let her stay." Tristan cursed himself. "I let her stay."

"You let a stranger . . ." Cook began, then swallowed hard, flushing scarlet at her own impertinence for questioning her master. "Even so," she said, "that don't necessarily mean the lady took him. He might be playin' one o' those games he's so fond of up in the attic. Says he don't disturb anyone there."

Tristan didn't need the mournful look in Cook's eyes to realize what the servant was saying. Gabriel took his games to the attic so he wouldn't disturb his father.

"I'm going out to search," Tristan said. "You rake through every inch of this house. If you find him . . ." *Tell him I'm sorry. Tell him I didn't mean it. Tell him I love him . . .* The words turned bitter in Tristan's mouth because he knew he'd never have the strength to say them aloud.

"We'll let you know when we find him, sir," the butler assured his master.

Tristan rushed out the front door. Last night's storm had left London a wonderland of white, drifts smoothing out the slope of the stairs and thickening the branches of the trees, crowning the lampposts and masking the cobblestone carriage circle.

Where was he even going to begin to look? Tristan wondered. His heart leapt as he noticed two pairs of footprints leading away from the house in the new-fallen snow. One the tiny imprint of a child's boot. Gabriel.

The marks rounded to the garden. Doubtless the woman had taken him out the back gate because she didn't want anyone to witness her abducting the child. Panic jolted through Tristan, and he ran, hoping that carts and horses and holiday travelers wouldn't have obliterated the footprints beyond the back gate.

He ran along the path his son had taken, praying in spite of himself. He'd just rounded a tangle of dead rose vines when he heard a sound, high-pitched, breathless. A cry of alarm? Gabriel? Had the boy realized Alaina was trying to steal him away?

Tristan charged past the brick wall that enclosed the garden, ready to throttle the woman who had dared take his son. But he'd barely breached the wall when he froze in his tracks.

He'd pictured a thousand horrifying possibilities in the time since he'd discovered his son was missing. Gabriel, struggling in Alaina MacShane's arms, terrified as she dragged him away, or, worse, his little boy oblivious in innocence, being cozened along the path to danger with peppermint drops or tales about star magic and heaven. But none of these visions prepared him for what he saw.

His solemn, earnest son was rolling in the new-fallen snow like a puppy, his frost-nipped cheeks red, his nose pink, his coat covered with snow, while Alaina MacShane heaped armfuls of downy whiteness over his squirming little body.

"You want a cheery snowman, Gabriel Ramsey," Alaina cried. "I'll make you into one myself!"

Another armful of snow rained down on the child, and his cherubic lips rounded over a squeal that struck Tristan to the soul.

Laughter. The sound he'd heard was his son's laughter. Tristan's heart cracked at the knowledge that it was a sound so rare he hadn't recognized it a moment before.

He stood, unable to move, staring at a child as different from the solemn ghost that drifted through the halls of Ramsey House as a unicorn was from a dray horse. And Tristan knew instinctively what enchantress had worked such astonishing sorcery—the woman whose face glowed with the rare beauty of a winter-born rose, her auburn hair tumbled in silken petals about her face, her cloak tangled and mussed from rolling about in the snow with his son.

"Stop, Laney!" the boy squealed. "I have to finish the snowman now! Papa'll miss his hat!"

She caught Gabriel by the toe of a boot, dragging him back to her, tickling his neck through the thick wrapping of his woolen muffler. "Your father will miss his hat, will he? Good! I can't wait to return it to him before he goes!" Gabriel howled in delight, but there was an underlying edge in Alaina's voice that the perceptive child didn't hear. One that displayed in crystal clarity what Alaina MacShane thought of the owner of that hat.

Gabriel wriggled away from her and scrambled to his feet, a fresh drift of snow cascading over his eyes, blinding him. "You can't catch me, Laney! You can't catch me!" he cried, scampering away in an effort to escape. Instead, Gabriel slammed headlong into the rigid form of his father.

Gabriel cried out in dismay as Tristan reached out to steady him, and the child's eyes rounded in alarm as they locked on his father's face. Tristan's gut clenched. Was he such a monster that he could drive the joy from his son's face in a heartbeat?

He strove with all his might to gentle the harsh lines of his features, yet the pain, the self-loathing, was so strong Tristan was certain Gabriel's too-wise eyes would discern it.

"P-Papa. I thought you were getting ready to go. To the office, I mean," the child stammered.

"Tristan!" Why did his Christian name sound so natural on Alaina's lips as she cried it out? She struggled to her feet, a halo of shimmering snow fluttering from every fold of her cape, her face alight with hope. "You decided to stay home? I'm so very glad."

For an instant, he drowned in the loveliness of her smile, warmed himself in the golden approval shining in those impossibly beautiful eyes. Then he remembered just how horribly frightened he'd been moments before, when he'd thought she'd taken his son. *Taken the son he was about to give away freely,* a grim voice echoed inside him. The thought made him angry, made him ache.

He leveled at her the glare that made the clerks at Ramsey and Ramsey quake in their shoes. "I was about to leave for the office when I discovered Gabriel missing, and—" What the devil could he say? *I thought you had stolen him away because I told you to make other arrangements for him?* Tristan felt like a fool. "Exactly what is this all about?" he demanded, gesturing to the maze of footprints and snowballs strewn across the winter-white garden.

Gabriel sidled away from him, pressing close against Alaina's snow-covered skirts, his chin thrust out at an uncharacteristically obstinate angle. "Alaina said that you were very sorry you had to go to work on Christmas. But since you did, she'd spend the day with me doing the most wondrous things."

Tristan's cheekbones stung at the knowledge that the woman had attempted to sugar-gild the truth—that Gabriel's father was such a selfish bastard he'd said Christmas be damned, despite his seven-year-old son. He started to protest, then stopped. Bastard he might be, but not enough of one to tell the cruel truth and extinguish the starshine in his child's eyes.

"We've already bought some holly from a holly cart and some gingerbread for breakfast. The cookie was so cunning, Papa, made in the shape of a tiny little man with currant eyes and buttons. It made me sorry to nibble off his legs and arms, but he tasted so very good I couldn't help myself."

"I see." Tristan did, far too well. The woman was still defying him. Defying him, but also making his little boy laugh.

"And we made a snowman, Papa, that was s'posed to look like you, with your hat and walking stick and all. But when

Alaina made the face it was all scowly. I told her it couldn't stay that way."

Alaina shook back her snow-dusted fall of curls. "Gabriel was just about to fashion the bits of coal into a smile." Why did those words weigh like stones in Tristan's soul? Alaina patted Gabriel's cheek. "You run along and do it now, young man, so your papa can see it."

Tristan wanted his son to wheel around and race to the snowman towering beside a stone bench. He hadn't realized how much he wanted Gabriel laughing and hurtling about, flinging armfuls of snow while his eyes sparkled like the ice-bright flakes that drifted to the ground. But Gabriel walked to the snowman and earnestly began to fashion the coal-chunk frown Alaina had made into a lopsided smile.

Silence fell, so heavy Tristan felt as if he couldn't breathe. In the end, Alaina broke it, her voice so soft Gabriel almost couldn't hear it. "That is all the child wants in the world, Tristan. To see you smile."

Tristan's hands knotted into fists as the words splashed acid on the guilt and resentment he had carried so long—from the year that Gabriel had been born and his own dreams had died.

But that inner death wasn't Gabriel's fault, a voice railed within him. It had never been Gabriel's fault.

Alaina's voice jarred him from the thought. "Do you remember how badly you wanted a pony the year you were twelve?" she asked. "And when you got it—all golden and cream—how elated you were?"

How could she know him to the core of his soul, know so many secrets? Tristan turned burning eyes to hers, shaken, old wounds ripped open. "I remember. But how could you possibly—"

"When I overheard Gabriel's Christmas wish last night, he offered to give up everything—Christmas and puddings and

241

playing Snap Dragon. Even the pony he wants so desperately. He said that he'd trade it all away if his papa would just smile again."

It would have been more merciful if she'd thrust a dagger in Tristan's chest.

"It broke my heart to hear him, Tristan. But what drove me to—to break into your house last night, to bring the kissing bough and the ribbons, was what Gabriel said last of all. He'd been talking to his mother, you see, up in heaven. He said there wasn't any magic, Tristan. And if that was so, then maybe there weren't even any angels."

Tristan raised one hand to the burning void where his heart had once been. God in heaven, he'd never known he could hurt so damn deeply.

"Papa?" Tristan started at the sound of Gabriel's voice. The child had taken the top hat from beside the snowman, carrying it upside down by its brim. Tristan's eyes devoured the sweet curves of his son's little face, the cherub-pink lips, the dark-lashed eyes that had stared out the window so often of late. Now Tristan knew what Gabriel had been searching for. Angels. Magic. The mama who would never return.

"You'll need this when you go to work," the little boy said. "Alaina picked the very shiniest bit of holly for the brim. She said you deserved to look your very handsomest since you are going to work on Christmas."

"Did she, now?" Tristan knew exactly what Miss MacShane thought he deserved. Whatever torment she'd devised, it wasn't bad enough.

"She worked and worked on it, and was so excited about taking the hat back in and putting it on your shelf to surprise you. She said she couldn't wait. Isn't she the nicest angel?"

She'd dealt Tristan the most savage blow his heart had ever

known. Yet Tristan could only thank her for it—for opening his eyes, for showing him the vast emptiness that had once been his heart. And for making him see Gabriel—really see him—for the first time since Charlotte had died. He'd be damned if he'd hurt the boy further in what little time was left to them.

"The hat is . . . quite festive." Tristan reached for it, but Alaina intercepted it.

"Please, Mr. Ramsey. Allow me." She made a great show of brushing the snowflakes from top hat's brim with her mittened hand. Tristan watched her, suddenly wary at the light in those amber eyes. There was such understanding, compassion, forgiveness, and something that shook him to the core—something akin to . . . love?

No. That was absurd, moon madness that had crept into the window with Alaina and Christmas wishes and Gabriel's dreams. He needed to get away for a little while, to pull himself together, to sort out what this all meant. Alaina and the magic, angels and kissing boughs, and Gabriel, willing to sacrifice everything just to see his father smile. Once Tristan reached Ramsey and Ramsey, he'd be able to think straight again.

Tristan raised the tall-crown beaver to put it on his head. A hatful of snow cascaded down his face. It chilled his cheeks, spilled into his mouth, and slipped beneath his collar to rain a frigid path down his bare skin. Gabriel gaped at him, aghast. But the infernal woman beside him was positively beaming.

"You see, Gabriel," she said, smiling up at Tristan with soul-searing delight. "I told you I couldn't wait to return your papa's hat. In fact, I'm sure he knows exactly how much I was looking forward to it." She looked so damned pleased with herself—brash as a pickpocket who had just filched a particularly plum watch.

He should be furious with her or at least under white-faced

control, not allowing her to know she'd ruffled him. He should be stinging and angry and hurting. Why did the frigid wash of snow cool the hot guilt inside him, soothe his regrets?

Tristan felt his mouth widening in the first smile he'd been tempted to since Charlotte's death. He removed his snow-spoiled hat and examined it for a long moment. Perhaps he really *had* run mad, Tristan mused.

Moved by devils he couldn't name, he methodically filled the hat with snow again, then turned it over on top of Gabriel's head. The boy laughed and skittered away under a miniature avalanche, the oversize hat dropping almost to his nose.

"But I didn't play the trick on you, Papa!" he cried, thrusting one mittened hand at Alaina. "She did!"

"Is that so?" Tristan stalked Alaina with a measured stride, his gaze fixed on hers. Just as she scooped up her skirts to run, he lunged, capturing her in his arms. "You know so much about me, Miss MacShane, perhaps you remember the penalty for throwing snow at Ramsey House. No one was better at revenge than I was."

He scooped up a handful of snow from the bench and planted it squarely on that cheeky grin. Alaina laughed and sputtered, not even trying to get free. Tristan drank in the warmth of her, the vitality, the pure joy in snowflakes and holly sprigs and snowmen that Gabriel made smile.

Suddenly she stilled, her face spangled with melting snow—glowing pink, her eyes wide, her lips trembling. Tristan felt a wrenching in his chest that he couldn't deny, felt himself drawn along the crystal magic this woman had spun on a Christmas morning.

He wanted to kiss her. Wanted it with a ferocity that made his chest burn, his throat ache.

This was madness. Impossible. These feelings she was unleashing in him, the way she plunged deep into his heart. Who was she? he wondered with raw desperation. Where had she come from?

Yet, for the first time, he found himself almost as bewitched as Gabriel, afraid to reach his hand through the veil of magic to grasp reality. Damnation, what was happening to him? A frisson of pure terror sizzled through him.

"Gabriel." Tristan bit out the child's name more harshly than he intended. The boy's eyes widened, and he stood very still. "Take my hat in to Burrows to see if he can dry it." Gabriel's rosy face turned crestfallen.

"Yes, Papa. But please, please, don't be angry with Alaina. Maybe angels don't know any better than to fill hats up with snow. I'll watch her more careful, I promise. I won't let her get in any more mischief if you let her stay!"

"Do as I told you, Gabriel." Tristan battled to gentle his voice, hating the unhappiness that flooded his son's face. "But mind that you tell Burrows to take care with my holly," he added. "And have Cook stir up some chocolate for you, nice and hot."

"But, Papa, my angel—"

"Miss MacShane and I have some matters to discuss— alone."

"But you won't leave without saying good-bye, will you, Laney?" the child pleaded. "You promised not to leave me all Christmas Day!"

"I keep my promises, Gabriel."

For a moment the child hovered in an agony of indecision. Then he cast one more glance at the woman who had made him believe in magic. He turned and ran out of the garden.

Tristan watched his son go and battled for inner balance, groped for some hold on all that had happened since Alaina MacShane had tumbled from a tower of chairs into his arms and into his life. In the end, he clutched on to blessed logic. He was a reasonable, rational man. Surely there must be a way to handle one small boy and a woman who crawled in through unlocked windows.

"You deliberately defied me, Miss MacShane," Tristan said in measured accents. "I suppose I could be angry with you. However, I hope I'm man enough to admit when I am mistaken. You were right to stay with Gabriel. I see that now."

"You do?" Had there ever been such wide, welcoming eyes? Such a soul-melting smile? It was all Tristan could do not to reach out and touch it.

"Gabriel has been lonely for some time. He needs a governess for the remaining time he is at Ramsey House."

"A-a governess—but you barely know me."

"And what I *do* know about you hardly qualifies you as the kind of steady, responsible woman who should be in charge of a nursery. But it's obvious someone needs to look after the boy. Normally, I'd ask for references, but you've already demonstrated your skill with Gabriel. He's become quite attached to you."

"He's a darling child. Affectionate and so tenderhearted. Any governess would be lucky to have a child like Gabriel put in her care. But I . . . I intended to leave London altogether after last night."

Why was the notion of her leaving suddenly alarming? "I'm hardly asking you to move in permanently. I will need you for two weeks only. After that, Gabriel will be joining my sister's household. I suppose even a lunatic . . . *or an angel* couldn't get in too much trouble in such a short length of time." He softened the words with a half-smile.

"I-I don't know what to say." Alaina gazed up at him with an eternity of secrets in her face, secrets that seemed to plumb straight to Tristan's soul, to make him want to discover what lay beyond the sunlight-on-honey hue that was her eyes.

"You were willing to commit larceny on my son's behalf," Tristan said gently. "Surely you could be persuaded to take gainful employment? I will make it worth your while. However, there are conditions."

"Conditions?"

"No more of this Christmas nonsense. I won't tolerate it."

"Surely it can't hurt to play a few games—"

"Play anything you wish as long as you do so far away from me. And no more nonsense about angels or magic. I don't want the boy disillusioned when you go away."

"Do you really believe I could hurt Gabriel?"

"Let's just say that, unlike my son, I do not believe in angels, wishes upon stars, or miracles that drop from heaven, even when they come tangled up in holly and ivy and kissing boughs."

A sudden, sharp sorrow stung her features.

"I don't know who you are or why you've come," Tristan continued. "But I do know that Gabriel needs you for a little while. Of course you did say you had somewhere else to be. If so, Gabriel can be made to understand that you have another commitment."

She gazed up at him, something unnerving in her eyes. "I thought my work here was finished. But maybe I was wrong."

Tristan's brow furrowed. She spoke as if she'd come here for some purpose. Drifted down on moonbeams.

Tristan's jaw clenched. Damn the woman, why was she looking at him that way? Luminous eyes, bruised with disappointment, as if he'd failed her somehow. As if she were hoping—for what? Miracles from him? Miracles he'd never been able to give to anyone, not even his wife or his son?

It didn't matter, he told himself sharply. He wouldn't even have to see her in this huge house. It was only for two weeks. Two weeks, and then Gabriel and his angel would be gone.

Five

THE ATTIC BLOOMED LIKE A CHAOTIC FLOWER GARDEN, BURST-
ing with color. Ballgowns and petticoats well past their first
blush, outmoded frock coats and impossibly bright waistcoats,
blossomed in disarray over the edges of the trunks Gabriel had
pilfered for costumes to use in the game of charades that had
whiled away the afternoon.

His grandmama's turban had graced the head of the dread
infidel Saladin, while silver gauze had gilded Richard the Lion
Heart with regal magnificence. Marie Antoinette had lost her
head, and Sir Lancelot had saved his Guinevere from the flames.

Dozens of games and hours of laughter had almost disguised
the fact that it was Christmas and that almost every other house
was bursting with family and laughter and good cheer.

Alaina looked down at her small charge, who had curled
himself up on a mountain of cast-off clothes, his last ginger
cookie drooping from his fingers as he slept. She wished that
Tristan could see him.

Tristan, with his sad eyes and his implacable mouth, his
broad shoulders carrying pain he wouldn't acknowledge even to
himself, let alone anyone else. Tristan, who had smiled for just a
heartbeat in the garden, snow sprinkling his ebony hair and
glistening in angel kisses upon the chiseled contours of that
starkly beautiful masculine face.

She'd been so angry with him the night before, this man who
had become so hurt and disillusioned in the years she'd been
away from the window. But in that stark moment in the garden
when she'd stared into eyes that were suddenly naked, vulnerable, she saw a shadow of the Tristan she had known: a man,

sensitive, kind, loving, staring at her through cold bars of a prison of guilt and self-loathing.

Her heart had broken for him, and she knew that if she held the deed to every star in the heavens, she would gladly have traded all their shimmering beauty to put the light back in Tristan's eyes.

She ranged about the attic, her gaze tracing a rocking horse with a crooked leg, too unsteady for another child's play, yet too beloved to be cast into the rubbish heap. The nook beneath the eaves was filled with cherished memories, bits and pieces of childhood, legacies of first dances and weddings, mourning brooches and castaway dreams.

Alaina wandered to the corner, searching for pieces of the Tristan she had loved for so long—letters home from the years he'd been a scholar at Harrow, an abandoned cricket bat.

A leather-covered volume was tucked beneath a broken fan, and Alaina drew it out, running her fingers over the legend embossed in gold upon the cover: *Charlotte Sophia Koenig, Her Journal.*

Alaina tensed, catching her lip between her teeth. Charlotte . . . this journal had belonged to Tristan's wife. She should put it back among the cobwebs, where layers of dust could dull the edges of the broken dreams it held. A life cut short, a love robbed by death.

She had no business prying through its pages. And yet, where else would she have a better chance to discover the truth, the secrets that had changed the Tristan who had given Alaina his Christmas guinea so long ago?

I can't, she cried inside herself, *can't bear to read how he kissed her, courted her. How they fell in love. It would hurt too much . . .*

And her imagination had already tormented her with images

of the delicate blonde in Tristan's arms, his mouth dipping down to capture her mouth in love's first kiss.

But the journal might hold the key to helping him . . .

She let it fall open to the middle, the inked lines spinning into focus. *Tristan asked me to marry him today . . .*

The words were like a knife to her heart. She shut the book and shoved it back onto the shelf, almost tripping over a sheet-draped mound in her haste to get away.

A wooden clatter sounded; something had tipped over beneath the mound and landed a sharp blow on her instep.

She reached down to straighten it, caught a glimpse of something dull gold beneath the white cloth. Guilt jabbed her as she took hold of a corner of the drape. What was she doing, prying into things that were none of her business? Why was she so compelled to keep rooting around the attic, searching for pieces of a childhood she'd never experienced, keepsakes of the family she'd never been part of, yet claimed as her own?

One peek only, she assured herself, slipping the sheeting back from what it concealed. She gasped as the faint light from the window fell upon a cluster of paintings, some framed, others mere canvases, jumbled together as if someone had shoved them here, pell-mell, to get them out of sight.

The first canvas portrayed a cream and gold pony caparisoned like a knight's steed of old, a childish Beth Ramsey seated upon it in the guise of a fairy-tale princess. The scene was so real, so filled with the beauty only children could see, that it stole Alaina's breath away. In the corner, the name *Tristan Ramsey* had been signed with a flourish.

She moved that portrait aside, her gaze scanning a still life of roses, a slipper, a fan, and a filled dance card with the name *Allison* painted on it—a tender tribute to the first ball of the sister Tristan had adored.

A boy's voice echoed in her memory, his boast ringing out against a crisp winter wind: *I'm going to be the greatest artist who ever lived.* . . .

She had believed in him, with every fiber of her child heart, but never had she imagined the reality of such remarkable talent, Tristan's own unique vision. Shape and color cast a spell so real her finger stole out to touch a drop of dew on a rose petal, and she half expected her skin to come away wet.

He was brilliant, Alaina thought numbly, his paintings holding that indefinable quality that would make eyes hunger to see them as long as there was a forever.

The next image elicited hollow pain in Alaina's chest: the young woman Tristan had loved, garbed in the gown she'd worn when he'd made her his wife. Every brushstroke was alive with hope and tenderness. Every hue glowed with passion and promise. How had everything gone so horribly awry? Had he been unable to paint because Charlotte had died?

Had Tristan lost his gift of painting as Alaina's father had lost the melodies that wound like a silver ribbon through his soul, too wounded to care anymore, to try anymore? Yet Thomas MacShane had been weak, for all his brilliance, where Tristan's dark eyes had blazed with inner strength. And the tiny numbers scribed in the corner of the paintings didn't record dates up to the time of Charlotte's death, but rather ended abruptly three years after Tristan's marriage.

Alaina started to pull the drape back down over the image, unable to bear looking at her another moment, when suddenly a small canvas toppled over. She straightened it, then froze. Of all the paintings she'd seen, this one pierced to the core of her heart.

An angel. Pale silver-gold curls haloed a face like a pink and white rose—perfection was captured in dark, laughing eyes as a chubby hand reached up to capture a star. Yet the hand wasn't finished, the dream unfulfilled. The brushstrokes ended, leaving only the artist's sketch of that grasping little hand forever longing for what it could never have.

What could have possessed Tristan to leave this unfinished? It was a masterpiece. One that could make heaven itself cry. It was like staring into Tristan's own heart, and it made her aware of just how much this man had lost.

There was a creak on the stairs, but Alaina didn't even look up. Her eyes were too filled with tears.

"Gabriel? Alaina?" Tristan's voice—uncertain, searching. She knew instinctively he'd been drawn to the attic by forces he couldn't resist. She knew, too, that she should cover the paintings, like a wound too raw to be touched by air, but she couldn't bring herself to extinguish the rare force of Tristan's world captured on canvas.

"It's past time for supper—" His words broke off, and Alaina could feel Tristan's eyes on her where she stood, silhouetted against the paintings he had done. She felt as if he'd caught her prying inside his soul.

"Tristan." She turned to him, aware of everything about him—his wind-tossed hair, his square-cut jaw, the muscle-honed perfection of his body, yet mostly, the raw expression in his eyes.

"I suppose I should say that I'm sorry," she stammered. "But I'm not. They're the most brilliant paintings I've ever seen."

"Not many artists up in heaven, eh? One would think Michelangelo would have received some special dispensation after all the work he put in on the Sistine Chapel." He was attempting to make light of his childhood dream. But she could still see the emotion stripped bare in his gaze.

"Tristan, I mean it. Your paintings are magnificent. I knew

you wanted to be an artist. I just never suspected you were this gifted. These should be displayed where people can see them, not stuffed in the attic."

Tristan gave a bitter laugh. "The attic is where they belong. They're nothing but rubbish—a waste of time and effort."

"How can you say that? Surely if you have the skill to create such wondrous things, you have the ability to recognize true genius when you see it. You must have had every artist in Rome ready to teach you."

"Rome?"

"You were going to Rome, to study. It was all you'd ever dreamed of. I remember—"

"I do my damndest to forget." His eyes clashed with hers, uncertain, confused, yet this time he didn't bother to question how she knew. He jerked the cloth until it spilled back over the jumble of paintings. It was as if he'd reached up and snuffed out the sun. "Those dreams and aspirations were a boy's fantasies. They were never real."

"I don't believe that! Your trunks were packed. You were leaving for Italy. You and your bride—" Alaina choked out the words, remembering the slashing pain that had accompanied the knowledge that Tristan was married. Remembering how she had run away from that stark reality, devastated herself, and yet glad that Tristan at last had everything he wanted. "Why, Tristan? Why didn't you go?"

His features drew into a grim mask, one that almost hid the half-forgotten sense of loss. "There was some difficulty at Ramsey and Ramsey. I found I had a knack for straightening it out. A head for business, my father called it. There was money to be made, deals to be struck. Things that were far more important than dabbling at art."

There was more, so much more, but Alaina knew he

wouldn't tell her. Not now. She looked into those dark, guarded eyes and wondered if he would ever tell her the true depths of his pain.

"It's time to eat. Cook prefers that her dishes be served while they're still warm." He turned to his son, shaking the child gently by the shoulder. "Gabriel, wake up," he said. "It's dinner time."

Gabriel yawned and blinked and smiled—a cookie-crumb-dusted smile that Alaina could see struck Tristan to the heart.

"Papa? We played the most delicious games. Alaina got her head cut off, and I got to rob the rich."

"Wonderful. Next Miss MacShane will be teaching you housebreaking," Tristan muttered.

"No," Gabriel said. "Next we get to set the house afire. She promised."

"Did she?" Tristan arched one brow at Alaina.

"I promised we could play that delightful game where you snatch things from a bowl full of flames. You know the one— you were always so good at it."

"Snap Dragon?"

"That's the one! Cook promised if I came in after dinner, she would help me fix it up."

"I'd wager the woman would do anything you asked. You've already got her singing your praises."

Alaina smiled. "I wish you would join us, Tristan."

For a heartbeat she could see a flicker of yearning in those chocolate-colored eyes, as if he were tempted. Then he shook his head. "No. I've a great deal of work to do before morning." He turned and walked down the stairs.

Alaina cast one more glance toward the paintings. It was so easy to imagine him up in a garret, painting until his eyes blurred and his hand trembled with exhaustion, so easy to imagine the satisfaction that would transform his face as he completed each image. Why was it she couldn't imagine him barricaded in some shipping office, monitoring voyages to places he would never see, counting up bolts of silk, bales of tobacco, and kegs of brandy he didn't care about?

Alaina stood, her knees aching from the hardness of the floor. She peeked one more time beneath the veiling of white sheet at the angel reaching for a star. How had Tristan Ramsey had lost his dream?

Glancing after Tristan and Gabriel, she took the leather diary from its shelf and tucked it in her apron pocket. Somewhere in the journal she just might find the answer.

The kitchen was a shambles, piles of dishes and pots and pans littering the large worktable in the center of the room, when Alaina poked her head through the door after dinner. Cook glanced up from her washbasin, a smile of welcome softening her old face, while Burrows, the dignified butler, helped her to dry a large platter. The two had embraced her as if she were their long-lost daughter the instant they had heard Gabriel laugh.

And Alaina had adored them on sight, their honest, hard-working faces beautiful to her because of the warmth that radiated from them both.

"I came to get the bowl for Snap Dragon," she explained, "but you're obviously much too busy—"

"Too busy for you, missy?" Cook said, casting aside her washrag and drying chapped hands on a towel. "May none o' me breads every rise again if I'm too busy to help an angel the like of you."

Alaina flushed. "Please, I—"

"Don't go tryin' to pretend you haven't worked a miracle, dearie. We've got eyes, the both of us. We've seen what you've done for our little Gabriel today. And it's passing grateful we are."

"I only played a few games with him. He's such a darling."

"That he is. But he's always been a somber little mite until today. Laughin' and squealin' and runnin' about, like a real child should."

"I hope we didn't disturb you."

"Disturb us? By St. Stephen's wounds, it was music to our ears, miss," Burrows said. "I only wish Master Tristan had been here to listen. I'd wager he's forgotten what it sounds like— laughter in this old place. There was a time when not a day went by without sounds o' joy."

Alaina peered up into that wistful old face. "What happened—to make the laughter stop? Tristan—I mean, your master doesn't seem to care about it anymore. And he has a child that needs it so desperately."

Burrows frowned. "You mustn't be blamin' Master Tristan, miss. It weren't his fault. He was never made for shippin' lists and hours and hours locked up in that office o' his father's."

"But he must like it. He said—"

"What'd he tell ye? That he took a dip in the pool o' commerce an' came out pure thirstin' for a lifetime o' it?" Cook asked. "Well it's a lie he's been tellin' himself for nigh on eight years now, an' the weight o' it's crushed him inside until sometimes I don't hardly recognize my boy any longer."

"I don't understand. I know he had dreams once of being an artist. But he can't even look at his artwork anymore."

"Buried it, he did. Would've done better t' bury that wife o' his instead," Cook grumbled.

Alaina's hand strayed guiltily to the weight of the journal in her apron pocket. "What was amiss with his wife?"

"Never saw a more clinging, weak-spined—"

256

"Mrs. Burrows, that's enough," Burrows warned. "It's not right to speak ill of the dead. Besides, there would still have been his father to tend."

"His father?" Alaina echoed.

"You want the truth o' what happened to Tristan, miss? He'll never tell you. The old master never thought much o' Tristan's love of art, but Tristan was so determined there was naught old Mr. Ramsey could do to dissuade him. I think he even pushed marriage on the boy in hopes that it would settle him down and he'd take to business. But Tristan was determined to go to Italy, to learn from some fancy-man painter who'd seen his work and loved it. Trunks were all packed, an' Miss Charlotte, his bride, had even swallowed up her unease about foreigners and was ready to go, when some o' the men who did business with Ramsey and Ramsey called Master Tristan down for a meetin'."

"To try to convince him to stay? That wasn't fair! Surely he could have gone forward with his plans."

"Only if he was willin' for the rest o' the family to go to ruin." Cook *tsk*ed mournfully. "Poor boy. Poor, kind boy."

"Tristan's father had headed the shipping company for years, an' his father before him. It was his pride an' joy. But the years were telling on the old master. Something—something in his mind was just broke, miss. Nothin' could fix it. An' the master, he just couldn't see what everyone else saw so clear. He'd made mistakes—little ones, but they mounted up at a dangerous rate. An' he wouldn't listen to no one—took it as a blow right to his dignity if any dared question him. Had the most horrendous temper-fits. The doctor told Master Tristan he'd seen the condition before. The mind just slippin' away, like the tide from the shore, real slow and easy, year after year until a person could look on the face o' their own mama and not know her at all."

Alaina closed her eyes, remembering the bluff, blustery man who had been Tristan's father—the man who had gotten Tristan the pony and beamed with pride in his son. The man Tristan had watched with such adoration, shored up by the mountainlike strength of his father—the rock of security who had given Tristan the strength to build his own dreams.

What must it have been like to know that he was going to lose that father, one memory at a time?

"Nothin' in the world could have kept Master Tristan away from his painting, Miss Alaina. Nothing except the need to guard his father's dignity."

"But after old Mr. Ramsey died, why didn't he go then?"

"Gabriel was born, and Master Tristan's wife was difficult. Didn't want to take her baby to some foreign land. Didn't want Master Tristan to paint at all."

Cook grimaced. "I always found it odd, don't ye know? The girl was from Germany, for pity's sake, an' she acted like she'd never traveled farther than Hyde Park. Tristan tried for a time to work with his pa in the day, then stay up late, painting when everyone else was asleep. But Miss Charlotte couldn't tolerate that either. She spurted tears like a blasted fountain every minute of the day, hanging on Master Tristan's sleeve, grudging every brushstroke as if he were stealin' the food out o' her mouth.

"They had a terrible row one night, Miss Charlotte crying and Mr. Tristan—well, he wasn't ever a boy given to anger. But that night, he was shouting something fierce. The next night I slipped into his studio, just like I done for fifteen years, to treat him to some chocolate and sweet cakes. He wasn't there. Nothin' was. The paints, the easel, the cunning picture he was painting of the baby. An angel, it was, reaching for a star. Worst of all, he'd gone through the house and stripped down every last painting he'd ever done. I think he couldn't bear to look at 'em because it hurt his heart too much."

Alaina tried to swallow past the knot in her throat. *Dear God, it must have destroyed him.*

"'Spected the impossible o' himself, that he could give away every dream he'd had an' not feel the loss, not feel resentful or angry or hurt. And above all, he'd never ask anyone else for help t' deal with all that had fallen on his shoulders. He just took on responsibility for all of it, silent as a stone, an' no one ever asked him if the load were too heavy." The old woman peered at Alaina. "I know he can seem hard and cold, but he's a good man, miss. Just tired and sad. Lost his way, that's all. If ever a man was deservin' of a guardian angel, miss, it's Tristan Ramsey."

Alaina swallowed a lump in her throat, her eyes burning. "I know."

"You made Gabriel laugh today," old Burrows said. "If you could do the same for my Tristan, I vow, I'd claim you was an angel myself."

Here was another person, wanting so desperately for Tristan to find joy. How many Christmas wishes had drifted up to heaven carrying that plea? Alaina wondered. Surely such prayers must be answered.

She scooped up the bowl of dried fruits Cook had prepared, the plums all covered with brandy, ready for the touch of a spark to turn the bowl into a snapping dragon so that Gabriel could attempt to snatch treats from the blue flames.

She knew now how Tristan had lost himself—once again trying to be kind and giving—the wonderful boy she had fallen in love with on a winter-white Christmas day so long ago.

Surely if she tried hard enough, she could find him again.

Six

FLAMES LEAPT AND WRITHED, BLUE-SILVER, BRIGHT ORANGE, in the darkened room, dancing above the plump bits of fruit that lay in tempting disarray beneath. Gabriel popped one in his mouth, smacking his lips in delight. "It's your turn now, Alaina!" the child chirruped. "Just concentrate real hard and grab!"

Yet Alaina couldn't concentrate on anything except the man sequestered in his study down the hall.

"Alaina, is there something the matter?"

She looked down to see Gabriel's babe-soft brow furrow, his mouth turn down in a frown of concern. How good had the boy gotten at reading the shifting moods of his elders? His mother's disappointment, his father's hidden pain? How often had Gabriel struggled to mend the tears in his family with hands too small for such a daunting task?

She forced a smile and plunged her hand into the bowl, scooping out a handful of the slippery fruit, but the flame nipped at her sleeve, a tiny tongue catching hold of the cloth.

"Alaina! You're on fire!" Gabriel cried in alarm, but the flames had barely licked at her skin before Alaina extinguished them. "I'm fine," she said nursing the reddening patch on her finger and wrist.

She heard heavy footsteps rushing into the room and was stunned as Tristan grabbed her arm, dousing it in a pail of water Cook had set nearby.

"How did you get here so quickly?" Alaina demanded. "One would think you were right outside the door!"

A dull flush crept up his cheekbones. "I happened to be passing by on my way to—to get a drink."

Alaina's heart stopped, and she smiled at him, hope fluttering inside her. He must have been watching them, wanting to join them, though he'd never admit it.

"I burned my finger," she said, displaying it to him in the light spilling from the corridor.

"That's what happens when you get too greedy, madam. Gabriel, go outside for a cupful of clean snow. That will cool Miss MacShane's finger."

"I always pop my finger right in my mouth," Gabriel suggested.

"Do as I asked, please."

The boy skipped out, leaving Alaina with Tristan, one of his strong hands enveloping her burned one. But the fire she felt inside was far more disturbing than the nip of the tiny flame. Heat shimmered out from where those long fingers cupped hers. It swirled along the delicate skin of her arm and flowed in hot, pulsing waves into her breasts.

"Isn't greed one of the Seven Deadly Sins, Miss MacShane? You'd best be careful or you'll not be allowed back through heaven's gates."

"The plums just looked so good, I couldn't help myself."

Tristan smiled and scooped a bit of fruit from the flaming bowl without so much as singeing his knuckles. "Open your mouth," he said in a low, husky voice. Her lips parted, and he slipped his prize inside, his fingertip lingering on the bottom swell of her lip, stroking the moist curve.

"Odd, sometimes I'm not even certain you are real," Tristan said.

Alaina's gaze flashed up to his, and he caught a spark of mischief, then her teeth caught his finger.

He laughed. "So angels bite, do they? Most uncharitable."

"You're right. Perhaps I should do penance by kissing it better." Hardly believing her own daring, Alaina caught his hand and kissed the tip of his finger, wishing she could heal the wounds that cut him far deeper.

Ever so gently, she let her kiss whisper to him things she could never say—love secrets and fragments of dreams, encouragement and gratitude.

He stared at her, transfixed, the other fingers of his hand uncurling, then easing up to caress her cheek. His own lips parted. Hunger—it flared in his gaze, stripping the wariness from the ebony depths of his eyes.

"If angels can bite," he rasped, "then is it possible that they can . . . kiss? Mouth to mouth?"

"I don't know. I've never tried." Alaina felt her heart beating its way out of her chest, her lips burning with the need to taste Tristan's.

He leaned forward, and she could feel the brush of his breath, the sibilant throb of need.

At that instant, a golden-curled, snow-spangled Gabriel rushed in. "Alaina, I brought the snow to cool you off!" he cried.

Alaina knew if the child buried her in a glacier, it wouldn't extinguish the fires Tristan had lit inside them both.

She leapt up, flustered. "I think I've had enough of this game."

"Then it's time for the dancing, isn't it, Papa?" Gabriel insisted. "We all go out and dance and dance under the kissing bough."

"I don't know how to dance," Alaina protested.

"I'll show you! Aunt Beth says I am 'most dashing.' But we'll need music. Papa, please will you work the music box, 'cause I'm not allowed to touch it?"

Tristan's brows lowered, his voice gruff. "I suppose I could. But just for a little while."

In a heartbeat, Alaina was in the drawing room where she'd first tumbled into Tristan's arms, her whole body thrumming with the memory of how he had felt against her—hard and strong, ridges of muscle, rasping breath, the weight of him pressed into her soft, woman curves, fitting with the perfect harmony of stars against the heavens.

Tristan crossed to a small table on which a music box sat and tinkered with it for a moment. Light, ethereal, the music wafted through the chamber, filling it with an aura of magic. The song was familiar, plaintive, an airy tapestry of words and melody that captured the poignancy, the pain and pleasure, of first love.

Alaina took the child's small hands and capered about with him, Gabriel stumbling and laughing, swaying and turning. Yet with every movement, she was excruciatingly aware of the man standing silent by the table. His melting gaze seemed to reach out and touch her with every step she took.

After Gabriel collapsed in a fit of giggles on a chair, Alaina looked up to see Tristan crossing the room, as she'd dreamed a hundred times, the harsh planes of his face devastatingly handsome, his eyes dark with intent. She stood, breathless, hoping for something she couldn't even name. Something she'd craved forever.

His lips curved in a shadow of the smile she'd loved so well. "May I have this dance?" he asked with an elegant bow. If he had asked her for her soul, she would have given it to him gladly.

She couldn't speak. She only nodded, her heart stopping as he closed the space between them. He took her left hand in his strong right one, then curved his other arm about her waist, splaying his fingers in the hollow of her back. She barely reached his chin, and she could see the throb of his pulse in his throat, hear the uneven rasp of his breath.

"Look at me, Alaina," he said, ever so softly. She did. Her bones melted, every fiber of her being seeming to catch the rhythm of his heartbeat. The music whirled about them, and then, suddenly, Alaina felt herself floating, swirling, to a music all their own—one that seemed to sing from her heart to his.

Never had she felt so vulnerable—as if every secret were his for the taking, every corner of her soul revealed to this man who held her so tenderly, imprisoning her heart with no more than a smile.

It was more beautiful than any dream to be in his arms, to feel the power in him, the promise, as well as the pain that she would have given her own soul to heal.

After a moment, his booted feet faltered. He fell still, his eyes on hers—dark and hot as coals.

"Papa, you danced her under the kissing bough!" Gabriel cried, clapping his hands.

"I know," Tristan admitted low in his throat. Alaina trembled as his eyes narrowed, thick dark lashes drooping down to obscure confusion and need, passion and pain.

His lips closed on hers for a heartbeat—slick silk, tasting of all the dreams she'd never dared to have. Hot and moist and seeking. Supplicant and yet demanding. Promising, yet tinged with the slightest tang of fear.

Fear of what? That he was making yet another mistake? That love was impossible, like the dream he'd once had of painting masterpieces in his garret?

The kiss was over in mere seconds, but Alaina knew it had changed her forever.

"Papa?" Gabriel's worried query broke in. "Papa, I'm not certain it's all right to be kissing angels. Maybe it's against the rules. You might get struck down with lightning or something."

"I was," Tristan murmured, staring at her with astonishment, and a dark, unquenchable thirst for her shimmered in his gaze. She had dreamed a million times of seeing just such an expression on his face, yet seeing it now only made her pulse race with alarm.

She had to remember that nothing could ever come of her love for Tristan. She had known that from the beginning. Now he was reaching out to her, ever so tentatively. But even angels couldn't afford to keep their heads in the clouds. Soon she would have to leave him.

"Laney, what *are* the rules up in heaven?" Gratitude flooded through her as Gabriel's voice shook her from her troubled thoughts. "If I threw my ball way up in the sky, all the way to the stars, would God throw it back?"

"I think He would," Alaina managed shakily. "Have you ever thrown a ball up and not had it come down?"

Gabriel smiled as if she'd just unlocked the secrets to the universe, then suddenly he sobered. "I wish I could throw something up and have it stay there forever. I wish my mama could catch it."

Alaina saw Tristan wince, but he asked gently, "What do you wish you could give her, son?"

"A letter to wish her happy Christmas. They must have Christmas in heaven, since that's where it all began. But I think she might be lonely there, even with all the angels."

Alaina's throat constricted, and she remembered a solemn-eyed little Gabriel leaning out the window, wishing on the stars.

"Maybe there is a way," Alaina offered. "Tristan, do you remember when you would send your wishes up to Father Christmas? Perhaps if Gabriel wrote his letter, we could send it to heaven the same way."

A slow smile spread across Tristan's features; the sensitivity that had graced the features of the boy she'd loved was even more beautiful in the strong features of this man. "I remember," he said softly.

Gabriel looked up at him, an angel child and a hurting father, a boy fragile with dreams and a man who had abandoned them. "Will you show me what to do, Papa?"

Alaina's heart wrenched as the child slipped his small fingers into the engulfing warmth of his father's.

Tristan led the boy into his study. Alaina trailed behind. The desktop was stacked with a mountain of ledgers, neat rows of numbers on creamy sheaves of paper. Tristan shoved them aside and drew out fresh paper.

"I want you to write down everything you want to say to your mother—just as if you were sitting on the stool beside her chair. Remember how you used to do that?"

Gabriel nodded. He took up a pen, dipped its tip in the ink, and started to write. A horrible scratching sound broke the silence, a blot of ink spreading in a stain. Gabriel stared at it, horrified. "Papa, I ruined it!"

"Inkblots don't matter at all in heaven," Tristan said softly. "They melt away."

The boy gave him an uncertain smile. "Aren't you going to write to Mama, too?"

Tristan looked away, and Alaina could see the bleakness in his face—sensed that Tristan and his wife hadn't really spoken in the years after he had walled himself off with work, long before sweet-faced Charlotte had died.

After a moment, Tristan nodded. "Yes. There is something I've needed to say for a long, long time."

Gabriel worked industriously while Tristan scribed his own letter—one line, Alaina could tell, came straight from his heart. Then Tristan folded up the scrap of paper into a neat square.

Gabriel followed his father's lead, his own square lopsided, blotted, and crumpled—the kind of notes mamas had tucked away in treasure boxes since time began.

"What do we do now, Alaina?" Gabriel looked up at her expectantly.

"Let your papa show you."

Tristan guided his son to the hearth, where flames crackled and danced. "We put the messages into the flames. If the smoke goes up the chimney, then the messages float all the way to heaven. Your wish will be granted."

"But what if it isn't?"

"Then we'll have to wish again later."

Gabriel scrunched up his face and thrust his note into the flames. The edges curled and glowed as the three of them watched it burn. Alaina couldn't breathe as she willed the smoke to curl up into the chimney. The thin tendrils wound straight up as if drawn by an angel's hand.

"Papa! Papa she heard me! Mama heard me! Just like she did when she sent Alaina!" The little boy positively glowed. "Put yours in, Papa!"

Tristan knelt down and fed his own note to the flames, his shoulders rigid, his eyes dark and intent and sad.

The note burned to ash, and he watched until the last bit of smoke spiraled up on its path to the sky.

Gabriel sidled over to him, leaning against Tristan's side. "Papa, what did you ask Mama for?"

"Forgiveness." Alaina barely caught Tristan's raw whisper.

"Papa, what for?"

"Because I didn't—wasn't a very good husband to her, Gabriel. Nor a good father to you."

"I think you're a wonderful papa. It's just that you're busy and worried a lot."

"You didn't have a Christmas, Gabriel," Tristan reminded him with ruthless self-loathing.

"I got something even better. You smiled, Papa, three whole times. And besides, there'll be lots of other Christmases when you don't feel so sad."

A choked sound rose from Tristan's throat. Lots of other Christmases . . . No, this would be the last, Tristan thought with a sick clenching in his chest. The last he'd ever share in this house, alone with his little boy.

Next year everything would change. Gabriel would be with Beth and her husband, stolid, kind Henry Muldowny. Henry's hand would be the one Gabriel would hold; Henry's arms would offer comfort to the boy when Gabriel fell. Henry would teach Gabriel to ride and to play cricket, and what it meant to be a man.

The future stretched out, a bleak wasteland, and Tristan realized just how much he would be giving up when he sent Gabriel away.

The pain cut so deep, Tristan feared he'd shatter. But Gabriel would be better off without him. He had no other choice than to let him go. Tristan fought back the impulse to hold the child in his arms forever, knowing that if he did so, he'd lose the courage to send Gabriel away.

"It's time for you to go to bed, son," he said. Gabriel shot him a smile full of trust, then gave Tristan a quick, rare hug. The child had lavished hugs on Burrows and Cook, his mother and Alaina, yet so rarely on his own father.

Tristan clutched the precious weight of his son in his arms and carried the child to bed. He tucked Gabriel under the coverlets; the rag-stuffed horse was nestled on the pillow beside him. When Tristan raised his eyes, his gaze caught Alaina's as she paused in the doorway. Her eyes clung to his for a heartbeat, seeming to peer straight into his soul. Then she turned in a rustle of dove-gray skirts and disappeared.

His heart swelled and ached, burning in his chest, as if it were coming to life again for the first time in more years that he could count.

It was Alaina's doing. Alaina's. Who was she—this woman who had tunneled past his defenses, who had reached past his pain and into the secret grief of his son? Gabriel had claimed her as his angel. But as Tristan knelt there, beside the child's bed, he wondered. Had Alaina MacShane come to answer Gabriel's prayers? Or Tristan's own?

Seven

THE NIGHT WAS VAST AND DARK AND LONELY. ALAINA PRESSED her fingertips to the drawing room window and stared out into the blackness, her nightgown a gossamer whisper against her skin. The old house sighed around her, asleep like the graceful old dowager it was.

It had been hours since she had left Tristan alone with his son, hours during which she'd read the green leather journal by flickering candlelight. An eternity in which she'd paced the confines of her room, tormented by the words Charlotte Ramsey had written so long ago.

Words that had haunted her until even her lovely bedchamber became too small to hold the restlessness of her thoughts, the discoveries she'd made that would give her no rest.

All the years she'd spent peering into Tristan's window, she had drunk in the warmth of the fire, the brilliance of candle-shine and laughter, the cozy familiarity of well-worn books and beloved trinkets. And she'd believed that anyone inside that magical chamber never had to face the darkness. But she had been wrong.

Tonight she had seen just how deeply loneliness could carve

itself into a man's face. How barren his eyes could be. How cold and alone he could be even when stout bricks and rivers of light and decades of security surrounded him.

In the pages of Charlotte's journal Alaina had traced the slow destruction of his dreams and discovered how bitter the betrayal must have been when those dreams had been crushed by his own wife.

What had Tristan suffered in the years since Gabriel's birth? A loss so devastating she could still feel it pulsing through him. And yet, tonight in the drawing room, she had sensed the faintest stirring of hope as well—like flecks of gold sprinkled in a crystal-blue stream. He had reached out to Gabriel, blessed him with the comfort only Tristan could give, offered his son the gift of his own vulnerability.

A letter to heaven—Gabriel's had been filled with a child's love; Tristan's with pleas for forgiveness that curled up into smoke, rising to where the words could bring tears to the eyes of the angels. All angels. Even Tristan's wife?

No. Charlotte Ramsey had been no angel. Tristan had done all in his power to make her smile, protect her, love her. But she hadn't deserved that gift. She'd used it against him ruthlessly, destroying him because she was too afraid to face the world, even at his side.

Tonight, as the smoke curled up the chimney, Tristan had asked Charlotte Ramsey for forgiveness—a request that had sent anger pulsing through Alaina's veins. For what crime should he be forgiven? Not thanking the woman when she so wantonly demolished the last vestiges of his dream? For daring to show pain and feel resentment at surrendering the creative fire that God himself had molded into Tristan's fingertips with the loving hand of a master sculptor?

If Tristan had belonged to Alaina, she would have guarded his artistic gift as she would his sensitive heart—cherished it, a tangible reflection of the beauty in his soul and the passion of his body. The mystic union their love would have woven between them would have found expression in their bed late at night as his fire invaded her, filling her with rainbows and light. And pray God, a new creation would eventually have come into the world, blinking and awed and frightened until Tristan gathered it into a father's loving arms.

But that dream had always been impossible. She'd known it from the first moment she'd scrubbed away the frost on Tristan's window and peered through that melting ice circle to watch him. She'd been more painfully certain with every brush of his thigh against hers as they'd danced to the music box's enchanted melody. She'd felt the utter hopelessness of it all—in the soul-searing abrasion of his callused palm engulfing her hand and in the bone-melting sweetness of his kiss.

It was said Eve had cast paradise away for a taste of the forbidden. Alaina understood that fall from grace completely now. For she would have let the clouds and stars, the heavens themselves, run through her fingers for one taste of Tristan's love.

If only Alaina dared to take up Tristan's hand, to kiss magic back into its supple strength, to slip the smooth wooden handle of a paintbrush between his fingers in benediction. If only she could reach out her arms to Tristan as women had offered themselves up to the men their hearts had chosen since the beginning of time. But she and Tristan were from worlds apart—as distant as Gabriel had been from the star he'd wished upon.

She crossed to the music box, raising its lid so that music spilled, silvery, shimmering, into the night. Inexpressible longing welled up until her whole chest felt raw with it—each suppressed tear crystallizing, cutting deeper and deeper into her soul.

She'd believed she'd known everything about Tristan Ramsey —the flicker of mischief in boyish eyes, the fierce inner strength that had radiated from every long, lean muscle, the fiery resolve that had awed and bewitched her from the first moment she'd looked upon his face.

I'm going to be the greatest artist who ever lived—a boy's boast? No. There had been a willingness to sacrifice, to labor, to give all for his art, a man's determination to fulfill destiny. Until Tristan's father had lost his way, wandering blindly into oblivion, on a nightmarish journey he would have had to take alone, if Tristan hadn't taken his hand.

She'd never realized that walls that could shelter could also entrap, that love that could warm could also suffocate. Yet even as a child, gazing up at her own father, she'd known that dreams shriveled into bitter things when they could never be fulfilled. She could only be grateful her mother had never seen the agony she had—watching the man she loved treading his stygian path to a living death.

"Please, God," she said aloud, "help Tristan. He needs You to help him."

"Gabriel would say that was why God sent you."

"Tristan!" She shut the music box with a guilty click, then wheeled to find him standing in the doorway.

Black breeches clung to his lean hips. His shirt spread across his chest in smooth ripples, the front open, exposing a wedge of burnt-honey skin dusted with dark hair. His face was carved in haggard lines of strain, yet so desperately beloved, it stripped her emotions raw.

If he painted her at this moment, Alaina knew what he'd capture on the canvas. Every brushstroke would reveal a tender, wistful yearning for the impossible, the pulsing anguish of a passion that could never be fulfilled.

She wanted to race across the space that separated them, to

take him in her arms, press him close to her heart. But she knew that even if she held him forever, she could never bridge the chasm between them.

Heat stung her cheeks, and she was excruciatingly aware of the thin cloth of her nightgown drawn taut over her breasts. "I didn't mean to wake you."

"You didn't wake me." His gaze trailed over her, from the crown of her head to where her toes peeked from beneath the gown's delicate hem. He didn't seem surprised or shocked that she was wandering about his house in nothing but a whisper of cotton. Rather, there was an odd sense of acceptance in him, as if he'd not be surprised to discover wings upon her back or a halo concealed in the ripples of her hair. If only he knew the truth . . .

Tristan cleared his throat, crossing to the hearth. On the mantel a half-dozen miniatures were clustered—portraits of the family Alaina had watched for so many years.

Beth Ramsey, smiling in her bridal finery, sturdy Henry Muldowny at her side.

Tristan's mother looking distinctly uncomfortable garbed in the height of style, a single rose seeming out of place in a hand fashioned for drying tears and brushing dirt from scraped knees.

Tristan, astride a cream-colored pony, ready to go off adventuring—to battle with the Green Knight, to vanquish the Titans, or, perhaps, to journey to the Continent to enchant generations, not with a sword, but with brush and canvas and the colors of his own imagination.

"Strange," he said softly, fingering the frame of gilded roses about his mother's portrait, "you seem to know everything about me, my family—where the Christmas greens were hung, the games we played. Even my pony Galahad, the most wonderful present I ever got. But never once have I heard you speak about your own family or Christmases in your past."

"I never celebrated Christmas. The closest I came was watching other people."

Tristan stared at her, touched by the bittersweet sting of her words—watching Christmas, barred from the magic circle of laughter and warmth and light.

"You watched us?" he asked, suddenly realizing how she had known so many things about his family, his life.

"I watched through the window. Your family was always so happy and beautiful and loving. The oddest thing of all was that I was never cold while I stood there. It was as if the warmth of that love was so strong it slipped through the pane to curl about me."

"It's so strange, Alaina. Sometimes I feel as if—as if I've known you forever. As if some rare magic—Christmas magic— brought you here."

Firelight gleamed on her face, her hair, the delicate rose blush of her skin tantalizing him through the thin cotton nightgown. Her small breasts pressed against the fabric in delicate perfection, and he wanted to touch them, like a penitent touching something ineffably holy.

But it was the golden glow of her eyes that drew a hard knot of need into Tristan's throat. Never had he seen such light in a mortal's eyes. They shone, almost as if she loved him.

Loved him.

The thought echoed a desperate longing in the deepest reaches of his heart. Dear God, this was insane. He was falling in love with her, and he wasn't even certain she was real.

He wanted to tear down the wall of mystery that separated them, wanted to spill everything he was into her hands. But what kind of a man would soil an angel's hands with the soul of a sinner?

No. He couldn't touch her, couldn't taint her. But maybe,

just maybe he could reach out to her with words, tell her things he'd not confess to anyone else, share things he'd only begun to admit to himself. He sucked in a steadying breath, reaching out the only way he knew how.

"Ever since Gabriel fell asleep, I've been in the attic," he said at last.

Alaina's heart wrenched at the image of Tristan amid his half-finished paintings. Had he gone there trying to find his dreams again? Or had he gone there to mourn their loss?

"Did you find what you were looking for?" she asked.

"I don't know. I just . . . sat up there, thinking—about so many things I hadn't considered for a very long time. Charlotte. My father. Gabriel—all the time I missed spending with him when he was small."

"You were wonderful with Gabriel tonight. Did you see his eyes shine when you helped him send a message to his mama?"

"Did it reach her, Alaina?" He was regarding her with dark, intense eyes.

"Wh-what?"

"The letter. Did it reach heaven?" His gaze plumbed to the core of her, earnest, a little afraid. The sight of that shadow of fear devastated her. "Am I forgiven?"

Dear God, did he really believe she had the answers he needed to hear? What did he want to be forgiven for? For sacrificing too much? Loving too deeply? Being too strong?

"Tristan, I—" She lifted her chin and peered straight into his eyes. "Yes. You are forgiven."

Blasphemy—the wrath of heaven should pour down on her for daring to say such a thing. Why, then, did she feel such absolute certainty?

He swallowed hard, and Alaina realized he'd been holding his breath, waiting for her answer, as if she had the power to lift him past heaven's gates or plunge him into hell. "Are you my guardian angel, Alaina MacShane?" He lifted his fingers to her hair, twining an auburn strand through them as if he were weaving enchanted chains to bind her to him. "I've been waiting for you a very long time. I'd almost given up."

"I'm here now." She cupped her palm against his jaw, feeling the stubborn strength in it, his warm breath melting along the fragile underside of her wrist.

"Can you show me the way, angel? Why is it that I feel if I just take your hand—" His voice broke on a laugh, and he let her glossy curl slip through his fingers. "I'm beginning to sound like Gabriel—concocting fairy stories about wishes and enchantment and some wild, magic place that drifts angels down to heal a man's empty heart."

"If I could heal you, Tristan, I would."

"There is so much yearning in your voice and in those wide golden eyes of yours when you say you would heal me—if you could. Have I fallen so far from grace, then? Is it impossible?"

"I can't heal you. No one can. You have to decide yourself to let the wounds heal."

"Heal myself?"

"Do you want the pain, Tristan—more than you want to love your son? To watch him grow up? Is your guilt over the past more important than all the years that lie ahead? It's one thing to make mistakes, have regrets. It's another thing to cast away a child's love because of some crazed sense of self-loathing. I've watched you raking open all the guilt and the pain and the regrets inside you. All of heaven could forgive you. Charlotte, your father—even Gabriel. But it will mean nothing until you decide to forgive yourself. What do you want, Tristan—from now until forever?"

His gaze met hers, his voice ragged. "I want—I want this Christmas back again. I want the kissing bough and music. I want to bring Gabriel a pony so beautiful he'll never forget the first moment he saw it, to lift him up and set him astride it and see his eyes shining up at me."

Hope, joy, burst like bright-winged butterflies in Alaina's breast. She caught his hand, held it fiercely in her own. "Then take Christmas back, Tristan."

His eyes betrayed just how agonizing the past days had been for him, barren of Christmas candles and his family's laughter and Gabriel's boyish delight. "It's too late," he said. "Christmas is over."

"Only if we allow it to be." She pulled away and ran to where the mantel clock stood, ticking away inexorably. Standing on tiptoe, she tugged on the tiny key in the glass door that protected the clock's face. It opened, and she reached in, moving the black clock hands backward, one hour, two hours, three, until it stood at a minute before midnight. Then she caught the pendulum, stopping time itself. "I'm magic, Tristan. Remember? There is still time to make wishes come true."

Eight

SUNLIGHT REACHED THROUGH CRACKS IN THE NURSERY'S curtains, like the fingers of eager children trying to snatch ginger nuts from a favorite uncle's pocket, and the promise of delight curled, warm and sweet, in Tristan's chest.

He should have been exhausted from lack of sleep, harried from the crazed pace he'd set since he and Alaina had left the drawing room, bent on working a miracle for Gabriel. Instead, he felt as if he had been reborn sometime during the night.

He crossed to the window and tugged open the drapes, letting sunlight splash over his sleeping son. Gabriel wriggled and croaked a protest, burrowing deeper into his coverlets, but Tristan strode to the side of that small bed and stole them away.

"Wake up lay-a-bed!"

"Papa?" The boy rubbed his eyes.

"Happy Christmas, Gabriel."

"Christmas?" The dimpled fists fell away, and eyes like melted chocolate popped open. "Christmas is over."

"Is that so? We'll just have to see about that." Tristan strode to where a clock sat on the nursery mantel. His fingers closed on the tiny gold key, and he tugged, opening the glass door that protected the timepiece. "Gabriel, come here at once."

The child clambered out of bed, his dewy brow creased in puzzlement, his stuffed horse clutched under his arm. "Papa? What's the matter?"

"I need your help." Tristan leaned down and scooped Gabriel up in his arms. The child smelled of dreamland and cinnamon, milk and innocence. Tristan buried his face for a moment amid the tumbled gold of Gabriel's curls.

"What help do you need, Papa?"

"Turning back this infernal clock. It says Christmas is over. Reach up and stop that pendulum at once." Gabriel gaped at Tristan as if he feared his father had gone mad. Tristan's mouth widened in a grin. Gabriel smiled an uncertain answer and did as he was bid, the clock giving one disgruntled tick before it went still.

"Now turn the hands backward," Tristan instructed, as the boy carefully swept the clock hands around, his eyes darting warily to his father.

"There! Stop!"

The boy jerked his hands back as if the clock had suddenly transformed into a dove and taken flight. "Papa—what—what is it? You're acting so—so strange."

"Happy Christmas, Gabriel."

"Ch-Christmas? Christmas is over, Papa."

"No, son. It's just beginning. And we aren't going to waste a single moment."

The child's eyes glistened. "It's the magic, isn't it? Alaina made magic!"

Tristan's throat constricted at the knowledge of how true his son's words were. "Yes. Alaina made the magic. Don't you want to see?"

Gabriel scrambled down and bolted for the door, but Tristan caught the tail of his little nightshirt. "Oh, no, young man. Put on your breeches."

"But, Papa!"

"You can't very well race all over London in your nightshirt." He bent down to whisper in Gabriel's ear. "Your bottom would turn blue with cold."

The boy stared at him for a moment, then a peal of laughter rang out—silvery as bells, more beautiful than any sound Tristan had ever heard. It was the first time he had ever surprised laughter from his son.

Tristan's eyes burned. The little boy darted about, dragging off his nightshirt, tugging on his clothes. But his small, eager fingers were trembling too much with excitement to fasten the buttons on his shirt.

"Papa, will you help me? I'm all crooked, and they won't go through their holes."

Tristan knelt down and treasured each small button, each wriggle of delight Gabriel gave as he danced from one foot to the other in impatience.

"Where is Alaina? She missed Christmas yesterday, too. No! I mean today! She almost missed Christmas."

"Alaina is attempting to set the house afire again." Tristan grinned, savoring the secret as he fastened up Gabriel's little boots.

Then he gathered his son in his arms and carried him down the wide stairway to where the drawing room doors stood closed.

"Alaina?" Gabriel called out. "Alaina, where are you?"

Tristan shoved open the door. Gabriel froze in his arms as a rush of pine-scented air swept out to greet them.

There, atop a table covered with bright red cloth, stood a tree in a bucket of sand, the evergreen branches laden with cookies and gilded nuts, candies and ribbons, and a myriad of tiny burning candles that glinted like stars upon the branches.

"Oh, Papa! Wh-what is it?" Gabriel gasped in awe. "It really is magic!"

"When your mama was a little girl, back in Germany, they celebrated Christmas by bringing a tree into the house and filling it with treats and presents. The first year she came to live with us, I made her a Christmas tree so she wouldn't be so homesick."

"Did it make her happy, Papa?" Gabriel asked breathlessly.

Tristan felt a bittersweet stab of memory. "She cried."

Gabriel laid on soft palm against his face. "That wasn't your fault, Papa. You tried to make her happy."

It was as if the child, with his too-wise eyes and his gentle soul, were speaking of so much more than the tree Tristan had constructed so many years ago.

Tristan forced his lips into a smile. "I hope you're not going to cry."

"No! I want to see it, all of it!"

He set Gabriel down, and the boy raced to the tree, the candleshine not half so bright as his eyes, his fingers reaching out to touch a bright orange bound with ribbon and a tiny gingerbread cookie shaped like a rocking horse.

"You can pluck your breakfast right off the tree," Alaina said, stepping from behind the branches.

"No! It's too pretty ever to eat! Can't we keep it just like this forever and ever?"

"I'm too hungry to wait," Tristan said. "I have to taste something or I might be tempted to try a helping of little boy!"

Gabriel plucked off a cookie and pushed it into Tristan's hand. "Here, Papa. I want you to have the first taste."

"There are presents, too. Can you find them?" Alaina asked.

The child turned to the tree again, dancing around it. He gasped as he found a brigade of lead soldiers taking cover among the branches—then a bright red top—and a pair of ice skates. Tristan's heart swelled at each jubilant cry as he lifted the boy to pluck off his presents.

Then suddenly, Gabriel gasped. "Papa, look!" He pointed at something hanging from one of the topmost branches. Tristan's brow furrowed in confusion as he lifted Gabriel to pluck it down.

"I don't remember putting anything like this on the tree," he observed, looking down at the small circlet of dull silver that glinted in the boy's hand.

Tristan gazed down at it—four swans woven of Celtic interlacing formed the circle of what seemed to be a brooch, each of the birds wearing a tiny crown. A pin was thrust through the center of it, dividing it in half.

"What is it?" Gabriel asked.

"It looks like a brooch of some kind," Tristan said, turning to Alaina.

"It's a penannular. The ancient Celts used them to fasten their cloaks," Alaina said. "This one represents an old Irish tale, the Children of Lir."

"What is Lir?" Gabriel fingered the gleaming brooch with wonder.

"Lir was a king who so loved his children that their wicked stepmother grew jealous and turned them into swans. So they must spend forever traversing the lakes of Ireland, longing for their beloved father."

"It's exquisite." Tristan's voice roughened at the poignancy of the tale. He hurt for the father, his children forever beyond his reach—as Gabriel soon would be.

"The penannular should be beautiful!" Her cheeks pinkened, her eyes a little shy. "My father always told me that it was the clasp to a fairy's cloak."

"A-A fairy? But I thought you were an angel. Are fairies and angels friends?" Gabriel asked.

"Of course! Unless they crash into each other while they're flying about. Then they quarrel."

Gabriel's mouth rounded into a soft O. "How did it get here?"

"My father stole it away on a misty night from the fairy king himself," Alaina said. "Da always said that was why our family had to flee Ireland. Now it belongs to you, Gabriel. So that you'll remember . . . remember me when you see it."

A knot of panic rose in Tristan's chest as he imagined what it would be like when Alaina went away. And she would go away, he knew. Soon, too soon.

"I don't need a fairy brooch to remember you, Alaina," Gabriel said. "I've decided Papa and I need you. Even if you go up to heaven, we'll go too, and we won't be the teensiest bit afraid."

Tristan's heart wrenched. What would it be like for Gabriel when he was forced to watch Alaina walk away? What betrayal would Gabriel's eyes show when his own father put him in a coach that carried him to his aunt's house—far from his nursery and Cook and Burrows and Tristan himself?

He couldn't bear the thought, so he turned back to the tree, reaching up to grab a gingerbread lady from one of the top branches.

"Be careful!" Alaina warned, but it was too late. A heavy object tumbled down through the branches, breaking cookies, scattering candies; the box landed with a thud at Tristan's feet.

"What the devil?"

"It's for you, Tristan." Alaina looked up at him, with such tenderness, such understanding, such shimmering hope, his fingers trembled.

He hunkered down and picked it up, unfastening the tiny catch that held the wooden box closed. He opened it, and his heart stopped. Paints—all pristine, their colors vivid and untouched, glowed like jewels in the candlelight. Brushes, their bristles silky sable, lay pillowed among whatever supplies he might need.

When in God's name had she bought them? Had she slipped away while he was gathering presents for his son? How had she hidden them on the journey back home? How much had they cost her—this woman with her threadbare garments, her agonizingly familiar eyes, and a heart far more generous than her purse's contents must be? Could she possibly know what the gift meant to him?

"Alaina," he choked out, "I don't know what to say."

"Don't say anything. Use them, Tristan. It wasn't too late for Christmas. It's not too late for this."

The possibility was too astonishing to grasp. He stood there, clutching the box, searching for words—words that had failed him as his eye and his brush and the colors of his imagination never had.

"But, Papa, we didn't get anything for Alaina," Gabriel whispered.

What could you give to an angel? What possible gift half so precious as the treasures of the heart Alaina had given him?

Suddenly Tristan froze, his eyes captured by the light twinkling through a waterfall of glass prisms decorating one of the candlesticks. He crossed to where they hung, picking one of the bits of shining glass from its hook.

"Here, Alaina," Tristan said, tucking it into her hand.

"You don't have to—I don't need anything—"

"Papa, you should give her the whole candlestick," Gabriel said. "What can she do with just one prism?"

"Whenever things get too dark, she can pull it out of her pocket and hold it up to the light." He dangled it before the candle flame, a hundred bright bits of blue light dancing across the room. His gaze caught hers, held it. "You'll always have a star to wish upon."

Alaina flung her arms around Tristan, holding him tight for a long moment. As if she never wanted to let him go. How long had it been since anyone had clung to him this way? Not to chain him, but rather with fierce emotion, opening the sky to him, handing him wings disguised as paintbrushes and vivid colors. He could feel the sweet wetness of tears dampening his shirt, seeping deep into the broken places in his heart. A shudder went through him as the coldness cracked, the bitterness forever sweetened.

"What would you wish, Alaina?" He breathed against her fragrant curls. "—if I could promise it would come true? I'd give you anything in my power."

A tiny cry tore from her breast. "I can't have my wish. I can't ever have it. But I'll keep your gift forever," she whispered against his heart, her words making Tristan agonizingly aware she would be far away, beyond his reach, when she made crystal stars dance upon the sky.

A sudden knock at the door made Tristan straighten, and he cursed the interruption, knowing he would trade half of his life if he could just stand in this room, with Gabriel's face shining and Alaina in his arms a little longer.

"I wonder who the blazes that could be?"

At that instant, Burrows tapped on the entryway, the old man's face beaming. "It's a gentleman for Master Gabriel, sir."

Tristan shook himself inwardly, releasing Alaina, feeling as if she'd taken his heart with her. "You'd best go see who it is, boy."

Gabriel rushed out to the door, Tristan and Alaina following in his wake. The boy tugged open the door, revealing a portly gentleman with straw in his hair.

"Is this the residence of Master Gabriel Ramsey?"

"I'm Gabriel Ramsey."

"There be someone in the garden right anxious to make yer acquaintance, young sir."

"Papa?" Gabriel glanced up at Tristan doubtfully. Tristan ruffled the child's hair.

"Go on, boy," Tristan urged.

Gabriel took a step out into a wonderland of ice crystals and snow like spun sugar, kissed by the morning sun. He made his way along the garden path, wandering as if he were entering the fairy king's domain. As he rounded the rose vines to where the lopsided snowman still grinned, he stumbled to a halt. There, beside it, was tied a glorious black pony, wearing a silver-mounted saddle.

"P-Papa?" Gabriel whispered.

"He's yours, Gabriel," Tristan said, an odd thickness in his throat. "Happy Christmas."

The boy whooped in delight, racing toward the pony, flinging his arms about its neck. Golden curls glinted against the animal's sleek midnight coat. The patient beast snuffled against him, nudging him with a velvety muzzle, eyes soft and wise with that special expression the best ponies always had—as if they were listening to a child's private pain and fears and dreams that would never be shared with another soul.

Tristan ached, wondering what secrets Gabriel and this pony would share. Would he cry into that silky mane when Tristan sent him away?

Tristan banished his melancholy thoughts and strode over to his son, catching the boy beneath the arms and lifting him into the saddle.

"Papa, this pony has the same name as you do! It's right here in silver: Tristan!"

"The name is on the saddle because it was mine when I was a little boy. You see, I got a Christmas pony once, too."

"What was your pony's name, Papa?"

"Galahad. I wanted my pony to have a properly noble name before we went out to tame dragons." Dragons spun of a child's imagination, far easier to vanquish than the kind that stalked a man's soul.

"I'm going to name my pony Galahad, too. And we can go riding together in the park and check to see if the swans have crowns like on my fairy pin."

"Any swans in the lake now would have their tail feathers frozen."

"In spring and summer we could ride every day together," the child said, suddenly weighed down by some emotion that stole a measure of joy from his face. "Unless you were too busy working. Then I would just wait real quiet in the hallway until you can come to play."

"Or maybe you could come right in and tell me to get the devil outside, there are important things to do. Knights to slay and dragons whose fire needs to be extinguished."

A shimmer of hope burned in the child's eyes. "Do you really think—Oh, Papa, can we wait an extra day for Christmas every year?" Gabriel asked.

"Why would you want to do that?"

"Because I want every Christmas to be just like this! With a tree full of presents, and Alaina and you and me all together. Papa, I always wondered what heaven was like. If it was angels and harps and clouds and things. But I was wrong. Heaven's the most wondrous place you could ever choose to be. Maybe we got heaven right here since Alaina's come."

Tristan stole a glance at the woman who stood in the snow, her blue gown like a splash of sky, her golden eyes brimming with tears. Heaven . . . had she drifted it down to them on angel's wings? Carried it with her through the window, along with the kissing bough? Or had it been in her eyes forever?

Tristan wanted to close the space between them, gather her into his arms and beg her to stay in a world where Christmas never ended and Gabriel laughed and Tristan could feel the colors and shapes and images welling up inside him, like a melody about to be sung.

Maybe we got heaven right here since Alaina's come . . . Gabriel's words echoed through Tristan's mind. There was only one cloud marring the beauty of this day. How were they ever going to let Alaina go?

Nine

THERE HAD NEVER BEEN A MORE PERFECT DAY. TRISTAN cradled his son in his arms, carrying that precious burden up the stairs to bed. He was certain it was past midnight, but he didn't care if the clocks never started again and time stood still forever at Alaina MacShane's command.

Laughter—the old house had rung with it. Joy—it had bubbled over in delicious abandon. And Tristan knew that in all of London no one had had a Christmas stuffed with more delight than he had.

For the first time in seven years, Tristan had truly gotten to know his own son. And the child he had discovered was a treasure beyond imagining—a tenderhearted, sensitive, brave little boy who had fought his battles too long alone. A winsome waif whose droll observations had made Tristan laugh inside until his heart ached with the sweetest pain he'd ever known.

Knights had been vanquished, enchanted swans transformed back into princes and princesses, during wild gallops through the snow-drifted park, Tristan's gelding keeping pace with the energetic bobbling of the pony Gabriel had christened Galahad. They'd returned at dusk, wind-stung and breathless, to find a feast stirred up by Cook and a flour-splashed Alaina, who had invited both servants to share the table that meal.

By the time that night was done, Burrows and Cook had been regarding her the same way Gabriel did—as if she were an angel fallen down from heaven. And Tristan was certain he'd never forget the picture of her—laughing and rosy and breathless—kneeling down to claim Gabriel's kiss beneath the sphere of candles and greenery that had been her first gift to the two of them.

It felt so right to come home to that lovely, animated smile of welcome, the light dancing over the freckles sprinkled like fairy dust across her nose. It had seemed so perfect when she had scooped Gabriel into her arms, heedless of the snow feathering over her gown and onto the floor. And when her eyes had met Tristan's own, alive with heart-stopping tenderness, he felt the luminous beauty of a new vision shivering to life, a fragile picture more beautiful than anything captured on canvas—a cluster of auburn-haired little moppets frolicking about Alaina's skirts, their faces bright with mischief, as she came to welcome him into her arms, into her bed.

"Papa . . ." Gabriel's groggy voice jarred Tristan from his thoughts as he bent to nestle the boy in amid the coverlets. "Promise me . . . you won't go to heaven for a long, long time. Promise you'll stay with me forever."

"I'll always be with you, Gabriel. Loving you, watching over you, no matter where you are."

"But if I'm at Aunt Beth's, I won't be able to lie outside your study with my books and soldiers so I can hear your voice when I play."

Tristan's blood froze in horror. "You—you knew about that?"

"Yessir," Gabriel mumbled, snuggling closer against Tristan's shirt, his cheeks staining pink. "When I was playing by your study. I heard you and Burrows talking."

Tristan's stomach churned at the image of Gabriel standing alone in the corridor, hearing that his world was coming to an end, and the child damming up all the pain and hurt and fear inside him for weeks, realizing that each day that ticked past was one more out of the tiny store of time he had left in his own home before his own father—the father who should have comforted him, cherished him, soothed his childish fears—sent him away.

"That's why you insisted on staying here for Christmas." Tristan squeezed the words past the lump of self-condemnation blocking his throat. "Even though there wouldn't be any celebration."

Those old-soul eyes met his, and Tristan could see the shadows of the sorrow he'd caused his child. "I wanted to show you I could be quieter, Papa, so I wouldn't disturb you. I wished and wished that you would smile. Because if you smiled, maybe you wouldn't send me away, even though I know I'm a terrible bother to you."

"A bother to me?" Tristan's lungs were afire. "God in heaven, boy! From the moment you were born, you were the one good thing in my life."

"But Mama said that was why you looked so—so angry all the time—because you had important business to take care of and we were in your way. But she said that was all right because she had me to take care of her."

Tristan froze. Had Charlotte manipulated Gabriel, twining her love about him like a vine, suffocating the child beneath the weight of her neediness? Tristan had always known she was jealous of any attention he'd paid others—his father, his sisters, his mother. But had she been jealous of her own son?

Anger broke free in Tristan, at memories of Charlotte scooping Gabriel out of the room whenever Tristan entered it, banishing him to the nursery for his supper, memories of the stiff, wary, almost wistful expression on his son's face when he came to bid Tristan good night on those rare occasions Tristan had been home from the office before the child was abed.

"Nothing is more important to me than you are, Gabriel. Nothing."

Gabriel grew quiet, a shadow staining across his features. "I didn't do a very good job of it, did I, Papa?" he asked in a small voice. "Watching over Mama, I mean. Mama died, no matter how I tried to stop it. Is that why you're going to send me away to Aunt Beth's? Because I didn't watch over Mama close enough?"

The words lanced Tristan's soul—God, that his son, his innocent son, should be wrestling such guilt in the night alone, that Gabriel had believed himself responsible for Charlotte's unhappiness and her death. While Tristan had wrapped himself in sackcloth and ashes and bitterness, selfish, so utterly selfish, in his guilt.

"No, Gabriel. I was the one who failed, not you. Failed your mother. Failed you. I thought—You looked so unhappy, Gabriel. When I'd catch you staring out the drawing room window, you were so sad I couldn't bear it. I thought if I sent you away from all this, you could be happy. You'd have Aunt Beth to love you and other children to play with, and not just— just a bitter man who didn't deserve you."

"But, Papa, if I went away, you'd get sadder and sadder. There would be nobody here to make you smile. That's what I gave all my wishes for. I promised never to wish again if the angel would just make you happy." His voice dropped low. "Even if it meant I had to go away."

"Oh, God! Gabriel!" Tristan's voice broke as he gathered his son in his arms, crushing the boy against him, the embrace crumbling years of bitterness, an eternity of lost dreams, leaving him one, fresh and bright and new—a son he'd never really known. "I love you, boy. More than life. More than anything the world can offer. We'll stay together, if you'll let me begin again. I'll do better this time, Gabriel. I swear it. If you'll just give me a chance."

"I'll give you all my chances, just like I gave you my wishes, except . . ." His mouth turned down in a frown. "I almost wish that I could get one of them back—my wishes, I mean—so that Alaina could stay forever and ever, too. But maybe you haven't used up all your wishes yet, Papa," he said, brightening. "Maybe you could wish her to stay."

"I haven't dared to wish for a very long time, Gabriel. Maybe it's time I tried."

Constellations nestled in the heavens in half-finished portraits of scorpions and lions and myth-veiled heroes, the winter night so still Alaina was certain she could hear Gabriel's angels whispering to the moon. She had climbed out the window of her bedchamber onto the sloping roof below. Making a nest of a thick blanket, she'd settled herself on a perch that was like her familiar childhood retreat. Sitting on the roof of the broken-down inn where she and her da had a room, she had been high above the dirt and the noise, in a place where even hunger's pinching fingers couldn't reach her.

She could sit forever, her legs tucked up, banded by her arms, her chin resting on her knees, and she could look out across the winking lights of the city toward the street where he lived. She could imagine him looking out at the same night sky, capturing the moon in a silvery net of brushstrokes, stringing the stars in a shimmering necklace across a painted sky. She could picture herself in a flowing blue gown, curling up on a stool at his feet to sing to him the haunting ballads her father had taught her so long ago.

Yet never in her wildest imaginings had she created a day as perfect as this one had been—from Gabriel's first cry of delight to his last drowsy whisper when Tristan had carried him up the stairs, the child hugging, not the familiar stuffed horse, but the awkward bulk of the newly polished saddle.

Her heart had shattered at the tender timbre of Tristan's baritone as he'd warned Gabriel he could sleep with it only this once, that in the future, it would remain in the stable on its own peg, alongside his papa's saddle.

She had slipped away, embroidering into the deepest places of her heart the picture the two had made—Gabriel, wreathed with the rare, drowsy delight of a child stuffed with all the joy and love he can hold, while Tristan sat upon the edge of the nursery bed, one strong hand of his clutched by one of Gabriel's small ones, mirroring the hold Alaina knew the child held on his heart.

If only Tristan would listen to his heart and keep Gabriel at his side, to tame dragons astride the black pony and build smiling snow-papas and chase away the shadows that crept from beneath the bed at night.

A soft, almost hesitant rap on the door made her turn to where the window was open to the night.

"Alaina?" Tristan's voice, soft, uncertain. She felt a surge of joy at its sound, and a sting of loss.

"Come in," she called back.

He opened the door, and she could see him through the window as he entered the room, then stilled. "Alaina? Can you come downstairs for a moment? There's something I want to give—Alaina, where the blazes are you?"

She leaned over into the frame of the open window, candle-light spilling across her face. "I'm out here. On the roof."

"The roof? Are you crazed?" She heard his boots thud in a path to the window, then he braced his palms on the window ledge, leaning out into the frosty kiss of night. "What is it with you and windows, lady? Are you determined to break your neck? Or has Gabriel filled your head with so much of this angel nonsense, you're ready to try to fly?"

"The roof has always been my favorite place, from the time I was a child. Come out. You can see forever."

"It's bloody cold out there! And the roof's full of snow. We'll both break our necks."

"You thought you wanted to cancel Christmas, too, Mr. Ramsey," she teased. "But no one had more fun than you did today. Just think what delights you might find out here if you had the courage to try it."

Her heart warmed as his scowl shifted, the planes of his face transformed by a smile. "Oh, damn," he said, shrugging one broad shoulder. "After everything else I've done today, why not finish it by freezing my hinder parts off?" He levered himself up, broad shoulders filling the window, his long legs unfolding into the snow. His glossy boots scrabbled for purchase on the roof tiles, then he settled himself on the blanket beside her, so close his arm brushed hers.

The warmth of him shimmered through Alaina like flecks of silver, his closeness her heart's most cherished dream. Never as a hungry-eyed girl had she ever imagined that Tristan would someday sit on the roof beside her, gazing out at the stars.

When he looked beyond the garden gate, above the city to the blue-black canopy of sky, his breath caught. "The stars— they're so close it seems you could pluck them from the sky."

"I'd rather have the stars that you gave me."

"I wish there was something I really could give you, Alaina, to show you how grateful I am for all you've done for Gabriel."

"I didn't do it for Gabriel. I did it for you, Tristan."

"For me? But Gabriel's wish—I thought you said—Why, did you help me, Alaina? What could I possibly have done to deserve your kindness?"

"I doubt you would remember. You were constantly being kind and generous. Every time I peeked through the window, I would catch you slipping peppermint drops into your mother's sewing basket or ribbons between the pages of Beth's music books. The year you made Charlotte the Christmas tree and gathered up little presents for everyone in the house, even Burrows and Cook and the little scullery maid—the one whose apron pockets you filled up with coppers until it was so heavy the pocket tore."

He stared at her, his eyes filled with yearning, his cheeks darkened with embarrassment. "You saw all that? I thought—"

"You thought no one knew. You'd pretend to be so gruff, as if you didn't care two figs about what some 'mad prankster' was doing about the house. But everyone knew, Tristan. We all knew it was you."

"It was just a stupid game I played—a boy's tricks. Nothing special. I'm astonished you remember. I'm certain everyone else has forgot. I hope to God they have."

"I was well acquainted with boys' tricks when I was a child. Shoving and pinching and poking with sticks. What you did was—magnificent. You showed me that there could be goodness in the world. Kindness. That hands didn't have to be rough and cruel and heedless. That sometimes they could be warm and healing."

Despite the darkness, she could see his cheeks flame. He looked away, raking his fingers through his hair. "I lost all that somewhere, didn't I? God, how disappointed you must have been when you saw—"

"You didn't lose it. It was taken from you, one tear at a time—by Charlotte, and by the kindest act you ever performed."

"Charlotte? Charlotte did nothing. I'm the one who failed in our marriage. She was so blasted unhappy. From the first day my father brought her back from Germany, she needed someone to protect her. She was so afraid, so fragile; she needed a husband to cherish her and—"

"And sacrifice his entire life to her weakness?"

Tristan stiffened. "What the—It was my fault the marriage failed. I didn't give her what she needed—security . . . enough love."

"She is the one who failed, Tristan. She took your love and she used it like a weapon against you. She knew your dreams from the very first, Tristan, watched you spend hour after hour weaving magic on canvas. She knew what your art meant to you. But she willfully stole it from you and flung it away, not caring that she was destroying the part of your soul that made you so beautiful."

"Alaina, I—"

"You loved her so much, felt so responsible for her, that you sacrificed everything for her. And she took away everything that mattered to you. Your art. Your son."

"I never loved her. I only wanted to—to protect her. And I'm the one who stayed away from Gabriel. I was too involved in working to—"

"You were attempting to save your father from humiliation and ruin."

Tristan's eyes widened. "You know? About—about my father?" In that instant, Alaina knew how much it had hurt him to watch his father sink deeper and deeper into the hazy half-world that was engulfing him. Helplessness, rage at fates and the heavens and his own inability to stem the tide—they had scarred Tristan's heart.

"You made choices, Tristan, hideous choices no man should have to make. You did the best you could with the dragons that beset you. You didn't turn away from your father or your wife. I can't believe you would have willingly turned away from your little boy. Charlotte built walls between you and Gabriel. Gabriel was too small and you were too overwhelmed to realize what was happening until it was almost too late. But it isn't, Tristan. Tell me it isn't too late for you and Gabriel."

Tristan turned his face to hers, candlelight and moonshine limning the sensitive curve of his lips, the hard ridges of his cheekbones.

"He knew, Alaina." She could see the confession wrench at Tristan's very core, see, too, the fragile dawning of awe. The rapt expression of a man scooping up a palmful of water in his cupped hand and discovering that it was liquid silver. "Gabriel knew from the first that I was going to send him away. But he's forgiven me. My son has decided to give me another chance, just like he gave all his wishes to make me smile. And I—I'm going to make the most of it, I vow. I don't know how I can make up for all the lost years—"

She pressed her fingertips to the full curve of his lips. "By not wasting another moment on regrets." Yet her own heart was filled with them, brimming, hurting, stinging. He was going to keep Gabriel in his arms and in his heart. He'd found his son and, in doing so, rediscovered himself, peeling away the hard rind of bitterness and resentment, revealing the tender heart of the boy she had met on a snow-spangled Christmas so many years ago.

Her work here was done. The enchanted moment she had stepped through Tristan's window and into his world was over.

But how could she leave him? With his kiss still warm on her lips? His touch still branded in every fiber of her being? How could she leave him when she'd loved him forever? As an adoring girl worshiping a bright-eyed boy who had seemed to be every hero she'd ever dreamed. And now, as a woman, loving a bewitchingly tender, beautifully flawed person, with all the pain and heartache, the stubbornness and the regrets, of a man of flesh and blood, not some fantasy-spun hero.

An anguished cry rose inside her. *I love you, Tristan! If you were mine, I wouldn't ever chain you away from the light and the magic and the beauty buried deep inside you. I would give you wings to soar to the sky. . . .*

But they couldn't stay on the roof forever. Before a new dawn broke, they would climb back through the window into a world where Alaina could never belong, where she would forever be a grubby-faced urchin, and Tristan would be the master of this house with its gilded frames and its pianoforte and its library stuffed with books.

Tristan turned to her, one large hand sweeping up to brush her curls back from her cheek. His palm lay against her skin, the touch perfection, like a dream. But he was warm and hard and real, smelling of bay rum and Gabriel's gingerbread and of hope reborn. "Alaina, how can I thank you? For all of this," he murmured. "For Gabriel. For the most magical Christmas ever. Wish upon a star, angel. I swear I'll make it come true."

Her eyes sought his, her heart thundering. There was only one thing she wanted before she said good-bye forever, if she dared to ask for it. The yearning in Tristan's dark gaze gave her courage.

"Kiss me, Tristan," she whispered.

His gaze flooded with tenderness, with need. He cupped her face in his hands and took her mouth in a kiss so tender it seared her very soul. His mouth traced hers with the loving touch of a sculptor with his masterpiece, his tongue easing along the crease of her lips, tasting her, treasuring her.

She gasped with pain, pleasure, and his tongue dipped into her mouth, stroking hers in a dance that built need, fed fires, turned her molten and liquid. Her fingers swept up to thread through the dark satin strands at his temple.

"So sweet, Alaina," he murmured against her mouth. "So sweet. God, how I want you."

The words shimmered through Alaina like the strains of a timeless love song, until her joy, her pleasure was too great to hold. It burst inside her, drawing from her lips words so bold she could barely squeeze them from her throat.

"Tristan. I have one last wish."

"What is it, angel? Anything—"

"Love me, Tristan. Tonight. I want to be in your arms, in your bed just once."

He didn't say a word. His eyes burned hot as coals, a groan tearing from his throat. He clasped her hand tight in his and drew her through the bedchamber window, in from the cold to where her dream was waiting.

Ten

FIRELIGHT WOVE SHADOW-LACE ACROSS THE WIDE BED. Candleshine danced through prisms in a symphony of color. Alaina shivered as Tristan lifted her through the window, setting her feet to the ground as gently as if she were spun crystal—a treasure that might be shattered in a moment's carelessness, a dream he never wanted to be awakened from.

Shadow and light loved his features as much as she did, gilding them with a nobility of spirit, a strength, an inner beauty not even the greatest artist in Christendom could capture upon canvas.

I love you . . . The words beat an erratic rhythm in her heart as Tristan raised his fingertips to her kiss-stung lips.

"Are you certain?" he rasped. "Certain that you want this?"

I've been waiting for you forever. And this is my last chance. Give me one night to hold in my heart when I'm gone. She couldn't tell him, didn't dare let him know the truth—that she was a ballad seller's child. And he, he was as far beyond her touch as the stars shimmering above. Yet Tristan had taken a waterfall of stars and tucked them into her hand to keep forever. She would trade them all away if she could keep Tristan instead. She groped for words that could tell him just enough, free him to seek the release they both so obviously wanted, needed.

"You promised me you'd grant any wish in your power. Touch me, Tristan. Please."

With a groan, he caught her in his arms, dragging her against him, kissing her with a fierce passion that drained the strength from her legs and made her cling to him with desperate hands.

His tongue delved into her mouth, not tentative this time, not tender, but with a man's need, thrusting and withdrawing in a dance that matched the one their bodies would soon indulge in.

His hand caressed her back, unfastening her gown, each button that surrendered to his touch making her quake with desire, each brush of his hand against bare skin sizzling to the core of her femininity.

Her own fingers trembled as they found his buttons, fumbling them through their holes until the cloth gaped, revealing honey-bronzed skin, a dark dusting of hair that tantalized her fingers, ridges of muscle her fingers burned to trace.

She had spent so much of her girlhood fending off the attentions of the men in the slums, to whom virginity was merely a resource being wasted, an avenue that could lead to coins that could keep flagons filled with gin. She'd defended her virtue like a tigress because of an impossible dream, that Tristan Ramsey would be the man to show her passion. That he would take her to his bed and touch her, delight in her, and she could truly belong to him one day.

But today had been a day of dreams come true. In this, her final dream, she could trace the contours of his body, plunder the honeyed sensuality of his mouth, delve into the hidden sensitivity that clung about his dark lashes.

She whimpered as Tristan stripped her gown down her shoulders, letting her garments float one by one to the floor, like the fallen petals of a lily.

Tristan groaned, his gaze devouring as it moved from her tumbled curls to the creamy column of her throat, then lower, to where her breasts shone, alabaster in the candlelight, their crests budding rosy-pink, yearning for his touch so fiercely they ached from it.

"You're beautiful, Alaina," Tristan breathed, reaching up one finger to trace the curve of her breast, his fingertip brushing the pearled tip of her nipple. "You're so damn beautiful. I don't deserve this gift."

"It's not yours to deserve. It's my wish, Tristan. My gift."

"Then why am I on fire for you, Alaina? Why have I never felt such craving to touch, to taste? Why do I want you so much I can't bear to wait another heartbeat?"

He scooped her into his arms, and she curled against his bare chest, kissing whatever she could reach—his jaw, the cords of his throat, his beard-stubbled cheek.

He lifted her onto the bed, then straightened, stripping off his shirt and flinging it over a gilt-legged chair. His eyes never left her face, their dark depths alive with hunger as his deft artist's fingers worked the fastenings of his breeches, then dragged them off as well.

He stood at the bedside, gloriously naked, every dip and plane and steely curve of his body gleaming in the candlelight. Never had Alaina seen anything so breathtaking. He was more beautiful than the image of David that Michelangelo had discovered, hidden in a block of marble. More entrancing than the slumbering Adonis who had captured the love of both Persephone and Aphrodite. For what perfect hero of myth or statue of marble could radiate such passion, such vulnerability, such strength and tenderness with the merest flicker of his eyes, curve of his lips?

Astonished at her own boldness, Alaina reached out a fingertip to touch him. She could feel a shudder of pleasure, raw, untamed, jolt through Tristan. She leaned toward him and pressed her lips against his thundering heart.

He climbed into the bed beside her, drawing her into his arms, kissing her with such hunger it humbled her, awed her, his lips finding the pulse beat at the base of her throat, then trailing fervent kisses to one of her breasts. One large hand engulfed it with worship-filled tenderness, shaping it until the nipple just brushed his lower lip. His breath was hot and hungry and sweet, and she quivered, arching her back, pressing the aching nub between his lips. He took it into that dark, wet haven, suckling her with a tender ferocity that made her tremble, made her moan.

One sinewy thigh eased across her hips, drawing her tighter into his embrace until she was body-long against him, every inch of her burning with the imprint of hard masculine flesh. Chest and thigh, belly and hips, the hard ridge of his arousal cradled against the downy cove between her thighs.

And she wanted more of him—to drink in every sensation, every caress until she couldn't breathe, couldn't speak.

"Ah, Alaina, so soft, so warm," he murmured. "Do you know how badly I've wanted this? From the moment you first fell into my arms."

She whimpered in pleasure, pain, wishing she could tell him the truth. That she had loved him for an eternity. That she had dreamed of making love with him forever.

He traced the delicate arc of her rib cage, ghosted his touch along the slight swell of her belly, then dipped lower.

She cried out, arching against his hand as his fingers found tender, pink flesh, the callused pad brushing a place where every desire seemed centered.

"Open for me, love. Let me show you . . ."

She let her legs fall farther apart, allowing Tristan and his magic to consume her, trusting him utterly, loving him completely. He teased her, tormented her, treasured her, and Alaina could feel the cold walls he'd built to shield his artist's soul trembling, melting, shattering with each slick, honeyed circle he made on her tender bud.

"I want . . . need you inside me, Tristan, a part of me forever. I can't—can't bear it—" she choked out, her own fingers seeking the hard length of him, the surging power between his thighs. He arched against her hand, his breath hissing between clenched teeth.

"Now, angel. Let me take you now." He knelt between her thighs, pressed the tip of his sex against her. Alaina arched, writhed, her fingers clutching at the rippling muscles of his back.

"Please, Tristan—"

He thrust his hips forward, and Alaina gave a choked cry of pain. She felt it lance through him, felt him stiffen, a muffled curse breaching his lips as he breached her untried body.

"What the—No! You've never . . . Why, Alaina? Why didn't you tell me?"

She drifted her fingertips across the lines of sensitivity carved about his beautiful mouth.

"Because then you wouldn't have granted my wish. And I wanted you, Tristan. Wanted you buried deep inside me." *The way you are buried in my heart.*

"Please, Tristan," she whispered. "My wish was that it would be wonderful. No regrets."

His lips curved with gentle awe. "How could I regret finding you? Your hands touching me, the dreams in your eyes that make me believe . . . in angels and miracles and love, Alaina. Love . . ."

He touched her as if they had forever instead of just this night. He savored every caress as if this were the only chance a man would get to make love to a woman in all of time. Every sweep of his hands was as filled with magic as the stroke of brush upon canvas. He poured all the colors of his imagination into her soul as he thrust into her body again and again, painting for her one perfect night when there was no pain or hunger or dream that couldn't come true.

She rose up to meet him, drawing him into the sheath of her body, as if she could banish all pain and bitterness, give back to him the years he'd lost, the passion he'd sacrificed, the joy that had once been as much a part of him as his sensitive hands and generous heart.

She would have given anything to freeze time, stop it forever. Instead, she clung to him more fiercely, trying to brand every sinew of him into her memory, for the long, lonely nights ahead.

She sought out the hot splendor of his kiss, her soul whispering secrets to his, secrets locked away far too long, like the paintings in the attic—love so intense even eternity couldn't dull its luster.

And when she shattered, pleasure exploding through her in exquisite waves of fulfillment, she held him fiercely in her arms as he sought his own release.

It burst upon him, tearing a groan from his chest. And he flung back his head, driving deep into her body, spilling his very soul into her again and again and again.

He collapsed against her, a delicious weight she never wanted to be free of. They lay there, and Alaina could taste Tristan's awe because it mirrored her own.

It seemed an eternity before he rolled to one side, carrying her with him, nestled against his sweat-sheened chest. His voice was raw, uncertain, yet filled with something new—hope.

"Who are you, Alaina?" He breathed the question into the passion-tossed billows of her hair. "I know I remember you— something about you from the first moment I saw you in the drawing room. I feel as if I've known you from the beginning of time."

Alaina buried a small, heartbroken smile against his skin, knowing the price she'd pay for this night would be an eternity of reaching for him in the darkness and the savage pain of discovering he wasn't there.

"I'm only a face in the window, Tristan," she said.

He looked at her, heaven in his eyes. "You're more than that, Alaina. Much more. Tomorrow you'll tell me. I'll love you until the truth spills out."

Tomorrow. She wouldn't be here tomorrow, Alaina thought, aching with the pain of it. Tomorrow she'd be gone.

Tears burned her eyes, but she refused to shed them. She had the rest of her life for tears. But tonight was hers.

She kissed Tristan, stroked him, joy soaring inside her as she felt his passion rise. A low growl rumbled in his chest as he rolled her beneath him. And as the pearl of a moon drifted on its path to the newborn day, they made love again and again, as if it were the last night on earth.

Dawn was a peach-hued promise upon the horizon when Alaina stole from the bed, not even daring to give Tristan a parting kiss. She couldn't risk waking him. It was better this way, that she slip out of his life before he opened his eyes. She couldn't bear to say farewell to him or to the boy who lay slumbering in the nursery.

To answer the questions he'd asked the night before would be to see the light die in his eyes as he realized that there could be no future between a ballad seller's child and a businessman respected by half of London. These people would scorn Tristan if he dared to love her, would shun him.

She should be grateful for her Christmas of magic, take comfort in the fact that she'd had enough miracles to last her a lifetime. She drew on her gown and stood a moment more, watching Tristan dream. The planes of his face had been gentled in their loving, peace brushed in light and shadow about his handsome features. She had given that peace to him. This should be enough for her.

It might have been, if her body hadn't been crying out for one more touch, one more kiss. If her heart hadn't been breaking at the thought of never looking into those dark eyes again and seeing awed passion reflected back at her.

No. Her task was finished here. Her work was done. Together, Tristan and Gabriel would build a life full of painting and promise and wishing on stars. If only she could be there to see Tristan's hair turn silver at the temples, watch his eyes glow with pride in the man Gabriel would become one day. If only she could share all the joy and sorrow the years would bring, give him more children to fill the house with mischief, and when life was through, cling to Tristan's hand, her heart filled to the brim with sweet memories when she closed her eyes for the last time.

She crushed the image that was shattering her heart. No. It was impossible. There was no place for her in Tristan's world. She'd known from the time she was a child there never would be.

She crossed to the desk in the corner, took pen and ink, and scribed a brief message. On tiptoe, she crept to the side of the bed, laying the note upon her pillow. Then she slipped from her pocket the most precious possession she had: a guinea, dulled by child fingers that had clung to it in the dark of night like a talisman. The coin's top had been pierced by a nail long ago, a frayed ribbon strung through the hole so she could wear it next to her heart.

You'd better take it. It's my wish that you do, and Christmas wishes are magic . . . The echoes of a bold boy's voice rippled through her memory as she lay the makeshift necklace tenderly upon the pillow beside him.

"Good-bye, Tristan," she whispered. "You'll be all right

now. I know it. But you and Gabriel will have to watch over each other now that I'm gone."

She turned and fled the room, tears streaming down her cheeks, a lifetime of sobs bursting in her chest as she hastened down the sweep of staircase.

At the drawing room doorway she paused, peering at the Christmas tree one last time. Its branches were plundered, the candles extinguished, the table littered with playthings and gingerbread and a set of paints that had made Tristan's eyes shine with the possibility that there was still time to recapture what he'd lost.

There, tucked beneath the tree lay a new object, wrapped in white cloth. A bit of paper lay atop it. *For Alaina . . .*

Echoes from last night rippled through her. *Come downstairs, I have a surprise for you . . .*

A gift from Tristan. She reached out a finger to touch it, knowing that if she did, she'd never have the strength to leave him. Her fingers curled into a fist. No. The time for presents and dreams was past.

Time . . . Her gaze snagged on the clock above the mantel. Silent. Still.

She stole over and opened the tiny glass door, setting the pendulum in motion. The magic was over. Time was beginning again.

Eleven

TRISTAN STIRRED AWAKE TO THE SHIMMER OF SUNLIGHT, AN unfamiliar eagerness pulsing through him: hope, Alaina's gift, during their night of loving.

He rolled to his side, one hand closing on the place where

Alaina had slept the night before. Only a crackle of paper answered him.

She was gone.

He forced himself upright, his heart hammering as his gaze locked on the pillow, a dull throb of panic beating at his temples. His fingers caught up the note, his eyes scanning it in desperation.

Dear Tristan,

Even we could not stop time forever. You asked who I am, why I came to aid Gabriel when he made his Christmas wish. It is because you changed my world one Christmas long ago. I return to you the Christmas guinea you gave to me. The coin was magic, just as you said, because it showed a whole new world to me. One filled with kindness and gentle voices. A place where there were always arms to hold you when you cried.

Because of you, I worked to make myself fit for that world, learned to read and to sew and to speak as a lady might. But we both know that can never change who I am—the ballad seller's child who followed your Christmas pony through the snow.

Tristan closed his eyes for a heartbeat, the memory flooding through him: Huge golden eyes with a shimmer of pride buried deep. A thin, grubby hand stroking the creamy mane of his pony. A sudden, startling kinship of spirits forged in an instant. A ragged urchin who had haunted him long after Christmas had passed, until he had curled up at his sketchbook and captured the image of that same little girl in one of Beth's angel-white dresses, curled up on a stool beside a pencil-drawn fire.

How many Christmases had he wondered about that little girl as the years passed? Wondered if she had enough to eat, if she was still so very brave. He dragged his gaze back to the letter, his chest aching.

I had never had a Christmas before, but this was so beautiful it will last a lifetime. Give Gabriel my love, and tell him that his father was truly the angel—my angel when I was lost and hungry and cold. You promised me that Christmas wishes are magic when you gave me this coin. Keep it and my wish for you. Be happy, Tristan. Even when I am half a world away, I'll be watching over you.

                                                                    Alaina

"No!" Tristan's voice tore, ragged. He bolted from the bed, snatching up his breeches and shirt, dragging them on. "Alaina?" he bellowed, racing down the stairs. "Alaina! Don't leave me! You can't leave me!" As he reached the drawing room, he heard it, his heart stopping at the sound—the delicate chime of bells that struck the hour. She'd started the clocks again. The magic was over.

Agony poured through him, fiercer than anything he'd ever known. He flung on his cloak, shoved his feet into boots.

"Papa?" Gabriel stood at the head of the stairs, his eyes wide and alarmed. "What's wrong?"

"It's Alaina! She's gone!"

"Did she go up to heaven without even saying good-bye?" The child's lower lip trembled.

"If she did, boy, I'll follow her there. I'll bring her back. I swear it."

He plunged out into the winter chill, calling her name.

It was past midnight when he trudged home, soul-weary, half frozen. He'd searched every coaching inn, every train station and shipyard, every place he could think of. He'd plunged down into the twisted labyrinth of Fleet Street, where the poor clustered in their misery. But it was as if God himself had reached down his hand to carry her away.

Burrows met him at the door, mournful. Tristan didn't even have to tell the old servant that he'd failed. "You'll find her tomorrow, Master Tristan," Burrows said, removing the snow-spattered cloak. "I'm certain that the dear miss couldn't have gotten far. You've countless business connections. It should be easy enough to get up a search."

"For one threadbare woman among countless others? Where could she be? God, where would she go? She must be hurting so badly, leaving Gabriel, believing that I—that I would have rejected her the moment I knew the truth about who she was, where she'd come from."

He crossed to the drawing room, where the tree still shimmered, its beauty barely faded, his gift to her tucked beneath it, unopened; the kissing bough still dangled, its ribbons bright in the firelight. Curled there beneath the shadow of the tree, Gabriel lay sleeping in his nightshirt, his rag-stuffed horse cuddled close, the fairy pin glinting on its shabby coat. Had the boy spent the whole day in this chamber, wishing for his angel to return?

Trudging to the wing chair, Tristan sank down on it, burying his face in his hands. "Where are you, angel?" he murmured against his palm. "God, if I could only tell you . . . But you're not here anymore, watching me through the window. I'll spend forever staring out, wondering where you are. If you're safe and warm. If you're hungry. Where would you run to, Alaina, when you're hurting?"

Gabriel whimpered in his sleep, and Tristan stripped off his frock coat, nestling its warm folds about his son. As he straightened, his gaze snagged on the sparkling expanse of the window.

It shimmered, a hazy reflection of firelight and the spreading branches of the Christmas tree—the fairy-tale vision that had comforted a little girl as she stood shivering in the snow.

Tristan gave a strangled cry, hardly daring to hope. Then he dashed out of the chamber, down the hall. He flung open the door, bolting into the snow.

The chill stung him, but he barely felt it, the night dark as he ran around the corner of the house to where the panes of glass shone against the brick—a golden beacon in the dark of night.

It was then he saw her, huddled beneath her cape, curled there in the shelter of the hawthorn bush.

"Alaina!" He cried out her name, and she spun to face him, her features white and horrified in the moonlight. She wheeled away, started to run, but he caught her in three long strides. His fingers bit into her arms, and he swung her around to face him.

"No!" she cried, struggling. "You have to let me go! I shouldn't have come back. I only wanted to watch you one last time—"

"Before you disappeared again, forever?" Tristan demanded, his voice ragged. "How could you come to my bed, share what we shared, and then turn and walk away?"

"What else could I do? I can't stay! It's impossible!"

"Not if you marry me."

"M-Marry you? Are you mad? Do you have any idea what people would say? The men you do business with. Their wives. Everyone you know."

"You'd be my wife. I don't give a damn what they think."

She looked so broken, so battered, as if she'd been battling with dragons far too long alone. "I've spent a lifetime trying to drag myself out of the London slums," she said, "but even if I were garbed in full court dress, they'd still look at me in horror, sneer at me behind their fans. They will never let me be anything other than the ballad seller's child. That's why I was leaving England. To get away. So that I can be—be someone else."

"What a tragedy that would be, Alaina MacShane. Then you wouldn't be Gabriel's angel. You wouldn't be the woman who bludgeoned her way into my life and made me feel again—joy and anger and hope and fear."

He could see the effort it cost her to thrust her chin up at that valiant angle he so loved. "I'm glad, Tristan. Truly glad if I helped you. But that doesn't mean you have to marry me. Or that I'm fit to be your wife. You need to find some lovely woman to be Gabriel's mother. You'll forget about me. You'll both forget about me in time."

"You truly think Gabriel will ever forget his first Christmas tree? His first pony? Or the woman who gave him a pin from a fairy king's cloak?"

"Tristan, please, I—"

He captured her hands between his own, urgency lacing his voice. "I hadn't forgotten you in all these years. I wondered what had happened to you when you took the coin and ran through the gate. There were so many things I wanted to do— to stop you and take you into the kitchen for some of Cook's sugar buns, to wrap you in one of Beth's warm cloaks. But you were already gone. I even sketched you, Alaina, sitting on the hearth, warm and safe with a plateful of pastries on your lap."

"On the other side of the window," she breathed.

"I'm asking you to enter the enchanted door, Alaina. To stay on my side of the window forever. I need your strength when my faith falters. Your wisdom when I'm uncertain. Your love, even when I fail. You gave me the gift of your belief in me when the paints tumbled from the Christmas tree. You made me dare to forgive myself, to let go of the bitterness that all but destroyed me."

He caught her chin tenderly with his fingers, forcing her to look into his eyes, to see the love shimmering there. "Every day, I watched my son look out that window with the same hopeless longing, the same soul-deep sadness that you must have shown when you peered in. Every day I tried to find the courage to go to him, comfort him. But I didn't believe I had the right. I felt so damned helpless. Then you tumbled into my arms, and everything changed." His voice broke, his eyes burned.

"You didn't come to answer Gabriel's prayers, Alaina. You came to answer mine. That I could start over again, without mistakes, without regrets. That I could paint and love my family, cherish my wife and make her understand that my love for her was the canvas that held all the colors of my dreams. That without her, there was nothing but darkness."

Tears pearled Alaina's lashes, trickling onto her cheek. "Tristan—oh, Tristan—"

He kissed away the salty dampness, hoping that he'd have a lifetime to ease her heartaches, share her joy. "I thought I was wishing the impossible, Alaina. To turn back time, the way you turned back the clocks to make it Christmas again. But I was wrong. For the first time in a long time, it was the future I was dreaming of. A future with you, Alaina. You aren't Gabriel's angel. You're mine. I lost you once, that long-ago Christmas. Please don't ask me to let you go again."

"But I—Oh, how can we . . . We don't know what will happen. If we were so foolish as to marry—"

"I don't know what will happen if I dare to take up painting again, but I'm going to find out. I'm resigning from my position at Ramsey and Ramsey."

A smile widened that soft mouth that had kissed him, healed him. "Oh, Tristan!"

"I love you, Alaina. But you may be trading a new life in America for one as the wife of a struggling artist."

She gazed up at him, her eyes filled with dreams come true. "I've been poor before, Tristan. I'm not afraid. It's not the treasures inside the house that make a home. It's the treasures of the heart. If we have love, we'll have all the riches in the world."

He laughed, swooping her up into his arms, marveling at how chilled she was, vowing to himself that she would never be cold again. He carried her along the path to the front door and flung it open.

"Gabriel?" He called his son, his voice resounding with shimmering joy. They reached the drawing room to see the child sit up, rubbing his tear-reddened eyes with his plump fists. "Gabriel, I've brought you your angel back." Tristan lowered Alaina until her slippers touched the ground.

The boy stared as if he expected her to disappear again in a puff of stardust.

"This time I'm going to stay, Gabriel," she said softly. "Forever and ever."

"Forever?" Gabriel breathed. "But, Papa, how? How did you find her?"

Tristan scooped his son up into his arms, Alaina embracing them both beneath the glistening green of the kissing bough.

"I made a wish," Tristan said, his eyes burning as he turned them to the window, alight with shimmering stars. "Don't you know, Gabriel? Christmas wishes are magic. Now, we need to give Alaina her present." He crossed to the tree, brought her the white-wrapped object.

Alaina unwound the cloth ever so carefully, her heart brimful as the candlelight illuminated a canvas. It was the portrait of Gabriel, a baby angel, but no longer did the painting whisper of hope unfulfilled, dreams uncaptured. A slender feminine hand had been painted to curve around the angel's, tucking a star treasure into his painted fist.

"Oh, Tristan." Tears streaked her face. "You finished it!"

He looked into her face, happily-ever-after in his eyes. "I call it *Alaina*," he said.

KIMBERLY CATES, hailed as "a master craftsman" by *Romantic Times,* is the author of *Crown of Mist, Restless Is the Wind, To Catch a Flame, Only Forever, Crown of Dreams, The Raider's Bride, The Raider's Daughter,* and *Stealing Heaven.* A native of Illinois, Kimberly taught elementary school for three years and married her high school sweetheart. She is currently working on her next historical romance, to be published by Pocket Books.

Andrea Kane

Yuletide Treasure

To my own greatest treasure: my family—
who, every day and in more ways than I can count,
teach me what love is all about.

One

Dorsetshire, England
October, 1860

SHE WAS BACK.

The thunderous knocking at the front door, followed by the flurry of departing footsteps, could mean nothing else.

With a violent curse, Eric Bromleigh, the seventh Earl of Farrington, shot to his feet, exiting the sitting room and taking the hall in long, angry strides.

He didn't need to guess the identity of his arrival. He hadn't a doubt who it was. A visitor was out of the question. No one dared visit Farrington Manor—not since he'd closed it off to the world five years ago.

Except those who came to deliver a universally unwanted package.

Eric kicked a chair from his path, oblivious to the splintering of the lattice-backed Sheraton as it smashed against the wall. Fire raged in his eyes as he bore down on the entranceway door—a menacing warrior set to confront an unshakable foe.

Flinging the door wide, he waved away the cloud of dust kicked up by a rapidly retreating carriage—the second carriage this month and the twenty-second in four years.

The dust settled, and automatically Eric lowered his blazing stare to meet that of the three-and-half foot hellion standing on the doorstep, who returned his stare through brazen sapphire eyes that held not the slightest hint of contrition or shame.

"Hello, Uncle. Fuzzy and I"—she gripped a somewhat tattered stuffed cat—"are back. Mrs. Lawley said to tell you I'm beyond . . . beyond"—she wrinkled her nose—"re-damn-sin."

With that, she shoved her traveling bag aside, shrugged out of her bonnet and coat, and cast them to the floor. An instant later she fired past Eric like a bullet.

"Redemption," Eric ground out, gazing bitterly at the discarded garments. "Beyond *redemption*. Dammit."

On the heels of his oath, a crash reverberated through the house.

Eric whipped about and stalked after the sound, confronting it in the green salon, where his niece stood beside the unlit fireplace, a shattered antique vase at her feet.

"Fuzzy wanted to sit atop that side table." She indicated the now-vacant surface. "Your vase was there. So I moved it. Fuzzy hates to share."

"Noelle." Eric's fists clenched at his sides. "What did you do to the Lawleys? Why did they bring you back?"

An indifferent shrug. "Their dog tried to bite Fuzzy. So I bit him."

"You bit their . . ."

"It was only his tail. Besides, he's fat and ugly. So is his tail."

"The Lawleys were the last decent family left in the parish," Eric roared, ignoring the wrenching pain in his gut spawned by Noelle's uptilted face—an exact replica of her mother's. "What the hell do I do with you now?"

"Don't say hell or else you'll end up there."

A vein throbbed in Eric's temple.

"Unless you came from hell to begin with, like Mrs. Lawley says. She calls you the Devil himself. Are you?"

Something inside Eric snapped. Abruptly, he reversed the vow he'd made the day he'd imprisoned himself inside Farrington, never to emerge.

"Come here, Noelle," he ordered.

"Why?" The keen gaze held no fear, only curiosity.

"Because I command you to. Fetch your coat."

Clearly intrigued, she arched her brows. "We can't be going anywhere. You never leave Farrington."

"I do today. With you. We're going into the village. It's time to resolve your living arrangements once and for all. Follow me." He strode to the door, pausing when he reached its threshold. "I suggest you obey. If I'm forced to repeat myself, I won't be nearly as pleasant as I'm being now."

Noelle folded her arms across her chest. "Even if you thrash me, I'm not going anywhere without Fuzzy."

"Fine," Eric thundered. "Collect your scraggly plaything. I'm bringing around my phaeton."

For an instant, Noelle's chin jutted up, and Eric thought she meant to defy him. Then, shutters descended over her eyes, and she shrugged, picked up her stuffed cat, and trailed silently past Eric into the hall.

He fought the rage that surged inside him like a dark, suffocating wave.

The torment had to end. And, even if making this trip meant rekindling the very fires of hell, he'd ensure that end it did.

Two

"DO YOU REALIZE WHAT YOU'RE ASKING OF ME?"

Rupert Curran gripped the side of the wooden pew on which he sat, raising his eyes to the church ceiling—whether to beseech God or warn him, Eric wasn't sure.

"I believe I made myself quite clear, Vicar," Eric responded. "You needn't quake nor beg for mercy from some alleged

Higher Being. I haven't come to slay you or your parishioners. As I explained, I've come to seek a suitable governess for my niece—a service for which the right candidate will be handsomely compensated. Further, to show my gratitude, I shall donate the sum of five thousand pounds to your church, which"—Eric cast a quick glance about the deteriorating sanctuary walls—"is obviously needed."

"Perhaps some people can be bought, my lord." Curran came to his feet, indignation etched in his every aged feature. "I cannot. Material gain means nothing if the price is sacrificing a young woman's life."

One dark brow rose. "Sacrificing her life? And who is it you fear will destroy her, Noelle or me?"

"Such a question deserves no answer."

"Nevertheless, I'd like one. Having severed all ties with the rest of the world, I'm curious as to whose reputation is blacker, mine or my niece's?"

"Your niece is a child, my lord," the vicar responded distastefully. "I'm convinced that, had she been offered four years of proper love and guidance, she'd be a happy, well-adjusted little girl and this entire conversation would be unnecessary."

"Really? Then tell me this, Vicar: If Noelle requires no more than proper guidance in order to thrive, why has every virtuous family in your parish returned her within a period of . . . let's see—" Eric tapped his fingertips together thoughtfully. "The longest duration was just shy of six months. That was with the Willetts. I'm sure, if there truly is a heaven, those gentle souls have ensured themselves a shining place within its gates. On the other hand, there were the Fields, who endured Noelle for a mere day and a half, until she set fire to the kitchen—and the cook. Overall, I'd estimate my niece's average stay at one residence to be three months."

"There are reasons for a child to behave as Noelle does," Curran said quietly. "But a man like you would have no knowledge of those reasons, nor understand their cause. Therefore, I shan't attempt to explain."

"Fine. Then, if it isn't Noelle's reputation that strikes terror in the hearts of your parishioners and prevents you from fulfilling my request, I assume it is mine."

For a moment, the vicar stared silently at the altar. Then, he replied, "You haven't emerged from your estate in five years, Lord Farrington. And before that—Well, I needn't tell you how shocked the parishioners were at Liza's death, nor how horrified they were by the part you played in driving her toward her untimely end. Most of your former servants still pale when they speak of those final weeks. It was a heinous tragedy, unparalleled in our small, quiet parish. To be blunt, the entire village is terrified of you. No one, regardless of how poverty-stricken they might be, would agree to relinquish their daughter into your hands."

Eric's features had hardened to stone at the mention of his sister's name. "I disagree, Vicar. For the right sum, people will do anything. Even negotiate with the Devil himself."

Curran shook his head. "You're wrong, my lord. Nevertheless, there's another, equally daunting, obstacle we have yet to discuss. Farrington is deserted, save, of course, you—and now Noelle. You dismissed your servants directly after Liza's death and have never replaced them, I presume?"

"Correct. And I have no intention of altering that arrangement."

"That decision is yours to make. However, I assume you expect Noelle's governess to reside at Farrington?"

"Governesses customarily reside at the home of their charges."

"Indeed they do. But this is not a customary situation. You

are an unmarried man suggesting that a respectable woman share your home, unchaperoned and unaccompanied by anyone save a four-year-old child. Even if your past were untainted and your reputation flawless, no proper young woman would accept such unorthodox living arrangements."

A black scowl. "I hadn't considered that. I suppose I should have." Swiftly, Eric reassessed his options. "Fine. I shall amend my offer." Determination glittered in his eyes, laced his tone. "I'll double my donation to the church from five thousand pounds to ten, and, rather than a governess, consider my offer to be for a wife."

"A wife?" Curran's head shot up, and he raked both hands through his silver hair. "Just like that?"

"Just like that." Eric rose. "I'm sure you know that I'm an exceedingly wealthy man. My circumstances have more than reversed themselves over the past five years. I've not only recouped my fortune, I've doubled it. As my wife, the woman in question will have access to all my funds. She needn't limit her spending, nor answer to me on her purchases, since I myself have no use for extravagances. She can send for whatever she wants: jewelry, clothing—a whole bloody wardrobe if she chooses—and whatever other insipid vanities women require. I don't give a damn what she buys—nor what she does, for that matter. So long as she does it within the bounds of my estate and solely during those scant hours when Noelle sleeps. It goes without saying that her conduct must be above reproach, given that she will be Noelle's only role model—and her only contact. The right candidate must understand that Noelle will be exclusively hers. Not only to oversee, but—to be blunt—to keep as far away from me as possible. And one thing more. Make certain the young lady you select is not the restless type. There will be no excursions to London, no balls or soirees, no outings in the country. In short, I remain at Farrington, and as my wife, so will she."

"To translate, she'll be your prisoner."

Eric's eyes flashed. "No, Vicar, she will not be my prisoner. She'll be Noelle's guardian. Which, whether you believe it or not, is a full-time job."

"What about the young lady's family ties?"

"They'll have to be severed. No one is permitted to visit Farrington."

"Why can't *she* visit *them?* With Noelle, of course. Certainly, you agree it would be good for the child to have a change of scene now and again."

"No!" Eric's fist slammed against the pew, the wood vibrating from the intensity of his blow. "I want no link with the world, no matter how indirect. Farrington—and all its occupants—remain where they are. As for diversion, Noelle will have hundreds of acres to destroy. That should be enough, even for her."

Dragging his hand through his hair, Eric brought himself under control. "Now, given those unnegotiable terms, who would you recommend I interview?"

Curran blinked in astonishment. "I cannot provide you with a candidate instantly—if ever. You'll have to give me some time."

"And during that time, do you trust a blackhearted sinner like me alone with Noelle?" Eric asked in an icy, mocking tone. "Because, quite frankly, I don't."

The vicar had just opened his mouth to reply when an unladylike shout permeated the church.

"Damn her." Eric's head snapped around.

"Lord Farrington," the vicar denounced with righteous indignation. "Need I remind you that you're in a house of God?"

"With a demon outside, threatening to break down its

hallowed walls." Eric was already heading for the door. "I instructed the little hoyden to remain on the lawn and amuse herself during my meeting. By now, she's doubtless annihilated your gardens and every living creature within it."

"She's scarcely four years old." Curran urged his aged body into motion, walking stiffly in Eric's wake. "She shouldn't be left unattended."

"Fulfill my request and she won't be."

He was reaching for the door when a terrified shriek rang out, followed by shouts of "Whoa!" and the sound of scrambling hooves.

Eric exploded from the church in time to see Noelle crouched in the road, paralyzed with terror as an oncoming carriage swerved from side to side, its driver trying desperately to avoid running her down.

"Christ." Eric took the church steps in two long strides, knowing even as he did that he could never reach her in time.

Out of nowhere, a flash of color darted from the opposite side of the road, snatching Noelle and rolling away as the horses reared—once, twice—tossing their heads in protest.

The carriage stopped.

Silence ensued, broken only by the disoriented snorts of the horses and Eric's harsh, uneven breaths as he battled a wild, immobilizing surge of emotion.

From somewhere behind, he vaguely heard the vicar approach, heard his murmured, "Thank God."

Oblivious to their presence, Noelle lifted her head and stared, white-faced, at the young woman in whose arms she was now clasped—a woman who had just saved her life.

With a howl of outrage, she began to struggle and beat at her rescuer's shoulders. "Let go of me! Fuzzy is under there. I've got to find him."

Unflinching, the young woman warded off the blows. "Stop

it," she commanded quietly, catching Noelle's small, trembling fists. "You can't rescue—Fuzzy, did you say?—if you're flattened beneath a carriage wheel." She squeezed Noelle's hands—a tender gesture that belied the severity of her tone— then raised her head and calmly regarded the sweating carriage driver, who looked as if he'd seen a ghost. "It's all right," she soothed him. "The child is unharmed. But I'd appreciate your keeping the carriage stationary a moment longer. Would that be possible?"

Mutely, he nodded.

"Thank you." The woman stood, still clutching Noelle as she brushed the road dust off her simple, mauve-colored frock. "Now," she addressed the child, "suppose you tell me what kind of animal Fuzzy is. Then we shall find him."

"He's a cat." A mutinous spark ignited in Noelle's eyes, and her chin jutted out belligerently as she clarified her statement. "A stuffed cat."

"Excellent. Now I know what I'm searching for." Disregarding Noelle's stunned expression, the woman nodded matter-of-factly. Then, shifting Noelle's weight onto one arm, she marched closer to the carriage, squatting to peer beneath. "Is Fuzzy fawn-colored?"

"Yes." Noelle strained to see. "Have you spotted him? Is he there?"

"Indeed he is. There and intact. A most fortunate cat." Noelle's rescuer turned to face her wriggling bundle. "I'll offer you a deal. If you promise to return to that pile of leaves you were playing in, I promise to rescue Fuzzy. However, if you venture back into the street before I reach your side, I can't be responsible for Fuzzy's fate. Is it a deal?"

Noelle stared at her as if she'd lost her mind. "Did you hear what I said? Fuzzy's not a real cat."

"I heard you. I repeat, do we have a deal?"

A slow, astonished nod. "Yes."

"Good." The young woman set Noelle on the ground and gave her a gentle push. "Go ahead."

Noelle sprinted to the grass.

Her rescuer smiled her approval. Then, shoving unruly chestnut curls behind her ears, she dropped unceremoniously to her knees. With calculated caution, she crawled alongside the carriage, keeping a healthy distance from the wheels, lest the horses bolt. At last, she stopped and groped beneath the vehicle.

Scant seconds later, Fuzzy emerged, gripped tightly in her hand. "Success," she called out, grinning. Her grin faded as Noelle lunged forward. "Stop." One palm rose to ward off Noelle's advance. "Our deal was for you to remain on the grass. One more step and Fuzzy will resume his precarious position beneath the carriage."

Noelle halted in her tracks.

The dazzling smile returned. "Wonderful. I appreciate a person who keeps her word." She glanced back at the driver. "Thank you, sir. You can be on your way."

The befuddled man was wiping his brow with a dirty handkerchief. "Thank you," he croaked.

"Thank *you*, sir." She waved, then headed toward Noelle.

The clattering of the departing carriage shattered Eric's paralyzed state.

Rage, vast as a storm-tossed wave, erupted inside him. He charged toward the roadside, where, at that moment, Noelle's rescuer was placing Fuzzy in the child's arms.

"Here you are," she said brightly. "Fuzzy survived his adventure and is none the worse for it."

Noelle snatched her beloved toy, her eyes still wide with disbelief.

"My name is Brigitte," the woman offered, patting Fuzzy's tattered head. "What's yours?"

A heartbeat of silence. Then: "Noelle."

"Well, Noelle, being that you're obviously quick on your feet, I'm sure you would have escaped that carriage unharmed. But I'm not nearly as sure about Fuzzy. For his sake, perhaps you could be a bit more cautious in the future."

"I suppose." Noelle glanced up to see her uncle bearing down on her. "I'm about to be chest-ized."

Brigitte stifled a grin. "And who is going to chastise . . ." Her mouth snapped shut as Eric loomed over them.

"Noelle, I ordered you to remain on the church grounds," he thundered. "What the hell were you doing in the middle of the street?"

Chewing her lip, Noelle regarded him solemnly. "That's twice in one morning," she pronounced. "I think you'd best not say *hell* again, Uncle. Even God has his limits."

A choked sound emerged from Noelle's rescuer—an obviously unsuccessful attempt to smother laughter.

"You find recklessness and impudence to be amusing traits, young woman?" he roared, unleashing his outrage on her full force.

To his astonishment, she raised her chin, meeting his ferocity head-on. "Recklessness, no, Lord Farrington. Nor impudence —at least not in its mean-spirited form. However, in this case, I must admit to finding Noelle's observation—albeit outspoken —to be amusingly valid."

Anger was eclipsed by surprise, and Eric's brows drew together. "You know who I am."

"I do."

"How?"

"I have a remarkable memory, my lord. And five years is not

so very long a time. While your appearance has altered somewhat"—she indicated his unshaven face and unruly hair—"on the whole, you look much the same."

"I don't remember you."

An ever-so-faint smile. "No, I don't suppose you do."

Pensively, he scrutinized her. "Since you know who I am, I assume you're also familiar with my shrouded past, and my ultimate—and permanent—seclusion."

"I'm aware of your reputation, yes."

"Yet you're not afraid of me?"

"No, my lord, I'm not."

"Why is that?"

A peppery spark lit her eyes, warming them to a radiant golden brown. "Stupidity, probably. But, you see, I've spent the past year and a half teaching children—two dozen of them, in fact, ranging in age from four to fourteen. As a result, it seems I have become impervious to both shock and fear. Even in the case of a notorious man like yourself."

"Brigitte!" The vicar's anxious voice interrupted, as he finally made his way to the roadside. "Are you all right?" He reached for her hands, clasping them in his.

"I'm fine, Grandfather," she assured him gently. "Dusty and disheveled, but fine." She rubbed one smudged cheek. "We all are—Noelle, Fuzzy, and me."

Grandfather? Eric's eyes narrowed on her face as a wisp of memory materialized at last.

A tiny child with a cloud of dark hair, trailing behind the vicar at every church function. A skinny girl in a secondhand frock giving out coins and sweets to the parish children as they exited after Christmas services. A gawky adolescent smiling shyly at him as he passed through the streets, gazing at Liza as if she were some sort of exalted angel.

The vicar's granddaughter.

How old had she been when last he'd seen her? No more than twelve or thirteen at the most.

Well, it was five years later. And the skinny girl, the gawky adolescent, were no more. To be sure, the forthright young woman who stood before him, her nose streaked with dirt, bore traces of the child she'd once been. Slender and petite, the crown of her chestnut head scarcely reached his chest. Her features, too, had remained dainty, from the delicate line of her jaw to the fine bridge of her nose to her high, sculpted cheekbones. Her manner of dress, a result of financial hardship he suspected, was also unchanged; her gown, beneath its newly acquired layer of dirt, was as plain and well-worn as ever.

And yet—Eric's probing gaze continued its downward scrutiny—despite the gown's faded, rumpled state, it could not detract from the feminine curves it defined; curves that had not existed five years past and which completely belied the hoyden-like behavior he'd just witnessed.

This unexpected whirlwind was a far cry from the person in his dim recollections.

"My lord?"

With a start, Eric realized she was speaking to him—and he looked up swiftly, seeing the uncertain expression on her face. "What?"

"I merely noted you seem a bit unnerved, which is understandable given Noelle's narrow escape. May I offer you something? A cup of tea?"

His decision burst upon him like gunfire.

"Yes, you may offer me something," he pronounced. "But not tea." He caught her elbow, staying her initial steps toward the church, curtly dismissing her objective in lieu of his more pressing one. "Miss Curran—it is Miss Curran, is it not? I see no wedding ring on your finger."

She glanced bewilderedly at his viselike grip on her arm.

Instantly, he released her. "I'm not going to harm you," he affirmed, sarcasm lacing his tone. "In fact, my intentions are uncharacteristically honorable. Now, is it or is it not Miss Curran?"

"It is, my lord," she confirmed, brows drawn in puzzlement.

"Excellent. You're unmarried. Next, are you betrothed? Bound to one suitor? Promised to . . . ?"

"Lord Farrington, this has gone far enough," the vicar broke in. "I'll save you time and trouble. The answer is no."

Eric cocked a brow. "No? Meaning your granddaughter is not spoken for?"

"No. Meaning she is not going to become your wife."

Brigitte gasped. "Wife? May I know what you two are talking about?"

"Indeed you may." Eric silenced the vicar's protests with an authoritative sweep of his arm. "Enough. Your granddaughter is a woman grown. Let her speak for herself." With that, he returned his attention to Brigitte. "Miss Curran, I'll be blunt. I've just made your grandfather a business proposition, one that would benefit both the church and the entire parish—and one he seems reluctant to accept."

"What was this proposition, my lord?"

"I offered him ten thousand pounds in exchange for finding me a suitable governess for my niece, Noelle. Further, since the chosen candidate would be expected to reside at Farrington— which is deserted save Noelle and myself—I agreed, for propriety's sake, to make the appropriate young woman my wife. This would render her the Countess of Farrington, complete with mansion, title—albeit a tarnished one—and more wealth than she ever dreamed possible.

"In return, she would be expected to shoulder the difficult and distasteful job of overseeing Noelle, who, as you've just witnessed firsthand, is an uncontrollable demon. Since gossip travels quickly, I'm sure you know that Noelle's been taken in by every respectable family in the parish and, just as quickly, turned out. As of today, the supply of decent families has been exhausted. Hence, my need for a drastic and immediate solution. Frankly, I've never seen anyone manage Noelle as well as you just did. You mentioned having experience teaching children. Being the vicar's granddaughter, I'm certain your character is above reproach. Tallying all those factors together, I'm prepared to offer you the position I've just described. Would you be interested?"

Brigitte's eyes had grown wider and wider with each passing word. "You'd give ten thousand pounds to the parish and take on a wife you don't know or want just to provide care for Noelle?"

"Exactly."

"Why not care for her yourself?"

Eric's jaw clenched. "That, Miss Curran, is my concern, not yours."

"What about your own life, then? What if, in the years to come, you find someone you truly love? You'd never be able to give her your name, having already bestowed it upon your governess."

A crack of mocking laughter. "You need not worry on that score. With the exception of today, I never intend to leave Farrington or to rejoin society. Therefore, I shan't have the opportunity to meet this alleged keeper of my heart. Your answer, please?"

She blanched. "My answer—now?"

"Certainly, now. I don't see a need to procrastinate, nor to explore absurd, farfetched ramifications." A sudden possibility made him scowl. "*You* don't harbor any romantic illusions of marrying for love, do you? Is that why you posed that ludicrous question about my awaiting the perfect bride?"

Brigitte's lashes drifted to her cheeks. "I harbor no such illusions, my lord. In truth, I thought never to marry."

"Why is that?"

Her lashes lifted, but shutters descended in their wake. "To echo your sentiments, that is my concern, not yours."

He felt a spark of admiration at her audacious response. "As you wish. Very well, then, let's circumvent your reasons and get to your decision. Are you or are you not willing to forgo your expectations to remain unwed, and to accept my terms? Simply answer yes or no."

"Lord Farrington, we're discussing marriage, not a business venture."

A shrug. "In this case, they are one and the same. I've made you an offer, defined the conditions that accompany it. Assuming both of us are amenable, we'll finalize our agreement."

"Just like that?"

"Just like that." Eric ignored her baffled incredulity. "After which there will be no further need for us to interact. You'll keep Noelle occupied and out of my sight. I'll sustain my solitary life. As a result, Miss Curran, you'll have no reason to fear for your own."

An odd light flickered in Brigitte's eyes. "You're determined to further this illusion, aren't you?" she asked softly.

Eric went rigid. "What in hell does that mean?"

"Three times," Noelle piped up. "Now you said that bad word three times."

Eric tore his stunned gaze from Brigitte to glare unsteadily at his niece.

"Noelle." Brigitte interceded, squatting down and stunning Eric yet again—this time with her direct and effective manner of handling Noelle's insolent tongue. "Your uncle is an adult, and adults cannot be ordered about nor reprimanded by children."

"Why? He said a wicked oath."

"I agree. Nevertheless, the rule I just gave you holds true even if the adult in question happens to be wrong. I know it seems very unfair, but that doesn't change the fact that a rule is a rule and must be followed."

Sullenly, Noelle kicked the dirt.

"You're angry. I don't blame you. I get angry when I have to follow rules I disagree with, too."

That made Noelle's chin come up. "What rules do you have to follow? You're a grown-up. You can do what you want."

"Oh, if that were only true." Brigitte sighed, shaking her head. "But it's not. Let me tell you something. Not only do adults have rules to abide by, just like children, but ofttimes our rules are far harder to obey—and the consequences far more dire if we don't."

A spark of interest. "Really?"

"Really. For example, if your uncle continues to utter profanities, 'tis true that you and I can do nothing to stop him. But I know someone who can." Solemnly, Brigitte raised her eyes to the heavens, then rolled them pointedly at Eric. "Thus, were I Lord Farrington, I'd guard my tongue. After all, you never know when He might be watching . . . and listening."

Noelle looked thoroughly pleased with that prospect.

"Brigitte," the vicar interceded, "before you foolishly entertain the notion of accepting Lord Farrington's offer, you should be aware of one detail he has yet to mention. The young woman he weds will be forbidden to leave his estate, with or without Noelle. She'll be a veritable prisoner in a mansion that is no home but a mausoleum. I, better than anyone, understand your tender heart and its selfless intentions. But I also understand that the same tender heart would suffocate within so barren a life. Thus, my answer is still no."

"We've heard your answer and your sentiments several times, Vicar," Eric snapped with icy derision. "But, as you are not the one I've asked to wed, I'd like to hear from your granddaughter. Miss Curran?" He lowered his expectant stare to Brigitte, who still crouched next to Noelle. And waited.

Brigitte met his gaze, looking from him to her grandfather and, finally, to Noelle, who abruptly bowed her head and began whispering to Fuzzy.

The last seemed to trigger Brigitte's decision.

She came to her feet.

"I accept your offer, Lord Farrington." As she spoke, she squeezed her grandfather's forearm—whether to reassure him or silence him, Eric wasn't certain. "—with a few stipulations."

Caution eclipsed relief. "Name them."

"I shall gladly take charge of Noelle and fulfill my part of the arrangement. I'll even comply with your less-than-appealing mandate that, once wed, I'll remain permanently at Farrington. However, I refuse to sever ties with my grandfather."

Eric's jaw clenched. "And I refuse to have my privacy invaded. I also refuse to allow you and Noelle to go traipsing to the village to be ogled and grilled about the savage with whom you reside."

Another profound flicker in those damned golden eyes, followed by—of all things—an impish smile. "Are visits by delivery men excluded from your definition of privacy invasion?"

"Pardon me?"

"Delivery men. They'll be arriving at Farrington in droves. Otherwise, how will I receive all the extensive purchases due a countess?"

Taken aback by her obvious teasing, Eric cleared his throat. "I see your point." A pause. "Very well, Miss Curran," he conceded, frowning as he sought a solution he could live with. "Your grandfather may visit you—once a month, and alone. Further, as no one is permitted to enter my *mausoleum*"—he cast a derisive look at the vicar—"your visits must take place on the grounds, not in the manor. Unless of course you elect to emulate the delivery men. In which case, you have my consent to meet at the mansion's rear entrance."

Her lips curved again. "Fair enough."

"Also, I expect, during these visits, that you will not neglect your responsibility to Noelle. She is to be in your company—and in your sight—at all times." His mouth twisted into a mocking grin. "Think of it this way: You can see to Noelle's well-being, while the vicar is assuring himself of yours."

Brigitte's smile vanished. "You have my word that I'll never neglect Noelle. Will that be sufficient?"

"It will."

"Thank you," she replied solemnly. "To continue: Before we wed and leave for Farrington, I shall require several hours in the village, both to visit the homes of my students—who deserve an explanation for my sudden departure—and to speak with a friend of mine who currently instructs in her home, but who would be elated to take over my job at the schoolhouse. Frankly, she is the only person I'd entrust with my students."

"You care that much for them?"

"I do."

"Very well. Consider your first two stipulations granted."

Brigitte gripped the folds of her gown, raising her chin a notch—and alerting Eric to the magnitude of her next condition. "You said I could spend your money freely, at my discretion. To be frank, I require nothing. But the parish does, more over the course of time than even your ten thousand pounds can supply. So, I'd like your word that I can provide for the church, the children, the village—any aspect of our parish I might deem worthy—not only now, but for all the years to come."

"My word," he repeated woodenly.

"Yes. Just as I gave you mine."

"What makes you think my word can be trusted?"

"Instinct."

A heartbeat of silence.

"My word, then. You may provide for the parish in any way and at any time you choose. Continue with your stipulations."

"I have but two more. First, I want my grandfather's future ensured, his appointment to our church guaranteed for the rest of his life. Is that acceptable?"

Eric nodded. "It is."

"And last, I'd like Noelle's blessing on our arrangement."

"Nothing more?"

"Nothing more." Brigitte glanced down, tucking a strand of sable hair behind the child's ear. "Noelle?"

"What?" Noelle muttered into Fuzzy's fur.

"How do you feel about my coming to live with you and your uncle?"

A shrug.

"I could help keep Fuzzy out of trouble."

Noelle unburied her face, assessing Brigitte with probing sapphire eyes. "I s'pose."

"Then it's all right with you?"

"I s'pose."

"Excellent."

Eric cleared his throat. "Does this mean your decision is final?"

"It does."

"Good." He veered toward the church, sidestepping both Brigitte and the disconcerted vicar. "I'll await your return. After which, your grandfather can perform the ceremony." He paused, his back to her. "Miss Curran?"

"Yes?"

"Thank you for saving Noelle's life."

Three

"NO. UNEQUIVOCALLY NO. YOU WILL NOT TAKE THIS FRIGHT-ful step based on some misplaced sense of duty to me and your students. You'll be helping no one by committing yourself to a blackhearted beast like Farrington."

The vicar leaned unsteadily against Brigitte's commode, watching as she arranged her meager wardrobe in the open traveling bag on her bed.

Responding to the anguish in his tone, Brigitte abandoned her task and went to him. "Grandfather." She lay her palm alongside his jaw. "The earl is not a 'blackhearted beast.' We both know that. If not in fact, then in here." She pointed to her heart. "It's not duty alone that's prompting my decision. I truly want to wed Lord Farrington."

"Why? Because of your romantic childhood notions? Brigitte, surely you can't still be clinging to those?"

"Why not?" She inclined her head, searching her grandfather's face. "Don't you recall what he was like before . . . before . . ."

"Yes—before," the vicar replied grimly. "And, yes, of course I remember. But that was years ago. Then came Liza's tragic death and the earl's self-imposed seclusion—events far more destructive than time. Lord Farrington is not the same man who filled your girlhood dreams."

"I realize that. Which is all the more reason for my decision."

Brigitte silenced her grandfather's protest with a gentle shake of her head, wondering how she could make him understand, when he lacked knowledge of a vital piece of the truth. But then, she'd never shared that conversation with him, for there were some memories too painful to discuss, even with this beloved man who'd raised her. "Grandfather, our parishioners come from miles around to seek your advice, easing their burdens simply by sharing them with you. Why? Because of your compassionate heart and open mind. Please, Grandfather, won't you offer those same gifts to me?"

The vicar sighed. "I'll try, child. It's not as easy when you love someone as much as I love you."

"I know. I feel the same way about you. And about our church. That love alone would propel me to accept the earl's offer. But I'd be lying if I professed that to be my only reason for doing so." Her gaze swept the ceiling, as if consulting the heavens, then lowered to meet the vicar's. "I understand your concerns, and I love you for them. But the earl is in pain. As is Noelle. They need me. It's my responsibility—no," she amended softly, "my privilege—to help them heal." With solemn reverence, Brigitte clasped her grandfather's hands. "How many times have we pondered the source of my restlessness? How often have we wondered why I feel so empty inside; as if I'm missing my calling—some unknown purpose that would give my life meaning?"

A flash of pain crossed the vicar's face. "I thought you'd filled that void with your teaching."

"Partially, perhaps. Fully? Never. Not that I haven't adored teaching the children," she hastened to add. "I have. And, yes, they've needed me. But Norah is equally qualified to fill that need. The two times she visited the schoolhouse, the children clustered around her like eager cubs. She's a fine instructor, and a caring one. My students will thrive beneath her guidance.

Whereas Noelle . . ." Brigitte's voice quavered, emotion surging inside her like a great, untamed wave. "You've always said that when a person's life is at its bleakest is the time when God's hope shines through. Perhaps now is that time, for both the earl and Noelle. Perhaps God is offering me this opportunity to bring joy back into their lives, to help make them a family. And maybe, just maybe, to open Lord Farrington's heart to love. Noelle needs him so badly. You and I both realize that beneath her sassy, devilish facade she's no more than a forsaken child."

"True. But is the earl capable of offering her that which she needs? Can a heart as cold as his learn to love?"

"Lord Farrington's heart needs to be reawakened, not taught. Think, Grandfather. Remember the stories you told me— about how the earl saw to Liza's upbringing?"

Staring off, the vicar's thoughts traveled back more than two decades. "That was a lifetime ago, but yes," he murmured. "Liza was a babe, the earl scarcely in his teens, when their parents were lost at sea. Lord Farrington refused to give Liza up to the countless families who offered to raise her. With the help of his servants, he himself provided her with care, education . . ."

"And love," Brigitte finished. "Even I recall that—not from the onset obviously, since Liza was two years my senior—but from the time she was about six or seven. She and Lord Farrington attended church weekly, arriving just before your service began. Oh, how eagerly I'd await their carriage. I'd watch them alight—a beautiful princess and her guardian, straight from the pages of a fairy tale. Lord Farrington was everything a princess could dream of: protective, devoted—and so handsome it was hard not to stare. His smile—I remember that most of all. It would begin at his eyes, then travel to his mouth. It was so dazzling it could melt the winter's snow." A reminiscent light dawned in Brigitte's eyes. "Every year during your Christmas service he would slip a gift into Liza's coat pocket, undetected. It wasn't until they were leaving the church that she'd find it. Then she'd squeal and hug him, and he'd break into that wonderful rumbling laughter . . ." Brigitte's voice faltered.

The vicar cupped her chin, raising her face to meet his gaze. "Your preoccupation with the earl began earlier than I realized."

"I suppose it did. But, preoccupied or not, what I beheld was fact, not sentiment. Lord Farrington was an exemplary brother. He doted on Liza. A man like that doesn't need to be taught to care."

"Brigitte," the vicar said quietly, "all that altered near the end. The earl changed after he lost his fortune; he became angry, bitter. His transformation must have been dreadful—and I'm not only referring to his physical transformation, although that alone was intimidating enough. But his unkempt hair and unshaven face were eclipsed by the hollow darkness in his eyes, his soul. How many times did we hear of his torrents? The way he cast the manor in darkness, permeated with silence, but for his terrifying fits of rage? 'Tis no wonder that less than two months later Liza ran off."

"If she was so afraid of her brother, why did she return?" Brigitte demanded.

"She was alone and with child. She had nowhere else to turn. So she sought refuge at Farrington, where she gave birth to Noelle on Christmas Day. Again, according to the servants, the weeks that followed were torturous. Torturous and violent."

"Liza died abroad, Grandfather, not at Farrington."

"Yes, I know. But what caused her to flee again? What if it truly was fear? What if the earl does have a temper as dangerous as the servants claim? What if that temper did, in fact, provoke Liza's flight and, ultimately, her death?"

"I don't believe that. Lord Farrington would never hurt Liza. Didn't you see the pain on his face just now when he looked at Noelle? That wasn't guilt, Grandfather, that was anguish— anguish that makes it unbearable for him to have her near. Why? Because she's the image of her mother. He's never gotten over losing Liza."

"Even if that's so, Noelle is the one now being hurt."

"I agree. Noelle sees only her uncle's rejection, not the pain beneath it. She's far too young to understand. But I *do* understand. I want to help. Please, Grandfather, let me do this. I know in my heart it's the right thing. And, at the same time, I'll be offering our parish the funds it needs to survive. Not only now, but always."

The vicar smoothed Brigitte's hair from her brow. "Child, even if I disregard my qualms about Lord Farrington, I'm still not at ease. You have no idea what it means to be a wife. I've never prepared you . . ."

"I know what's entailed," Brigitte interrupted softly. "However, your worry is most likely unfounded. Lord Farrington gave us no indication that he wants anything more than a governess—someone to share his name, not his bed."

"Still, you're a beautiful young woman. And the earl *is* a man." Curran frowned. "I should have anticipated this day and better planned for it. But somehow the years dashed by without my notice. One moment you were a shy little girl. The next, you're a woman grown, eighteen and ready to begin your own life." He shook his head in wonder. "Did I fail to see the signs? Have there been gentlemen who've shown interest?"

"No," Brigitte returned adamantly. "At least none whose interest I've returned."

"Because of Lord Farrington?"

Utter candor shone in her eyes. "Yes."

The vicar fell silent, wondering why all his supposed wisdom wasn't sufficient to provide him with the insight he needed right now. Torn between reason and affection, he sought a higher voice, beseeching Him for advice.

In the end, he wasn't sure which was more compelling, God's will or the appeal on Brigitte's face.

"All right, child," he relented. "I'll marry you to Lord Farrington. I only pray I'm doing the right thing—for you and for Noelle."

"You are." Brigitte gave him a fierce hug. "Thank you, Grandfather. I'll hurry and finish packing. I have only three students left to visit. Then I'll be ready."

"I'll await your arrival in the church." A hint of a smile appeared. "That is, if it's still standing. The earl and Noelle have been there for hours. By now the entire structure may be reduced to a pile of debris."

Brigitte grinned. "Then we'll rebuild it."

"Structures are far easier to rebuild than lives."

"True. But the results are not nearly as rewarding." Gently, Brigitte kissed her grandfather's cheek. "Don't worry," she whispered. "I shan't be going to Farrington alone. I'll take with me your most precious gifts: love, determination, and an abundance of faith. Armed with those tools, how can I fail?"

TWO HOURS LATER, BRIGITTE'S CONFIDENCE WAS SUBJECTED TO its first test.

Before her loomed the tangible evidence of her onerous challenge: Farrington Manor.

Slipping off her coat, she took a long look about her new

home. The entry hall was barren, devoid of furnishings or objects, other than one upset chair that sprawled across the wooden floor and a small traveling bag—Noelle's, she assumed. The light was minimal, the ceiling high, the walls bare.

Walls it would be up to her to fill.

She drew a fortifying breath, reminding herself that no task was insurmountable. Farrington was hollow, not cold. Its heart was asleep, its soul encased in darkness.

But how to awaken it?

"You and Noelle may do as you choose," Eric pronounced, tossing his coat in a nearby cloakroom. "As you can see, the manor is quite large. The grounds surrounding it are extensive. Most of my time is spent in my quarters. Therefore, there's little worry that we'll cross paths." He bent, gripping the handle of Brigitte's one and only bag. "I'll place this in your room." With that, he headed toward the staircase.

"Wait."

Shoulders taut, he pivoted to face his bride. "What is it?"

"Before you take your leave, I have several questions I need answered. For one thing, where *is* my room? And Noelle's, for that matter? Not to mention the kitchen and the schoolroom?" As she spoke, Brigitte lay a restraining palm on Noelle's shoulder, perceiving—and understanding—the child's restlessness. After all, she'd been confined for hours: first waiting in the church with Eric, next standing by while the vows were being exchanged, and last, sitting still for the carriage ride home. As a result, she was a coiled spring ready to explode. And if she did . . . well, Brigitte wasn't eager to see Eric's reaction.

"I won't take much of your time, my lord," Brigitte continued, using her unoccupied hand to scoop up Noelle's bag. "But as you yourself just said, the manor is huge. So unless you have a map to provide me, I will need some instructions."

Eric's gaze delved into her's, his expression unreadable. At last, he nodded. "Fine." He stalked back and relieved her of Noelle's traveling bag. "Follow me."

"Fuzzy and I aren't staying in that pink room," Noelle announced as they rounded the first-floor landing. "It's ugly and Fuzzy hates it. He doesn't much like the green room either. It's filled with dumb statues that don't do anything. Except break."

Brigitte saw the corded muscles in Eric's neck go rigid—the only indication that he'd heard Noelle's outspoken stipulations. She herself had to bite her lip to keep from laughing.

They headed down a seemingly unending hallway.

"The blue room is my favorite," Noelle continued. "It has a big window and long drapes. When I'm bored, I use them to climb down to the ground."

"You destroyed those drapes during your last stay," Eric returned icily. "You cut them to shreds to make a winter coat for *that* tattered thing." He jerked his head in Fuzzy's direction, never stopping or breaking stride.

"Fuzzy isn't a 'that.' He's a 'he.'"

"Nevertheless, the drapes are gone. The remnants have since been carried off by real animals. Ask your governess to order new ones." Abruptly, he halted. "The blue room," he announced, flinging open the door and depositing Noelle's bag within.

Brigitte peeked inside. "It's lovely," she murmured, appraising the canopied bed and wide—though blatantly curtainless—windows with a smile. "Very well, if this is to be Noelle's room"—turning, she glanced thoughtfully across the hall—"I'll take the chamber directly opposite it." In a flash, she sprinted over and reached for the door handle.

"No!"

Eric's command fired like a bullet. Jolted, Brigitte backed away, her eyes wide and questioning.

"That room is not to be disturbed," he thundered, advancing on her. "Ever. It is locked. It will remain so. Is that clear?"

Wordlessly, Brigitte nodded.

"Good. If you wish to be near Noelle, take the room next to hers." Eric gripped Brigitte's elbow and ushered her down to the next room. "I'm sure you'll find these to your liking. If not, there are a dozen other bedchambers to choose from. One will doubtless suit you."

Catching her breath, Brigitte inquired, "Which chambers are yours?"

His brows arched, anger evidently eclipsed by surprise. "None of these. I reside in another wing. Why?"

"Because I want to know precisely where Noelle and I are prohibited from entering. That way, we can prevent unpleasant displays of temper like the one you just subjected us to."

A flicker of something—was it admiration?—flashed in Eric's dark eyes. "I suppose that's prudent. My quarters are at the far end of the corridor in the east wing. As to your limitations, other than the bedchamber you just approached and, of course, my own, you're welcome to frequent any room you like." He cleared his throat. "Treat the manor as your home."

"Thank you," she replied soberly, searching the harsh lines of his face. "Now, if you will just tell me where the kitchen is, I shan't trouble you again. Noelle, Fuzzy, and I will settle in and begin to get acquainted. Perhaps we'll explore the grounds. Unless, of course, Noelle shatters that lovely lamp on her nightstand—the one she's rolled to its side and Fuzzy is vaulting over. In which case, we'll spend the afternoon sweeping up slivers of glass. Right, Noelle?"

Noelle jumped, stunned to realize Brigitte was aware of her actions. "How did you know what Fuzzy and I were doing?" she demanded, staring at Brigitte's profile. "You're looking at my uncle."

"I'm smart." Brigitte grinned, turning to face her. "And so are you. So I'm sure you'll agree it would be a shame to waste the remainder of this crisp autumn day scooping up pieces of the very lamp by which I planned to read you a bedtime story. I admit that Fuzzy's antics are amusing. But are they worth sacrificing an outing *and* an hour's reading adventure? The choice, little tempest, is yours. And, of course, Fuzzy's."

Noelle's eyes grew wide as saucers. "You're not going to punish me?"

"For what? You haven't done anything—yet." A conspiratorial wink.

Slowly, Noelle stood the lamp back in its original spot. "Fuzzy likes to jump," she informed Brigitte, twining a lock of hair about her finger. "But he likes leaf piles better than lamps."

"I can understand that. Dashing about the woods presents far more exciting, and safer, possibilities than skipping about a small nightstand." Brigitte's smile reached out to Noelle, enveloped her in its warmth. "If you'll give me a moment with your uncle, I promise to help you amass the tallest mound of leaves you've ever seen—one that will impress even Fuzzy. Would that be acceptable?"

A decisive nod.

"Excellent. And, Noelle," Brigitte added with undisguised pleasure, "I'm proud of you. That was a mature and responsible decision. Fuzzy is lucky to have you looking out for him." With that, she turned back to Eric, nearly laughing aloud at his stunned expression. "The kitchen, my lord?"

"*H-m-m?* Oh, the kitchen." He dragged a hand through his thick hair. "It's directly beneath the pantry area—which is down the stairs to your right. Groceries are delivered once a month, as is coal, wood, and whatever other supplies I require. I presume you can cook?"

"Of course."

"Fine. Because my own needs are meager and I see to them myself. However, I pay the delivery men well. So order whatever additional groceries you want for you and Noelle. They'll see you get them."

"Excellent." Brigitte's eyes sparkled. "You may leave us now, my lord."

Eric's lips twitched ever so slightly. "Clearly, I can." With a mystified glance from Brigitte to Noelle, he swerved and headed down the hall toward the east wing.

"He likes you," Noelle piped up.

"Pardon me?"

"Uncle. He likes you."

Brigitte folded her arms across her chest. "Really. How do you know that?"

A matter-of-fact shrug. "The way he looks at you. And even though you made him mad, he almost smiled after he chest-ized you."

"*Ah.* I see."

"You like him, too. Don't you?"

Brigitte gazed wistfully after Eric's retreating back. "Yes, Noelle, I do. Very much."

"How come you don't lie?"

"What?" Brigitte's attention snapped back to her inquisitive young charge.

"Grown-ups always lie."

"Not all grown-ups. And certainly not always."

"You're different," Noelle countered. "You don't lie. You don't talk to me like I'm too dumb to understand. You don't ignore Fuzzy. And you don't even hate me."

"Hate you?" Brigitte felt a knife twist in her heart. "Why would anyone hate you? You're intelligent, witty, and spirited."

Another shrug. "Papa hated me. I heard Mrs. Lawley say he never even wanted to meet me. 'Course, Mrs. Lawley hated me, too—just like all the other families who brought me back to Farrington. And Uncle? He hates me most of all. He never keeps me for more than a day. Then he finds another family for me to live with. But they always return me, and it starts again." Noelle stared at the tip of her shoe. "My mama didn't hate me. I could tell in the picture of her I saw. She was too beautiful to hate me. But she's dead. That's probably why I'm beyond re-damn-sin." Noelle's lashes lifted, and she inclined her head quizzically. "What's re-damn-sin?"

Brigitte wasn't certain she could speak. "Who said you were beyond redemption?"

"Mrs. Lawley. What does it mean?"

"It means Mrs. Lawley is a terrible judge of character," Brigitte managed, striving for control.

"Is *she* beyond re-damn-sin?"

"I hope not. But at this moment, I'm not at all certain."

"Her dog is. He tried to bite Fuzzy." Noelle considered the matter. "Whatever re-damn-sin is, it must be a very bad thing to be. It has two wicked words in it—well, really only one. 'Sin' is only bad when you do it; saying it doesn't count. 'Damn' is bad all the time."

Thank God for Noelle's precociousness, Brigitte reflected as she dissolved into laughter. Without it, she might have stormed over to Mrs. Lawley's house and slapped the woman across her thoughtless face—she and all the other supposedly fine, decent families Noelle had been subjected to these past four years.

The truth was, this remarkable child had been passed about like a sack of grain, given only food, clothing, and a roof over her head.

Meager substitutes for encouragement, constancy, and love.

Suddenly, Brigitte knew what she must do.

"Neither of those words, wicked or otherwise, pertains to you." She grasped Noelle's hand, leading her back inside the blue room. "Let's select appropriate romping clothes for you, shall we?" Squatting on the floor, she opened the traveling bag, assessing Noelle's meager wardrobe.

Clothing was the farthest thing from her mind.

"You know, Noelle, your uncle doesn't hate you," she remarked offhandedly. "In fact, I think he loves you more than he knows. More, in fact, than he wants to."

The last captured Noelle's interest, and she plopped down on the rug beside Brigitte. "What do you mean? Uncle *doesn't* love me. He doesn't love *anyone.*"

"You're wrong. And not only with regard to you. Your uncle loved someone else. Very much, in fact."

"Who?"

"Your mama."

"My mama?" Noelle's eyes widened into huge, glittering sapphires. "Really?"

"Really." Brigitte sat back on her heels, abandoning all pretense of sorting through clothing. "You're right about your mama being beautiful. She was. In fact, you look just like her."

"Mrs. Willett told me that, too. The Willetts kept me longer than anybody. Mrs. Willett even liked me. She said I was real smart. But Mr. Willett didn't like smart girls. He wanted a boy. They yelled at each other a lot, especially when they thought I was asleep. And Mrs. Willett would cry. Finally, they brought me back to Farrington. That day, in the carriage, she told me I looked like Mama. I guess she was just being nice, so I wouldn't feel bad that she was returning me."

"No," Brigitte countered, determinedly squelching her own distress. "She was being truthful. You have Liza's eyes, exactly, and her delicate nose and chin. Even your hair is the same color—black as night."

"Did you know her?"

"Yes I did," Brigitte answered cautiously. "In fact, I knew your uncle, too. He doesn't remember me, because I was very young. But I remember him. And what I especially remember is how much he loved your mother." That much was true. Reaching out, Brigitte took Noelle's hand. "Darling, this is going to be hard for you to understand. Lord knows, you're wiser than most adults, but you're still only four."

"Three and ten months. I won't be four 'til Christmas."

Brigitte's lips curved. "I stand corrected. *Nearly* four. Anyway, I'll try to explain. Your uncle was your mama's older brother. He took care of her throughout her life. When she died, it was like a part of him died, too. Not on the outside, but on the inside. Can you understand that?"

Noelle nodded. "I felt like that when Mrs. Lawley took Fuzzy away. She said I couldn't sleep with him anymore 'cause he was too dirty and I couldn't play with him anymore 'cause I was too old. I cried a lot that night, and my tummy hurt really bad. So, when everyone was asleep, I sneaked downstairs and fetched Fuzzy out of the rubbish." She pursed her lips. "But Uncle couldn't do that—fetch Mama back, I mean. So his tummy must have kept hurting."

"Exactly." Tears stung Brigitte's eyes, glistened on her lashes. "I think his tummy still hurts, Noelle. And everything that reminds him of her makes it hurt more."

Another sage nod. "The night Mrs. Lawley took Fuzzy away, one of the maids heard me crying. She brought me another toy. I didn't want it 'cause it reminded me how much I missed Fuzzy. Does Uncle feel like that when he looks at me?"

"I think so, yes. Except that, in your case, the new toy was a stranger. In Lord Farrington's case, you're a part of Liza—the wondrous legacy she left behind. So, yes, it hurts—maybe too much for him to endure. But that hurt stems from love, not hate. He loves you, Noelle; he just doesn't know how to welcome that love without allowing in the hurt that's always accompanied it. It's our job to help him. We're going to succeed. I know we are."

Noelle studied Brigitte with keen, probing eyes. Abruptly, her gaze lowered, and she began playing with Fuzzy's collar. "After that, will you go away?"

Brigitte had been expecting that question. Given the circumstances, it was more than natural.

So was her answer.

"No, darling, I won't. Not then. Not ever. I'm married to your uncle now, and Farrington is my home. I'm staying right here with you and Fuzzy."

Relief swept over Noelle's face. "That's good." A tiny pucker formed between her brows. "But what about your mama and papa—won't they miss you?"

"They can watch over me at Farrington the same way they always have," Brigitte replied softly. "They're in heaven, just like your mama."

Noelle's head came up. "Oh! I thought the vicar was your papa."

"Almost, but no. Actually, he's my papa's papa—my grandfather. He raised me the same way your uncle raised your mama."

"Do you remember your parents?"

"Only my father, and only vaguely. Mama died when I was born."

"Same as my mama!"

At that instant, Brigitte actually hated Liza for abandoning this precious miracle—a miracle she didn't deserve. "Yes, Noelle, much the same. Then my father died in a carriage accident when I was two. Grandfather has been both mother and father to me. He's a wonderful man. I've been truly blessed."

"I heard Uncle say the vicar could visit you at Farrington."

"That's right. When he does, I'll bet you and Fuzzy love him as much as I do." Brigitte rose, lifting a simple, loose-fitting dress from the bag. "Speaking of Fuzzy, didn't we promise him some exercise? Let's get you changed so we can go explore the woods. Together we'll find the perfect spot to erect a huge pile of leaves. Then, Fuzzy can jump to his heart's content."

Peals of laughter drifted into Eric's chambers, invading the darkness and the privacy he'd safeguarded for years.

Brigitte Curran.

Damn the guileless chit for intruding upon his life. She was supposed to be supervising Noelle, not permeating the sanctuary that was his and his alone.

What were they laughing about anyway?

With a will of their own, Eric's legs carried him to the window, and he moved the heavy drape aside so he could peer out. From his vantage point, he could see the entire section of woods surrounding the manor's east wing.

He didn't have far to look.

There, pouncing from the lowest branch of a nearby oak to a towering mound of leaves below, were his niece and his bride, alternately climbing and rolling about, leaves clinging to their hair and gowns.

His bride.

Eric released the curtain as if he'd been burned.

What the hell was wrong with him? What was the cause of this unanticipated reaction to Brigitte Curran and the sight of her bounding about like a child?

A bloody beautiful child. Vibrant and spirited, frolicking with a little girl who was the image of Liza.

Resurrecting a flood of memories long since buried. Memories—and feelings.

Everything inside him went taut.

He'd expected the past to haunt him—at least so long as Noelle was underfoot. That's why he'd married Brigitte. To rid himself of the unthinkable task of rearing Liza's daughter. Brigitte was the perfect candidate for the position: unattached, untainted, uncomplicated by shallow expectations and false hopes. Plus, she related to Noelle in a way he'd never before seen, much less imagined.

What he hadn't anticipated were the emotions she evoked inside him—not merely pangs over what had been, but over what could be.

She was a glimmer of radiance in an interminable hell.

She was also his wife.

In name alone, he reminded himself, scowling. To permit more would be insane. She wasn't one of his occasionally summoned, well-paid courtesans. She was a sheltered innocent who knew nothing about coupling and less about how to separate physical need from emotional involvement. To take her to bed would be cruel.

But, God, she was beautiful. Beautiful, exuberant, and as uninhibited as she was tenderhearted.

Would she be uninhibited in his arms?

With a muttered oath, Eric slammed his fist against the wall, squelching that tantalizing concept in the making. To bed his wife would be an unacceptable complication, threatening not only her mental well-being, but his own. He'd achieved what he'd sought: a governess for Noelle and peace for himself. Anything more was inconceivable.

He moved away from the window, closing his mind and heart to the ongoing shouts of laughter.

But at night, they haunted his soul.

Five

"WE HAVE TWO MAJOR CELEBRATIONS COMING UP," BRIGITTE informed Noelle, kneeling alongside the tub.

"What celebrations?" Noelle's nose wrinkled in concentration as she watched Brigitte lift Fuzzy from his first bath. Snatching him away, she squeezed him free of water, then began vigorously toweling him dry. "Fuzzy looks grand," she declared, holding him up to admire. "Now even Mrs. Lawley couldn't say he was dirty."

Brigitte was still reeling from the implications of Noelle's question. "Did you say 'What celebrations'?" she demanded. "Why, your birthday and Christmas. Or have you forgotten December is but a month away?"

Noelle's motions slowed. "November only started a week ago."

"Yes, but Advent begins at month's end—that's less than three weeks. A scant four weeks later is Christmas Day and your fourth birthday. We have hours of preparation ahead. Baking, selecting gifts, planning a party—"

"Fuzzy doesn't like parties," Noelle interrupted, retying the ribbon about his neck. "He likes to spend holidays alone with me. Besides, Uncle won't allow guests at Farrington. He doesn't see anyone—you know that."

"Only too well." Brigitte sighed, feeling utterly discouraged by the lack of headway she'd made with Eric.

In the fortnight since she'd arrived at Farrington, he'd made no attempt to see her or—worse—to see Noelle. In fact, they'd spied him but thrice, each time by accident and each time only

356

until he noticed their presence and vanished. Never had he ventured into their wing. Not even to investigate when Noelle's antics resulted in ear-splitting crashes that could wake the dead: the oriental vase she'd used as a croquet mallet, the flock of bird figurines she'd sailed over the second-story landing to prove they could fly, and the half-dozen other "incidents" that had accompanied her gradual but steady transition from a behavioral nightmare to a normal, high-spirited little girl who no longer needed to destroy her surroundings to receive the attention she craved. That attention, a natural expression of Brigitte's love, was now given freely, supplanting the reprimands of Noelle's numerous foster families.

How much easier Noelle's transition would be if her unyielding uncle would allow her into his heart.

But with or without Eric's help, Brigitte was determined to offer her precious charge the joyous elements of childhood that she deserved—Christmases and birthdays.

On that thought, Brigitte returned her attention to Noelle. "Even if your uncle maintains his rules *and* his seclusion, that doesn't preclude us from having our own private birthday party. We'll take tea and cake on the grounds—in the snow if necessary—followed by a rousing puppet show. Wait until you see how superb Grandfather is at puppetry . . ."

Panic widened Noelle's eyes, and she clutched Fuzzy to her chest. "He can't use Fuzzy as a puppet. No one holds Fuzzy but me."

"Of course not. Fuzzy will be a guest. What kind of cake does he prefer?"

Silence.

Comprehension struck like a douse of cold water. "Noelle, have you never had a birthday celebration?"

Noelle buried her face in Fuzzy's fur.

Brigitte fought her rising anguish. "Noelle." She stroked the child's shining dark head. "How have you spent the past four Christmases—and where?"

A shrug. "I was born on my first Christmas," she mumbled. "So I s'pose I spent it at Farrington. I don't remember my next one—I was at some family's house, I guess. When I was two, I was at the Reglingtons'. They sent me up to the nursery without dinner 'cause I squashed a few of the presents when I was playing in the sitting room. When I was three, I was at the Ballisons' house. I clipped the needles off their Christmas tree and spent the rest of the day in the cellar. Do you promise the vicar won't take Fuzzy away?"

"I promise, darling. No one will take Fuzzy away." Brigitte's stomach was in knots. After a fortnight of stories such as these, she'd thought herself beyond shock. She wasn't.

Lifting Noelle's chin with one damp forefinger, she probed the matter, needing to verify her suspicions. "You've never decorated a tree? Baked mince pie? Sent Christmas cards? Gone caroling?" Seeing Noelle's negative shake of the head, she sucked in her breath. "And what about your birthday? Surely the families with whom you lived didn't ignore it entirely?"

"They didn't know it was my birthday. The only person who knew the date was Uncle—He's the one who told me I was born on Christmas Day. 'Course, my name is Noelle, so I kind of guessed. Which is good, 'cause he didn't really want to tell me. I just pestered him 'til he did. But he never told anyone else. And as for parties, Uncle never celebrates anything, 'specially the day I was born, which he tries to forget."

That did it. Brigitte's final heartstring snapped.

"Noelle, it's time for you and Fuzzy to rest." Tossing down the towel, she guided Noelle from the bathroom into the blue bedchamber, pausing only to draw the newly hung curtains. "We've been racing about since we finished your morning studies. A short nap will do both you and Fuzzy good—especially Fuzzy, who's probably exhausted from the ordeal of his first bath."

Noelle settled herself beneath the bedcovers, blinking her huge eyes at Brigitte. "You're going to see Uncle, aren't you?"

Had she truly hoped to fool her brilliant young charge?

"Yes, Noelle, I am. It's time he and I had a talk."

"You've been here two weeks without talking. In fact, we've only seen him three times. But he's seen us a lot more."

Brigitte's brows drew together. "What do you mean?"

"'Xactly that—We've only seen him three times," Noelle repeated patiently. "Once, when we came in the back door after collecting our groceries, and twice more in the kitchen when we were preparing dinner. You remember—He disappeared the instant he saw us." She cradled Fuzzy to her cheek. "You were right, you know. Fuzzy looks ever so much nicer now that he's clean. And he didn't mind the bath nearly as much as I thought he would."

"I'm glad." Brigitte perched on the edge of the bed. "I know we've only seen your uncle thrice. What I meant was, why did you say he'd seen us a lot more than we've seen him?"

"Because it's true. He watches us from his window whenever we play in the woods."

Brigitte's spine stiffened. "Are you sure?"

"Course I'm sure. I spy him all the time. He only watches for a while. Then he goes away."

"Does he now . . . ?" Brigitte's mind was racing. So Eric wasn't as immune to his niece as he liked to pretend. He *did* care—whether or not he wanted to. "Noelle, thank you. You've just given me the ammunition I needed."

"Ammunition?" A puzzled frown. "Isn't that for guns?"

"Only sometimes," Brigitte retorted. "Sometimes it's for people." Leaning forward, she smoothed the blanket beneath

Noelle's chin, gently kissing her brow. "Now, go to sleep. Fuzzy, too."

Noelle nodded, her eyes sliding shut. "Good luck with Uncle," she whispered. "And don't use too much ammunition when he chest-izes you. He really likes you an awful lot."

Five minutes later, Brigitte silently contested Noelle's assessment.

"I apprised you that my chambers were never to be violated," Eric snapped, glaring at Brigitte from his doorway.

"I didn't violate them. I knocked. I intend to see you. Where we speak is entirely your choosing."

His eyes flashed like glittering chips of obsidian. "Seeing and speaking to me are not part of our arrangement."

"Nevertheless, I aim to do so." Brigitte stared up at him, undeterred by his towering height and formidable temper. Further, she could see beyond the harsh features and unruly appearance, beyond his bitter facade. The man who'd ruled her girlhood dreams was still there, buried deep inside this dark, caustic stranger. "You won't succeed in frightening me, my lord," she informed him. "I wasn't afraid of you before, and I'm far too upset to begin now. So you might as well let me in. I have something important to say, and I don't intend to leave until I've said it."

With a stunned expression, Eric eased open the door. "Make it brief."

Brigitte stalked in, too troubled to feel awkward about the fact that she was in Eric's bedchamber for the first time. She whirled about to face him. "It concerns Noelle."

"In that case, it does not concern me. Good day."

"Cease this absurd pretense, Lord Farrington. It's pointless. You're fooling neither of us."

"What the hell are you rambling about?"

"About you. About this supposed loathing you feel for Noelle. And about the nonsensical myth you insist on furthering that you're a blackhearted tyrant." She paused to catch her breath. "You're a fraud, my lord. A fraud and a fool. Both of which are your doing. Nonetheless, if you choose to retreat from life, that decision is yours to make, so long as it hurts only you. However, in this case, it hurts Noelle more. Thus, I've given up waiting for you to come to your senses, and decided to intervene."

Eric looked torn between disbelief and eruption. "Have you gone mad?" he thundered, slamming the door so hard the walls vibrated. "Has a fortnight with my niece stripped away your senses?"

"Quite the contrary, my lord. A fortnight with your niece has enlightened me beyond my wildest expectations. She's a brilliant, sensitive child—but of course you wouldn't know that, would you?" With a quick prayer, Brigitte pressed onward. "In fact, you don't know her at all."

"Nor do I intend to, you insolent—"

"I questioned Noelle about the type of birthday celebration she prefers," Brigitte interrupted. "It appears she's never had any celebration whatsoever."

A sardonic laugh. "That doesn't surprise me. The small amount of time she's spent destroying each house in which she's resided left little time for festivities."

"Whose fault is that?"

His jaw clenched so tightly Brigitte feared it might snap. "I'd suggest you watch your tongue, Miss Curran."

"With due respect, my lord, I'm not the least bit interested in what you suggest. I'm interested in Noelle, and her well-being. She needs a normal life: not just studies and discipline, but a family, strolls in the park, other children to play with. Why do you think she's so attached to Fuzzy? Did it ever occur to you he's the only constant in her life? She's been tossed from house to house like an unwanted object since the day she was born. Now she's a virtual prisoner at Farrington. All she wants is a real home—friends, laughter . . ." Brigitte paused. "Love."

"Are you quite finished?" Eric bit out.

Utterly incredulous, Brigitte shook her head from side to side. "You're not going to give an inch, are you? You're going to let your own anguish destroy that little girl's life."

Something inside Eric seemed to snap.

"Celebrate her bloody birthday then!" he stormed, crossing the room to seize a half-filled goblet of brandy from a barren writing table. "Invite the vicar. Bake a cake. Jump in the leaves from dawn till dusk, for all I care. Now get out."

"And Christmas?"

The goblet banged to the desk. "No."

"No? No what? No church? No tree? No gifts? No . . ."

"No Christmas." He wheeled about to face her. "And that is nonnegotiable. So far as I'm concerned, Christmas does not exist. It ceased to be five years ago."

"I understand your pain, my lord. But Noelle is a child. Surely—"

"No!" Eric roared, hurling his goblet against the wall.

Brigitte jumped, totally unprepared for the violence of his action. Taking an inadvertent step backward, she watched shards of crystal shatter, cascading onto the oriental carpet in a glittering spray.

Simultaneously, she became aware of her surroundings for the first time. Her unnerved gaze took in the doused lamps, the naked furnishings, the tightly drawn drapes. *Grandfather was right,* she reflected numbly. *It is a mausoleum. Other than the pile of books alongside the nightstand and the rumpled bedding, it's as if no one lives here at all.*

"Are you frightened, Miss Curran?" Eric put in, his tone menacing. "Or merely scrutinizing my quarters? Because right now I'd be very frightened if I were you."

His taunting words found their mark, and Brigitte's stare returned to his, assessing him, not with alarm but with comprehension. *He's challenging me,* she realized. *He wants to scare me away. He's fighting to protect himself.*

All her girlhood dreams surged to life, mingling with the compassion and insight afforded by maturity.

"No, my lord, I'm not frightened," she denied, with a decisive set of her jaw. "I'm also not 'Miss Curran'—at least not any longer."

Eric's eyes narrowed. "No, you're not, are you?" Purposefully, he stalked forward. "You're the Countess of Farrington." He loomed over her. "My wife."

"Yes. I am."

"In name only," he reminded her. "At least thus far."

With the innate knowledge that she hovered on the brink of her future—and Eric's—Brigitte sealed her own fate. "That choice, my lord, was yours. Not mine."

Anguish tore across his face. "Damn you," he muttered through clenched teeth. "And damn me for wanting you."

With that his arms shot out, dragging Brigitte to his chest, trapping her against the powerful contours of his body. Roughly, he seized her chin, lifting it to meet the descending force of his mouth, crushing her lips beneath his before she had a chance to breathe, much less protest.

Physical sensation, coupled with fierce emotion, crashed through Brigitte, taking her under in a huge, engulfing wave. Whimpering, she accepted—no, welcomed—Eric's assault, her dazed mind wondering how many nights she'd dreamed of this, at the same time knowing no fantasy could ever come close to this incomparable reality. Eric's lips moved over hers with a burning intensity, urgent, reckless, but more like that of a drowning man than an angry one.

She moved closer, somehow needing to soothe his turmoil. Her fingers uncurled, glided up his shirtfront to rest over his heart. "Eric," she whispered, a balm against his fevered mouth. "Oh, Eric."

A hard shudder wracked his body, and his punishing grip relaxed. His fists unclenched, his palms drifting up and down her spine, caressing rather than hurting. Urging her closer, he gentled the kiss, his lips circling hers, lingering, silently demanding hers to part.

Brigitte understood his plea.

With a natural, innocent ardor, she complied, opening to his penetration, quivering with anticipation as his tongue slid in to mate with hers.

And then she was lost.

Eric's mouth possessed hers with unabated hunger, stroking every tingling surface, awakening nerves that had been forever asleep. Inundated with sensation, Brigitte stood on tiptoe, granting him better access, pressing closer to his powerful frame.

A low groan vibrated from Eric's chest, and he took what she offered, possessing her in a way Brigitte had never in her wildest imaginings fathomed. His hands moved down to cup her bottom, and urgently, he lifted her from the floor, fitting her soft curves against him, pressing the rigid lines of his erection as deep into her as the confines of their clothing would allow.

Pleasure—dizzying, drenching—poured through her body in torrents of liquid heat. Had Eric not been holding her, she would have collapsed, her limbs weak with sensation, unable to function. As if reading her mind, Eric swept her into his arms, gripping her tightly as he headed toward the bed. An instant later cool air, welcome on her feverish skin, assailed her as he lowered her to the sheets.

"Brigitte."

It was the first time he'd said her name, and her heart sang at the sound.

"What?" Her lashes fluttered open.

"Are you sure?"

Sure? She'd been sure forever.

"Yes. I'm sure."

His breathing was harsh, strained, and he leaned over her, bracing himself on his forearms. "Do you understand what's going to happen?"

No coldhearted man could ever be this tender.

"Yes, I understand."

He swallowed, every tendon in his neck strained, taut with need. "If you want to change your mind, do it now. Because once I'm in this bed, once I have you under me, there will be no turning back."

She reached up, her palm stroking his bristled jaw. "I don't want to change my mind. Make love to me."

Those mesmerizing eyes narrowed into piercing obsidian chips. "Love? This has nothing to do with love," Eric cautioned, dragging air into his lungs, clearly struggling to regain a control that was far beyond his grasp.

With a hard shake of his head, he capitulated.

"I'm a bloody bastard for doing this to you." Fervently, he tunneled his fingers through her hair. "You're a beautiful, romantic innocent who believes that what we're about to do is rooted in some miraculous emotion. It's not, Brigitte. It's based in physical need. I want you. I'm insane with wanting you. I've wanted you since the moment I saw you outside the church. My body is screaming to be inside yours, to pour an eternity of pent-up hunger into your womb. But that's lust, my softhearted bride, not love. So, I repeat, if you want to leave, do it now. Because nothing is going to change if you stay, not even after we've burned each other up in bed. Not our lives nor the barriers that divide them. Nothing."

Liquid heat shimmered through Brigitte's veins. "Burn each other up? Is that what we'll do?"

"That—and more."

"Show me." Brigitte's arms curled about Eric's neck, her fingers lacing through the long hair at his nape. "I don't care about the rest."

"You might later."

"If that's the case, the burden will be mine. Just as the decision is now." She gazed up at him, seeing the fine man Eric deemed dead and gone. "I'm your wife. You can hardly be accused of ruining me. Further, since I don't believe in infidelity nor want to exist without ever knowing passion, you're the only man who can offer it to me. Please, Eric, I know what I'm doing."

"Do you?" he demanded, lowering his weight onto hers. "Because, Lord help me, I don't."

His kiss was consuming, his hands blindly unfastening her gown, tugging it away from her body. With awkward fingers, she unbuttoned his shirt, parting the edges to explore the warm, hair-roughened skin of his chest.

With a muttered oath, he pushed her hands away, flinging his shirt to the floor, dragging off her undergarments in several hard, fierce motions. He moved away only long enough to shed the rest of his clothes, devouring her with his eyes in a way that made Brigitte feel as beautiful as he'd claimed she was.

He came down over her, his whole body shuddering at the first contact of their naked flesh, his mouth capturing her moan of pleasure.

Brigitte couldn't form a coherent thought, so intense were

the physical sensations coursing through her. She clutched at his arms—desperate to please him, uncertain how.

Eric raised his head, staring down at her.

"Teach me," she beseeched, more demand than plea.

The harsh lines about his eyes softened; an odd light flickered in their inky depths. "You need no teaching. I'm already undone."

"But . . ."

"Hush." He brushed each corner of her mouth with his, muttering, "Let me." His hands moved to cup the silky weight of her breasts, a sound of pure male satisfaction rumbling from his chest as he felt her inadvertent shiver. "This, at least, I can give you. Let me, Brigitte. I want to watch those incredible golden eyes of yours shimmer with the wonder of discovery." His lips found the pulse at her throat. "I want to feel you shudder with a pleasure you never dreamed possible. Brigitte— let me."

She tried to answer, but at that moment his thumbs found her nipples, teasing them with featherlight strokes until Brigitte couldn't speak or think or even breathe. Oblivious to anything but feeling, she sank into the bed, eyes sliding shut as she wordlessly gave Eric the permission he sought.

He sensed her surrender, and acted on it.

Lowering his head, his mouth replaced his thumbs, and Brigitte had to fight to keep from screaming as he surrounded her nipple, bathing the sensitized peak with his tongue, tugging it rhythmically with his lips.

"Eric . . ." It was the only sound she could muster, and it emerged like a strangled sob.

He didn't answer. Not with words. Instead, he shifted to her other breast, lavishing it with the same seductive caresses as he had the first. His hands moved lower, tracing the curve of her waist and hips, savoring the softness of her skin. His knees nudged her legs apart, settling in between to grant him the access he sought.

At the first brush of his fingertips on her inner thighs, a floodgate of desire erupted inside Brigitte. Disregarding the tiny inner voice that branded her a wanton, she parted her legs wider, whimpering as he traced erotic circles higher and higher up her trembling limbs.

"Open your eyes, Brigitte."

Her lashes lifted at his command and, by doing so, discovered something even more wondrous than the exhilaration of his touch.

He was as affected as she.

Damp wisps of hair clung to a forehead that was slick with sweat, his features whip-taut with desire. Most wondrous of all was the inferno blazing in his eyes—an inferno rooted in something entirely different from anger.

"I want to watch you," he muttered thickly, his thumbs stroking the sensitive area where her thighs ended and joined her torso. "From this moment on, I want to see the beauty of your passion as it unfolds." His thumbs crept a fraction closer to where her entire being screamed for him to be. "Show me, Brigitte."

Reaching out, she clutched his wrists, urging him higher, her gaze wide and fixed on his.

It was enough.

His fingers opened her, found her, and he made a rough sound deep in his throat as he explored the velvety folds. "Perfect," he managed, his breath coming in shallow pants.

Brigitte cried out, undulating against his hand, pinpoints of pleasure radiating out from her very core. Eric was watching her intently from beneath hooded lids, and he deepened his caress, somehow knowing just where to touch, how to heighten the ecstasy. Engulfed in sensation, Brigitte tossed her head on the pillow, certain she was dying and not giving a damn. She was already as close to heaven as one could get.

Until he stopped.

"Eric?" Her dazed eyes searched his face—needing a reason. Needing him.

"I want to be inside you when it happens," he rasped, coming down over her until his rigid shaft was poised where his fingers had been. "Christ, I'm not even sure I can wait." He shuddered, his hips moving of their own accord. "Brigitte, I'm going to have to hurt you."

"I don't care." Her arms stole around the damp contours of his back, tugging him down to her, her untried body's demands more powerful than her mind's fears.

Another profound emotion crossed his face, then vanished in the wake of physical craving.

Eric entered her slowly—as slowly as their straining bodies would allow—pausing every few seconds to give her time to adjust to his penetration. When he reached her maidenhead, he stopped, staring so deeply into her eyes that Brigitte wondered which possession was more absolute.

"I swear I'll make it worth it," he growled. Raising her hips, he lunged forward, tearing the thin membrane of her innocence in one powerful thrust.

Brigitte's breath suspended in her throat, the pain an unwelcome intrusion. Determined not to destroy the miracle of their joining, she battled back her cry of pain, biting her lip until tears stung her eyes.

"Don't." Eric kept himself perfectly still, his knuckles grazing her cheek. "Don't hide from me. Not now." He lowered his mouth to hers. "Ah, Brigitte, I'm sorry," he breathed into her lips. "So damned, damned sorry."

The agony in his tone was more painful than the rending of

her body. "Don't be," she whispered fiercely, her meaning as vast as his. "It's so beautiful. How can you be sorry?"

On the heels of her words, she moved—tentatively lifting her hips to his, stunned by the breathless resurgence of desire that resulted.

Easing back, she stared dazedly into Eric's eyes, repeating the motion only to find that the pain had subsided, supplanted by a frantic need for completion. The friction was unbearable, magnified threefold by the thick, full feel of him pulsing inside her, stretching her inside and out.

She gave a harsh whimper—and Eric's patience snapped.

"Yes," he groaned, pressing his forehead to hers. "Again— when I tell you." He withdrew slowly, then stopped. "Now." He thrust downward, cupping her hips as she arched up to meet him.

This time she sobbed aloud, and Eric gave a feral shout.

"Again," he commanded. "And again, and again, and—"

His voice shattered, along with his control. Gripping the headboard, he plunged into Brigitte, over and over, and she met his wildness with her own. The bedsprings grated with each frenzied thrust, the sound punctuated only by their broken cries and labored breaths.

Something was about to happen. Brigitte could feel it. It was as if she'd scaled a magnificent rainbow and now hovered just shy of its exquisite peak.

"Eric . . ." She moaned his name, silently willing him to take her where she so desperately needed to go.

He did.

Clenching her bottom, he lifted her up—hard—drove deep into her core, ground himself against the very damp, throbbing flesh that yearned for him.

Brigitte splintered into a million fragments, explosion after explosion crashing over her, radiating out in hot, convulsive spasms. As if from a distance, she heard Eric groan, felt his grip tighten as he fought to prolong her pleasure.

Until holding back became impossible.

Lunging forward, he surrendered to his climax, swelling to massive proportions before he erupted, shouting Brigitte's name in conjunction with the pulsing surges of his release.

Please God, Brigitte prayed during that brief, final instant when Eric was truly hers. *Let this miracle last. Please.*

Hers were not the only prayers being offered by a resident of Farrington at that precise moment.

Two halls away, tucked in her bed, Noelle cradled Fuzzy on the pillow beside her. "She's still in his room, you know," she advised her plaything with a sage nod. "And Uncle's not angry, or we'd hear his shouting way down here. We have to pray, Fuzzy." She squeezed her eyes shut, accomplishing the same for Fuzzy by covering his button eyes with the palm of her hand. "God—I know I do lots of bad things," she began. "But I promise I'll stop. I'll listen and I won't break stuff, and I'll never need chest-izing again. Only please"—her lips quivered, and two tears slid down her cheeks—"please don't take Brigitte away."

Six

"NOELLE, NOT SO CLOSE TO THE POND," BRIGITTE INstructed, simultaneously reaching up to collect another sprig of holly.

"But Fuzzy wants to learn how to sail." Flat on her stomach, Noelle crept a bit closer to the water's edge, straddling Fuzzy across the piece of driftwood she intended to serve as his boat.

"And he wants to learn now, before it gets too cold and the water freezes."

"How very ambitious of him." Abandoning her task, Brigitte approached Noelle with a pointed lift of her brows. "But tell me, can Fuzzy swim? Or, more important, can you?"

Noelle frowned. "No. We can't."

"Ah. Well, you're in good company—neither can I. And, since I suspect that pond is far taller from top to bottom than either you or I—and certainly Fuzzy—I'd prefer not to tempt fate. All right?"

"All right." Grudgingly, Noelle rose, rubbing her dirty hands on her mantle, thereby transferring stains from the former to the latter. "What are you doing?"

"Gathering holly."

"Why? You said Uncle won't let us celebrate Christmas."

"He won't." Brigitte grinned. "I'm hoping he'll change his mind." She squinted at her rapidly growing collection, visualizing Farrington's sitting room alive with the spirit of Christmas: Its barren walls decorated with wreaths of holly and mistletoe, its fireplace reawakened and aglow, its floor piled high with gifts. And in the center of it all, she, Eric, and Noelle, standing about a glorious evergreen heralding the season.

On cue, Brigitte's gaze shifted to the magnificent fir she'd selected for that all-important role, the perfect nucleus of a perfect fantasy.

"Brigitte?" Noelle's voice interrupted her daydream. "'Cept at his window, I haven't seen Uncle for more than three weeks—since the day you talked to him. Have you?"

The fantasy shattered into bitter shards of reality.

"No, love." Brigitte shook her head. "I haven't. Apparently, your uncle needs more time alone."

"More time? He's always alone. He didn't even come out

when your grandfather visited. Though I'm positive he knew the vicar was here—I saw him watch the carriage arrive."

A slight smile. "Noelle, you spend far too much time spying on your uncle's window."

"It's only too much 'cause he's there too much. If he weren't, it wouldn't matter how often I looked, 'cause he wouldn't know I was looking." On the heels of that bit of reasoning, Noelle pursed her lips. "Why don't you visit him anymore?"

Brigitte sighed. "You and I have discussed this. I didn't *visit* him at all—not even the one time I went to his chambers. I merely went to ask if we could celebrate your birthday, and he agreed."

"I didn't hear him shouting. Neither did Fuzzy."

"That's because he didn't. I explained the situation, and he gave his consent."

"Then if you weren't arguing and you weren't visiting, why were you in there such a long time?"

Heat suffused Brigitte's body as she recalled the answer to *that* question.

Those moments in Eric's arms had been the most unexpected and exquisite of miracles—excruciating pleasure and equally excruciating anguish. Oh, he'd warned her, been honest with her from the start. Not only about his motives for taking her to bed, but about the aftermath, how it would affect her. He'd been right. They'd dressed and parted like strangers, leaving her emotionally raw, bereft, craving something Eric was unable— unwilling—to give.

But he was wrong that the ache would result in regret. It hadn't. Anguish or not, Brigitte wouldn't erase their lovemaking for anything on earth. She was Eric's wife now, and even if he chose to denounce it, they were bound in a beautiful and irrevocable way that was hers to cherish for the rest of her days.

Lonely days, if Eric had his way.

"Brigitte?" Noelle was tugging at her skirt. "Can't you remember what you and Uncle talked about?"

Brigitte's flush deepened. "We didn't talk about much, Noelle. Other than celebrating your birthday, which he conceded to—and Christmas, which he did not."

"Why do you think you can change his mind about Christmas?"

"Because I'm a fool," Brigitte answered, gazing wistfully down at the lush greenery in her hands.

"No you're not!" Noelle's defense was fast and furious. "You're just up-to-mist . . . ick," she added. "Up-to-mist-ick. I always forget the 'ick' 'cause I can't understand how such a yucky word got to be part of a good one."

Brigitte grinned. "I see your point. And, yes, I am optimistic. However, I'm also playing with fire. Your uncle will doubtless become livid when he learns of my plans."

"You're not afraid of Uncle, are you, Brigitte?"

"No, Noelle, I'm not."

"What *are* you afraid of?"

"*H-m-m?*" Brigitte blinked at the sudden change in subject.

"You must be afraid of something. Like Fuzzy and I are afraid there might be big monsters under my bed. We check every night to make sure it's safe. What are you afraid of?"

"Heights," Brigitte confessed.

"Heights?" Noelle's eyes widened in surprise. "You mean like high up places?"

"*Um-hum.*"

"Wow." Noelle sounded incredulous. "Didn't you ever climb trees before you got grown-up?"

"Only short ones." Brigitte caressed Noelle's smudged cheek. "Come. Help me gather a few more sprigs of holly. Unfortunately, it's clustered in this area—far too close to your uncle's chambers to grant me peace of mind. Let's be done and on our way before he catches a glimpse of us." She returned to her task.

Glancing at the manor, Noelle was on the verge of telling Brigitte that it was too late, that, judging from the angle of the window curtain in her uncle's chambers, they'd already been discovered, when a brilliant idea struck her.

" 'Only short ones' . . ." she repeated, chewing her lip. "How short?"

"What?" Brigitte was tugging at another bough.

"You said you only climbed short trees. How short?"

"Very short."

Noelle pressed her face into Fuzzy's fur. "Now's our chance," she whispered.

So saying, she inched away until she came up against the thick bark of the oak tree that loomed beside the pond. Tilting back her head, she gauged her distance, then flung Fuzzy up as high as she could.

He landed—and caught on the lowest branch.

In a flash, she shimmied up the tree, snatched Fuzzy, and—just to be on the safe side—climbed several limbs higher. After counting to ten, she called, "Brigitte!"

Brigitte spun about, her gaze darting everywhere at once. "Noelle, where are you?"

"Up here."

Following the sound, Brigitte tipped her head back until she spied her charge. "What are you doing up there?"

"Fuzzy got stuck. I climbed up to get him."

"Well, you can climb right back down."

"I can't. I . . . My dress is caught on the branch, and I can't pull it free."

"Noelle . . ."

"I know you're afraid," Noelle interrupted in a soothing tone. "So why don't you get Uncle?" She pointed helpfully toward the manor. "Just throw a stone at his window. He'll hear it. He's probably standing near there anyway."

Brigitte gaped. "Why you little imp. You planned this."

A grin. "Get Uncle, Brigitte. He'll help you."

"I'll do no such thing. You come down here this instant."

"No." Shaking her head, Noelle inched farther out over the water. "The branch gets real thin out here," she announced. "You'd better not take any chances. You'd better fetch Uncle so he can—"

Noelle's sentence ended on a broken scream as, with a loud crack, the branch gave way, toppling both its occupants directly into the center of the pond.

"Brigitte!" Noelle shrieked, flailing about in genuine terror.

Her dark head vanished beneath the surface.

"Oh, my God." Brigitte kicked off her shoes and flung the holly to the ground, racing forward and splashing into the pond without thought or strategy.

She struggled her way to the spot where Noelle had now resurfaced and was thrashing about in an attempt to save herself. Frantically, Brigitte grabbed for her—once, twice—but each time Noelle's battling limbs evaded her.

Panic took over. Relinquishing all attempts at retaining her footing, Brigitte lunged at the child, grabbing hold of Noelle's waist and catapulting them both headlong into the center of the icy pond.

Frigid water slapped Brigitte in the face, stinging her eyes and nose. She strove to regain her balance, but Noelle's wrestling limbs and her own sodden layers of clothing were too ponderous to overcome. Blindly, she fought for their lives, her arms and legs growing weak after what seemed like an eternity of effort. Finally, with her last bit of strength, she thrust Noelle upward, praying it was far enough for the child to break the surface and breathe. Her own lungs were bursting for air and a dark roaring pounded through her skull as she kicked at her gown and cloak, her feet searching desperately for the muddy bottom.

Abruptly, Noelle was yanked from Brigitte's grasp. A split second later, a powerful arm anchored beneath her legs, hauling her up and out of the water.

Air, frosty or not, was the greatest of gifts, and Brigitte sucked in one huge breath, then another—dissolving into harsh spasms of coughing.

"Slowly," Eric commanded. "Breathe slowly. Don't try to speak."

"Noe . . . Noelle . . ." Brigitte rasped.

"I told you not to speak." He deposited her on the bank, Noelle coughing and wriggling beside her. "She's fine. As are you. Reckless and stupid, but fine."

With that, he turned and waded back into the pond, emerging at the exact instant that Noelle choked out, "Fuzzy!"

Brigitte propped herself on her elbows in time to see Eric toss the saturated plaything at his niece. "Here. He's in better condition than you are."

Staring at her uncle with eyes the size of saucers, Noelle snatched her toy, then succumbed to wracking coughs.

Kneeling, Eric leaned Noelle forward, rubbing her back and forcing the water from her chest. "Don't be frightened. You swallowed almost half that pond. You're merely returning it."

Hugging herself to still her shivering, Brigitte wondered if she'd died and gone to heaven. Not only had Eric saved their lives—and Fuzzy's, for that matter—he was tending to Noelle, carefully ensuring that her breathing returned to normal and, miracle of miracles, *teasing* her.

If this were heaven, Brigitte decided, it was every bit as wonderful as her grandfather had always claimed.

In the wake of that assessment, she dissolved into another fit of choking.

Eric's head snapped around. "Are you all right?" he demanded, frowning as Brigitte's coughs were replaced by uncontrollable shudders.

Mutely, she nodded.

"Dammit, Brigitte." He released Noelle, tearing off his own saturated coat and wrapping it around his wife, fierce emotion glittering in his eyes.

Instantly, Noelle burst into tears. "Don't chest-ize Brigitte. It wasn't her fault; it was mine."

"I know very well whose fault it was." Eric scooped first Noelle, then Brigitte, into his arms. "I've got to get you both inside before you freeze to death." His dark stare swept over his wife, then flickered to the grass behind her. "Since I can only manage two hoydens and one bedraggled cat at a time, I fear the holly will have to wait."

So saying, he strode off toward the manor.

With a contented smile, Brigitte gazed over Eric's shoulder, watching until the rapidly retreating boughs of holly had disappeared from view.

Miracles, she mused, might be gifts from heaven.

But they happened right here on earth.

"Noelle, drink that entire cup of warm milk and climb into bed."

Leaning against Noelle's bedchamber wall, Brigitte massaged her own pounding temples.

Noelle gave her a worried look. "Your cheeks are real red, Brigitte. I think you're a whole lot sicker than me."

"I'll be fine," Brigitte assured her. "As soon as I have you tucked in, I'll go to bed. By morning, I'll be myself again."

Dubious, Noelle complied, swallowing her milk then scrambling between the sheets, Fuzzy beside her. "Uncle was a hero, wasn't he, Brigitte?"

A small smile. "Yes, love, he was." With an enormous effort, Brigitte propelled herself into an upright position, crossing the room to kiss Noelle good night. "I shudder to think what would have happened had Lord Farrington not chosen that precise minute to glance out his window."

"He didn't choose that precise minute to glance out his window," Noelle refuted matter-of-factly. "He'd been watching us for nearly an hour. That's why I climbed the tree when I did—I was counting on his help. But you'd already guessed that part." She chewed her lip. "The next part was a surprise to me, too. I didn't 'xpect to fall in the pond. That was real scary. Uncle must have run awfully fast to get from his chambers to the door and across the grounds to the pond in so short a time."

"It didn't seem short to me," Brigitte replied, feeling the room sway. "It seemed an eternity."

"He didn't chest-ize me for what I did. He didn't even chest-ize you about gathering holly." Noelle screwed up her face thoughtfully. "Where's Uncle now?"

"I don't know, Noelle. Back in his chambers, I suppose. Although—should he emerge—I wouldn't suggest alerting him to the fact that you plotted his heroic appearance. I don't think he'd take kindly to it."

"No. He wouldn't," a deep-timbred voice affirmed. "So rest assured, Noelle, you'll be duly chastised for your antics— tomorrow."

Brigitte jumped, staring incredulously at the doorway as if seeking confirmation of the impossible.

Hovering just inside the room, Eric assessed his niece with an expression Brigitte's feverish brain classified as none other than tenderness.

"For tonight, all conversation will cease," he commanded. "Go to sleep."

"But, Uncle, Brigitte is sick," Noelle protested.

Eric's attention shifted to Brigitte, who continued to gape at him as she tried to absorb the reality of his presence.

"My niece is right. You *are* ill," he pronounced.

"I must be." She blinked. "Not only ill, but delirious. I could swear you're standing in Noelle's room."

Eric didn't smile. "You have a fever. A high one, I suspect. You belong in bed."

"Obviously I do." Brigitte pivoted, wobbling a bit as she headed toward her room. "Very well. I'm on my way, my lord. I'm sure by daybreak I'll awaken and realize this was all an up-to-mist-ick dream . . ."

In a dizzying surge, the floor rushed up to greet her.

Seven

"DON'T." BRIGITTE TOSSED HER HEAD, FENDING OFF THE chilly compress that persisted in finding her face.

"Lie still and stop fighting me, dammit." A firm hand gripped her chin, and that dreadful cloth resumed its path.

"Too cold," she murmured.

"I know it's cold." His grip gentled. "But you're burning up. It's the only way to bring down your fever."

With immense effort, Brigitte cracked open her eyes. "Eric?"

"*H-m-m?*" He applied the cloth to her nape.

"Am I in bed?"

380

"Yes."

"In my quarters?"

"Of course."

"And you're tending to me?"

"I'm the only other adult at Farrington."

Her eyes slid shut. "I *am* in heaven. How wonderful. At last I can savor this dream. I've awaited it forever."

"Stop it," he ordered vehemently. "You're not in heaven. You're at Farrington. And you are *not* going to die."

The fervor of his tone only minimally penetrated Brigitte's semiconscious state. She turned her lips against his forearm, burrowing into the warmth of his skin. "Do you know how long I've loved you?" she murmured. "Forever. Can you guess how many nights I've pictured your coming to me?" A breath of a sigh. "Dozens. Hundreds. But the fantasy was never this real. Certainly not before. Not even after. No dream could re-create the sensations I discovered in your arms." Hazy mists clouded her mind. "Do you remember that afternoon, Eric? The afternoon we were together? I do. Every extraordinary detail. Nothing . . . ever . . . felt . . . so . . . wonderful."

Reclaimed by her feverish slumber, Brigitte missed the tormented look on her husband's face as he caressed her fiery cheek. "Yes, Brigitte," he replied in a rough, ragged voice. "I remember. And, no, nothing ever felt so wonderful."

He fell silent, watching the rise and fall of her breasts as she slept, unable to deny the wrenching emotions her confessions had evoked—emotions he'd thought himself incapable of feeling.

Rising, he paced aimlessly about the room, facing the incomprehensible truth.

He could lock himself away, seal his door to the world for the duration of time. But he couldn't seal his heart from this selfless, beautiful angel who was his wife.

Brigitte.

For more than a month now he'd evaded her, scrutinized her, wanted her. Initially, the battle was arduous. Since the day he'd taken her to bed, it was futile.

How ironic. His worry had been for Brigitte—that it would be she who'd be unable to cope with the aftermath of their passion. Instead, what had happened? She'd accepted his conditions, resumed life as it had been before that unforgettable afternoon in his arms. While he, on the other hand, spent every waking moment, every sleepless night, yearning for her. And not only in bed. He yearned for her laughter, her spirit, the fiercely protective way she stood up for Noelle.

Noelle.

For the first time, Eric found himself able to contemplate his niece without anguish, separating her from the events surrounding her birth. That in itself was a miracle.

So was the change in Noelle.

With utter disbelief, he'd watched as Brigitte transformed her from an uncontrollable, rebellious child into an exuberant, loving little girl, giving her a home, a future.

A mother.

Swearing softly, Eric averted his head, his jaw clenched in self-deprecating recall. If anyone was to blame for the past, it was he. That's why he'd done what he had to, taken the only route he could.

Banished Noelle from the desolation that was his life.

After what he'd endured with Liza, he'd been dead inside, incapable of giving or feeling—especially to the newborn babe his sister refused to acknowledge.

Refused to acknowledge? Hell, she'd wanted to erase Noelle's birth, as if it were some unwanted gift that need only be returned to be forgotten.

Eric squeezed his eyes shut, asking himself for the thousandth time what he'd done wrong. What had happened to the precious Liza he'd raised since infancy, showered with love, lavished with attention? Dear God, what had he created? A selfish woman with no sense of honor or commitment, neither to her brother, nor to her own child?

Whatever his mistakes, he couldn't allow Noelle to be subjected to them—or to him, for that matter. She deserved more than a blackhearted uncle who had nothing inside him but emptiness and self-hatred.

And now she'd have more—thanks to Brigitte.

A muted whimper from the bed brought Eric's head around, and he frowned when he saw his wife thrashing about, the bedcovers a tangled mass at her waist. Crossing the room, he resettled her, tucking the blankets beneath her chin.

"Noelle," she cried out, fighting the weight of the covers. "Must reach her . . . She'll drown . . ."

"Noelle is safe, Brigitte," Eric murmured, wondering whom he was comforting—his wife or himself. "And so are you."

"Eric?" As if from a great distance, she whispered his name.

"I'm right here. Nothing is going to harm you, or Noelle. Now sleep."

She quieted at once, her beautiful features relaxing into a deep, trusting slumber.

How in the name of heaven could she trust him?

Or love him.

The memory of Brigitte's admission made Eric's chest tighten.

Do you know how long I've loved you? Forever. Can you guess how many nights I've pictured your coming to me? Hundreds. But no dream could re-create the sensations I discovered in your arms.

It had to be the fever talking. After all, "forever" was impossible; they'd known each other less than two months.

Thus, the remainder of her vows must have been equally groundless.

Not those describing their passion.

Those, Eric reflected with a hot rush of memory, he himself could attest to. Never in his wildest imaginings, much less experiences, had he encountered such excruciating pleasure, a wild, incomparable storming of the senses that preoccupied his thoughts to the point of obsession.

Evidently, they preoccupied Brigitte's thoughts as well.

But lust, as he himself had apprised her, did not signify love. So whatever Brigitte was feeling—or *thought* she was feeling—couldn't be love.

Could it?

With a weary sigh, Eric dragged a tufted chair to the foot of the bed. Then, he dropped into it, tossed a blanket over himself, and closed his eyes.

His last thought before drifting off was that he'd have to conjure up some halfhearted punishment for his precocious tempest of a niece. Nothing too severe. In truth, the little troublemaker had done her job well. . . .

"Brigitte!"

The shriek pierced through Eric like a knife.

Scrambling to his feet, he shook his head, trying to orient himself. Where was he? Who had screamed?

"Brigitte . . . don't leave me!"

Noelle.

Memory jarred into place.

Swiftly, Eric glanced at the bed, assuring himself that Brigitte was deeply asleep, oblivious to the world and everyone in it. Then, he dashed from her room and down the hall to Noelle's, flinging open the door to find the child sitting up in bed, crying as if her heart would break.

"Noelle—what's wrong?"

Coming to her knees, Noelle didn't question his presence, just reached out for him, her small body wracked with sobs. "Uncle . . . I had a bad dream . . ." She broke off to catch her breath. "About Brigitte. She was so sick when you put her in bed. And Mama died of a fever. Mrs. Lawley said so. I dreamed I tried to wake Brigitte up, and I couldn't . . . and she never woke up . . . and . . ."

Eric crossed over to the bed in four strides, gathering Noelle in his arms. "Brigitte is fine," he assured her fiercely.

"Do you promise?"

"I promise." Eric could feel the tension ease from Noelle's shoulders.

"Did she wake up at all?"

"*Um-hum.* In fact, she just had a bad dream, too."

"She did?" Noelle raised her tear-streaked face, the terror of her nightmare temporarily held at bay. "But she's a grown-up."

"Grown-ups have bad dreams, too, Noelle." Eric stroked her hair, paternal instinct reawakening from its lengthy slumber. "Nightmares are just fears that lie in wait for our other thoughts to rest. Then, when the path is clear, they dash out and wreak havoc in our minds. And, since everyone has fears, everyone has nightmares."

Noelle digested that information with a loud, shuddering sniff. "If Brigitte is right and grown-ups have to obey rules, and you're right and grown-ups have fears and nightmares, what's the difference between being an adult and being a child—'cept the fact that children are shorter?"

An ironic smile touched Eric's lips. "Not much," he confessed. "Except that children don't try to hide their feelings behind stupid walls of self-delusion and self-protection."

"Brigitte doesn't hide her feelings. You just don't look hard enough to see them. Actually, you're not real good at seeing your own feelings either." Noelle plucked the handkerchief from her uncle's pocket. "May I use this?"

"Feel free." Eric frowned. "What do you mean? What don't I see?"

"How much you like Brigitte." Shrugging, Noelle blew her nose with an unladylike honk. "Or how much she likes you."

Eric shook his head in amazement. "Are you certain you're only going to be four?"

"That's what you told me. You said I was born on Christmas Day, 1856."

"You were." He tipped up her chin. "You were tiny and beautiful. You were also loud. You began wailing and kicking the instant you were born."

A grin. "Really?"

"Really."

"Uncle, how did Mama die?"

Meeting Noelle's gaze, Eric replied, "A fever, just as Mrs. Lawley said. But it wasn't like Brigitte's fever. It was much worse. She had influenza, it was a very cold winter, and I wasn't there to take care of her."

"Wasn't she at Farrington?"

"No, Noelle, she wasn't."

A thoughtful silence. "Mama ran away, didn't she?"

Eric tensed. "Who told you that?"

"The Willetts. They didn't actually tell me. I just overheard them during one of their arguments. I covered my ears, 'cause I didn't want to hear the rest." A resigned sigh. "But I guess I always knew the truth. Even Mama didn't want me."

An emotional knife pierced Eric's heart. "It wasn't a question of . . ." He broke off, desperately seeking the right words to say. "It wasn't that simple, Noelle. Your mother was beautiful and spirited, just like you. But she was very young when you were born—very young and very confused. She couldn't cope; she wasn't strong enough." Staunchly, he sustained the myth that would keep Liza's name as untarnished for Noelle as it was for Farrington's one-time servants, for the villagers, for everyone who believed him an ogre. "The fault was mine, Noelle. I was cruel to her. Angry and cruel. My rage frightened her and, eventually, drove her away."

"Brigitte's not frightened of you."

A corner of Eric's mouth lifted. "No, it appears she isn't."

"Neither am I." Noelle climbed into his lap. "Do you know what I think? I think Brigitte's right. I think you loved Mama a whole lot. I think you just pretend Mama's running away was your fault 'cause you want people to hate you. That way they'll leave you alone and you won't have to remember and your tummy won't hurt. You're doing that adult stuff you were talking about—shelf-illusion and protection. But you know what, Uncle? I don't believe you. You're not cruel." To Eric's amazement, Noelle wrapped her arms about his neck and hugged him. "You're a hero," she whispered. "You saved my life." Groping behind her, she grabbed hold of a clump of damp fur, shoving it unceremoniously in Eric's face. "Fuzzy's, too. We love you."

Were those actually tears he felt burning behind his eyes?

"Thank you, Noelle." That shattered voice bore no resemblance to his own. "I didn't think I needed that, but it turns out I do. Very much."

"I'm glad." Noelle dried her cheeks, the look she gave him one of profound wisdom. "Maybe, if you add Brigitte's love to mine and Fuzzy's, you won't be so angry anymore. Maybe that bad shelf-illusion will go away. And then maybe you can be happy." With that, Noelle gave a huge yawn. "I think I can go back to sleep now." She wriggled between the sheets, sighing contentedly—until she felt Eric's weight lift from the bed. "Are you returning to your chambers?" A flash of fear darted across her face.

"No. I'm using a lumpy chair in Brigitte's room as my bed. That way, I can keep an eye on her and also be nearby if you need me. Is that more to your liking?"

A broad smile. "Much more." Noelle nestled into the pillows. "Uncle?"

"*H-m-m?*"

"Will you come to my birthday party?"

Silence.

"I won't chest-ize you if you can't," she continued sleepily. "But it would be a whole lot easier for you if you could. That way, I won't have to fall out of trees to get to see you and you won't have to rescue me from drowning in ponds."

A chuckle rumbled in Eric's chest. "I see your logic, little schemer. I'll consider the invitation."

"Good night, Uncle."

"Good night, Noelle."

"Uncle?"

"Yes, Noelle."

"What's my punishment going to be?"

"Swimming lessons. For you, Brigitte, and Fuzzy. Given by the most grueling of instructors. Me."

Eight

A NOISE OF SOME KIND PERMEATED BRIGITTE'S CONSCIOUSNESS.

Frowning, she opened her eyes, wondering if Noelle had called her. It was obviously late at night, judging from the darkness of her room and the depth of her slumber.

Anxious to check on Noelle, Brigitte sat up . . . and just as quickly sank back into the bed. Why in the name of heaven was she so weak?

Memory flooded back in a rush. She'd been ill—very ill—for how long, she hadn't a clue. The last thing she remembered was collapsing in Noelle's chambers.

No. She remembered Eric, sitting at her bedside, bathing her face, forcing sips of water down her throat.

Or had she dreamed all that?

Gingerly, she tried rising again, this time slowly, swinging her legs over the side of the bed and coming cautiously to her feet. She groped at her nightstand until she found the lamp, turning it up so she could see.

Her room was empty, the grandfather clock by the wardrobe telling her it was nearly two A.M. Shivering, she glanced down at her thin linen nightdress and automatically reached for her robe, only to discover it wasn't in its customary position at the foot of her bed.

Her gaze fell on the tufted chair, its indented cushions and rumpled blanket a clear sign that someone had been using it as a cot.

Eric.

With a tender smile, Brigitte ran her fingers over the chair's elaborate wooden trim. So it hadn't been a dream. Eric had been with her, tending to her while she'd been sick, actually sleeping in her room lest she need him.

Joy swelled inside her.

The noise slashed the silence again.

Brigitte's head came up, her smile vanishing as she focused on the harsh, abrasive sound. Noelle?

All else forgotten, Brigitte dashed down the hall and flung open the door to Noelle's room.

She halted at the threshold.

The room was dark, quiet, the even sound of Noelle's breathing telling Brigitte she was fast asleep.

Relieved, Brigitte shut the door, leaning against it to regain her strength—and to analyze her persistent feeling that something was amiss. With a will of its own, her gaze traveled across the hall to the room she'd been forbidden to enter—the room she'd known from the outset had been Liza's.

The door was ajar, a shaft of light escaping through it . . . along with an echo of the rasping sound that had awakened her.

Reservations cast aside, Brigitte crossed the hall and slipped into the room, somehow knowing she was taking another irrevocable step, this one more pivotal than those she'd taken the day she'd agreed to marry Eric and the afternoon she'd shared his bed.

The room was in shambles.

Broken furniture, shattered glass, splintered paintings—shrouded in four years of dust—covered the carpet in a blanket of debris. In the center of it all stood Eric, head bent, shoulders heaving with long-repressed emotion.

"Eric." Brigitte said his name softly, coming up behind him and wrapping her arms about his waist.

He went rigid. "What are you doing here?" he demanded, his voice raw, harsh with pain.

"I love you." She lay her cheek against his shirt. "I want to be here with you. And I won't leave, no matter how hard you fight me."

His muscles went limp, and he turned, crushing her against his chest. "I have no more strength to fight. But Brigitte"—he swallowed—"look around you. For God's sake, see what I've done, what I am. Run from me while you can."

"I don't want to run. And I can see perfectly well what you've done. I can also see why. Perhaps you managed to deceive your staff, the villagers, even yourself. But you can't deceive me. As for who you are, you're the one who's blind to that truth, not I." She tilted back her head, meeting his tortured gaze. "Stop destroying yourself. None of what happened was your fault. Eric—" She lay her hand against his jaw. "Liza wasn't worth it."

Shock supplanted anguish. "You don't know what you're saying."

"I most certainly do." Brigitte stood her ground. "My fever is gone, my head perfectly clear. As for my assessment of Liza, I know a great deal more than you think I do, possibly more than anyone else does. You see, my lord, I had the unique opportunity to see the cruelty your sister kept so carefully concealed behind her engaging veneer. I knew her priorities, her coldness, even the extent to which she'd go to ensure her goals were realized."

A vein throbbed at Eric's temple. "How?" was all he managed.

"For reasons of her own, Liza decided I was a potential threat to her future. So she relinquished her facade in order to keep me in my place." Brigitte's smile was sad. "I must admit, she did a fine job."

"You knew each other?"

"Only from a distance. We spoke but once—when she sought me out to warn me away. I'll never forget that day."

"Warn you away? From what?"

"From you." Seeing Eric's stunned expression, Brigitte gave a bemused shake of her head. "Oh, Eric, I've been in love with you since I was a child. First, it was infatuation. I had to force myself not to dash outside and watch when you'd ride into the village, not to stare when you and Liza attended church. You were a knight in a fairy tale, sheltering Liza as if she were the most precious of treasures. I would have given anything to trade places with her, to be your adored little sister. Until I got older. Then my feelings changed from worship to something stronger, something even I didn't fully understand. All I knew was that I no longer wanted to be your sister. I wanted . . . more. I wanted to be one of the lucky women—no, the *only* lucky woman—on whom you bestowed that dazzling smile. I tried so hard to conceal it; never meeting your eyes, never allowing myself to so much as brush against you as you passed. But Liza was a very shrewd young lady. She perceived my feelings. And if there was one thing she didn't intend to share, it was you. Therefore, she cast aside her angelic mask and allowed me to see the ugliness of her character."

"When?" Eric asked hoarsely. "When did this happen?"

"The year before Noelle was born, just after Grandfather's Christmas service. I was thirteen—nearly fourteen, actually—and Liza was past fifteen. I'd gone around back of the church, to check and see if there were any children who hadn't received their Christmas treats. Liza followed me." Brigitte paused, feeling the pain as keenly as she had the day Liza shattered her adolescent dream to bits. "She said she had come to put an end to my flagrant infatuation, to—in her words—relegate me to my proper place, once and for all. I can still picture her eyes; those frigid sapphire chips appraising me as if I were a pitiful, unwanted bit of rubbish. She minced no words, telling me how pathetically obvious I was, and how laughable. She reminded me that you were a fabulously wealthy earl, while I was not only a child, but a wretched waif—the poor granddaughter of the local vicar. She then pointed out that my tattered gown wasn't fit to polish your silver, nor my social graces refined enough to grant me entry to Farrington as your scullery maid, much less your paramour. She suggested that I wait until I matured, then cast my eye on your coachman, or any one of your hundred other male servants—excluding, of course, your valet and butler, who would shudder at my lack of breeding."

Even after all these years, memories of Liza's cold tirade brought tears of humiliation to Brigitte's eyes. "I remember my stunned disenchantment—where was that fairy-tale princess I'd envied for so long? Then, Liza's words sank in, and I realized that, cruel as her intentions might be, her assertions were correct. We're all equal in the eyes of the Lord, but not in the eyes of others. Therefore, regardless of how good and honorable I was, I had no place in your life.

"Keeping that in mind, I heard your sister out, then gathered up the skirts of my less-than-acceptable gown and marched off. I held my chin high, not because I felt defiant, but because I refused to cry in Liza's presence. Nor did I—until I reached my home and my bed. There, I wept and wept until my tears and my dream had washed away."

"Brigitte . . ." It wasn't until Eric said her name that Brigitte realized he was holding her face, his thumbs capturing her tears.

"That confrontation didn't change anything, you know," she whispered. "Not really. Liza destroyed my hope, but not my love. I never stopped loving you, Eric. I never will. Especially since that afternoon in your chambers." Brigitte smiled softly. "Regardless of how little our physical joining meant to you—to me, it meant everything."

Squeezing his eyes shut, Eric groaned, stark emotion slashing his features. Then, he enfolded Brigitte against him, pressing her cheek to his heart. For long moments he said nothing, just held her, stroking her hair with a shaking hand.

At last he spoke.

"Everything you've said about Liza is true. With one exception. Who she was, what she became—*was* my fault. I was the one who molded her character. I catered to her every whim, purchased the world for her in order to compensate for our parents' deaths, devoted my entire life to her happiness."

"What about *your* life?" Brigitte asked the question that had plagued her for years. "Friends? Acquaintances?" A pause. "Women?"

"I was thirteen when my mother and father died. In truth, I never missed them; most likely because I scarcely knew them. I was raised by a governess and sent off to school the instant I could read. Even during holidays, my parents weren't home. They were far too restless to remain at Farrington; they were always dashing off on one adventure or another. I thought Liza's birth would encourage them to settle down. It didn't. When she was four months old, they sailed on an expedition to India. There was a horrible storm. Their ship sank. Suddenly, I was the Earl of Farrington—overseer of a neglected estate, faltering businesses, and a newborn babe. My childhood—whatever there was of it—came to an abrupt end. Thus, to answer your question, I had no time for diversions, no time for anything but work and Liza. Acquaintances? I had scores of them through my business dealings. Friends? I had none. Women?" Roughly, Eric cleared his throat. "When I needed one, I sought one out."

If Brigitte loved her husband before, she loved him all the more now—now that she understood the magnitude of his sacrifice. "So Liza was unused to sharing you with anyone."

"Indeed. She was also unused to sharing my money." Eric inhaled sharply. "Shall I tell you why she ran off?" He didn't wait for a reply. "Because I lost my fortune. It was that simple. When Liza was sixteen, I made one immense, unwise investment, and suddenly my wealth vanished. I waited until I had no choice but to tell her—although, fool that I was, I assumed her sisterly allegiance would prevail. I explained that we were far from destitute, but that luxuries would have to be forfeited, at least for a time. Instead of compassion, she looked at me with an expression that proclaimed me the Devil himself. She accused me of intentionally squandering her inheritance, and of being a brutal and unfeeling brother. Then, she locked herself in her room. The next morning she was gone. No note, no message, nothing. I didn't hear from her for months. Until, one day, she reappeared on my doorstep, begging for my help."

"She was with child," Brigitte inserted quietly.

A bitter nod. "She'd met a superbly wealthy Italian aristocrat who'd promised her the world. Instead, he filled her with his seed, then discarded her to return to his home . . . and his wife. Throughout her confession, Liza wept and wept, swearing to me that she'd learned her lesson, that she'd changed. God help me, I allowed myself to believe her." Eric swallowed, his arms tightening reflexively about Brigitte. "Evidently, Liza inherited my parents' restlessness. Three weeks after Noelle's birth, she announced she had no patience for motherhood and no tolerance for my unexciting, frugal existence. In short, she was bored and, thus, had decided to leave England and travel abroad. When I brought up the subject of Noelle, she shrugged, repeating that she hadn't the patience for an infant, nor had she a clue about child-rearing or an inclination to learn. She suggested I raise Noelle myself or, if my poverty precluded that choice, I farm Noelle out to some barren woman who would rejoice in the chance to nurture a child of her own. Quite frankly, Liza didn't really care who reared Noelle, so long as she herself didn't have to do it. I was jolted into a heinous reality I'd tried desperately to deny: that the sister I'd raised from infancy was a shallow woman with an empty heart and a hollow soul. I went insane. I bellowed until the walls shook, smashed Liza's room to bits, threatened to lock her in whatever remained of its confines until she came to her senses. I did everything short of striking her—and, God help me, sometimes I thought myself capable even of that. Nothing worked. When Noelle was six weeks old, I was summoned to London on urgent business. I was gone one night. When I returned, Liza had vanished, leaving behind a newborn babe and a staff that cringed the instant I walked through the door."

"Lord only knows what lies Liza told them," Brigitte inserted furiously.

Eric shrugged. "At that point it didn't matter. I didn't blame them for their fear. All they'd heard for weeks was Liza's sobbing and my savagery. I'm sure she had little trouble convincing them I was a madman. And, as I had no desire to amend their misconceptions, I dismissed them. They were weak with relief and lost no time in fleeing. Within hours, Farrington was deserted—except for Noelle. I packed her things into my phaeton and drove her to the home of the closest decent family I knew: the Gonerhams. I scarcely recall what I said when I thrust her into their arms; something about Liza being frightened and running away. They were too stunned, and too terrorized by my precarious state of mind, to turn Noelle away. I retreated to Farrington, intending never to emerge." A shudder ran through him. "I did precisely what I'd denounced Liza for doing: abandoned Noelle. But, Lord help me, I had nothing left to give her—no love, no tenderness. Nothing but bitterness and resentment. And, how could I risk creating another Liza? Making all those irreparable mistakes again?" He shook his head. "I couldn't.

"Some three months later, I received word that Liza had contracted influenza and died. I felt nothing. It was as if she'd died already—and taken me with her." Eric gave a hollow laugh. "The irony was that the urgent business that summoned me away and gave Liza the opportunity to escape turned out to be an announcement from my solicitor. One of my ventures had reaped an enormous profit. I'd recouped my fortune, plus some. Had Liza waited one day longer, she'd have been a rich woman again, and Noelle would have had a mother."

"Yes, but what kind of mother?" Brigitte demanded. "One who would forsake her own child? Eric, consider what you're saying. Your reasons for relinquishing Noelle were entirely different from Liza's. Yours were selfless; you were recoiling in pain and thought yourself incapable of giving Noelle what she needed. Liza's were not merely selfish but downright cold-blooded; she chose to sever all ties with her newborn babe in pursuit of an unencumbered and exciting life. How can you compare the two?" Saying a silent prayer, Brigitte fought to recapture all her husband had lost. "Eric, you said I was wrong, that if I truly knew who you were I'd feel differently than I do. Well, I wasn't and I don't. You didn't create Liza's character; she was born with it. Your only sin was to love her—which is no sin at all. You've condemned yourself to an undeserved hell and, in the process, deprived yourself of the one true treasure Liza did create."

"Noelle," Eric supplied, the lines of tension about his mouth easing ever so slightly. "She *is* quite a character, isn't she?"

"She's rare and special. I know it—and so do you. What's more, other than their physical resemblance, she's as unlike Liza as day and night. Noelle is sensitive and exuberant, bursting with life and laughter. And love. Love she's aching to give—and to receive. She needs a real parent, Eric, one whose heart is worthy enough to embrace her. She needs you. What's more, you need her." Brigitte reached up, her fingertips gently stroking his lips. "It's time, Eric," she stated softly. "The past is gone. And the future could be filled with such wonder."

"Brigitte." Eric's breath warmed her skin. "You almost make me believe miracles are possible."

"They are—if you allow them to be."

He captured her palm, pressed it to his lips. "Have you any idea how precious you are?"

Gazing up at her husband, Brigitte abruptly realized that, in the end, Liza *had* lost. For there in Eric's eyes was a rekindling of the very blessing Brigitte believed had been wrested away five years ago.

Hope.

"I love you," she breathed, somehow needing to say the words again.

Eric exhaled sharply, his hand trembling over Brigitte's. "You said earlier that our physical joining meant everything to you," he said, his voice hoarse with feeling. "It meant everything to me as well."

Brigitte gave him a small, tremulous smile. "Not merely lust then?"

"Not lust at all. Love. I love you, Brigitte—more than I can say. More than I ever believed possible." Profound emotion slashed across his face, echoing in Brigitte's heart. "When you fell sick—Christ, I was terrified. Then I couldn't seem to bring down the fever. Not until tonight. It's been three days, and you've done nothing but fade in and out of sleep, rambling on about being in heaven."

"I was. Because you were beside me."

A muscle worked in Eric's jaw. "I was frantic. I paced. I swore. I even prayed." His fingers tightened around hers. "I'd only just found you. I couldn't—*can't*—lose you."

"Nor will you." Brigitte wanted to shout her joy to the skies. "Not now. Not ever."

"Even Noelle was alarmed, and you know she's practically fearless. That first night she had a gruesome nightmare. She dreamed you'd died. I could scarcely stop her sobs. She loves you so bloody much . . ."

"You went to Noelle," Brigitte interrupted, her pupils dilating with joy. "When she awakened from her nightmare, you went in to comfort her."

"Yes. I did."

"Oh, Eric." Brigitte flung her arms about his neck. "You see? There are miracles." She closed her eyes. "Thank God."

Eric tangled his hands in her hair. "If God is to be thanked, it's for bringing you into our lives. Perhaps He finds me deserving after all."

"Oh, He does," Brigitte concurred fiercely. Leaning back, she caressed her husband's bearded jaw. "God sees you as I do. As I always have. As the man you truly are. A knight in a fairy tale: honorable, protective . . . extraordinary."

"But sadly in need of a princess to rescue." Eric brushed his wife's lips with his. "Would you know of someone who might fill that role?"

"Have you forgotten? It's already been filled—by your wife. You saved my life, remember?"

"I remember." Sweeping Brigitte off the floor and into his arms, Eric made his way through the debris—crossing the past's threshold and never looking back. "And in return, you gave me mine."

"Uncle?"

The hushed summons tickled Eric's ear.

"*H-m-m?*"

"Is Brigitte better? Is that why you're hugging her? Were you celebrating?"

Eric cracked open an eye, his arms tightening reflexively about his wife, now curved gently against him, the slow rise and fall of her back telling him she was asleep. Smiling, he recalled the exquisite hours preceding that slumber. "Yes, Noelle," he returned in a whisper, grateful that he'd heeded Brigitte's advice and donned his trousers while she'd scrambled into her nightdress—just in the event of such a predawn intrusion. "Brigitte's much better. And we were celebrating."

Noelle's sigh of relief was buried in Fuzzy's fur. "Then everything will be better, won't it, Uncle?"

"Yes, Noelle, everything will be better. Now go back to sleep; it's still night."

"All right." She hesitated. "Uncle? Remember what I said about how much Brigitte likes you?"

"Um-hum."

"Well, I know a way she'd like you even better."

Both Eric's eyes snapped open. "What?"

Noelle pressed her lips closer to his ear, her whisper loud enough to be heard across the room. "She thinks you're really handsome. She stares at you an awful lot. I think you should make it easier for her to see you."

Eric's lips twitched. "What do you suggest?"

"Shaving your face and cutting your hair. It would make you look ever so much nicer. Look how splendid Fuzzy looks since his bath. And I saw what a fuss Brigitte made over him. She'd probably make a fuss like that over you, too." A pause. "Well, maybe not *as* big a fuss, but then Fuzzy was a lot dirtier than you are."

"Thank you." Eric bit back his laughter. "That's excellent advice. I'll put it to use this very day."

"Good." A satisfied nod. "Uncle, are we a family?"

Eric's amusement faded, emotion knotting his chest. "Yes, Noelle. Thanks to Brigitte, that's precisely what we are."

"I thought so." She kissed his cheek with a loud smack. "G'night, Uncle."

"Sweet dreams." Eric reached up and tugged one tangled dark tress. "By the way," he said, "it's gotten quite cold these past few days. I think it might snow. Perhaps we should plan to move your birthday party indoors. My chambers are more than large enough to accommodate even the grandest of puppet shows."

400

Noelle's eyes widened. "Really?"

"Really. Now get some rest. We have a busy morning ahead of us."

The bright blue gaze narrowed questioningly. "We do?"

"Certainly. Didn't you hear me? It feels like snow. Therefore, we'd best fetch those numerous boughs of holly Brigitte so painstakingly collected—then abandoned when she dashed into the pond to save you. By tomorrow, they could be buried under layers of snow. If that should happen, and if the ground remains covered, we won't be able to retrieve them in time for Christmas. Nor are there enough boughs left on the trees to replace them."

The significance of Eric's words sank in, and Noelle flung her arms about his neck, hugging him fiercely. "Oh, Uncle, I'm so glad you learned how to celebrate."

"So am I, Noelle," Eric managed. "Very, very glad."

Lying quietly beside him, Brigitte smiled through her tears, giving silent thanks to the heavens.

In reply, a decision was made somewhere far above.

And the first snowflake deferred its descent one day longer.

Epilogue

"BRIGITTE, DID YOU SEE ANNE COREWELL'S EXPRESSION WHEN Uncle gave her the Christmas shillings?"

"Yes, Noelle, I did," Brigitte affirmed, cheerfully warming her hands by the sitting room fire. "I saw all the children's faces. They were elated."

"Are some of them truly coming to Farrington this afternoon?" Noelle demanded, prancing about their gloriously decorated Christmas tree—the very fir Brigitte had selected scant weeks ago when Christmas seemed naught but an inconceivable dream. "Just for my party?"

"Actually, quite a few of them accepted our invitation." Brigitte's heart swelled with gratitude as she recalled the generous response of the villagers, many of whom were postponing their own Christmas festivities in order to grant one precious four-year-old the first real celebration of her life. "And not only the children," she added. "Their families as well. After all, sharing Christmas with those you love is what makes the day so special—right?"

"Right!" Noelle's head bobbed up and down, pausing as another thought struck. "Brigitte, what about your grandfather? Is he coming? He's family—and he's *really* special. It's 'cause of him that so many people like Uncle again. I heard Anne's parents talking—They said the vicar's been come-mending Uncle and saying everyone should welcome him, not fear him." A tiny pucker formed between Noelle's brows. "What's 'come-mending'? Does that mean Uncle was broken and the vicar fixed him?"

"No, love." Brigitte grinned at Noelle's customarily inventive reasoning. "Your Uncle wasn't broken. Commending someone is praising them; the opposite of chest-izing them."

"Oh! No wonder so many people are coming to my party. The vicar must have explained how Uncle saved our lives. Now they all know he's a hero, too."

"Indeed they do. And, to answer your question, yes, Grandfather will be here."

Noelle chewed her lip. "Do you think he'll be too tired to run the puppet show? His Christmas sermon was awfully long. I know 'cause, even though I stayed awake through the whole thing, Fuzzy nodded off twice."

Brigitte's shoulders shook. "Grandfather wouldn't miss your

party for the world. Rest assured, he and his puppets are en route to Farrington even as we speak."

"Oh, Brigitte, Christmas is just as wonderful as you promised!" Noelle tossed Fuzzy in the air, where he bounced against a wreath and landed in Noelle's arms with an evergreen sprig about his neck.

"More wonderful," Brigitte replied, glancing up as Eric entered the room. "Who was that at the door?"

"Bladewell—the Farrington butler." A look of awed pleasure split Eric's clean-shaven face. "According to him, all the servants will be returning to Farrington by the first of the year. Not one of them refused my offer—my *request*," Eric amended softly, "to assume their previous positions."

"Oh, Eric, that's splendid!" Brigitte's heart sang at the wonder in her husband's eyes. "What else did he say?"

"*H-m-m?* Oh, nothing more." Swiftly, Eric averted his gaze, busying himself with readjusting the garland about the doorframe. "He had to hurry off to his sister's house. She's making Christmas dinner for their family."

Brigitte's brows rose. "I see. If that's all you discussed, then why were you gone so long?"

An evasive shrug, followed by a chuckle. "I had a private matter to attend to, my inquisitive wife."

"How many people will be living here, Uncle?" Noelle piped up, before Brigitte could pursue the subject.

"Lots." Eric rumpled her hair. "Hundreds, perhaps. Is that too many?"

"Oh, no," she assured him. "Fuzzy has decided he likes company after all."

"Does he like surprises?"

Instantly, Noelle's eyes lit up. "Yes. Is that what the 'private matter' was—a surprise?"

"*Um-hum.* Upstairs." Eric gestured toward the doorway. "Would you care to see it?"

"It's in your chambers, isn't it? You're finally going to show me the preparations you made for the puppet show!"

"Excellent guess. Unfortunately, however, it's only half right. Come." Amusement curved Eric's lips as he turned to his wife, who was eyeing him in utter bewilderment. "Will you be joining us, Lady Farrington?"

"Is there something more than I already know?" she demanded.

"Accompany us and find out."

"I fully intend to." Brigitte sprinted after Noelle, wondering what on earth Eric had done in his chambers, other than that which she'd helped him effect: arranging Noelle's tea party and hiding her gift. When had he found time to do more? He hadn't left their sides for more than a few minutes at a time; not since that pivotal moment in Liza's room. Nor had he spent a single night in his old room. Brigitte herself could attest to *that* fact, she thought with a warm, sated glow.

Of course, there was that hour every afternoon when she and Noelle would take their naps—an hour she seemed to require more and more as the days progressed. Perhaps Eric had used those intervals to work on his surprise.

Which reminded her that she had a surprise of her own to share.

Lighthearted, Brigitte dashed up the stairs, hearing Eric's rumbling laughter as he followed in her wake.

By the time they reached the east wing, Noelle was soaring at a dead run.

"Uncle, it's locked!" she called out, jiggling the door handle.

"Of course it is. How else would I keep prying young lad*ies*"—he tossed Brigitte a meaningful look along with his emphasis of the plural—"from inspecting my handiwork."

Brigitte was all innocence. "I?"

"You." He strode up, extracting the key from his pocket.

"I didn't even know of the surprise," she protested.

"What if you had? Would you have been disciplined enough to stay away?"

Silence.

"I rest my case." Eric inserted the key in its slot.

"I believe I've just been chest-ized," Brigitte muttered to Noelle.

"That's all right." Noelle patted her arm soothingly. "Remember what I said: Uncle always smiles when he chest-izes you." Her attention was recaptured by the sound of the bolt lifting. "Hurry, Uncle. Fuzzy and I are going to burst."

"In that case . . ." Eric swung open the door. "Go in and behold your surprise."

Noelle dashed in, Brigitte at her heels, and whooped with pleasure at what she saw.

Brigitte and Eric had set up the entire outer room of his chambers for Noelle's party, with a curtained stage for the puppet show and lots of chairs surrounding it, together with an elegantly clothed table laid out for the most exquisite of teas.

"Brigitte, did you help Uncle?"

"I did, indeed," Brigitte confirmed. "Given the meager number of hours you sleep, it took two of us to accomplish this by Christmas Day."

"It's perfect!"

Thrilled by Noelle's jubilation, Brigitte darted about behind her, watching as Noelle lingered over every loving detail of their preparations.

A towering silhouette of color in the inner room caught Brigitte's eye.

Puzzled, she pivoted—and her jaw dropped. "Oh, my . . . Noelle, look!"

Noelle's head jerked around, and she followed Brigitte's stare, gasping as she beheld the full effect of her uncle's surprise. Her eyes grew big as saucers, her mouth widening into an astonished O.

Eric's sleeping quarters were no more. The furnishings had vanished, but for a small side table upon which sat a diminutive version of Brigitte's fir tree, trimmed in full Christmas array.

Or maybe it just seemed diminutive because it was eclipsed by the dozens and dozens of presents that filled the room, some carefully wrapped, others open and on display, beckoning their admirers forward.

Toys, sweets, girls' clothing of every hue and variety, games, books—a floor-to-ceiling paradise of gifts awaited Noelle, each and every one of them with her name on it.

"Merry Christmas," Eric said, his voice rough with emotion.

"Are all these for me?" Noelle managed.

"Other than the ones on the far wall, which are for Brigitte. They're from me to you: for all the Christmases we missed and should have shared." He cleared his throat. "Well, tempest, what are you waiting for?"

It was all the permission Noelle needed.

She dashed forward, snatching up two dolls at once, together with an armful of outfits in which to dress them. Seconds later, she spied something and squealed, flinging the clothes aside, dropping to her knees to shove both dolls—and Fuzzy—into a three-level dollhouse large enough to fit another half-dozen miniature occupants.

"Eric . . ." Brigitte wasn't certain what to say.

"Aren't you going to inspect your gifts?" he asked, pointing to the thirty or more beautiful, fashionable day dresses and ball gowns that lined the far side of the room. "I hope they please you. I had the seamstress make a variety of styles, in case you prefer one over another. The boxes alongside the gowns contain accessories and undergarments, plus some fragrances and jewelry I thought you might enjoy."

"How . . . ?" Brigitte whispered. "When . . . ?"

"It wasn't difficult." Eric closed the gap between them, smiling at the look of stunned disbelief on Brigitte's face. "You and Noelle sleep quite soundly during your afternoon naps. I used that time to receive deliveries and ready my room— permanently." His ardent gaze delved deep inside his wife. "I no longer have use for separate quarters, do I?"

"No," Brigitte breathed. "You don't."

"As for the gowns, I sent your blue day dress to the seamstress, who used it for measurements." He framed Brigitte's face between his palms. "No one will ever mock your clothing again."

"I wouldn't care if they did."

"I would. Not because I give a damn what anyone thinks, but because what hurts you hurts me. And because I intend to shower you with every luxury life has to offer."

"I . . ." She swallowed. "Eric, I don't need all this."

"To enhance your value or your beauty, no—you don't. But for the new life I have in mind, yes—you do. We're going to be doing a great deal of entertaining; you, Noelle, and I. Today's party is just the beginning. Farrington has been asleep far too long. It's time we awakened it."

Brigitte twined her arms about his neck, her lashes damp with tears. "I love you."

"You're my own priceless miracle," Eric replied huskily. "And I love you more than you'll ever know."

With a slow, shaky breath, Brigitte offered her husband the gift she'd been savoring. "Would you mind dreadfully if the new gowns and the entertaining were to wait a bit longer?"

He blinked. "Why? Don't you like the dresses? I can have others made."

"I think that would be wise." Brigitte's eyes glowed through her mist of tears. "Much larger ones, I should think. Large and loose-fitting, to accommodate my Christmas present to you." Capturing Eric's hand, she placed it against her abdomen.

She watched his expression change from puzzlement to speculation to comprehension.

And then to joy.

"Brigitte." His throat worked convulsively. "Are you saying . . . ?"

"Merry Christmas, my love." She reached up to kiss him. "It seems our first joining yielded even more than our hearts. Our child will arrive this summer."

Wordlessly, he enfolded her against him, his awed fulfillment a tangible entity that spoke for itself.

"Uncle? Why is Brigitte crying?" Noelle asked.

"Because I'm happy," Brigitte answered, disengaging herself from Eric's embrace and kneeling down to face Noelle. "Noelle, how would you feel about having a brother or sister?"

Noelle inclined her head. "How could I have a brother or sister? I'd need parents for that."

"You have parents." Brigitte cupped her chin. "Us."

Realization struck. "You mean you and Uncle are getting a baby?"

"Is that all right?"

Worry furrowed Noelle's delicate brow as she considered the possibility.

"Noelle, I've never had a baby before, nor have I been one for many years," Brigitte confided. "You, on the other hand, were one yourself just a few years ago. You'll remember a lot more than I. I'm counting on you to help me, and the babe."

"Will it be a boy or a girl?"

"I honestly don't know."

"When will it arrive?"

"Sometime at the beginning of August. I'm not exactly sure."

"You really don't know much about babies, do you?" Noelle determined, frowning.

"I'm afraid not."

"Will I truly be the baby's sister?"

"Indeed you will."

"Can I call you 'Mama'?"

A lump formed in Brigitte's throat. "Nothing would make me happier."

"And Uncle 'Papa'?" She looked at Eric.

"I'd be honored," he responded.

Noelle grinned. "Then it's okay." Abruptly, she glanced down at Fuzzy, a pensive look on her face. "Brigitte—I mean, Mama—" she said at last, "we're a real family now. And families share, 'specially stuff that's special. So I think I'll share Fuzzy with my new sister or brother. After all, Fuzzy knows how hard it is being new to a family. He helped me get used to it. I'll bet he could help the new baby get used to it, too. Would that be all right?"

Brigitte thought her heart would burst. "I love you, Noelle," she said, hugging her new daughter tightly. "And, yes, it's more than all right. It's wonderful."

"What's more, your decision couldn't have come at a better time," Eric put in. "Because Fuzzy's not the only one who's going to be busy with a new charge."

"What do you mean?" Noelle asked.

With a secret smile, Brigitte rose. "That's right. I almost forgot about your birthday gift." So saying, she scooted off to a shadowed corner of the outer chamber. An instant later, she reappeared, a small wire crate in her hands. "Happy birthday, Noelle."

From within the crate, a golden kitten with huge dark eyes stared out.

"A cat! A real cat!" Noelle snatched the crate, yanking open the door and lifting out her new prize. "What's his name?"

"*Her* name," Eric corrected. "She's your kitten. You choose."

"She looks just like Fuzzy!"

On the heels of her words, the kitten—realizing she was free—sprang to life, bounding to the floor and tearing off. Toys flew everywhere, boxes tipped over, and the side table wobbled precariously as she slammed into its legs.

"She might look like Fuzzy, but she behaves like you," Eric observed dryly.

"I know! I'll call her Tempest!"

"An excellent choice, Noelle." Brigitte was laughing so hard she could scarcely speak.

"Tempest—come here," Noelle commanded.

In response, Tempest tossed them an insolent look, then sprang onto the side table and shimmied up the tree, knocking down one ornament after another as she climbed. Halfway to the top—and evidently satisfied with her level of destruction—she stopped, curling up on a branch and peering at them through arrogant, half-closed eyes.

"Aren't you going to chest-ize her?" Noelle demanded, turning to her new parents.

"No, Noelle." Eric gave a resigned sigh, resting his chin atop Brigitte's head. "Experience tells me Tempest is beyond re-damn-sin."

ANDREA KANE is one of the rising stars of women's fiction, garnering an enviable reputation for crafting incomparable romances. Her most recent novel, *The Last Duke,* appeared on numerous bestseller lists, and followed in Andrea's tradition of award-winning, bestselling titles:*Samantha, Echoes in the Mist, Masque of Betrayal, Dream Castle,* and *My Heart's Desire.* Her growing list of devout readers applaud her passion for romance and share in her realization that "as a child, I was an incurable romantic, a believer in fairy tales where happily-ever-after reigned supreme and true love conquered all. Everyone said I would outgrow it. I never did." Fortunately, Andrea continues to delight us with beautiful and exhilarating stories—her own special brand of fairy tales. She lives in New Jersey with her husband, Brad, daughter, Wendi, parakeet, Ariel, and Maltese puppy, Rascal (the canine hero of *Samantha*). She is busy creating her latest triumph, *Emerald Garden,* which will be released as a Jaunary 1996 Pocket Books lead title and will be on bookshelves in mid-December.

I love hearing from my readers! Drop me a note (include a legal-size SASE for a copy of my current newsletter) at the following address:

P.O. Box 5104
Parsippany, NJ 07054–6104

With love,

Andrea

Judith O'Brien

Five Golden Rings

For my big brother, Brooks, who always opened my Barbie dolls while I unwrapped his cars and soldiers.

And I didn't really mean to throw your blue St. Louis Cardinal baseball cap out the car window on the highway. It just happened.

One

"MISS GRAHAM! MISS GRAHAM!" THE CHILD RAISED HER HAND so high, with such ferocity, that Emma Graham had a mental image of her boring a hole into the ceiling.

"Yes, Jennifer K." Emma smiled. The half-dozen children who had not been called upon emitted the usual groan of disappointment.

Jennifer K., so labeled to distinguish her from the four other Jennifers in the first-grade class, preened the moment her name was called.

"I would like to be a Christmas angel," she announced, flipping a hand through her long blonde hair.

"Very nice, Jennifer K. I'll be sure to make a note of that should the need arise."

Emma had become an expert at judging the children in her classroom. Every class had a Jennifer K., the pretty girl all too aware of her own beauty.

This class was no exception. There was also the class clown, the smart kid, the tomboy with more skinned knees than all of the other kids combined, and so on.

Only one child didn't fit this year, the new boy, an enigma to her as well as to the other children. In her five years of teaching, she had never had a student like this one.

Today, as usual, he sat very still, with his hands folded on top of the desk. He was too quiet for a six-year-old, his eyes were too solemn.

According to the principal, his mother had died when he was still an infant. Emma had made a half-dozen attempts to contact his father, but either the messages never reached him or he had not bothered to respond. The boy's nanny always brought him to school and picked him up. He never went home with another child, never had play dates or party invitations at the end of the day.

Although there were plenty of children of divorce in her class, the new boy was the only child who'd had a parent die. The children sensed this difference and had avoided him since his first day. There was an unspoken fear, a feeling among the children that such misfortune just might be contagious.

Emma resumed speaking to the students. "I have divided the class into three groups. Some of you will be Hanukkah, some of you Kwanza, and the rest of you will be the Twelve Days of Christmas."

As if on cue, a universal moan and cheer swept the classroom like a stadium wave. The excitement was almost palpable. Christmas was a mere three weeks away. Toy catalogs had been making their way into the classroom, green and red construction paper was posted everywhere. Even the grumpy school custodian, with his ever-present push broom now decorated with wisps of tinsel, was seen sporting a red Santa hat. By mid-January he would be complaining about the holiday glitter embedded in every carpet and corner, but for now he joined all the rest of the school in a frenzy of anticipation.

All except the new boy. It was hard enough to be new to a school, but to be new at school at this time of year was very nearly unbearable. He was new, his mother was dead, and the most unfortunate thing of all—his name was Asa.

There was no need to distinguish Asa from any other Asa in the class—he was the only one. In fact, he was the only Asa in the entire school, perhaps in all of Brooklyn.

Emma tucked a strand of her coppery hair behind her ear as she bent over her desk.

"Miss Graham! Miss Graham!"

One of the Michaels was speaking. There were two Michaels, which was unusual. Usually she had at least three in each class.

"Yes, Michael R.?" She glanced at the clock. Fifteen more minutes until the final bell, and she had yet to pass out the assignments.

"Do you have a boyfriend?"

A silence fell over the room. Emma cleared her throat, accustomed to hearing that question at least once a week. During the holiday season, the question cropped up alarmingly more frequently. It was her own personal signal that the season had begun in earnest.

"No, Michael R., not at the moment. Okay, listen up. I have here a stack of letters to go home to your . . . Yes, Bobby. What's your question?"

"Miss Graham? My parents wrestle at night with their shirts off. I've seen them."

Emma bit the inside of her cheek to keep from laughing. "Thank you for sharing that with us, Bobby. As I was saying, the notes I'm passing out are to be signed by one of your parents. Each note is special, and . . . Yes, Sunbeam, do you have something to add?"

Sunbeam seemed surprised to have been called upon. No matter what, she always seemed surprised. Blinking, she stood up next to her desk.

"My father smokes a funny-looking pipe at night."

Sunbeam's father, a former roadie for the Grateful Dead, now a Wall Street banker, also wore tie-dyed underwear, according to his daughter, and had been arrested in college. Sunbeam brought in his mug shots for show-and-tell.

"Smoking is not good for you," said Billy. "It gives you cancer and they have to cut you up and then you die."

Sunbeam's lower lip began to tremble. "But he only takes one or two little puffs. He says it makes him happy. Will my daddy die?"

"No, Sunbeam. I'm sure your daddy will be just fine." Emma began passing out the notes. Asa did not move when she gave him the folded white paper.

"Asa," she said, "you get to do something very special. You get 'five golden rings.' Just bring in some old plastic curtain rings, and I'll help you paint them gold."

Slowly, without looking down, he took the note and jammed it into his Power Rangers backpack.

"You have to write the note to his daddy, since his mommy is dead," chirped Jennifer K., again flicking her hair.

Emma wanted to wrap the silken hair around her chubby little neck. Instead, she ignored the comment. She had learned during her first year of teaching that sometimes the best reaction was no reaction at all.

"Okay—the bell's about to ring. The sooner you guys bring the items into class, the sooner we can begin. And remember tonight's homework—a full page of capital Js."

The bell blasted, and the children grabbed their backpacks and lunchboxes and lined up by the door. Everyone had a buddy. Except for Asa. He stood alone, the last in line.

He was always the last in line.

Emma had wanted to be a teacher ever since she herself had been in first grade. There was never any question, never any doubt. Others wanted to be teachers for the short hours and the long vacations, but for Emma, it was the teaching she adored.

On the wall of her Park Slope apartment, just three blocks from her school, were class pictures of Emma and her kids. There were five photographs, neatly mounted in identical wood and acrylic frames, chronicling her rise from student teacher to full teacher. It was a large, blank wall, with plenty of space for the scores of pictures that would eventually hang there.

Most of her friends from college were married now, with children of their own. Emma was content with her temporary charges and a closet full of pastel tafetta bridesmaid dresses and dyed-to-match pumps neatly lined up in a row.

Emma collapsed onto the couch, exhausted, although it was only a little past five in the evening. She put everything she had into her job. There was nothing left at the end of a day.

It was good that she had no husband or boyfriend, she reflected. She couldn't possibly gather the energy it would take to meet a guy, much less cultivate a relationship. Of course, there had been boyfriends, especially in college. Things just hadn't worked out. Nothing tragic or catastrophic. She just had never met the right guy.

Her lips curved into a small smile. Who would the right guy be? He would have to be tall, at least tall enough to balance her own five-foot-eight frame, and athletic enough to want to bicycle with her on one of her summer trips. Smart, perhaps even brilliant, with just enough idealism to soften the edges. It would be nice if he could also be handsome.

The small smile became a giggle. "Yea, right Graham," she said to herself. "I'm sure there are tons of guys just like him, all waiting for you to make the first move."

She stood and stretched, catching her reflection in the hall mirror.

She was pretty, in an understated way, nothing flashy or showy. Perhaps that was her problem—she was too average. An average schoolteacher, in an average school, with an apartment that was functional and tidy, and average.

Suddenly her cat, a sociopathic tabby with the unoriginal name of Pumpkin, pounced on her feet.

"Okay, I'll get you dinner." She sighed, and the cat immediately skittered across the floor and slid under the couch.

It crossed her mind to call up some friends and go over to Dapper Dan's, a neighborhood hangout. But it took too much effort, simply too much work to get dressed and see the same old gang over the happy hour steam table. The limp chicken wings and potato skins did not quite balance out the overpriced beer and strained conversation.

Instead, she'd spend an average evening with the cat and Peter Jennings on television. An evening like a thousand others, and a thousand more to come.

Most of the kids remembered not only their homework but their holiday projects as well. Even Asa, silent, his large eyes ever-roaming, clutched a small paper bag filled with curtain rings. If he had been any other child, she would have teased him about being ready to change the words to "thirty-seven golden rings." But Asa was different. Emma simply smiled at him.

It wasn't until after school was over, when the kids were gone and Emma was about to turn off the light switch, that she noticed Asa's paper bag was on the floor.

She picked up the bag and opened it. There were a few dozen old curtain rings. His father must have bought new ones when they moved. On the top of the heap was a smaller hoop, already painted gold.

Curious, she pulled out the small hoop. It wasn't plastic. It was metal.

Emma brought it over to the light on her desk. Not only was

it metal, it seemed to be real gold. The ring was clearly an antique and had the burnished pink-gold of old jewelry. There was an inscription on the inside, but the engraved script was too worn to read.

"Funny," she muttered, placing the ring in her purse for safekeeping.

She needed to call Asa's father to let him know about the ring. Perhaps then she could find out more about the boy, ask the father if he had always been such a withdrawn child. Of course she would have to be gentle, diplomatic—a cautious path she had trod many times when speaking to parents.

Something flipped in her stomach at the thought. What was the little boy's father like? What kind of man must he be?

It was an unnerving thought.

In the end, the closest Emma came to speaking to Asa's father was leaving a message on his answering machine.

"You have reached eight three nine, seven five seven two," said a clipped, impersonal voice. "Please leave a message, and I will return the call as soon as possible."

The voice wasn't unpleasant, Emma mused as she took a breath to answer. But just before she spoke, she inhaled the piece of gum she had been chewing.

"Ah, I . . . Hello," she choked. After a brief series of gagging sounds that resembled Pumpkin coughing up a fur ball, she was able to continue. "I'm your, *ahem, ah*. That's better. Hello. I'm Asa's teacher, Emma Graham, and I have . . ."

A bleep interrupted her sentence. Was that the signal to begin speaking or end the message?

"Damn it," she snarled into the receiver.

"Hello?" It was his voice, the voice of Asa's father. "I just walked in the door, and . . ."

421

Emma did not hear anything else. She did the mature thing, had the adult reaction to being caught off guard: Emma slammed down the receiver.

"Why did I do that?" she moaned at the silent telephone.

Immediately her telephone rang. Could it be him? Oh, my God, she thought. Did he have caller identification? Had she left her number?

Hesitantly, she picked up the phone. "Hello." She used a different voice, the sultry, deep voice of someone who just woke up.

"Emma? Is that you? My goodness, you sound awful. Do you have a cold?"

Immediately she relaxed. "Oh, hi, Mom." Emma fell back against the sofa cushions. "No, I'm fine."

During the conversation with her mother, Emma kept on thinking of Asa's father and wondering what he could possibly think of her.

Emma yawned, gazing at the television as she sipped the last of her hot chocolate. Pumpkin was under the sofa, brutally shaking a felt mouse by its neck, bells jingling with every quiver.

Idly, she reached for her purse. The ring was there, safely tucked into the zippered coin compartment.

It was a beautiful ring. Had it been Asa's mother's? No. That didn't seem right. The ring was too old and fragile to have been worn anytime recently. Whoever had worn this ring had done so for years, decades perhaps. Emma imagined an old woman refusing to part with her ring, refusing to take it off during chores and laundry and baking gingerbread for the grandchildren.

So soft, so gently worn, the ring was smooth as polished satin. Emma placed the ring on her own left hand, the vacant ring finger. So soft, so smooth.

Pumpkin emitted a high-pitched wail. Emma ignored the cat.

The metal felt warm to the touch. It slid perfectly down her finger, as if it had been made for her. Her whole hand felt warm. A delicious drowsy feeling radiated up her arm and encompassed her entire body.

Emma's eyes closed. She would sleep right here on the couch, she thought to herself. She would sleep.

The mattress was lumpy.

Emma tried to fall back asleep. She was having a wonderful dream, although she couldn't recall any details.

An unfamiliar scent brought her back to consciousness. Something smelled of animals. Emma sat up.

"Pumpkin? Does your litter box need cleaning?"

The moment she opened her eyes, the words died on her lips.

She was in a small room. It had wide-plank floors, and there was a large wooden wardrobe in one corner. A ladder-back chair with a woven cane seat stood on a rag rug.

It was a rustic bedroom, and she looked down at a handmade quilt. She could now smell straw and coffee and corn bread, the odors coming from beyond a calico curtain that hung in a doorway on a thick wood rod.

Just beyond the calico curtain she heard footsteps. They sounded thick and booted, clanking on the planks.

Embers glowed in the fireplace, but still the room was cold. Thick sheets of ice covered the window, on both the inside and outside.

Before Emma could even react to her strange surroundings, a large hand divided the calico curtain. In stepped one of the most handsome men she had ever seen—tall, superbly built, wearing a loose white shirt and thick trousers held up by leather suspenders.

His hair was coal black, but sprinkled lightly with flecks of gray. Yet at that first, startling moment it was his eyes Emma noticed, brown eyes that had laughed and cried.

"The doctor says we can try again, Em." His voice had a strangly flat accent. "When the time is right we can try again."

With that he withdrew from the room as swiftly as he had entered.

One extra detail managed to filter into her mind. The man had also been wearing a ring. From a single glance she knew his matched the ring on her own left hand.

Two

EMMA HAD NO IDEA HOW LONG SHE SAT IN THE BED, QUILT tucked under her neck, eyes fixed numbly on the calico curtain.

She had heard of the term "clinical shock" before, and now she knew exactly what it meant. Time seemed suspended, and she was unable to move or speak or feel anything. Her mind numbly toiled to explain where she was. Perhaps she had been kidnapped and taken to an elaborate theme park, or she had gone overboard on this year's Pioneer Day celebration at school.

But this was real. Every detail was too perfect to be a museum or some sort of illusion. The smells were sharp and pungent, the sounds echoed. No airplanes roared overhead, no highway hummed in the distance. Somehow, Emma had traveled back in time.

Eventually she heard the man leave. He didn't say a word to her, no "good-bye" or "have a nice day" or "what the hell is a strange woman doing in my bed?" Nothing.

Little by little she took note of her surroundings. The mattress was lumpy and seemed to be filled with corn husks.

The quilt she gripped in her hands was slightly faded. Every knot and stitch was visible, quaintly uneven.

There were animals outside. She could hear clucks and squawks, a vibrato neigh. More than once she heard what sounded like a wagon rolling by. The wheels crunched on snow and gravel. The drivers clicked a rein or spoke soothing words to the horse.

Finally Emma noticed a small hand mirror resting on a trunk. She jumped out of bed, slightly light-headed for a moment, and grabbed the mirror to see her reflection.

It was she, all right. Even in the dark and spotted mirror surface she recognized her own face. Her expression was one of confusion, her blue eyes reddened and a little swollen; her hair was braided and tied with strips of cloth. But it was unmistakably Emma Graham who stared back from the mirror.

A small triangle of cloth poked out from the closed trunk. Before Emma replaced the mirror, she opened the trunk to tuck it back in place.

A refreshing fragrance wafted up when she tilted the heavy lid back, a smell of flowers and springtime. On top of neatly folded clothes were dried flowers, their stems tied with bright ribbons. Just below the ribbons was a small leather-bound book.

It was a diary. Emma knew that immediately. She began to close the trunk lid, then halted. For a moment she simply stood, barefoot and in a loose cotton nightgown. Then she grabbed the diary, closed the trunk, and jumped back into the wadded warmth of the bed.

The red diary had no lock. Emma anticipated a musty smell when she opened the leaves, but the only odor she could detect was one of flowers.

The pages were clean and white. After a few blank pages, the entries began. Blue ink, crisp, precisely formed letters.

In Emma's own handwriting.

There was no mistaking it and no possible explanation. Emma had written the exact same way since junior high school, the same sharp angles, the same distinctive slant. The writer of the journal was Emma herself.

She rubbed her eyes, painful eyes that felt as if she had been crying. Then she began to read.

The writing was Emma's, but these were the words of a complete stranger.

The entries began in March 1832, in Philadelphia. The writer did not identify herself, but spoke of her infant son and her husband and the journey west they were about to embark upon.

There was a strange tone to the entries, a self-conscious caution to every word. No names were mentioned. No specifics.

The baby will turn one year old on our journey. My husband hopes we will be in Indiana by then. He will begin working with Judge Isaiah Hawkins immediately. Those who have worked with my husband in Philadelphia express surprise and not a little dismay at his abrupt departure. As a lawyer, he is generally considered amongst the most promising in Philadelphia, if not the entire East Coast. Yet his choice of clients is capricious as the March wind, and every bit as impoverished. He seems determined not to accept clients who can afford his worth. He longs to go west, to face frontier law rather than city law. The baby frets.

The next entry was even briefer.

The canals are frozen, so we wait. I know no one, nor do I wish to make anyone's acquaintance. Our fellow travelers are an appalling lot, rough and slovenly of both appearance and manner. I can only believe the further west we travel, the further our surroundings will deteriorate.

A few lines described her husband's excitement. "He knows not how I feel. He will see naught beyond his own happy idealism. He wants to help others, but I fear it will be at his family's expense."

The next passage was dated May 1832. "The heat is fierce. I thought Overton Falls would be a town, but there are only a handful of houses. My baby would be a year old now, had the Lord not called him to His side. Would he be taking his first steps?"

Emma put the journal down. There were no other entries. The other pages were fresh and blank.

"The baby died," she mumbled to herself.

Emma simply stared at the room, at the coarse furniture, the valiant attempts at comfort. Suddenly she had to get outside, to see where she was, and if she could find her way home.

There were women's clothes in the wardrobe, and she pulled out the warmest-looking dress she could find. There were stockings, all black and cotton and misshapen, and a heavy petticoat. In the bottom of the wardrobe, under scraps of cloth, were two pairs of shoes. Apparently they had not been worn for a while; both pairs were free of mud and dirt. She slipped on the sturdiest ones, black leather with thick buttons on the side and clunky soles.

Just below the clothing in the trunk were a brush and a tin box of hairpins. They were lethal-looking spiked things, with a light crust of rust, as if they, too, had not been used in a long time. Emma did the best she could with her hair and was quite pleased when she shook her head and only a handful of pins tinkled to the floor.

Stepping through the doorway and into the next room,

Emma was surprised at how tidy the husband had managed to keep the place.

The primitive room contained yet another fireplace—this one was cold—with a kettle on a large hook hanging from the chimney. There was a plank table and a stone sink. Along one wall was a bench with folded bedding on the seat.

This was where he had been sleeping.

Next to the bench was a spindly pine table with a clay pipe, a pottery jar that read "tobacco," and a stack of heavy-looking books. She picked them up and examined the titles, *The Columbian Orator* and *Blackstone's Commentaries.* They seemed to be legal volumes. Although there was no paper, there was a small bottle of ink, corked and frozen, and a bedraggled quill pen stained at the tip with indigo ink.

Clothing and hats hung from a peg by the door. Once she had taken her students to a period room at the Brooklyn Museum, and there had been a similar peg with carefully preserved clothes. She had explained to the children that people had no closets back then. The kids pressed their noses against the acrylic barrier, and someone pronounced it "weird." Standing now before the strange clothing, rough to the touch, she was inclined to agree with her student.

This was all very weird.

There did not seem to be any women's coats, but there was a weighty shawl. Emma assumed it was what she was supposed to wear and drew it around her shoulders.

"I'm hungry," she announced to herself, and stepped over to the sink. There was no food there. Dishes were soaking, a thin layer of ice having formed over them. A red-levered hand pump was stationed over the sink. Emma gave it a few yanks, but nothing happened. Using both hands she tried again. A drop of icy water sputtered out and nothing more.

Rewrapping the shawl, she was about to leave when something caught her eye.

Under the table was a wooden crib.

"Oh, no," she whispered. In the crib was a tiny quilt and a small infant's smock. Instinctively, she picked up the smock and held it to her face.

His smell was still there, the sweet fragrance of a baby. She knew it was the smell of her own child, a child she would never know. Her child, and the child of the man with the marvelous eyes.

Her knees buckled as she sank to the ground, the little shirt still pressed to her face. A feeling of loss encompassed her, such pain as to make living almost unimaginable. It came like a physical blow, as if she had been struck in the middle by a tree trunk.

A moan escaped her lips, and she closed her eyes, savoring the fresh perfume of a baby.

Emma didn't hear the door open or feel the cold blast of air from outside.

"Em."

She looked up. Her husband stood on the threshold. He wore a wide-brimmed hat dusted with snow, a large, dark brown overcoat that seemed too tailored and fine for their new life in Indiana.

"Em," he repeated. He took a step toward her and stopped. "You are out of bed."

She nodded and smiled, embarrassed, and refolded the smock and placed it back in the crib.

Her husband's expression remained blank as he closed the door and fastened the large wooden latch.

"Why are you wearing the horse blanket?"

She began to stand, and he reached out a cold hand to assist her.

His hand, large and callused, was perfect. It wasn't the hand of a sedentary man. It was the hand of someone who would fight for what he believed in, fight for what he loved.

Part of her wanted to cry again; the other part wanted to laugh with sheer joy. This was him. This was who she had been waiting for.

Her own hand grasped his, and he looked at her with mild surprise. "You are wearing the horse blanket."

"I am?" She beamed, placing her other hand on top of his. She could feel the strength there, the warmth returning. There was a tracing of veins on the back of his hand, and she ran her thumb along the ridges.

She stopped and looked up at him.

Their faces were only a few inches apart. Although his face was unlined, he was lean, his cheekbones prominent beneath those astonishing eyes.

His skin was slightly dark, yet it was too late in the year for the color to be from the sun. In spite of his overwhelmingly masculine stance, his rugged build, his facial features were almost delicate. There was a fine, patrician quality to him, a nobility she had never before seen in a man.

He was waiting for her to respond.

"I'm wearing the horse blanket because I was cold."

He did not blink. The snow on his hat remained white and fluffy. The room was cold enough for it to stay, unaltered, on the brim forever.

Then he did something wondrous. He smiled. It was not an all-out guffaw grin, nor was it a flash of white teeth. Instead, his mouth curved up slightly, and a luminous sparkle came briefly into his eyes. Then it was gone.

"Well, Em. That sure makes sense."

With that he took off the hat. Clumps of snow fell to the

430

floor, and she stared at his hair. There was something fascinating about a man so young, perhaps in his early thirties, with so much gray in his hair. It wasn't just at the temples, where one would always imagine a young man with dark hair to gray. It was all over, silvery and thick and unrepentant.

"I'll fetch you something to eat." He shrugged off the coat and hung it on the peg. He was wearing the same white shirt and trousers he had worn earlier, only now he wore a dark, slender tie, limply knotted into a bow, and a narrow-lapelled coat.

She was about to comment on how nice he looked, when she realized two strange facts. One was that he, the husband, was making her a meal. Wasn't that the job of the wife?

The second fact was more disturbing. As he spoke she had been trying to place his peculiar accent. But it wasn't his speech, the way he formed the words, that was so odd. He seemed to have a typical eastern accent, a little more pronounced, but not unusual. The odd thing was the way he spoke, the flat manner. He spoke every word without a shade of emotion. No passion, no warmth, no anger—just straightforward, methodical words.

And there was something similarly peculiar about his eyes. Other than the swift glint of humor she had seen a few moments before, they, too, were completely devoid of feeling.

There had to be a reason for his strained manner, the hesitant, precise formality. What on earth could have happened to him?

The meal passed in complete silence.

Emma was actually relieved. There was so much she wanted to ask, yet clearly she was supposed to know all the answers. There were everyday details she hadn't the faintest clue how to ascertain.

"Did you have a good day at the office?" Her voice sounded unnaturally cheerful. His head snapped up, eyes wary.

"I will most likely ride the circuit come spring, Em. It will be the usual three-month tour, same as the one I would have ridden in the autumn if . . . well, if things had been different. Until then, we will continue to barter for all we need."

"Oh—that's not what I meant!" She swallowed the dry corn bread and took a sip of the tepid coffee. "No, I really want to know, Michael. Are you enjoying the work?"

Michael. She just called him Michael. Oh, God. Was that his name? Or had she just blurted out the most common name she could think of?

He had been about to take a bite of bread when those deep brown eyes of his leveled at hers. Slowly, deliberately, he placed the bread back on the pottery plate.

"Why thank you kindly, Em, for your concern." There was no sarcasm to his voice, nothing at all. "I believe I will enjoy it once I start riding the circut. Now I am beginning to prepare some small cases. Squabbles between neighbors, boundary disputes, that sort of thing."

He bent his head again and continued eating.

But was that his name? She had to know.

"That sounds great." She cleared her throat. "Michael."

He did not react. Instead, he picked up his empty plate and mug and began to carry them to the sink.

"Oh, I'll get those. Michael."

He paused, his back stiff as he took a deep breath. Then he continued on to the sink and stacked them on the side.

"Thank you." He then walked to the peg, where he slipped on his coat and hat. Snow was still on both.

"Good-bye. Michael." She waved uncertainly from the table.

At last he looked at her, and that strange almost-smile again played on his lips.

432

"Good-bye to you, Emma."
And with that he left.
She sat motionless, staring at the closed door.
Michael. Her husband's name was Michael.

Three

HER HANDS STILL STINGING FROM THE HARSH SOAP AND COLD water she had used to wash the dishes, Emma decided to explore the town of Overton Falls.

She stepped from the cabin, fumbling with the large wooden latch, still wrapped in the horse blanket that Michael found so amusing. The brightness outside, the sun reflecting off the silvery snow, made her wince, as if she had not been out-of-doors for a very long time.

Instead of retreating back into the cottage, she straightened her spine and hugged the blanket closer.

"I live in Brooklyn," she muttered between clenched teeth. "I'm not afraid of Indiana."

With that, she was slammed to the ground by something large and strong that had walloped the back of her knees.

The wind was knocked from her, and as she gasped, she came face-to-face with the most horrible visage she had ever seen. Tiny, piercing eyes rendered her motionless. Fetid breath engulfed her, pungent and hot.

"Jasper! You come on and join the rest!" A young man pulled the creature away from Emma.

It was a pig. Perhaps a hog. Whatever it was, it was something monstrous and unshaven from the porcine family.

"Sorry, ma'am. Jasper's just a little excited about his walk."

The boy could not have been more than twelve or thirteen.

He helped her up with a bony, cold hand. Then he was gone—chasing Jasper and a half-dozen other pigs down the street.

She regained her limited composure while her eyes adjusted to the blinding white. The view before her caused her to take a step back.

It was a small village, with wagons and dogs wandering through the street, a bustle of activity within yards of the cabin. Apparently no one had noticed her run-in with Jasper the perambulating pig. Or if they had noticed it, no one seemed to think it out of the ordinary in this strange little town.

Each of the dozen or so buildings had smoke puffing from its chimneys. Some were clearly homes, and one, set back in suburban splendor, was surrounded by a grand whitewashed fence. The other structures were close to the unpaved road. There were tradesmens' signs on a few, painted boards, squeaking as they dangled on their hinges. All seemed to have been rendered by the same hand—clear and neat, free of any artistic pretenses. On one sign a letter had been omitted. Instead of painting the entire sign over, the missing letter had been squeezed above the word, a tiny arrow pointing to the correction.

An open door just yards away revealed a blacksmith's shop; the constant clanking and pinging of the two workers was inescapable as it echoed through the streets. She walked slowly, trying not to draw attention to herself, yet mesmerized by all she saw.

A pair of children ran through the streets, laughing and pulling a smaller child on a sled. Why weren't they in school?

The wind whistled between the buildings, unhindered, as if on the open prairie. There were no tall buildings to buffer her from the cold, no smoky car exhausts or steaming manholes. The feeling of frigid, unheated air could not be forgotten.

There was no escape from winter—not even a temporary reprieve—until spring.

She walked toward the center of the town, a fork in the road where horses were tethered and wagons were being loaded.

The other pedestrians were beginning to stare at her. The women huddled closer to each other, bonnet brims concealing their expressions as they spoke in hissing urgency, pausing only when they passed Emma. The men offered nods and hesitantly tipped their hats, fancy hats and plain, fur-trimmed and knit.

A clapboard building had a sign in golden lettering, Zollers' Fine Dry Merchandise, and Emma entered. She felt warm inside, warmer than she had been since waking up in the cottage.

For a few moments she saw dancing spots, then gradually the interior of the store became clear.

It was a large single room. In the center was an iron stove, the source of the glorious heat. The walls were painted a gentle blue-gray, and every inch of space contained shelves or barrels or open burlap bags.

The shelves were packed with pottery and china. Although the blue and white china was lovely—delicate and transluscent —the pottery was fantastic, rough but imaginative. A glazed candlestick doubled as a ring holder, and a jug was covered with paintings of elves and wood creatures.

Emma reached out a finger to touch the jug.

"*Ah-em*," rasped a male voice.

She jumped. An older gentleman in a canvas apron gave her a courtly bow.

"Good morning, ma'am. I am so pleased to find you up and about at last."

Emma gave him what she realized must have been a blank stare, and he continued.

"I am Hans Zoller, proprietor of this establishment. I am well aquainted with your husband, ma'am, and I believe I can speak for all of Overton Falls when I say how proud we are to have a man of his ability among our citizens."

"Oh?" Emma smiled uncertainly. "He is quite a guy, isn't he?"

"Why, yes." Mr. Zoller nodded. "He has managed to stop an out-and-out war here, he has. I have not a doubt that had it not been for your husband, there would have been bloodshed on the fair streets of Overton Falls. You mark my words."

She wanted to know more, to ask for details, names, anything that might help her understand Michael. Perhaps then she could understand why she was there.

Instead, she turned her attention back to the shelf. "What lovely pottery." There. That seemed appropriate. No one in Overton Falls could fault her for being overly bold.

Mr. Zoller made a strange face, one of sympathy. Emma did not see it. When he spoke, she had no idea that anything was amiss.

"Yes, ma'am. That pottery was made right here in the Falls by the Larsons. They live just yonder past the Hungry Boar Tavern."

"How nice," she replied, staring at more objects. There was a shelf holding a hideous tea set in a gruesome shade of greenish silver. Mr. Zoller followed her gaze and pointed with pride.

"That is genuine lusterware, straight from St. Louis." He beamed. "It's pottery, but glazed to look like the finest silverware in the world. Fit for royalty, it is."

Emma again smiled. There was no reason for her to be in the store. Just as she was about to leave, she turned to ask him a question. This was important. She had to make it good.

"Thank you, Mr. Zoller. By the way, what is the easiest way to get to my husband's office? My sense of direction is terrible."

She hoped that a dazzling smile would make the question seem perfectly rational.

Mr. Zoller's face remained impassive. "Why, I reckon just walk outside, up Main Street a house or two, and you will see the shingle with Judge Hawkins's and your husband's names."

"Thank you." She tightened the blanket around her. It was then she spotted the blue spongeware bowl filled with old lemons. It was peculiar, a bowl of lemons that looked worse than anything she had ever discovered in her vegetable bin at home.

Again, the experienced shopkeeper saw her curiosity. "Have you ever seen those before, ma'am? Real oranges! They're special, of course. Only get them on the holiday."

"The holiday?"

"Yes, ma'am. Christmas is just shy of a fortnight away."

"Christmas," she repeated. "Oh, thank you."

The moment she left the store a gray-haired woman scurried into the room.

"Well, Hans! Tell me—tell me all about her! Did you see what she was wearing? Been here well on a half year and she hadn't ever been out of her bed. That poor man does it all, man's work and woman's work. What did she say?"

"Calm down, woman."

For thirty years he had stood by her side, ever patient with her gossipy ways. She was a good woman, just given to idle chatter.

His wife knew when to wait. She busied herself with rearranging the rock candy as Hans stared out the window. At last he spoke.

"Poor woman," he whispered. "Don't know as I've ever seen a young lady so distraught over the death of her young one."

"That's not all!" His wife fairly danced to his side, unable to keep her tidbit to herself for a moment longer. "They say the husband's a strange one as well. He's part savage—Delaware, I think. Did you know that? Old Emil Jenkins swears he heard him talking Delaware to a pack of Indians on their way to the reserved land."

Mr. Zoller wasn't surprised. There was an intensity to the young man that set him apart. Although the storekeeper was interested in his wife's information, he refused to admit it. Should he express an ounce of curiosity, he would never be able to keep her quiet. Instead, he gave her a stern look.

"Hush, woman," he growled. She paused, and he gave her an affectionate wink. "What do you say we sample some of that new cider?"

Emma wasn't feeling very well. Perhaps it was the cold, or the fact that she hadn't eaten since that small bit of corn bread earlier in the day, or the unfortunate run-in with Jasper the pig.

She saw the shingle. On top, in bold letters, it said Judge Isaiah Hawkins. In smaller letters it read Michael Graham, Attorney at Law.

So her last name hadn't changed. She was Emma Graham in Brooklyn, and she was Emma Graham in Overton Falls.

This was too much, all too fast and too strange. She was standing in the middle of a prairie town in 1832, sporting a horse blanket and uncomfortable shoes, married to a stranger.

"You all right, Mrs. Graham?" It was the voice of a young woman. Emma felt an arm reach around her shoulders, a strong arm. "Want me to take you over to Mr. Graham? He's just yonder."

"No. Please." Suddenly Emma did not want him to see her like this. She needed to think, to catch her breath.

"Come with me, then. I'll bet alls you're wanting is some vittles. Come with me, Mrs. Graham."

Emma allowed the young woman to half-carry her to a cabin.

They passed a weaver's shop, then a place with a large wheel in front that Emma assumed was a wheel maker's, and The Hungry Boar Tavern. Finally, they turned to a cottage even smaller than the one she shared with Michael.

If the other cabins were rustic, this one was downright primitive. There were two chairs in the single room, and the young woman shooed what appeared to be a small bear cub off one of the chairs before easing Emma into the seat. The room was musty, and a layer of dirty grime seemed to cling to every surface.

"There you go, Mrs. Graham."

Emma got a clear look at the woman now, as clear as was possible in the dark cabin. She was young, perhaps in her mid-twenties, and quite stout. There were very few stout people in Overton Falls, at least judging from what Emma had seen of the town. The business of day-to-day survival must have kept extra weight off most of the citizens.

Her dark hair was straight, parted in the middle and halfway down her back. Her dress was made from chamois, loose and stained.

"I'm Rebecca Larson, Mrs. Graham. My husband and me, we make all the pottery here in town."

"I've seen it." Emma sat up. "It's wonderful!"

Rebecca Larson shrugged her shoulders, a shy, dismissive gesture. "We try, ma'am. He makes the pottery, and I do all the painting. He's gone just now, tending to his brother in St. Louis. He'll be back in a piece. I'm here alone with our little boy."

Emma then noticed the little boy in the corner, sound asleep.

"He's all tuckered out, ma'am," Rebecca Larson explained, smiling fondly at her son. "Played all morning and now he'll sleep. Can I get you some of the stew in the kettle?"

The fragrance was marvelous, the smell of a luscious dish that had been simmering for hours.

439

"Oh, that would be great." Emma tried to keep the eagerness from her voice.

Rebecca Larson moved with surprising swiftness. After spooning some stew into a pottery bowl, she placed it on the small table, gestured for Emma to pull up her chair, and handed her a wooden spoon.

Emma was halfway through the dish before she realized that Rebecca had calmly seated herself on the floor, cross-legged, as she watched her guest eat. No napkin had been offered.

She also could see the bowl itself better now, and was startled by the beauty of it. Although the shape was flat and unremarkable, the ornate designs were nothing short of fantastic. There were figures of dancers and animals and magnificent flowers, all twined around a star. Rebecca had used only one shade of paint, a subtle blue. Yet the dish seemed to explode with vibrant life.

"This dish"—Emma pointed with her wooden spoon—"it's beautiful. You painted it?"

Rebecca nodded. "Just the other day. It's my newest one."

Emma finished her meal in appreciative silence. The stew was delicious, and Rebecca was clearly pleased when Emma mentioned it.

"Thank you, ma'am." It was difficult to tell, but she seemed to blush in the dim light of the cabin. The windows were shuttered, and the only illumination came from the glow of the fireplace.

After a second helping, Emma was beginning to feel human.

"I'm so sorry, Mrs. Larson," she apologized. "But that was about the best stew I've ever had."

"The secret is to cook it a good long while." She took Emma's plate and motioned to the kettle.

"Oh, no thank you. I'm full." Emma took a deep, satisfying

breath. "I really don't know what I would have done without your help."

"Aw, it ain't nothing." Rebecca Larson smiled, and Emma realized she was quite pretty. "I don't know what we would have done without your husband, Mrs. Graham."

"Really?" Emma leaned forward, wanting to hear more.

Rebecca thought she understood. "I don't suppose you know all that's been going on here, you being sick for so long and all that."

"No. I'm afraid I have no idea."

For a few long moments, Rebecca did not speak. The sounds from outside seemed distant, and Emma wrapped the blanket more firmly around her shoulders.

"You see, Mrs. Graham, me and Walter, we are plain people. We don't ask for nothing from nobody. We make pottery, good pottery. I can take you back yonder someday to see our work shed, if you want."

When Emma nodded in eagerness, Rebecca smiled a genuine smile. "You are a lot like him, Mrs. Graham."

"Like Walter?"

"No, ma'am. Like your husband."

"I am?"

"Yes, ma'am. It don't bother your husband none to be in here with us, or to let us walk into his workplace just like anyone else. Other people in this town ain't like you. They want us to leave. They are happy enough to use our pottery, because it's good and it's cheap, and when Mr. Zoller sells it to them, they can almost forget where it came from."

"I'm sorry, Mrs. Larson. I'm a little confused here. Why on earth wouldn't they want you to live in Overton Falls?"

"Your husband hasn't told you?"

Emma shook her head.

"Mrs. Graham, my Walter and me and our boy. Well, we're part Indian." Rebecca lowered her eyes.

It took a moment for Emma to realize that was it, the reason the good citizens of Overton Falls wanted them to leave.

"Why, I think that's just fine, Mrs. Larson," Emma said softly. "You should be very proud of your heritage. It's noble and magnificent, and nothing to hide from the world."

Rebecca remained silent for a long while, and when she looked up at Emma, there were tears in her eyes. "You are a lot like him. He's trying to make it against the law for us to be driven out of town. The whole reason we had to move here in the first place is because of something called the Indian Removal Act. Mr. Graham says that's why all these people from out east were allowed to take our reserve land. We had no place else to go. You are a whole lot like him, Mrs. Graham."

A strange warmth spread through Emma's midsection, a sense of wonder at what Michael was doing, a sense of pride at what he was attempting to do.

Another emotion began to rise, every bit as unfamiliar to her. She realized that after a few short hours, she was beginning to fall in love with Michael.

"Mrs. Larson," Emma said. She suddenly felt breathless and giddy—she wanted to see Michael. She wanted to do something for him. "Mrs. Larson," she repeated, her voice a little more even. "May I have that stew recipe? I would love to make it for Michael."

Rebecca Larson stood up, her face a ray of happiness. "Of course you can, Mrs. Graham! It's simple enough. I can't write none, but I'll tell you it. Now, the most important thing to remember is to cook it a long time."

Emma nodded.

"Add whatever vegetables you got in the house. But with

possum meat, you got to cook it good and long so the gristle don't stick in your teeth."

"Possum?" Emma's voice cracked.

"Yes ma'am. Sometimes I throw in a little squirrel, just for the flavor. You can make the stew with just about any critter you got. Stick it in a big pot, skin and all, and cover it with some water. Now, when the broth begins to bubble . . ."

The cabin door flew open, bringing a thankfully clean gust of air.

"Em?" Michael stepped toward her. "Mrs. Zoller told me you were out, Em, and that she saw Mrs. Larson bring you over here."

His voice had a new tone to it, gentle and soft. He reached forward and tucked a strand of hair behind her ear. "Let me take you home, Em. You look tired." His large arm wrapped about her shoulders as he pulled her to her feet. Yet she was still under his arm, in his embrace.

She closed her eyes for a moment.

"Thank you kindly, Mrs. Larson, for taking care of my wife."

"It pleasured me, Mr. Graham. Oh—would you like to take some of my stew home? Mrs. Graham took a real shine to my possum stew."

Emma felt Michael start, then recover. "She ate the . . . well. Why, thank you, Mrs. Larson. I'd be much obliged."

The sound of the stew being sloshed into a bucket was almost Emma's undoing. Michael sensed it and whisked her out of the door.

Now the people in the streets did not bother to hide their stares. The sight of Michael, a steaming wooden bucket in one hand and his pale wife in a horse blanket under the other arm, leaving the half-breed Larson's cabin was enough to cause a minor riot.

Emma snuggled closer to Michael. She glanced up at him. He wore a strange expression on his handsome face, rigid and set, his jaw so tight she could see a muscle working. His eyes were focused straight ahead.

"Are you angry?" It hurt to ask, but she had to know.

He maneuvred her around a cart, stopped her from stepping right into the path of a pair of horses, not answering until they were safely across the street.

"Angry?" She saw him swallow. "Nah, Em. I'm not angry." Michael seemed to be choosing his words carefully. "You just ate possum in the cabin of a half-breed. You took their hospitality when no one else will even acknowledge their existence."

Then he looked down at her. His eyes had a strange sheen, an inner glow, and Emma stopped breathing.

Suddenly he pressed his lips to her forehead, warm, dry lips that seemed to touch her very soul.

"Oh, Em," he whispered. "I'm so very proud of you."

And he smiled.

Four

SHE COULDN'T WAIT FOR HIM TO RETURN FROM HIS OFFICE.

After Michael made sure Emma was safely home, he went back to work, promising to be back well before supper.

"I hope you don't get tangled in rush-hour traffic," she called just as he opened the door to leave.

He gave her an enigmatic smile, adjusting the brim of his hat over his eyes. "Thank you, Em."

The smile faded as he turned, shaking his head in confusion.

Four hours later, Emma sat on the bench by the fire, standing up to peer through the window whenever she heard a noise outside. The brilliant afternoon faded to dusk, a brief gentle glow before darkness forced her to light an oil lamp.

The snow had begun to fall in earnest now, muffling some sounds, amplifying others.

At last the door opened. Michael's face was reddened from the biting cold, and he blinked when he saw her rise to her feet and help him with his coat.

"You're still out of bed?"

She had missed him. In the short time he had been gone, she had missed him with an ache that was almost tangible. He had been mere yards from their house, but just seeing him again made her breathless.

"I tried to make some corn bread while you were gone." She placed his coat and hat on the peg.

"You did?"

Emma nodded. "I burned it, Michael." She pointed forlornly to the table, where a plate of blackened bread was still smoking.

His gaze followed, while she focused on his face. A corner of his mouth quirked, and she saw two indentations—dimples— as he supressed his laughter.

Dimples. She never would have expected him to have dimples, but for some reason the sight of them elated her. She knew, instinctively, that the dimples had not appeared in a very long time.

"Why, Em. It looks delicious."

Without meeting her eyes, he reached over and took a piece. It crumbled to ash. He was not deterred and placed it swiftly into his mouth. Emma had the distinct feeling that had he thought for any length of time on the matter, he would have lost his fortitude.

His expression remained blank as he chewed.

"*Mmmm.*" He nodded, making a valiant effort to swallow.

She ran to the sink and poured him a mug of water. It had taken her a half hour to pump the water into a pottery pitcher. Already a sheet of ice had formed.

"Here, Michael."

He took the water gratefully.

"Well, how is it?"

After drinking the entire glass, he faced her, his countenance again serious. The corners of his mouth were blackened from the crumbs.

"I believe it needs a pinch of salt," he said somberly.

Emma clapped her hands together and began to laugh, her eyes watering as she tried to catch her breath.

"Oh, Michael! It was awful—I thought I had set the whole place on fire the way it filled with smoke!"

Instead of joining her hilarity, or even smiling, he simply stared. Slowly he reached out, his gesture tentative, and wiped a tear from her cheek.

"Em"—his voice was a rich caress—"I haven't heard you laugh for so long, for so very long."

The smile faded from her face. A feeling of regret washed over her as she watched his expression, so wary and guarded, yet so full of tenderness. She raised a hesitant hand and touched his shoulder, feeling the strength and warmth just beneath the fabric.

For a brief instant he remained motionless, arms slightly raised by his sides.

"I'm so sorry," she murmured. He stood so still he did not seem to be breathing. But he swallowed, and a shadowy darkness flickered in his eyes.

She kept her hand on his shoulder, savoring the muscles with her fingertips even as she watched his face. "Please forgive me."

At once he clamped his arms about her, his lips brushing against her temple. He held her with such feral need, his body

446

enveloping hers with its size and strength, that she felt her feet lift from the floorboards. Michael alone supported her full weight.

She had never felt such shelter, such fierce protection.

"I'm home," she whispered to her own wonderment. "My God, Michael, I've come home."

He put her down and pulled back so he could see her, focusing on her face, reading her emotions. Then his mouth descended upon hers, his forearm bracing the back of her head as she tilted to meet him.

Yet something was wrong, something was terribly out of place. She was suddenly afraid, not of Michael, but of her own emotions that threatened to engulf her. Would she be yanked from his arms as swiftly as she had arrived? Would this man who had so suddenly become the center of her world just disappear?

Gasping, she pulled back, her gaze unfocused.

"Em?" There was such fragile concern in his voice that she tried to stop trembling, but could not.

"I'm sorry, Michael," she explained. "I can't. I mean I'm not ready for this. I just can't."

She backed away, her arms crossed to prevent them from shaking, to hold on to something, anything.

At first he simply watched her. Then he glanced down and took a deep breath. "I understand, Em."

A thatch of hair tumbled over his forhead. Instinctively, she stepped forward to brush it from his eyes, but his own hand raked through the thick hair first. She again folded her arms, more tightly this time, closer to her body.

The fire crackled. He glanced briefly at the charred remains on the table.

"I'll go fetch some dinner," he said. Then he smiled gently, as if resigned. The dimples reappeared.

"Where can you get dinner?"

"The same place as usual." He looked away from her, and the tension eased. The painful ache that seemed to resonate between them finally abated.

He pulled his coat and hat back on. "Mrs. Hawkins always makes enough to feed an army. I'll step on over to the Judge's house and fetch us some supper."

"Doesn't she mind?"

"Nah. She's sort of adopted me. I'm about the age their son would have been if he'd lived."

The brittle smile fell from his face, and his gaze rested on the crib beneath the table. A look of interminable bleakness passed through his eyes. So swiftly did it disappear that she knew no one else would have even noticed it.

"I'll be back in a few moments." He then ducked outside.

"Michael." Her voice was a small plea. "Oh, Michael."

The Judge's wife was a fabulous cook.

They dined on roast chicken, sage stuffing, mashed turnips, and apple currant pie. Emma noticed the chicken had a more pronounced flavor than what she was used to, and there was very little white meat.

As she wrapped the leftover pie with a cloth, a thought suddenly struck her.

"Michael, something's been bothering me."

He paused at the fireplace, where he was adding more wood, his expression urging her to continue.

"I saw a lot of children on the street today. Why aren't they in school?"

"Ah. The school." He passed his hand through his hair, and again Emma couldn't help but admire the unusual blend of gray and black. "Do you mind if I smoke a pipe?"

"No, please," she said automatically, wondering if it was anything like the funny pipe Sunbeam's father was so fond of.

It was a long, thin clay pipe, the one she had noticed earlier by his law books. He dipped his fingers into the tobacco jar and placed a pinch into the bowl of the pipe, then lit it with a long stick of wood from the fire, pulling on it until the bowl burned amber.

"The school has been closed since late summer," he said, his words emerging with a puff of smoke.

"Why? Because of the weather?"

He shook his head. "No, Em. This is usually the only time of year the blab school has a full roster of students. The rest of the year most children are needed on the farms."

"Blab school," she repeated. One of her Pioneer Day lessons had been about the old-fashioned schools. He smiled.

"It's a one-room schoolhouse. They call it 'blab' school because children of all ages are there at the same time, talking and chattering their lessons."

"I've heard about them. But why is it closed?"

Michael raised his eyebrows, which remained dark and free of gray, making his face seem impossibly youthful when he smiled. "It's gossip, Em. If you want the full details, I suggest you ask Mrs. Zoller over at the dry goods store. She'll be more than happy to give you the story."

"Oh, tell me!"

Michael settled onto the bench and grinned, the pipe clamped between his white teeth. "It's not the sort of story a woman should hear."

"Then why does Mrs. Zoller know it?"

A bark of a laugh escaped his throat. It was the first time she had heard him laugh. She'd seen him smile, now she had heard him laugh.

449

"Point taken." He took a long pull on the pipe, his eyes fixed just beyond Emma in thought.

There was something terribly impressive about him, the concentration on his face. A fact came into her mind, a bit of information she must have already known on some level.

He's a brilliant lawyer, she said to herself. The moment the idea formed, she knew it was true. He possessed a remarkable legal mind mingled with something else, a native, intuitive intelligence that would make him a formidable opponent in a court of law. And a spectacular champion.

"Very well, Em," he said at last. "The school is closed because the schoolmaster ran off."

Emma understood. As much as she loved her job, there were many days that she, too, felt like running away. Such as the annual lice outbreak, when she was forced to examine every child's head each morning, or when the stomach flu made its round-robin appearance, always right after lunch, and always near her desk.

"So why don't they just hire another schoolmaster?"

Michael shook his head. "That's exactly what I suggested. I was defeated." His eyes met hers, and there was a sense of understanding between them. Their minds somehow worked in the same way, followed a similar thought process.

He continued. "Too many of the townspeople felt that to bring in another schoolmaster would be to bring in another corrupting influence."

"Now you have me completely confused."

"Ah. Well, here's the main point of their argument. You see, the schoolmaster did not just run off. He ran off with one of his pupils."

"You're kidding?"

"Nope."

"How old was the student?"

Michael took another pull on the pipe. "I suppose the pupil was about seventeen."

"Well, I guess that's old enough. I mean, she probably knew what she was doing and all. How old was the schoolmaster?"

"Henry? I reckon Henry was twenty-five or twenty-six."

"Well, that's not so bad, Michael. It's a shame they couldn't just live here in Overton Falls. Did her parents object to the match?"

He nodded.

"I think it's sort of romantic, don't you?" She sighed. Michael stood up and grasped her hand, and she immediately folded her fingers over his. Again she was struck by how very right it felt.

"Em, there was more than just a problem with her age." She looked at him, her eyes questioning. "The real problem was that she was engaged to be married to the Zollers' oldest boy. The wedding was planned, everyone in the town had already purchased gifts—from the Zollers' store, of course. So when the bride ran off with the schoolmaster, all of Overton Falls was in an uproar."

Dawning understanding lit her face. "Oh," she said quietly, then, more emphatically, "So the Zollers not only lost a daughter-in-law. They were stuck with gifts no one needed or paid for."

"Exactly."

"But that's no reason to keep the school closed, Michael. The children need an education, no matter who gets married to whom."

"Ah, but the Zollers don't see it that way. They are powerful in this small town, and their views are taken seriously. Not only did the schoolmaster take their future daughter-in-law, but it made their son Ebenezer a laughingstock."

"With a name like Ebenezer, he was probably already a laughingstock," she muttered.

451

Again Michael laughed. This time it was an easy, natural sound, and Emma smiled back. Their hands were still clasped together.

"That is the truth. Still, the Zollers control the store. Until we can establish a bank, their store is also the center of finance here. If they decide to deny credit to someone, it could make life very difficult. No one will go against the Zollers." He gave her hand a gentle squeeze. "So that's why the school is likely to remain closed."

Another idea came into her head. Her expression changed to a knowing smile. Michael lowered his pipe.

"Tell me now, Em. Tell me now so I can talk you out of it."

"I just had a brilliant idea."

"Oh, no."

"Why don't I become the new schoolmaster . . . or mistress?" Her voice became an excited rush. "I'm qualified, Michael. And since I live here, I wouldn't be a corrupting influence."

"Emma . . ."

"No, listen! I wouldn't ask to be paid. I'm a good teacher. Please, Michael. Whom do I ask? Who's in charge of the school?"

He did not say anything for a while, his face betraying reluctance at shattering her enthusiasm. "You would be wonderful, Em. You were quite a teacher in Philadelphia." Small lines formed at the corner of his eyes as he smiled in remembrance. "Miss Hamilton wept at our wedding not because of any romantic sentiments, but because she was losing the best teacher her school had ever had."

Emma paused, not surprised that she had been a teacher in Philadelphia. "Whom do I speak to about the position?"

"This isn't a good idea, Em."

"Why not?"

He began to open his mouth to speak, then stopped. "All right, I'll be blunt. You are a woman, and for that I am most earnestly delighted, but as far as I know there has never been a female schoolmaster in this state."

"I could be the first!"

"Emma, you taught at a small girls school where the students were prim little ladies. This is the frontier. The children here are rough, and you'd have boys as well as girls."

"I think I could handle it."

"Another problem is that many of the citizens of Overton Falls are beginning to despise me. Unfortunately, that feeling may touch you as well, through no fault of your own."

"How could anyone despise you?" Her voice was full of such sincere confusion that he paused.

"The same reason as in Philadelphia. It's me, Em. And the choices I've made. You know that I tend to represent the most unpopular defendants."

"So?"

"The wealthy ones, the ones with connections and well-placed friends, don't need a lawyer like me. The others do. They have already been condemned by circumstance, by birth and usually poverty. I try to even things out for them, which makes me less than socially favored. The notable lack of invitations in Philadelphia made that clear."

"I'm glad you choose the clients you do. I truly am. But that doesn't mean I shouldn't be a schoolteacher."

"Em"—he rested his hands on her shoulders—"Overton Falls is also like Philadelphia in other ways. It matters here about my background."

When she gave him a perplexed frown, he continued. "My grandmother. It doesn't matter where I was raised, where I was educated. What matters here is that my grandmother was a Delaware."

"Why should that matter?"

"Amusing, Emma. Quite funny." He at last let go of her hand and tapped the contents of the pipe into the fire. "The truth remains that I have Indian blood in my veins. We're only a half step away from joining the Larsons in being driven out of this town. If Judge Hawkins hadn't accepted us, and the Zollers, as well . . ."

Now it made sense. His compassion for others, the grace of his movements, the strange light in his eyes. All were from growing up under what must have been appalling circumstances.

Yet she knew she was meant to run that school, to teach the children. Somehow, she'd find a way.

Emma put on the nightgown as quickly as possible. It was freezing in the cabin.

She waited for Michael to come into the bedroom, but he didn't. Shifting under the quilt, she tried to get warm and watched the calico curtain for any movement. Still he did not enter the bedroom.

She combed and braided her hair; still he remained in the other room. Finally, she peeked through the curtain covering the doorway.

"Michael? Are you coming in?"

He had been reading by the fireplace, forehead resting on his palm. He jumped when she called his name.

"But . . . well. Are you sure?"

Of course. They hadn't been sleeping together. He had been banished to the bench.

"Please, Michael."

Slowly he closed the book and checked the fire to make sure it wouldn't flare during the night. He seemed nervous.

Once he entered the bedroom, he methodically removed his

trousers. The shirt was oversized, and wearing that alone, he silently climbed into bed.

"So," she whispered, her voice husky. "The doctor says we can try again."

He nodded. In the dim light she could see his profile, so beautifully sculpted. "That is what he said."

"When the time is right?" She moved closer, her hand on his chest.

He frowned. "Yes, Em. When the time is right."

"Well, how about now?" She couldn't believe what she was saying, but she needed him. Badly.

"Now?" His voice was uncertain. "It's snowing out."

"What difference does that make?"

"Well, because the ground is frozen." He yawned. "How can we plant rosebushes when the ground is frozen?"

"Rosebushes?"

"*Mmmm.*" Then he reached for her, pulling her close.

After the initial shock wore off, she smiled in the darkness. She was about to tell him what she meant, when she looked at his face.

He was asleep.

She pulled the quilt over his arm, and he held her close to his body. His leg shifted over hers, and she bit her lip.

In slumber his face was sublime, his chiseled features those of a storybook hero. His muscles relaxed, huge muscles that hinted at enormous physical strength. Unlike the selectively buffed physique of someone who worked out in a gym, Michael's limbs were large all over, his chest and back knotted and hard.

As she drifted off to sleep, she thought how odd, how very strange, that she couldn't tell where his body left off and hers began. They had such different bodies, yet as they held each other, there was no distinction between the two. It was almost as if she could feel his physical exhaustion, as if she, too, had been lost all day in the intricacies of the law.

She took a breath and realized that in his sleep, he did the same. His heart drummed next to hers, and the beats were indistinguishable, in perfect unison.

How very odd.

A PATTERN WAS BEGINNING TO ESTABLISH ITSELF FOR EMMA, strange in all its smells and sounds and movements. In a place her world had left behind, where long-ago people struggled for survival, she slipped out of the warmth of bed to get breakfast. Everything was different. The dawning light was fresh when shining through the thick glass. Corners remained dark without electric lights to switch on. No radio announced the weather or time; there was only the rustling of chickens and horses and pigs somewhere nearby.

It was utterly unfamiliar to Emma. At the same time it was comfortable, a morning routine that had nothing to do with her life before.

Unlike the previous morning, when Michael had left her still dazed and in bed, she awoke before he did. Cloaked in a haze of sleep, she was halfway through preparing breakfast before she realized what she had been doing.

"How did I know this?" Emma wondered aloud as she put the coffeepot on a hook over the fire. There was leftover corn bread—edible, made by the judge's wife. But how had Emma figured out how to make coffee? Even in Brooklyn she used instant, intimidated by the European names of most coffee machines.

456

She sat on the bench for a moment, her chin resting on her palm, trying to figure out why this did not feel as strange as it should. Instead of being paralyzed by fear and confusion, she was adjusting. And it was stunningly easy. Why wasn't she completely freaked-out?

At that moment, the reason walked in. Even wearing only a shirt, scratching his sleep-tousled head in confusion, he was breathtakingly handsome.

"You've made coffee," he said behind a yawn.

"I sure have. Don't ask me how, but I did."

For a moment he stood still, just looking at her.

"Don't worry"—she straightened on the bench, raising her chin off her hand—"I didn't attempt anything more ambitious than coffee. The corn bread is left over from Mrs. Hawkins."

His smile was startling, more potent than the sun's rays, more welcoming than a summer breeze.

As he turned around to get dressed, he paused. "I sure could use some of that possum stew this morning."

"No problem. Just fetch me a critter and let me cook it nice and slow, so the gristle doesn't stick in our teeth."

He halted and faced her, his eyes shining, the smile now lighting his entire face. "Em," he breathed. "How I've missed you."

Then he was gone, behind the calico curtain. He dressed in the bedroom, and as he pulled on trousers and suspenders and boots, he whistled a tuneless song. Emma hugged herself, staring out the window at the cold morning in Overton Falls, wondering what new miracles this day would bring.

Emma dressed with extra care, pinning her hair in a style similar to one she had seen the mother wear in the television series *Little House on the Prairie*. Of course, the actress on the show had hairdressers and makeup artists to give her that authentic look. Emma was forced to rely on her own inexpert hands and a spotted mirror.

At the bottom of the bedroom trunk she found a woman's coat, which wouldn't be nearly as warm as the horse blanket, but would probably be more appropriate in the prying eyes of Overton Falls. Again the red leather diary had been on top of the clothes. Before she closed the lid she reached for it.

She had to make an entry. The last words were so sad, so hopeless, that Emma felt she needed to change the tone. She retrieved the pen and ink bottle by Michael's books. The ink was no longer frozen, having been warmed by the heat of the morning's fire.

"My new life here is a challenge," she wrote, dipping the quill back in the bottle. "I feel with Michael by my side, anything is possible. Today I will do my best to get the school open—the children need it. Christmas is coming. Anything is possible."

She read over her words with satisfaction, blowing on the page to hasten the ink's drying. Then she slipped on the coat, a dark green, closely fitted, ankle-length garment with a velvet collar, and stepped outside.

The first place she went was Mrs. Larson's cottage, to return the wooden bucket and thank her for the stew. She knocked once, and just as she was about to knock again, the door opened.

A small boy, perhaps five or six, answered the door.

"Hello." She smiled.

He immediately stuck his middle two fingers in his mouth. Emma handed him the bucket. "I saw you yesterday while you were taking a nap. I believe this belongs to your mother."

Rebecca Larson then appeared at his side, wearing the same loose-fitting dress as the day before. The boy grabbed his mother's leg, still sucking his fingers and staring at Emma.

"Oh, good morning, Mrs. Graham!" Rebecca stroked her son's head with comfortable affection.

"Good morning to you, Mrs. Larson. Is this handsome young man your son?"

The mother laughed. "He sure is, ma'am. This is George Washington Larson. George, this pretty lady is Mrs. Graham."

At the mention of her name the boy pulled his fingers from his mouth. "Are you Mr. Graham's mother?"

Emma laughed. "No, George. I'm his wife," she answered. It still felt odd to be someone's wife, strange yet wonderful.

"Oh, where are my manners," Mrs. Larson stammered, backing into the cottage. "Would you like to come in?"

Emma shook her head. "I just wanted to return the bucket and thank you again for the stew. Also"—Emma leaned closer—"I wanted to ask you a question."

Rebecca Larson's eyes widened as she accepted the bucket. "What is the question?" Her voice was low.

"You and your husband do business with the Zollers. How on earth can I get on her good side? I want to reopen the school, and without their support, it will be all but impossible."

Rebecca stared at Emma for a moment. Only the slow dropping of her jaw gave any indication that she had heard the words.

"Mrs. Graham, you'd best come in here," she said at last. "This may take a while."

Emma cringed. "That bad?"

"Let's put it this way"—Rebecca held the door wide—"little George here may be sprouting whiskers by the time I'm finished telling you all."

Only little George smiled at the thought.

Michael's workday passed in a haze of activity. He seemed to work nonstop, paging through the judge's battered law texts, speaking with an elderly couple from Germany who wanted to purchase more land, trying to calm a young farmer who was certain his neighbor had been poisoning his well water.

Mrs. Hawkins, her incongruously girlish gray curls bobbing with every step, brought him the usual delightful midday meal. He ate it without much thought, simultaneously going over papers filed for an upcoming suit.

Emma. Warmth spread through his body as he thought of her, his wife. For so long now she had retreated into her own world, inhabited by her alone. He had feared she would never return to him, that she would live only in her mind, a sanctuary where death and pain could not enter.

Would they ever be able to speak of their little son? To remember him together, the shared memories of his short life. He was just beginning to walk when he died. This would have been but his second Christmas.

Michael shook his head. "Think of something else," he said to himself, clenching his fist, watching as his knuckles turned white.

At least Em was better. Perhaps by this time next year, they would have another baby. Perhaps.

The moment he stepped into the cabin, he knew something was very wrong.

Everything was just as it had been when he left that morning. There was no indication that anyone had been there all day. The fireplace was cold. He checked the larder, and last night's chicken was still there. She had said she would have it for lunch, yet it remained untouched.

Without taking off his hat and coat, he charged into the bedroom.

"Em?" He swallowed hard. Had she retreated again? If she left him now, she would never return.

But the room was empty, the bed neatly made.

It had been hours since he had last seen her. Where could she be?

He ran out the front door, leaving it open and swinging in the winter wind. "Emma?" he called.

There was no answer.

He started to run toward the center of town, his mind creating horrible images of what could have happened. Anything was possible in this untamed country. Tales abounded of people who were killed by wild beasts or drowned by fierce waters or simply vanished, never to be seen again.

Perhaps she had run away, unable to face all that had happened, unable to face her own husband. On some level she must still blame him for their loss, for everything that had occurred since they came west. She had to blame him. God knows, he blamed himself. There were days he felt he could no longer live with the guilt, weighing him down, tearing him apart.

He should never have left her alone. He should have let Mrs. Hawkins look after her. No. That wouldn't have been right. He should have stayed with her himself. He should have been brave enough to face the accusing hurt that was bound to cross her features, her exquisite features.

From somewhere he heard her laughter, distinctive, musical. He had almost forgotten the sound until the evening before, when she had laughed again, the glorious notes bringing warmth and beauty back into his life.

He listened, hoping to hear it again. Had he imagined it? Had he so wished to hear her voice that he conjured the cherished tones?

Again he heard her laugh, this time joined by an unfamiliar cackle. He turned in the direction of the sounds, and stopped, sure he must be imagining the sight before him.

Two figures were silhouetted in the dusk, lit from behind by the oil lamps of Zollers' Fine Dry Merchandise. They were so close they were all but touching. Moving closer, he realized one of the figures was his wife, radiant in her Philadelphia city cloak. The other was Mrs. Zoller. His wife had just said something, and Mrs. Zoller barked a dry laugh before turning toward him.

"Why, Mr. Graham!" Mrs. Zoller was smiling, her voice rich with coquettish delight. The effect was unsettling. "Your charming wife has come up with some clever ideas for our store. Such ideas! Why, we're bound to make . . . well!" Lowering her voice, she touched Emma's shoulder. "Mr. Graham, I've been thinking about something. Your wife would make such a wonderful teacher for our children. I understand she was quite the schoolmarm back in Philadelphia. That is just what this town needs, some city polish to take the coarse edge off some of our children. Not every boy is as accomplished as my Ebenezer. As a favor to all of us, would you allow her to reopen the Overton Falls School?"

Emma looked at him with such an expression of hope, of tenderness, that he felt something tighten in his chest. All he could do was nod. All he could do was get her back home as soon as possible to find out how she had tamed Mrs. Zoller in a single day.

"YOU DID *WHAT?*" MICHAEL ASKED AGAIN, CONVINCED THAT he must have heard her wrong.

Emma looked up at him, rubbing her cold hands over the new fire. The heat of the flames caused the loose strands of hair surrounding her face to lift and float. He reached forward to fasten a long curl behind her ear, not wishing it to catch a spark.

"I simply appealed to Mrs. Zoller's only two weak spots: her love of money and her innate snobbishness."

"And that bought you her support in reopening the school?"

"Sort of." She grinned, and he watched her face as he pulled up a chair by the fire. She was full of a gentle confidence he had not seen for a very long time. He wanted to simply watch her, to see her sit calmly without the darkness that had been there before.

Emma felt the pull of his stare, knowing he was observing her every move. She longed to touch him, to be physically near him. Without warning she stood up and promptly sat in his lap.

After his initial grunt of surprise, he adjusted her, pulling her closer, wrapping his arm around her back. It felt so natural, so complete.

For a moment she leaned against his chest, her eyes closed in contentment.

"You're not sleeping a wink until you tell me everything, Em," he whispered.

"*Mmmm*," she sighed, longing to stay forever in his embrace. Her arm went around his shoulder.

"I'm going to stand up now. I'm giving you fair warning. You're going to fall onto the cold, hard floor unless you satisfy my curiosity."

"You're beginning to sound like Mrs. Zoller." She refused to open her eyes.

"That does it." With startling swiftness he stood. Emma, who had, indeed, relaxed into a drowsy tranquillity, gasped and clutched frantically to avoid falling.

But his hold on her had never loosened. Instead, he cradled her tightly against his own body.

"Oh, Em. Don't you know I'd never let you fall?"

She reached up and touched his face, rubbing her thumb lightly along his cheekbone. "I know."

For a moment he simply looked at her, his remarkable eyes drinking in every detail of her face. She returned the gaze, bold, unblinking, savoring the features she could never grow weary of, never forget.

Slowly, his mouth touched hers, tentatively at first. His lips were warm, molding with ethereal perfection to her own.

Her hand had slipped down and cupped the back of his neck, and she felt as if she were floating on a cloud. The other hand stroked his upper arm, the knotted muscles now beginning to tremble.

With her still ensconced in his powerful hold, he carried her into the other room, through the calico-draped doorway and to the bed. He lowered her to the mattress carefully, not giving up his possession, remaining so close she could feel the heat of his body.

He trailed soft kisses from the corners of her mouth, along the line of her jaw, down her throat.

"Emma." His voice caressed her name. A magical, honeyed warmth seemed to course through her veins at the tone.

Her fingers began to unfasten the buttons on his shirt, clumsy in their haste. It was as if her fingers moved on their own, with no thought on her part. With every button she found it harder to stop trembling. She had to feel him, to experience his skin against her own. It was as necessary to her now as breathing.

He worked at releasing her, too, from her clothing. Finally her shoulder emerged, then the other shoulder was free.

She gasped at the cold of the room, a room where the fire had not yet been lit. In an instant, though, the chill had vanished, replaced by the fevered touch of his skin against hers.

His mouth descended on its fragile path, across her collarbone, then slowly, deliciously, covering her breasts. Her hands gripped his back, as if to pull him ever closer, as if to never let him go.

464

More clothes fell away, and they both ignored the sound of tearing cloth. Nothing else mattered. Only to get closer, ever closer.

She opened her eyes to take in the sight of him, just for a moment. He was perfect, in every way perfect. Skin glistening in the dark, the sculpted beauty of his form held suspended for her to see. His eyes were open too, and he held his breath as his gaze encompassed her. And then they were again touching, stroking, becoming one.

As it was always meant to be. As it would always be.

They lay entangled under the quilt. He smoothed her hair in a slow, rhythmic motion. She felt his mouth curve into a smile.

"Well?" She prodded, nudging him gently, pausing to enjoy the solid feel of him.

"I was just thinking." His voice was low and deep. "You have quite a way of changing the topic."

"I do?"

"You do, Em. You have yet to explain how you managed to get Mrs. Zoller eating from your hand."

"*Ah,* that."

"Yes, that." His words mingled with a chuckle. The two of them lapsed into a comfortable silence. She traced small circles idly on his chest, wondering how one person could have made such a difference in her life.

"Em?"

She stopped tracing the circles.

"I think we should get you a warmer coat." She shifted her gaze up to look at his face, and he gave her a small smile. "That old schoolhouse is drafty."

For a moment she could say nothing. Her throat tightened, and he pulled the quilt over her bare arm.

"Oh, Michael." She swallowed hard against the urge to cry. "Thank you."

He did not reply. He simply smiled.

The next morning was unexpectedly glorious, the brilliant sunlight warming the cabin. Emma had breakfast on the table by the time Michael had finished shaving and dressing.

He took a sip of coffee and leaned forward. The light caught his eyes, but he didn't blink. His full attention was on Emma. "So, will you finally tell me how you changed Mrs. Zoller's mind about the school?"

Her hand cupped the side of his face, still damp from shaving. "I went to Rebecca Larson's yesterday. We had a chat about Mrs. Zoller."

Michael nodded.

"Well, she told me that the Zollers are civil to the Larsons, not out of any kindness, but because the Larsons' pottery sells. The Zollers tried to sell some less expensive factory-made pottery, but it fell apart and everyone demanded their money back. So they keep stocking the Larsons' pottery."

"That makes sense."

"I also learned that Mrs. Zoller is something of an elitist. She feels she alone represents society in these parts. She went to a finishing school in St. Louis, you know."

"She should have stayed longer." Michael placed the mug on the table. "They let her out before she was finished."

Emma laughed. "I'm not sure that would have helped. Anyway, I suppose she found out that back east, my family has some vague social connections."

"Even though you married a half-breed?"

His voice had been matter-of-fact, a simple question rather than a stinging comment. Yet she felt the weight of his words, the importance of what he had said.

466

"I wouldn't have married anyone else." She tried to keep her tone light, but she realized it was the truth. "You're the only one."

"Em."

She glanced down and struggled to recall what she had been talking about.

"So I went over to the store and found Mrs. Zoller." He remained silent, so she continued. "I told her it crossed my mind that what this town needs is Christmas decorations. Everyone, simply everyone, back east decorates a tree in their house now. It's all the rage."

"I never noticed."

"Well, anyway, it will be all the rage one day. So I gave Mrs. Zoller the opportunity to be ahead of the times, to become a genuine trendsetter. It worked—she was suddenly all ears."

"That must have been an attractive sight."

Emma ignored him. "Then she began to panic. 'Why, Mrs. Graham,' she practically cried, 'where on earth can we get Christmas decorations when it's already mid-December?' Well, I told her that it just so happens that Rebecca Larson has made a dozen ornaments. Next thing I knew, Mrs. Zoller was out the door and on her way to the Larsons'."

"You must be joking." He leaned back, his face incredulous. "Mrs. Zoller actually went over to the Larsons' home?"

Emma nodded eagerly. "And that's not all. We ate lunch with Rebecca and her son at the cottage."

"I don't believe it." He shook his head. "No, Em. I just can't see Mrs. Zoller over there."

"She seemed to think it was all right. I suppose she thinks I may have been crazy these past few months, but I was brought up well. Insane, maybe, but always the lady."

"You were never crazy." His voice was low, and he reached across the table, folding his large warm hand over hers.

"Never mind. The important thing is that over lunch, I mentioned the school. At first Mrs. Zoller wouldn't even discuss it. But little by little, we wore her down. Every time she would get that scowl on her face, Rebecca would chime in with something along the lines of 'how about some cherubs—you could sell them for ten cents apiece, I'd give them to you for five?' And Mrs. Zoller would smile. Did you know those are artificial teeth she has? Made from cow teeth, she says. I wouldn't admit that, would you?"

"You were never crazy."

Emma leaned over and kissed him. "I love you, Michael," she said softly.

His hand gripped hers more tightly. "Em, I love you."

Outside a cart rumbled by, and the early morning voices reminded her that the workday was about to begin.

"I guess you had better go to your office." She reluctantly looked away.

Instead of answering, he rose to his feet, never releasing her hand, and pulled her close.

"In a while, Em." His mouth was next to her ear, his lips lightly touched her, causing a shiver to run through her. Then his mouth bent into a knowing grin. "In a while."

Seven

THE SCHOOLHOUSE WAS IN APPALLING SHAPE.

Emma stepped carefully over the threshold, amazed that a room could be both frigid and musty at the same time. There was dust and filth in every corner, and only by brushing the sole of her boot against the floorboards could she discover the floor was made of wide wooden planks.

The walls had been whitewashed, but the paint had started to peel away. The teacher's desk at the front of the room was speckled with ink stains, but the inkwell and quill holder were empty. There were rugged benches with slightly higher benches to serve as tables. Most were broken and splintered. The fireplace was jammed with rubbish, and when she took a few steps closer, she realized that an animal had made a nest there.

With all of the work Emma had accomplished in the past week, between helping the Zollers set up a proper "Philadelphia-style" Christmas display—which owed more to the windows at Macy's than to anything in Philadelphia—and watching little George Larson so that Rebecca could fill the Zollers' order, it had never crossed her mind that the log cabin schoolhouse would be in such a disastrous state. After all, it had only been empty for just under a year.

The school was to open in two days. Mrs. Zoller, while merrily selling her stock to excited customers, had indeed managed to convince most of the town's citizens to give the new schoolteacher a try. The previous teacher, Emma learned, charged up to five cents per pupil a week to attend school. Emma's fee would be a few sticks of kindling for the fireplace. Everyone was pleased, yet slightly suspicious, at the rates.

Meanwhile, Rebecca had come up with some unusual designs for ornaments. Emma explained some basic ideas to her, the tried-and-true Norman Rockwell images Emma had grown up with. Rebecca nodded and began to work.

The results were surprising. Her St. Nicholas sported a blue and green suit trimmed in plaid, with a bushy red moustache on his youthful face. The angels all wore broad smiles and top hats. And the manger scene was set in a tepee, surrounded by sturdy-looking buffalo, the baby Jesus holding an ear of corn. Yet the stuff sold like mad to the folks of Overton Falls, who had no preconceived notions and even fewer inhibitions about where to place the ornaments.

Emma Graham had single-handedly introduced commercialism to the celebration of Christmas. Although she felt more than a twinge of guilt and was given a stern lecture by the minister of a nearby Presbyterian church—where all giddy activities were frowned upon—it was hard to deny the joy everyone seemed to derive from the decorations. Especially the children.

As the day of the school's opening drew near, she met some of her new students. And a sense of panic began to knot in her stomach. It was a strange concept—one room, one teacher, all ages from five to sixteen. She had no idea what they knew, how to teach them, where to begin. As long as she was busy helping Rebecca, she could avoid dwelling on the reality of the job she had undertaken.

But standing in a filthy, frozen room, furnished with broken benches, tipped-over tables, her breath puffing in the cold as she began to panic, she realized that she was simply not up to the job.

"Oh, my God," she whispered to herself, swatting a frozen cobweb as she stepped toward the blackboard. There she saw the elegant tracings of a forgotten lesson. The handwriting was beautiful. The lesson contained four- and five-syllable words, old words, poetic words, the meanings of which she could not recall.

"I can't." She shook her head. What had she been thinking? This was not a well-run school, with a principal and a secretary or even a grumpy janitor. There were no books. There were no slickly bound guides or examples to follow or older teachers to consult in a crisis. Emma would have to be everything, provide the children—some of whom were on the cusp of adulthood—with all they needed. It was impossible.

She backed away from the blackboard. Her knees bumped into a rickety chair, and slowly she sat down.

Perhaps they could leave town. Michael could live anywhere, she reasoned. They could just slip away during the night, leaving a little note to Mrs. Zoller explaining that a relative in a distant state was ill, and they would be gone for a few weeks.

But Michael wouldn't do that to Judge Hawkins or his clients. He would never slip away, shirk his responsibilities. How disappointed he would be at her failure.

Tears began to blur her vision, to soften the horror of the room. In gentle focus the room looked inviting, rustic but warm. Perhaps one day someone could make the school as homey as it seemed with her eyes brimming with tears, but Emma could never be that person. She would have to tell Michael as soon as possible.

That morning while he shaved, he had whistled. It was such a light sound, so hopeful. He had no idea she was not up to the task she had set about with such impressive vigor. She was a fraud.

She wasn't even his real wife. She was a fake, an impostor. Michael deserved a real wife, not this shabby imitation who wasn't even capable of running a log cabin school or making him a decent meal.

Slumping forward, she sniffed once. Just as she was about to stand up to go and tell everyone it had all been a mistake, the chair creaked, then splintered into a half-dozen pieces. In an instant she was sprawled on the squalid floor.

That did it. Her small hold on composure vanished, and she burst into tears. It felt good to cry, to sob like a child, with sloppy abandon. The fear that had been building up in her was gone. In its place was the hollow realization that she was virtually good for nothing.

"Em."

His voice came from the doorway. She hadn't heard him enter, but suddenly he was there, at her side, gently pulling her to her feet.

"Go away, please," she said behind her hands, attempting to shield her face from his extraordinary eyes. "Please leave me alone."

"No."

Tenderly, he pried her hands from her face.

"Please go, Michael. I don't want you to see me like this." She tried to pull away, but he drew her into his solid embrace.

It wasn't until then that she realized he was breathing hard, as if he had just run a great distance.

"Michael?" Her tears seemed to vanish as she looked up at him. His hair was disheveled, his cheeks were reddened from the sharp December wind. "What's happened? Are you all right?"

She had been so busy wallowing in self-pity, and all the while he had needed her.

He nodded once, then took a deep breath. "I went home to see if you were there, Em. There are some new folks in town, and they have a baby. It's colder than they expected here, so I thought I would lend them our baby's blanket. I didn't think about it much. I went into the trunk."

The grasp he had on her shoulders was almost painful, but she didn't care. "What happened?"

"Your diary fell out. I started to put it back in, Em. It fell open to your latest entry. I didn't mean to read it, but my eyes seemed to take in the words even as I closed the book. I tried not to read it. But I did. And then I had to find you."

"Michael?"

He rubbed a hand over his eyes before he spoke again. "You don't know what your words mean to me," he said softly.

For a moment she tried to remember what she had written. Then it came back to her—that with Michael by her side, anything was possible. Had he seen the other entries as well? No. He had only seen the last one, the one she made a few days earlier.

"Michael." She reached up just to touch his face, and he grasped her hand and kissed her palm.

Then, without warning, he pulled her into a fierce embrace. She was about to speak, when she realized his shoulders were shaking, his broad, strong shoulders. Perplexed, she returned his hug, stroking his back, wondering what was happening.

He was crying.

Her own knees began to tremble, and she squeezed her eyes shut and held him, comforted him.

"I miss him, Em." His voice was broken. "I miss him so much. And all this time I thought you blamed me."

"No. Of course not."

It came like a splash of cold water, as she realized what he must have been going through. How could she have not seen it before? How he must have tortured himself, how he must have suffered alone, the double agony of loss and guilt.

For a long time they stood in the mess of a cold schoolhouse, holding on to each other, gently rocking back and forth in silent understanding. His breathing became even, no longer ragged and harsh, and she could not recall what had seemed so important before he came into the schoolhouse.

At last she spoke. "Did you give them the blanket?"

"I did." He hesitated. "It still smells of him, Em. I had almost forgotten that sweet smell, but it's there, in all of his clothing and blankets."

"I know." Her own voice wavered, then she spoke more firmly. "I know."

An image came to her mind, of a toddler with curly dark hair and eyes brown and deep, just like his father's. And of a smile, with new teeth just emerging, and a small soft hand patting her cheek.

"Do you remember the way he used to pat your face? Remember that, Em?"

She smiled and nodded. "I do." Another picture unfurled in her memory. "He had a rabbit that I knitted for him. The ears were so long. He used to put the bunny over his face, an ear covering each eye, when he'd sleep."

"The bunny is still in the trunk. I just saw it, but I couldn't pick it up. Not today, Em. But maybe someday I will."

Again they remained silent for a timeless spell. It was like viewing an old home-movie in her mind, flickering reflections of a very loved child and Michael laughing, holding the squealing form over his head in play, the child gleefully gurgling.

He took a deep breath and kissed her temple. "Emma?"

"Yes?"

"This school is a mess."

She was about to agree. She was about to confess that it was an impossible task, one she would never in the world be capable of, and to suggest they slink away in the darkness of night and never return.

But now those thoughts seemed absurd, even ridiculous. She glanced up at him, and he looked so very handsome and hopeful and young, far younger than he had seemed before. It was his eyes. The shadow was gone, the furtive shading she would catch like a forgotten nightmare. Then he smiled, an open, generous smile of love and strength and vigor.

"Oh, Michael," she whispered, "with you by my side, anything *is* possible."

Eight

THE STUDENTS FILED IN ONE BY ONE, SOME NODDING AT Emma, others making a pointed effort to avoid eye contact.

She turned her back to the class and wrote her name on the blackboard, oversized letters proclaiming "Mrs. Graham." Pausing for a moment, she took a deep breath and hoped her heart would stop pounding.

It was the ultimate first day. This would be completely unlike any teaching experience she had ever had. She was to be alone with children who were raised without television, without playgrounds or even books. Most had only heard music when the traveling dancemaster came through with his fiddle. Newspapers were rare and, when they reached the town, months out of date. There were no such things as hamburgers or pizza, no Toys "R" Us or Superman.

The truth was that she had absolutely nothing in common with these rural children from another century. She would be unable to draw upon her own childhood with these kids. It would be like teaching a room full of aliens from another planet.

With Michael's help, and the unexpected help of Mrs. Zoller—who had adopted the school as her own pet project— the school was now warm and welcoming. The fireplace was stoked, all signs of dirt and dust had vanished. Emma had put some of Rebecca Larson's ornaments—the ones that had chipped or cracked in the groundhog kiln—on the walls, and studied some of Michael's old schoolbooks for ideas on how to teach these children.

They hadn't helped much, but at least she now knew the

meaning of some archaic words with too many syllables to count.

"Good morning," she said in a voice full of false confidence.

"Good Morning, Mrs. Graham," they answered back.

Emma blinked. Somehow she hadn't been expecting a response, anticipating instead sullen silence. She looked at the rows of students, all still wearing their coats and boots, all shifting at their newly repaired desks. Michael had fixed the desks with astonishing speed and skill.

Every desk held a slate and two pieces of slate chalk for the students to write on. No paper in this school, only boards and chalk.

The students were all sizes, all ages. Her degree had been in early childhood education. How could she ever teach a fourteen-year-old boy?

A girl in the front row raised her hand. Emma smiled at her. "Yes. Please introduce yourself."

The girl pulled off her faded pink bonnet to reveal a magnificent head of blonde hair. "My name is Hannah." She flipped her hair and glanced at the other girls, as if daring them to speak.

Emma noticed another girl, with short brown hair, was staring straight ahead. She went to her desk and leaned over. "I'm Mrs. Graham," she said softly. "What's your name?"

At first the girl said nothing, then her lower lip began to tremble. "My name is Hannah, too," she said in a stricken voice.

"Why, that's a beautiful name."

The first Hannah flipped her hair back. "Thank you, Mrs. Graham," she replied.

Emma stayed with the dark-haired girl. "What's your last name, Hannah?"

After a slight hesitation, she said, "Robinson. My last name is Robinson."

"Then you will be Hannah R.," Emma said, bringing a small smile to the girl's face.

"My last name is Van Wyk," announced the long-haired Hannah.

"Then you shall be Hannah V."

Emma went around the room, asking each child to state his or her name and tell a little about themselves.

"My name is Asa Blake." The fourteen-year-old boy's voice cracked as he spoke. "I live just outside of town and I'm real good at checkers. I ain't good at ciphering none, so my Pa sent me here for a spell."

"I'm Elmer Jenkins," said the next boy. "I have hogs, and my favorite is named Jasper."

"*Ah.*" Emma folded her hands. "How is Mr. Jasper? I haven't seen him lately, Elmer."

"Well, he gets a little scared this time of year, on account of this being butchering season, and all. I believe the smell of smoking ham makes poor Jasper somewhat melancholy, Mrs. Graham."

Emma managed to hide her smile at the thought of a melancholy hog and went on to the next child. He was a little boy of about eight.

"My name is also Asa." He giggled. "I mean, not 'also Asa,' just Asa. My last name is Zimmerman, so I reckon I'm going to be Asa Z." Then he straightened. "My parents were making funny sounds the other evening. I swear, I couldn't sleep none with all the shouting and hollering they were doing."

"Were they fighting?" Elmer Jenkins asked.

"I thought so at first," Asa Z. answered thoughtfully.

"Mrs. Graham?" Hannah V. waved her hand in the air. "I once heard a story about a fellow named Mr. Bluebeard who

477

had all these wives and killed them. He hung them up in his barn, one by one, all in a row. I wonder if Asa Z.'s father was killing his wife?"

"No!" Asa Z. stood up. "That ain't so! I thought someone was being hurt, so I went in there, and they were just changing their clothes."

"Changing their clothes?" another child asked.

"Yep. They said it was time to put on some warmer clothes, and the sounds I heard was them trying to get the new clothes on. It was dark. I don't know why they didn't light a lamp, but it was dark, so they were having some trouble with the buttons and all. That's why they were hollering."

The fourteen-year-old guffawed, then became quiet when Emma glared at him. "Very well. Now, I'm going to put some words on the board, and I want all of you to write the words on your slates."

A moan went through the room, a familiar sound, the sound of reluctant students. Emma stopped. There was a smell now, too. It hadn't been there before, when the room was empty. But now it was unmistakable, the sticky-child smell she knew so well from Brooklyn. It was here, in 1832 Indiana!

She had begun to write, when the door opened. It was George Washington Larson, sucking his middle fingers, clutching a bucket containing his lunch.

"Good morning, George." She took his hand. The leather lace on his shoe was untied, so she bent down to fasten it into a bow. Two other children asked to have their shoes laced, and Emma silently longed for the speedy invention of Velcro.

Finally she was able to return her attention to George, who was looking very alone and frightened and sucking more vigorously on his fingers. She bent close to him to speak. "Where would you like to sit?"

There were several empty seats, and just as Emma was leading him to one, Elmer Jenkins stood up.

"Mrs. Graham, ma'am? George Larson, here, is an Indian, and I ain't supposed to be around none of them, on account of my Uncle Henry being killed by Indians. My mama says that if any Indians come to school, I have to go home. She gets worried about me."

Emma stood, momentarily stunned. George's face was expressionless. He simply stared straight ahead.

"I'm very sorry about your uncle, Elmer," she began. "George?" The little boy looked up, and Emma squeezed his hand. "Do you promise not to kill anyone at school today?"

There was a brief silence, and the children exchanged perplexed looks. George pulled his wet fingers from his mouth. "I promise, ma'am."

Elmer Jenkins turned red, and some of the children giggled, a bit uncomfortably at first. Then, as little George had to be helped into his chair, even Elmer Jenkins began to smile.

Emma paused by Elmer's desk. "I'll speak to your mother, Elmer. Maybe we can change her mind a bit."

She returned to the blackboard and began to write.

Somehow, the day passed, slowly at first, then with surprise she realized the day was over. The children lined up to leave, some shoving each other, Asa Z. pulling Hannah V.'s hair, then pretending another child had done the deed.

And then they were gone.

She sat in the strange silence of the room, the children's voices fading as they chattered outside. The board was covered with numbers and letters and phrases.

The schoolroom door opened, and Michael went to her side. "How was it?"

She sighed. "The same. I can't believe it, Michael. There was the stuck-up girl, the tomboy, the class clown. I think I even have a few difficult parents."

Her last words were cut off by a kiss. "I'm so proud of you, Em," he whispered. "So very proud."

Emma and Michael were exhausted by the time they returned to their own home. He had been silent during their walk from the schoolhouse, staring straight ahead as they trudged through the snow.

"Michael?"

"*Hum?*"

"How about if I plan a Christmas party at the schoolhouse. We could invite the whole town. It's already decorated with ornaments, and I saw some evergreens in the back. Perhaps I could make little gifts for the children."

"Gifts? Emma, no one celebrates Christmas like that, not out here." Then he stopped. "At least, they didn't before you came."

"But I'll bet the kids would love it," she sighed as they entered their cabin and hung their cloaks on the peg. "How about if I have them do a play to the 'Twelve Days of Christmas'? It would be a good way to combine numbers and words, and I could get an idea of their academic level without having to embarrass anyone. I think school should be fun for the children, don't you?"

"Maybe." Michael stacked the wood in the fireplace and lit the fire, blowing on it until the flame caught.

She watched him as he moved, the strong hands, the striking face in profile. As if he knew she was watching him, he stood slowly and faced her.

"Em." His voice was low.

She stepped into his embrace, her eyes closed as he rocked her in his arms, gently, tenderly.

"The doctor says we can try again," he whispered.

"I know. But the ground is frozen and it's snowing."

His lips pressed against her temple, then her throat. "I'm not talking about the rosebushes."

Later, in the orange glow of their bedroom, the embers in the fireplace crackling, Emma watched him sleep.

This was so right, being here with him. What extraordinary, magical force had sent her here? Or sent him to her. It must be magic, pure Christmas magic.

Michael took a deep breath and pulled her closer, yet she could not sleep. Her thoughts traveled back, far away, to another time and place that seemed as distant as a long-ago memory.

The ring. She held up her left hand and touched the ring. It was so soft, so smooth.

Before, she had not been able to read the inscription. The script had been faded and worn. What wondrous words had Michael inscribed? She slipped the ring slowly off her finger to read the etched letters. Just as it passed her fingertip, she felt him reach for her.

"No, Em! Don't!"

And then she was asleep.

Nine

THE WARMTH TICKLED HER NOSE. HALF-ASLEEP, SHE REACHED out. "Michael," she sighed.

And rolled onto the floor.

Gasping, she rubbed her eyes. The warmth that had tickled her nose let out a plaintive cry.

"Pumpkin." Emma stared as the cat arched against her hip. Outside a car alarm shrieked.

"No." Her hand flailed, and she knocked over the mug that had held her hot chocolate, now cold and empty. For a moment all she could do was stare at her furniture, at the television set that hummed with the morning news. "Oh, God, no."

The gold ring. She looked down at her hand. The ring was gone. "Michael?" It hurt to say his name, knowing there would be no answer.

It had all been a dream. The town, the life.

And Michael.

It had all been a glorious, terrible dream.

A weatherman on television announced a severe snowstorm watch, hazardous driving conditions, and ice on the roads. The time, he added, was seven-thirty.

She was late—she had to get to school. A feeling of nausea gripped her; shock and pain and a horribly sick hum seemed to vibrate through her body. Everything was off, everything was wrong.

She went through the motions of getting showered and dressed, feeding the cat, watering the plants. As if in a trance, she felt nothing, would not allow herself to think.

The ring was nowhere to be found. Even after she crawled on her hands and knees and peeked under every table and chair, she could not find the ring. The synthetic fibers of the carpet burned her palms, but it didn't matter.

Emma needed to cry. She felt the urge to sob rise in the back of her throat; the desire to simply crumple up and scream was almost overwhelming.

But she couldn't. A class full of first graders was waiting. And she knew that once she started to cry, she would not be able to stop. Not for a very long time.

Perhaps in the evening she could cry to her heart's content, shake her fist in the air and ask why she had to have such a dream. Because she knew that, after this dream of Michael, her life was ruined. Never again could she wrap herself in false contentment, never again could she convince herself that she was perfectly happy.

From now on, every small joy would be tarnished. Now she knew real joy, and it could never again be hers.

She followed the path she had so often followed, stopping at the muffin shop for coffee, checking her mail box in the school's main office. The routine of her normal day was hollow and meaningless, every motion seemed to be a cruel mockery.

The secretary said hello, and Emma supposed she returned the greeting. Someone's mother handed her a bag full of junk. Emma realized it was for some sort of Christmas project.

The classroom was exactly the same—the slightly messy desks, the fragrance of paste and construction paper, and a faraway aroma of something sticky. How could the classroom be the same when her whole world had been turned upside down?

The children arrived as usual, trickling in, shoelaces untied, hair askew and spiked by static. When she spoke, she heard the words echo, as if another Emma Graham stood beside her and uttered the same old words.

"Okay—who needs their shoes tied?"

A cluster of children shuffled to her, giggling and pushing each other. She tied a pair of *Beauty and the Beast* sneakers, Ninja Turtle boots, *Aladdin* sneakers, and two sets of *Pocahontas* moccasins. She paused at the moccasins, a terrible feeling in her stomach.

A small hand tapped her shoulder. She glanced up, and for a moment her breath caught in her throat. It was the new boy, Asa. There was something about him.

"Miss Graham? My daddy's here, and he wants to talk to you about the ring."

"Great," she muttered, as another foot was placed in front of her. This is all I need, she thought, to explain to a complete stranger exactly how his antique ring was lost. She had automatically tied the new sneakers into a sturdy double knot, when she realized these shoes were large and free of any cartoon characters.

She closed her eyes for a moment and tried to rub away the pounding in her temples. Trying to compose herself, she stood, wishing the day were over. Wishing she were still asleep. Wishing she were anyplace else but where she was.

"Em?" His voice was so soft she thought she had imagined it.

Her eyes opened, and there he was. Michael—her Michael.

Now he was wearing two sweatshirts, one over the other, and jogging pants. But it was unmistakably Michael. He seemed larger than life, strong and sure in a world of child-size furniture. Yet it was him, his lustrous hair, the beautifully sculpted face, and those eyes.

"I'm sorry," he said, squaring his shoulders, his voice flat. There were circles under his eyes. "You look like someone I know—someone I knew. I'm Asa's father."

He extended his hand, and she automatically took it. A warmth radiated from his grasp, a large hand. She knew.

"Michael." Her voice was shaking.

"Yes, Miss Graham?" One of the two Michaels in her class tugged at her skirt.

"No, not you. I'm talking to . . ." Her knees began to tremble, yet she held on to his hand.

"Em." Asa's father reached toward her with his other hand and tucked a strand of hair behind her ear.

"The gold ring," she said, "I can't find it."

He nodded. He, too, seemed stunned. "Asa told me he took

484

it to school. They're a set of wedding bands, they've been in my family. I checked the box last night, Em. They were both there." He swallowed. "They can't be separated. As far as I know, the rings have been welded together, linked, for over a hundred years." He glanced around the classroom before he spoke again. "I held them last night and had a dream."

"Indiana?"

He took a deep breath. "Yes. A prairie town in 1832."

"Overton Falls." This couldn't be happening. "The Larsons and Judge Hawkins."

"This is impossible." As he spoke his other hand rested on her shoulder. "Are you all right, Em? I mean, how do you feel."

"Fine," she said automatically. Then she shook her head. "Now I'm fine. This morning, when I woke up, I wanted to die."

He didn't smile. "So did I. I didn't know what to do, how to get through the day." He stepped back, his gaze again caressing her. "You got your schoolroom."

"Miss Graham has a boyfriend! Miss Graham has a boyfriend!" Emma couldn't identify the voice. She didn't care.

Finally he smiled, a smile that reached up and lit his eyes from within.

When she could again speak, her voice was a low rasp. "And you? What do you do?"

He looked down at his sweats and laughed, the rich laugh she thought would come to her again only in her dreams. Now it echoed in her classroom, mingling joyfully with the voices of the children.

"I was just about to jog in Prospect Park. I thought it might clear my mind." His entire body seemed to relax.

"It's snowing, Michael. The ground is frozen and it's snowing."

"I know. I was hoping to find a snowplow to run behind. I

guess I didn't think about it too carefully." Pushing a hand through his hair, he continued. "I'm a public defender, Em. I was a partner with a large firm for a while but realized that's not why I went into law."

Asa had been watching them. Emma suddenly realized the little boy had been staring at their entwined hands.

"We're planting rosebushes in our front yard in the spring, Miss Graham. It was my idea." He straightened his small spine. "It was all my idea. All my idea."

With an enigmatic smile that made him seem much older than six, he strutted back to his desk.

"What do you think happened?" Michael also looked down at their hands. "How could we possibly have had the same dream? And why doesn't it feel like a dream?"

As she looked into his eyes, the eyes she knew so very well, she could only swallow an urge to cry, this time with happiness.

"Maybe," she said softly, "maybe it's just Christmas magic."

JUDITH O'BRIEN's first book, *Little LuLu Goes to the Store,* was self-published when the author was in the third grade. Although the print run was a disappointing single edition, the illustrations won praise from the author's parents. Over two decades later a second novel, *Rhapsody in Time,* was published. Ms. O'Brien is a graduate of the University of the South in Sewanee, Tennessee, and a former writer for *Self* magazine. Her work has also appeared in *Woman's Day, Reader's Digest, YM,* and *Health.* Her other novels include *Ashton's Bride* and her latest, *Once Upon a Rose,* soon to be published by Pocket Books. She now lives in Brooklyn, New York, where she is working on her next wonderful romance.